THE RC AND THE RAKE

A NOVEL

By: Christopher Kahn

FOREWORD

I knew he would die heroically. It was the way he lived that made me think that, and I knew it like a diamond realization on a crisp November day in our youth when we stormed across a narrow trestle-bridge, racing an oncoming, snake-like train winding its way down the mountain. When it became clear that it would reach us before we would find the other side, we climbed over the side-rail, spider-men scaling the web of crossbeams, laughing as brothers do in absurdly dangerous situations.

It wasn't intentional, Cory's falling. Perhaps the vibration of the engine overhead was too severe to keep a grip. My own hands, bigger though they were, numbed from the ceaseless effort of grasping. But his release from the joist came with such apparent ease that the unknowing eye might have construed it as a jump. I knew him better than that. At least back then.

Most likely it was just a slipped foot on a wet reinforcement. A mistake. God knows he made more than his share, though none ever seemed to bear him consequence. And then that slow motion fall with limbs protracted, a spreading flow of lava, crumpled cellophane unraveling, a body plummeting eighty feet towards the canyon floor, towards a road that cut through the brown and brackened chaparral and whose asphalt followed the natural contours of the terrain.

I vividly remember the moment of his fall as if it were my own. He seemed to hang there in mid-air for just a pause, not reaching out for my hand, not groping for the slippery steel supports. The sweep of his blonde hair cut back across his forehead, shielding an eye. He just turned, as easily as one rolling over in bed wrapping the sheets into a tighter cocoon.

I screamed his name as I watched him recede, certain I was witnessing death for the first time. But as always seemed to be the case the hand of God slid under him. This time in the guise of a manure truck. Like some circus stunt he hit the bed of the Mac Hauler squarely and came up without a scratch. The one goddamn truck on the road that morning, not there to deliver dung but to save the charmed life of a thrill-seeking, angry kid. I can still see him smiling up at me through all that shit.

That's when I knew he would die heroically. It would take something extraordinary to kill him. This is the story of that extraordinary thing - a woman.

I, myself, Ray Sonne, had met a rosy-cheeked New Zealand girl with a heart of gold at the Sangrata Famiglia in Barcelona, Spain. I returned with her to the rural land down under and the peaceful, violence-free countryside. There I worked as a contractor in a setting where no one minded the slow grind of progress' wheels. Maybe it was running away. I suppose we're all running from something. Family you can never really escape. Although I never saw them again I thought about them often. Where was my brother? Was my mother really at peace after all that had happened? How did my father die before that?

We never wrote. Never called. For almost a decade I hadn't a shred of information about my brother. Last I saw him he was standing on the front porch with my mother, neither of them waving although it would be our last goodbye, me off to Europe, him just standing there in a tank top at the ripe age of sixteen, his burgeoning shoulders broadening before my eyes, she wiping her hands on an apron that read: Get Your Ass Out Of My Kitchen.

Then, in January of 1995, in an oncologist's office in Wellington, I saw him. On the cover of "Health and Fitness" magazine. Muscular and tan. A Cadillac smile white as northern winter. Possessing that Southern California "glow." I could just see the carrot juice and egg-white omelet on his breakfast table every morning. The digital sports watch that probably logged every aerobic to anaerobic heartbeat. I laughed out loud then indicated the cover of the magazine to the tiny woman sitting next to me so she would not think me possessed. "That's my brother." She took only a glance then eyed me with disdain and went back to studying her crossword and chewing on a pencil. I was strangely overjoyed for Cory. I tucked the edition in my shoulder bag when called then went inside to discover my illness.

Perhaps confronting my own declining health softened me. A tumor has a way of realigning you. I began to make inquiries about him. Some months after that I received this letter:

Dear Ray:

I regret that I have to be the apparent bearer of the most tragic news regarding your brother. Somehow, I can barely bring myself to write about it. In fact, even thinking about it now has brought such a flood of tears I cannot clearly see the page. It would be most helpful if I could meet with you in person or at least speak by phone. Enclosed please find my private phone number. Appropriate arrangements can be made for your travel to Los Angeles. I feel very strongly about this and hope very much to be speaking with you soon.

"Drill where there's oil." Cory always used to say.

Sincerely,

Georgia Hart

Georgia Hart

P.S. Plane fare enclosed if you need it.

The letter was startling enough. The check for the airline ticket, generous. But the author - Georgia Hart. Outside of Julia Roberts maybe the most beautiful and popular actress in the world. Even a kiwi outbacker like myself knew that. And married to one of the most financially successful movie directors of all time - Andrew Goldman. It was going to be a story I would never have believed.

I called Georgia and she talked me through the cursory details of Cory's death. I had to tiptoe through my inquiry to keep her from sobbing fits. I don't know why I needed to know any more than the basics; he had died for me in a small way thirteen years ago.

A trip to L.A. was arranged.

I had been fighting hard to recover from my surgery and praying there would be no recurrence of the esophageal malignancy. The flight across the Pacific was easy but the first time back on the continent in nearly a decade and a half left me balking on the mound of my own memory. My father had disappeared when I was eighteen. My estranged mother had died last year Georgia told me. Apparently, Cory was among only a handful of attendees at the funeral. They were much closer. Perhaps because they were both so beautiful to look at. I, on the other hand, inherited my barbarian father's wide nose, soft physique, and hairy back. (And his mechanical mind; I could fix anything - except relationships.)

The fear that I thought I had abandoned by leaving, crept over me the moment I felt the California sun. Could it be that apprehension is indigenous to a place? A ghostly hand wrapped around my throat as my duffel bag hit the taxi's back seat. Breathe. Breathe. I had never been so aware of my own pulse, the temples of my head caught in the pincers of some giant, invisible crustacean. I was unavoidably flowing into the form of my broken adolescence, towards a blind alley whose secrets I had been running from for thirteen years.

I tried to let the opulence of Beverly Hills distract me as the ragged cab wound its way up Benedict Canyon to the Goldman estate. I had never heard of anyone naming their home but there it was, emblazoned on the wrought iron gate - Chateau Rosebud.

So young. She had the look of someone's big sister caught in the middle of planning a surprise party. Her hand slid into mine before I even finished introducing myself. An impassive Hispanic named Raoul disappeared with my gear.

"Can I get you anything? A drink?" She asked punctiliously. Though I could sense her desire to get on with the conversation.

"No, thank you. I'm fine."

Georgia's recounting of the story began on the walk to the verandah. "My introduction to Cory began much the same way as yours." I craned my neck on the way through to get the full view of this palace - lavish, cavernous, European, baroque - a faux villa really. But it was the vision of Georgia that completed this picture and gave the house its gravity. So unabashedly youthful and beautiful in a way that the sun must be to a morning glory. She radiated warmth. I had always been suspicious of people in "the arts", especially performing arts. But I found myself giving in to her perceived kinship. I expected her to be aging then realized that she had been a star at the tender age of twenty-two, married her first director and bore his only child at twenty-three, a daughter named Lani. And yet, she appeared to be my own age. She could have been a schoolmate of mine or a buddy's ex-girlfriend.

Her body was lean; she moved like royalty. The somberness of the account she was about to give, perhaps. "Do you mind sitting outside? I do so enjoy the sun this time of day."

I shook my head. I was the tethered calf being lead to the milk of sadness.

In the bougainvillea-covered gazebo, with a panoramic view of an uncommonly blue-skied Los Angeles where the Santa Ana winds had washed the April smog momentarily away, she launched into her story.

Which was, of course, Cory's story.

The only interruption was Raoul's lunch tray. I'm sure there were countless phone calls inside and much business to be attended to. Georgia knew my brother, was close to him, intimate even, perhaps in a way I could never understand. It was almost unbearable, this woman, a titan in an industry with a global appeal, a statuesque Helen of Troy, pouring out a testimony from that place inside reserved for love's bravest charge. I had never known the geography of this place, never dared map it out. The boot heel of cultivated fear kept me pinned to my own emotional dirt. I was merely a listener now in the life of a brother I had once loved back in the buried bones of a past with a dense archaeology of pain.

"Cory was like a god..." she started.

CHAPTER ONE

He caught a glimpse of himself in the gilded hallway mirror. This was what it had come to. All those years of training. Pumping iron on two and three day splits. Mile after mile on the roads, on bike and foot. Accutane to get rid of the terrible acne. Bearing the necessary sting of the fifty dollar haircut and learning how to even out the tan. Brown rice and steamed vegetables. Boiled chicken and can after can of tuna fish. Star-Kist ought to present him with a plaque. But he loved what he saw every time he passed the looking glass. He was not Narcissus, however; he was Cory Sonne, and he had transformed himself.

An orange and green reptilian woman, as thin as a gulag's soup, slithered around circular colored patches on the canvass. The name was right there - Pissaro. It sounded famous; Cory knew it must have been. If this was in the foyer, what other famous paintings might the "Chateau" house? Andrew Goldman might even have an original of Cory's favorite artist - Norman Rockwell. This reverence for the "Saturday Evening Post" stylist was a holdover from one of the few savored moments of his childhood. Selling the most tickets for a Boy Scout-O-Rama and receiving an entire collection of silver commemorative coins of Rockwell's most celebrated pictures. The man did a lot of work for the Scouts. The scouts had been a safe haven for Cory from a father with a furious backhand that he frequently used.

Nothing could touch him now. Nothing. He had paid his dues, and now he was standing under the vaulted ceiling of a twenty million dollar home admiring the world's finest in furniture, antiques, and art. Andrew Goldman, a slice of Americana himself, had personally invited Cory. He thought to himself, "I should have saved that recorded message." To preserve the moment of his arrival. That's what he was thinking. It couldn't get any better than this. He would nail this job. He would become Andrew Goldman's personal trainer, and who knows what the possibilities would be from there?

There are moments that absolutely define life, that clearly indicate direction, irrevocably pull us out of one skin, reassemble our bones like a whole new hand in poker, and mold our new form. Rarely do we cause them to happen, have any control over them. They are like tumbleweeds pitched across our highway in the desert or a leaf that falls from an autumn tree precisely onto the line of prose we are reading, propped up on the trunk and a gnarled root. They come to us but they are never innocent, carrying the blood of temptation, the funnel of desire, the fragment of an unrealized dream. They wear the face of love or danger or both. Cory was seized by such a moment locked into the vision of Georgia Hart descending the stairs towards him.

His life would never be the same.

Her eyes came at him like parallel arrows. He would suffer them, pull them through his flesh, out the other side and wear their scars.

Before words, before the shaking of hands, there was the dance across the eyebeam, the silent sliding of one foot over another on the high-wire that connected them, their preter-selves passing through each other on the way to the platform of the other's being. Cory Sonne and Georgia Hart, who had never met before, balanced in front of each other desperately searching for that place they instinctively felt that both had been.

"I see you've met my wife." The bazooka voice boomed from the landing. Cory and Georgia turned toward Andrew, their bodies parting like church doors dismissing the congregation.

"Yes." Cory answered, though they had not exchanged words. The first lie. Or was it? He shook

Andrew's meaty hand. All business now.

"No use beating around the bush. We need you for a three month shoot in Poland. After what you did for Lisa Sanderson in 'Outside Force,' it seems you're the man."

"Andrew, he isn't inside ten seconds yet." Her voice was mellifluous and clear, obviously trained, with a hint of an odd accent, or fragments of stolen accents throughout the years.

Andrew was right. He was "the man." Outside Force had made nearly two hundred million dollars, and Lisa Sanderson was the new, female James Bond. Part of her appeal was the ripped chest and shoulders that Cory had given her after eight exhausting months in the gym and on running trails.

But Poland? Three months? Even with the fall of the Berlin Wall five years ago it was still Eastern Europe. And in the dead of winter? After seven years of building a business in L.A. with a dozen steady clients who had been putting bread on his table for over three years? Not to mention the stars that came and went according to their schedules. How could he leave them? "You didn't mention on the phone that it was out of the country."

"Why? Because I specifically want you. And in order to make that clear, I needed to meet your objections in person." Such slick confidence. 'Selling snow to Eskimos' his mother used to call it. But there was something quite likable in his open countenance. Probably what Georgia treasured about him other than his genius, his money, his irrefutable place in history. Cory stopped himself from making the mental list.

"But I'm dug in pretty deep in this community."

"Yes, I know. I made some calls." Andrew had spoken with most of Cory's clients, asking permission in an offhand sort of way. They were glad to consent and help out, though they must have all secretly enjoyed being "owed" by Andrew Goldman.

"Funny, no one mentioned it to me."

"There are things to know, and there are things to know. If you get my meaning." Cory was not one for the surreptitious. He'd called a spade a spade his whole life, suffered a little for it but slept like a rock at night. He didn't have the wading boots for the tide of bullshit so common in the Hollywood setting.

"I'd be giving up my entire income for three months, and having to live with the uncertainty that my clients may not be there when I get back."

"Oh, they'll be there. But I can understand your reluctance. And what would it take to overcome this apprehension?"

The deal-making, at last.

"Financially?"

"If that's you're ballpark." What could he have meant by that? What other considerations were there? Cory wondered if Andrew believed that secretly he wanted to be an actor. He'd been accused of that before, told he had “the look.” You couldn’t be young, healthy and reasonably attractive in L.A. without everyone assuming you were an aspiring actor.

Cory reassured him. "That's my only ballpark. Guaranteed." They understood each other.

He was not prepared to make or field an offer like this. The figures tumbled through his head. Number of workouts per week multiplied by the hourly rate. Be bold, he told himself. Ask for fifty percent over that. Georgia stared at him, tugging on the left lapel of her low-neck Armani shirt, her breasts surprisingly visible. Was she nervous? Doing it on purpose?

"At least three thousand a week." Cory served it up like a fastball.

Without a split second's hesitation, Andrew replied. "Done. Plus travel, accommodations, expenses, and standard per diem." Andrew had driven it over the center field fence. They were shaking hands. Georgia was smiling. Cory was going to Poland.

CHAPTER TWO

There were only two weeks to arrange the transition. Fortunately, for Cory, he had been training an underling, Jake Fields, to work with some of his client overflow, schooling him in the finer points of designing specific programs, understanding weaknesses and catering to them, maintaining safety, and most importantly, dealing with the wealthy. How lucky for Jake; his income would more than quadruple over the next three months. Then there was always the chance that the clients might prefer Jake's methodology over Cory's. Possible. The pleasant introduction of change could not be overlooked. No matter how hard Cory tried to keep up with the latest advances, equipment, and information, he often felt he wasn't doing enough for people who swore allegiance to his abilities. Variety. Core training, dynamic circuits, bands and flexballs, body bars and balance boards. He had to give them variety. He knew that much about human nature. Well, they were getting it now; they were getting a whole new trainer, a new face to look at. Yeah, he might lose them all. Possible, but not likely.

It was remarkable how much business there was to attend to. Mail, telephone, gas and electric, paying off credit cards in full, paying rent, car payments, insurance for three months in advance. Cory met Miranda, Georgia's haughty but perspicacious assistant, who would have been a linebacker had she copped a Y chromosome at conception and the proper dose of testosterone. Miranda told him it would be ten times more difficult to conduct business in the U.S. from Poland. No doubts about that. But being single and Spartan, Cory's ducks were easily aligned and his readiness in tow.

Setting up the gym in Krakow, on the other hand, was not so simple. Andrew had sent a team of interior designers over months ago. They were converting a former communist dignitaries' hotel into what amounted to a fancy, colorful dormitory for the film's inner circle of crew and the Goldman family. One whole room set aside for exercise. Cory had been making phone calls at one and two in the morning with companies in West Germany and Austria to ensure quality equipment, no matter what the cost. There would be little time for repair; no room for error. He even ordered a second treadmill and high/low pulley stack and had them put into storage at the hotel. Just in case. No way he was going to be without. They were shipping exercise equipment he was unfamiliar with to a place he'd never seen. He could only hope that it would all be set into motion correctly and effectively.

A copy of the script came in the package Miranda handed him the day after he had consented to the job. A Holocaust movie. Cory's first reaction was disconsolation. He envisioned it - Nazi uniforms, death camp locations, freezing weather, starving extras who "look the part", a general moroseness permeating the production. And why? Had there not been enough written and filmed about the atrocity? After Night and Fog, Shoah, QB7, Triumph of the Spirit, the eponymous and widely viewed Emmy-winning mini-series, and innumerable others, what else could be raked out of the heavy hearts of a world that continued to bear the pain of remembering. That would be Andrew's argument. To make sure they keep remembering. A jackhammer of a film, a truncheon over their collective head? Would they line up for this story again even with Andrew's name on it?

It was clear that this one was Andrew's shot at the big "O." The Oscar. The motion picture industry's big prize that had escaped him his entire career. Over two billion dollars at the box office. Wasn't that enough? Very few filmmakers in history had his track record. No. He wanted that Best Picture Honor. And with Eastern Europe open for negotiation, with the infamous script for the Pulitzer Prize winning Pillar Of Salt polished, and with Georgia matured and ripe for the role, Andrew was loading up his magic carpet ride to Krakow.

Cory had to get a jump on Georgia's training. His second trip to Chateau Rosebud was about getting down to brass tacks. Five feet ten inches tall and all leg, small boned, which was a big advantage, broad-backed, a disadvantage, narrow jawed - perfect. It didn't matter, though, because once you looked into that face, you would interpret her however she wanted you to. That was her gift as an actress. And those tits.

"What are we going to do about those tits?" Cory looked into the mirror to address her even though she stood right next to him, tramping away on her Stairmaster. She blushed.

"Cory!" She smiled and said it like she'd known him for years. "What's wrong with them?"

"Nothing. That's the problem. They're perfect. How long have you had them?" Georgia started with the look of 'whatever do you mean?' "Save it. I've been around bodies too long not to know the difference."

This was Los Angeles after all. Breast implant capitol of the world. He could spot them in a second. He'd spent enough time looking, pondering, lusting and looting women's breasts. Not to mention training a score of women before, during, and after surgery.

"Four years. I gave mother nature all the time she deserved then decided to make my own physics."

"Well, yours don't actually defy gravity; they give in just enough to make them look authentic."

"Then how did you know?"

"Bone width. Ninety-nine percent of the time your wrist and ankle widths have a direct correlation to your bodyfat potential. And remember, a mammary is all water and fat."

"You're taking all the eroticism out of them." She chided him then bent over a little, pushing them together until they practically spilled out of her leotard - a bodacious cornucopia.

"If you could sense the way my blood was moving now, you wouldn't have said that." Cory covered his mouth. Why did he say that? "I'm sorry. It just slipped out."

"Don't worry, Cory. I've heard worse over the vegetable stand at Gelsons, and I've been known to deliver an off-color remark or two myself. Just warning you."

"Fair enough." Cory responded.

Beads of sweat began their retreat down the pronounced nape of her neck. Sternocladymastoid, Cory would have called it. The muscle. But the Latin-derived name didn't take anything away from the beauty of it. The smooth shape, tapered like a rivulet of flesh, immaculately integrated into the whole of her upper torso.

He took her wrist. Found the pulse. Counted beats. She eyed him, fixed on his watch. “Twenty-two. This is the place you want to be when you perform any cardio-vascular workout for the next two weeks. We want to burn bodyfat at first without losing the metabolizing muscle. To guarantee that you work at the low end of your training heart rate for a longer period of time. “Georgia nodded and flipped back the rogue strand of hair hanging over her forehead.

"I've got to be unusually thin for this part. Concentration camp you know."

"Yes, I read the script."

Her eyes widened. "That was quick."

"Had to know what I was getting myself into."

"And do you?"

Cory smiled, “We’ll deal with your haunted, deprived look as we get further in. That will most likely push you into a very fragile place – mentally and physically. For now let’s try and stay healthy.” He changed the subject. "About the tits? What are you going to do with them? Anything?"

"I was thinking about having the implants removed for the part..."

"Oooh, brutal." Cory moaned.

"Hey, it's the role of a lifetime. What's a couple of

incisions for a shot at an Oscar?"

"What changed your mind?"

"Andrew. He loves them. Didn't want to part with them. I don't know why he never goes near them." The last words trailed off as if she had changed her mind about letting Cory hear them. "We're going to tape them down. He did it for Julie Height in 'McBert' when she played a man."

"Well, now I know what I'm dealing with."

"Your education is only beginning, pretty boy." Cory laughed but the remark circled around like a black boomerang and lodged in the back of his mind. There was recklessness behind her smile.

CHAPTER THREE

Francesca Duchesne worked in a beauty salon - Bunini of Beverly Hills. She knew how to ameliorate her appearance, to present a face that wasn't hers. And she came upon this impeccable knowledge gradually, with years of experimentation. The tricks. Contouring lip liner just dark enough to create fullness, light enough to blend seamlessly. Layering on the base to cover the natural patchiness of her skin tone and give uniformity, as if the countenance coming at you in the night hid no secrets - just plain and beautiful and brushed on. Covering the iris of a dull, gunmetal gray eye with a violet contact lens to inspire a sparkle that never came with the morning pillow. Fooffing the almond blonde hair, not her real color since the Junior

Prom, over the face to frame the bones that lacked classic lines. And the piece de resistance - the nails. Perfect. Manicured like a banzai. Always a hot breath away from red. Acrylic. Cory had been growing most tired of them, the tapping sound they made, a woodpecker on a Formica tree. Maybe he was looking for excuses. Georgia surely used make-up, just not like a rodeo girl waiting for her broken cowboy.

Cute, little Francesca. If she had possessed anything less than the sexual appetite of an entire harem, he would have relinquished the free haircuts long ago. But Cory knew the two of them were not right when the prospect of leaving Francesca for three months left him undaunted. Better to end it now. He waited until she shaved the fuzz on his neck.

Chin down, he spoke to the floor. "I've had an offer."

The sheering continued, unflustered. "What's that?"

"Andrew Goldman wants me to go to Poland and train on the set with Georgia Hart; it's three months, maybe longer." A long pause, just the hum of the electric razor. "I'm taking it."

Francesca buzzed off and looked into the mirror at her lover. The reflective other, a third person she suddenly felt she did not know. "What are you saying, Cory?"

"Three months is a long time. I'm saying don't wait

for me."

She picked up the soft brush, custom made from alpaca hair, and delicately cleared the cut locks from Cory's neck and shoulders, reining in the tears during her last act of kindness. She had swallowed so much her whole life. The hole in the lining of her stomach would widen, and through it would flow every drop she would not shed for Cory's satisfaction. At the bottom of her heart's garden, she knew this day would uproot. But she would sorely miss him; he had treated her well if a bit constrained. He never left a dirty dish on her counter, never complained about her cold feet on the back of his calves, and always let her come first and last. She would miss him all right, and she hated that most of all.

CHAPTER FOUR

"We've made a decision." Georgia handed Cory the dumbbells. Her biceps burned with the sting of fatigue after thirty wide grip curls. She was on the circuit, and Cory ushered her to the stationary bike.

"About what?" He asked innocently.

"Lani is coming with us to Poland. We're designing a curriculum in conjunction with her school here. A sort of semester in Europe thing."

"Pedal speed up." Cory rotated his finger. "That sounds cool. Use the continent as one big classroom. She'll certainly learn about the Holocaust."

"Yes, and she'll be writing papers and taking classes at the American School with an English speaking teacher we've hired especially for the girls."

"Girls?" He muttered? Emphasizing the 's.'

"Couldn't let her go it alone. She's bringing her classmate, Niki, along."

"Lucky girl."

"Both lucky. They're going to have you as a phys. ed. teacher."

"I see. Despite the fact that I'm not credentialed?" Cory cracked open an Evian bottle, removed the plastic ring, and handed it to Georgia. She spoke between drinks.

"Well, we told the school that you had expertise in this area and that it wasn't new to you. Do you?"

"Not in the prep school setting. But I instruct every day. And I've trained teenagers before."

"I know. They'll probably get more out of working closely with you than their gym class. Hell, I hardly went when I was in high school. Spent most of my time forging notes and smoking up behind the shop buildings. You can give them an introduction to fitness they'll take with them the rest of their lives."

"I can do nutrition, anatomy, physiology..." Cory gained enthusiasm.

"Why not?"

They locked gazes. Their eyes talking about something else. As if, in their foreshadowing of the expedition, they could sense some other sumptuousness. The same thought. But they dared not admit it to each other. The good, implacable fantasy is the second bird in the bush. Cory and Georgia shared the one in their hands - the training session. Cory was not the type to trade up on unbirthed dreams?

The sibilant cascading over her bottom lip changed tone. "Sssso. You need to get Lani and Niki together and started on a training program."

"I'm freed up in the afternoons beyond Thursday. No problem." Cory agreed.

"Great. They'll be so excited. I have to warn them not to fall in love with their trainer." Georgia laughed. Joy drew her cheeks back and put a scintillating generosity in her whirlpool eyes.

Attempting nonchalance, Cory inquired, "How old are they?"

"Sixteen."

"Sixteen? No problem."

"Don't kid yourself. Sixteen in these environs ain't sixteen in Joplin, Missouri."

A shot fired over Cory's bow.

CHAPTER FIVE

The subterranean gym of Chateau Rosebud was so thoroughly outfitted even the cleaning equipment had a hand-carved cabinet of its own. Cory scanned the racks of CD's, slipped in something he thought the girls would like - Prince - and adjusted the bass.

Vibrations.

The music. The muscle contractions. Quantum Physics. The Big Bang. The Soul. All vibration? He meandered through the brick-a-brack of his mind while he waited for Lani and Niki.

Resting a foot on the recumbent bike, ordered especially for Andrew and which he seldom used, he noticed the slim paperback on the floor next to the Stairmaster.

Robert Frost - "A Boy's Will." He opened to the bookmark. His eye immediately caught by what was underlined.

STORM AND FEAR

When the wind works against us in the dark,
And pelts with snow
The lower chamber window on the east,
And whispers with a sort of stifled bark,
The beast,
'Come out! Come out!'-
It costs no inward struggle not to go,
Ah, no!
I count our strength,
Two and a child,
Those of us not asleep subdued to mark
How the cold creeps as the fire dies at length,

How drifts are piled,
Dooryard and road ungraded,
Till even the comforting barn grows far away
And my heart owns a doubt
Whether 'tis in us to arise with the day
And save ourselves unaided.

Georgia. Had to be hers. Not exactly light reading for the cardiovascular workout. Everyone else seemed to prefer the trash novels - "easy reads" his clients always said. Danielle Steele, Stephen King, John Grisham. Cory wasn't an avid reader. Periodicals mostly. Discover, Muscle and Fitness, Sports Science. Poetry? Might as well have been Polish. Which reminded him to pick up a Polish/English dictionary.

The pelting rain slanted across the Florentine driveway. December rain that would soon be January snow in Krakow.

Georgia's voice preceded them into the gym. "Cory? Are you down there?"

"Yes." He scooted to the stereo and subdued Prince's "Sexy Motherfucka."

A beautiful mother, a stunning daughter, and her equally attractive friend descended the stairs. "I want you to meet Lani and Niki."

"Hello." The handshakes were mild, the smiles confessional. Georgia wore a double-breasted navy Armani suit with a burgundy beret. What the designer must have had in mind for the future elegance it would inspire. Standing there in her sophistication, out in front of the novitiates, she resembled the female heron bringing her egrets to water for the first time.

"You're not going to torture us are you?" Niki asked, squinting her brown eyes in their deep sockets. Gaspari was her last name. She was Italian, but Genoese. A lighter complexion, a narrow nose that squared at the point. Thin but on the threshold of a genetically superior inheritance - a well proportioned woman's frame. Unlike Lani, who had the roundness of her father but Georgia's face. Voluptuousness was unavoidable - the breasts were there in full force. But she'd have to be careful around the corner to thirty or she'd be saddled with a Rubinesque density no longer in vogue no matter how many pictures of Marilyn Monroe still rolled off the presses every year.

"No, we're just going to do a little fitness evaluation." Cory responded.

Groans. They would not be the last ones either. The black Mercedes pulled up outside. Cory caught it out of the corner of his eye through the glass slits at the top of the far wall that allowed a ground level view of the exterior. Georgia motioned with her hands that they were all his and exited.

"I refuse to weigh myself if that's what you're thinking." Lani demanded.

"Is that right? Well, let's get a few things straight right off the top. There is no democracy in my gym. It's a dictatorship. And what I say is the rule. Just to appease you, however, I don't put much stock in the scale either. Too many variables, especially for women. PMS. Menstruation. Water retention. I know all about it. But you are going to be weighed. If you don't want to know, cover your eyes. I won't tell you, nor anyone else. I'll just keep it for my own records, and it will go to the grave with me. But we have to have a standard, a starting point against which to compare, and for now this is it. We'll do electrical impulse testing later for body composition. Who's first?" They corroborated silently as teenage girls can do. Then Lani covered her eyes and stepped on the scale.

Cory relaxed and read the numbers. Inside he was relieved. He had won the first battle, established the hierarchy, instilled the first discipline. No small feat. It reflected a great respect for the mother, he thought. Trust in Cory by default from Georgia's loving daughter. He was pleased to see there was a bond between Lani and Georgia. And Niki fit right in.

The evaluation proceeded smoothly, even after the shrieks that came when Prince started singing "Woman, Oh Woman."

CHAPTER SIX

"It doesn't bother you? A high profile guy like Andrew Goldman, symbol of the decadent west, our Super Jew, rubbing it in their faces by making a Holocaust movie in Eastern Europe where god knows there's already enough unrest?"

"It's only a movie, Gabe."

It was Cory's last night in town and he chose to spend it with his closest friend at his favorite restaurant - Toscana. Stabbing at the gorgonzola gnocchi with his fork and waiting for his swordfish. Gabe pursued, sliding his Polo glasses up the slope of his long nose with his middle finger.

"Triumph Of The Will was only a movie. Jaws was

only a movie; it crippled the east coast ocean front resorts for years. Remember New Jack City? They rioted in Westwood." Gabe prided himself on being a pragmatist. He was a money man, an accountant with a formidable firm that catered to the entertainment industry. And capriciousness was a sin he scrupulously avoided. Unfortunately, he tried impressing this on everyone else, Cory included.

"Well, I'm not going to be in Poland when the movie opens, now am I, Gabe?"

"Cory..." Gabe pointed his spoon at Cory. In his passion, flecks of lobster bisque spat across the table, anointing his friend. "...Sorry. But come on. Ethnic Cleansing. Bosnia, South Africa, Rwanda. The New Tribalism. Hell, there are even young fascists claiming the Holocaust never happened. That's scary."

"What should I do? Stay here? Wait for the next Rodney King incident to incite the two hundred thousand gun-carrying gang bangers to maraud and loot at will?"

"All right." Gabe pondered the last piece of garlic bread in the basket. "You're right. I'm probably overreacting."

"Probably." Cory added sardonically.

"But do me a favor, keep your eyes peeled and don't trust anyone."

"I do that here."

They laughed.

Campy, the giraffe-like maitre d', brought over a bottle of wine. "Signore Cory, you must try this new Chianti. It is magnifico. I give it to you as a going away present." Campy was a generous, demonstrative Italian. A redundancy, Cory surmised. It had turned out to be one of his shrewder moves to offer training sessions to him over a year ago when the restaurant first opened in exchange for meals. Intended as a kindness for a pleasant and eager beginner, the gesture blossomed into a blessing of favor every time he dined at the popular Brentwood eatery.

Campy poured with his back to the commotion at the door, then turned and finished in a hurry. "'Scuze'."

"What's all the fuss?" Gabe rattled between sips.

Trent Tarver had arrived with a trail of sycophants. Hollywood's favorite up-and-comer.

"A star on the rise." Cory intoned.

"And the detritus behind him." Gabe added.

Campy was steering them near the corner table at the window. He was no fool. It was good business for the high profile clients to be seen by those passing by.

Gabe clicked his tongue - an idiosyncrasy on the cusp of annoyance. "Had to be a good reason for that open table when there are forty starving civilians waiting for a seat."

"I won't miss this bullshit while I'm gone."

"You'll get your version. It's indigenous to the movie business."

Trent Tarver chose the aisle next to Cory's table. It circled through more of the restaurant. Trent came towards him; would he recognize Cory? They had trained together four months in preparation for Trent's breakout film - Banger Street. And if he did remember, would he even say hello? Cory had learned never to expect anything from celebrities. That was the only safe way to play it. They had needs and behaviors better left to whores and analysts. They were, in a sense, whores themselves. Prostituting their talent and/or fame for adulation and adoration that never filled the vacuum of their insecurity. He wondered if deep down inside Georgia wasn't cut from this same loathsome cloth. It was his opinion and he never forgot that but he was always on the lookout for a circumstance to prove him wrong. He'd yet to find it.

Their eyes met. Some recognition. Even a small nod, not much more than a Greek fisherman confirming the weather. Perhaps the force of the chattering column behind him prevented him from stopping. But the nod was enough, and Cory stabbed back just his name, "Trent."

And they were gone. Catapulted into the Hollywood din of Toscana's deal-making table.

"A small victory." Gabe was right in tune.

"You saw it? I didn't just anticipate it?"

"Nope. That was a definite nod of recognition. The Lloyds of London chin dipped in your favor."

The swordfish arrived.

Campy swung around to the table and poured the remainder of the Chianti. "How's everything?"

"Superb. As always." Cory said.

"Benne'. I told Mr. Tarver about your trip to Poland. He says he work with you before. Si?"

"Yes. He's a decent guy." Cory added.

"Decent for now, eh?" Campy winked at him as he caromed off to his other clients. There wasn't a patron seated in his restaurant who he didn't know by name or association. Not on a Friday night. He was a pro's pro. And he took those little folded twenty, fifty, and hundred dollar bills with the ease of a painter's brush stroke. Campy was an artist and the sybaritic were his canvas.

The tap on the shoulder surprised Cory. He looked up. Trent Tarver stuck out his hand. "Swordfish. It figures." He obviously missed the gorgonzola gnocchi, Cory thought.

Cory pushed his chair back and stood. "Trent. You're looking good. This is my friend Gabe Rosen." They shook; Gabe didn't stand.

"I hear you're going with Goldman to Poland."

"Yeah, for Georgia mostly."

"I'd go to the south pole for her." He lodged a fist into Cory's shoulder, not gently. Firm enough to telegraph the message: 'I'm still working out, and I'm better than ever.' A macho gesture Cory inherently despised.

"It's a grim project. Auschwitz and all." Cory

wanted off the subject of Georgia fast. No opportunity for mistakes. Even prolonged conversation could lead to gossip, and there were plenty of jackals at these tables. He was instinctively looking out for her already, though he had no idea why.

Trent cleared his throat. Affectation. "Yeah. I read for Andrew. With Georgia. I was this close." He held thumb and forefinger together.

"Who is the male lead?" Cory asked, shocking even himself. He had never bothered to find out. Hadn't given it any thought. It flashed on him. Man, was he single-minded; he better get his head straight. Trent mumbled something. "I'm sorry?" Cory hadn't heard the name. It seemed to pain Trent to repeat it. Cory liked that.

"Sean McDonough. Friggin' Irishman. Get a load of that." It was uncharacteristic of Trent to publicly emote. He caught himself. "But he's good with accents, and there's a heavy German thing going on."

Cory nodded. Some moments of sticky silence. As if Trent expected Cory to be forthcoming with some private information. But there was nothing he could use, and so Trent terminated the conversation. "Well, good luck, and give my best to the Goldmans." He moved out of Cory's parting handshake - the recoil of a firing pin.

Cory resumed sitting. When Trent was well away, Gabe shook his head. "What?" Cory asked.

"Nothing." Gabe smirked; Cory chose to ignore.

"By the way, did I tell you I'm flying over on the Concorde?"

Gabe leaned in. "Do you realize where you're headed?"

Campy saluted Cory from across the restaurant. Cory wanted to say, "I'm the best. I'm the best fucking trainer in this goddamn city. That's where I am." But he sat there staring at his Jewish friend whose concern was legitimate. Did Gabe sense something Cory was too involved to notice? Gabe's was a question for which Cory had no answers.

CHAPTER SEVEN

The house on Decker Street was filled with the saddest melodies and bleakest landscapes growing up. Rebecca Sonne, Becky as she was known to all but the county registrar and her distant relatives, studied music and drawing at the community college before settling in to her role of wife and mother - an abandonment of sorts. She did, however, manage to escape a career with the tools of her brief arts education, a hand-me-down piano and a sturdy easel.

Cory never minded the music growing up. Though he sensed between the notes a longing for release his mother did not possess in her domestic labors.

The paintings were a different matter. The walls

were fettered with dull vistas, lacking clarity and depth as if the artist suffered from a kind of myopia and could never clearly see the object horizon. Cory had always thought she'd have been better off going impressionistic, rendering the image in her mind, freeing up her dependency on the "real." But Becky was never that brave. And she painted, in water and oil, mediocre canvases Cory came to resent. Especially the night his father, Eli, beat her over the head with an "Autumn Stream" screaming at her, "Cry me a river, schoolgirl! Cry me a fucking river!"

From this, Cory gleaned the lesson that whatever he did in his life he would do better than anyone else. There would be no mediocre sunsets on his walls nor in his acts.

CHAPTER EIGHT

A blazing, yellow-white tumbleweed working its way towards them from a great distance. That's the way Cory saw the sun from the window of the Concorde, sixty thousand feet above terra firma, two-thirds of the way to outer space. The dark desert behind it, the cape of the galaxy dappled with winking light, only dramatized the sunset. Was every star really a human soul telegraphing its love back to earth as his mother had often told him as a child? If so, who were these people who first showed up on the cusp of the night? The oldest? The most desperate? The most missed? Becky?

Cory looked down the row of seats. Lani, next to him, bobbed her head in time to the tune on her discman, a faint murmur to Cory's ears. Niki slept on her shoulder. He had agreed to escort the two of them, five days ahead of Georgia and Andrew, so they could get a jump on school in Krakow.

Paris. Stop number one. A driver from Warner Brothers International would meet them at baggage claim. Cory would need the help. For two girls who were supposed to have packed and shipped everything but the essentials over last week, they still seemed unnecessarily loaded down. Two big duffels, a backpack, a carry-on, and a laptop computer - apiece. Cory had done what he was told. One bag, one carry-on. He sensed this would be more than an isolated infraction of the orders from on high.

Sitting in his comfortable seat, he watched the Delta Wing of the plane keep things silky smooth. At ten miles up there was practically no weather; the meteorology happened below. The Mach Meter read: 3.2. They were quietly hurling through the sky at over three times the speed of sound, thirteen hundred miles per hour. Cory had once, along a desolate stretch of California highway, taken a Kawasaki Ninja 1000 up to 130 mph. Helmetless, his sunglasses had been yanked from his face and his eyes teared from the lashing wind, even as he ducked down below the meager fairing for some relief. This was ten times faster, and the caviar on his small square of toast lay undisturbed.

One week into January of 1994 and he was finally

moving up in the world, literally.

The lips were fuller, not quite Georgia's, not quite Andrew's. Somewhere in between. Lani must have sensed Cory's staring; her eyes popped open.

"What?" She asked without taking her headphones off.

"Nothing. Just seeing if you were asleep." Lani didn't hear him. With the music swelling down the tunnel of her ear, did she expect that she would?

"What?" She repeated, carelessly stripping the headphones.

"I was just checking if you were asleep." In a strange way he had grown fond of this spoiled princess. She may have been pampered and privileged but she was smart. And smart recognizes its own malfeasance even if it can do nothing about the maleficent outcome. She was mischievous often and contrite at just the right times. Cory could see that already in the dozen workouts with the two of them at the Chateau Rosebud Gym.

"I can never sleep on commercial flights," she intoned.

"As opposed to the chartered jets you're used to?"

Lani just sneered then smiled. The feigned and the literal. The sucker punch then the right cross.

"Did mom tell you Andrew's buying a new plane?"

"No, she didn't mention it."

"It was supposed to be ready for this trip but they

screwed up the paint job or something. A gold stripe that looked more yellow. Andrew hates yellow."

"Why?"

"Who knows. Maybe his mother dressed him in ugly yellow suits when he was a kid."

"And your mom?"

"What about her?"

"What was her childhood like?"

"You want the press junket version or the real version?"

"I always opt for the truth."

"Oh, you're one of those."

"Yeah. There are a few of us."

Lani shifted in her seat as if this were a more formal presentation, something she had wanted to tell him. Niki stirred but only slid to the other side of her backrest, her angel's hair swinging to the other cheek.

"There's something I like about telling this story, and it's one that I rarely get to tell. Seems no one is really ever interested in the whole story. They just like to hear about the mansions and the money and all that."

"I read somewhere that she was from Hawaii; is that right?"

"Are you going to interrupt me?"

"No, go right ahead."

"Well, in answer to your question, yes. She is from Hawaii..."

"What island?" Cory interrupted again. Lani's nostrils flared. "No, I'm just kidding. Go ahead."

"Kauai." She paused to see if the game would go on or if the story could continue unabated. Cory swept his palm up towards her, urging her to proceed. "Paradise. Or so everyone thinks when I say Kauai. Yes, the island is beautiful, the garden island and all that, but when she took me there a few years ago for her mother's funeral, not her real mother but the woman who raised her, her Hawaiian mother, she showed me the house where she was raised. It was a shack; I'm telling you. It was all overgrown, the plants had sort of taken over the property again. Wooden floors, tiny rooms she told me she shared with another hanai child. That's what the Hawaiians call a sort of 'adopted child', a hanai child. And they do this quite commonly - take in strays and make them part of the family.

"See, mom's real mother was a hippie, you know the sixties and all that, and she wanted to travel around the world with this guy she met in Honolulu on his boat so she left my mom with this guy's brother and his wife and their family and didn't return until six years later. By then, mom was so deeply entrenched, is that the right word, entrenched?" Lani asked, quizzically.

"Yeah. Sounds right to me."

"Well, she just ended up staying there until she was eighteen. Then she got a scholarship to college, the University of Hawaii, and, as she tells it, she left Kauai and never looked back."

"So it wasn't a happy childhood?"

"She never admitted it but just think about it. Abandoned as a baby. Raised with strangers, strange culture, four older Hawaiian brothers - 'mokes' she called them. Local boys who liked to drink, fight and treat women like shit. She once told me that she was always having to fight to keep them from fucking her. And her Hawaiian dad, Ricky, wasn't much better, though she said it never happened. When she was a teenager, he used to wait quietly in the bathroom for her to step out of the shower, masturbating, I think. She'd scream at him; he'd snicker then leave."

"She told you all this?"

"We're pretty close. I try to tell her everything. She feels compelled to do the same. Sometimes it gets pretty sticky. But she's a very good listener. You'll see."

"Does she ever visit them?"

"Never. She went back once I think for her best girlfriend from high school's wedding. But she said it was a mistake. They had no concept of how she had built a great life for herself. They only wanted to know why she didn't call and visit more often. They didn't get the picture. You have to remember, these are very simple people. I don't think they've ever even been away from the islands."

"And you mentioned a funeral?"

"Yes, Mama Keala's. That was when she took me.

They're pygmies, these people. Really tiny. Very mixed emotions. Mama Keala took her into her home, raised her, taught her much but had kind of an abusive side as well. Mom says she used to get beat, out of Mama Keala's frustration over Ricky's screwing around. There was sort of a Cinderella thing going on as well. Make the 'hauli' girl do all the cooking and cleaning."

"Wow. And Andrew was the rescuing prince."

"I know. Pretty amazing; isn't it? I mean to go from that to all this." Lani indicated the Concorde but what she meant was everything in her life that provided the means to travel on it.

"Then you came along pretty quickly?"

"Well, Andrew was already forty-six when they met. And he didn't have any kids."

"And Georgia was how old?"

"Twenty-two when they married. Twenty-three when she had me." Lani could see Cory doing the addition in his head. "No, I came along eleven months later; no shotgun wedding."

"Who could possibly hold the gun? Georgia didn't have a father and Andrew's was probably too old to shoot straight." Lani didn't laugh. Cory tried to cover his tracks. "Besides, she married a brilliant man, had a beautiful daughter, and built a great life."

"You know, contrary to what everyone likes to think, just because you have money doesn't mean life turns out peachy." Lani's tone of voice shifted from educational to accusing.

"You're right. I'm sorry. But despite what you might think, it still seems to me that they turned out one hell of a daughter." Sure he was brown-nosing her. But he'd been tyrannical enough in the gym; he could and should give a little ground. Lani seemed placated, for the moment.

A half a minute of prickly silence. Only the drone of Air France's metal bullet piercing the stratosphere. Out of nowhere she asked, "What's your story?"

If only he could say. If only he could really tell someone everything, unburden himself like a cement truck funneling out its heavy cargo to stiffen someone else's driveway. He lied. "Not much to tell really. Just your average, small town, all-American upbringing."

Lani nodded, a sideways motion really. As if she were trying to draw more out of him. At least that's what he thought. But his mouth locked shut when the image of his dead father, lying in a pool of blood at Cory's young feet, burst into his head. There would be no more words. Not now, not ever. Not on this subject. The spectacular hum outside dominated. Not even the Concorde could speed him away from his past fast enough.

CHAPTER NINE

The doorman at the Hotel Ritz in Paris must have thought the two teenage girls, dressed in their funky street garb and sporting camera's around their necks, were tourists. He placed his fat, French paw in the middle of their backs and shoved them right back into the revolving door before they stepped three feet inside the lobby of this grandest of hotels.

Cory had to straighten things out immediately with the concierge and accept a string of apologies from the red capped goon who was, after all, only doing his job. Still, Lani and Niki could not resist, on subsequent entrances and exits, brandishing a tongue or worse, adjusting the small flaps and lanyards of his pseudo-militaristic uniform. These girls could be brave and brutal when they were familiar with the terms or the territory.

Less than ninety minutes into the country, and they had checked in, changed, and holstered the No Limit Platinum American Express Card in their hip pocket sandwiched in a wad of French francs that could choke a mule.

Cory had barely emptied out his shaving kit along the black marble sink when the girls barged in, without knocking, and urged him to hurry up. There were only two hours left of prime shopping time. The normally indolent duo could show amazing alacrity when spending was the order of the day.

Stephan, the limo driver, was at the ready. He reminded Cory of an elongated Robert DeNiro right down to the bristling walk. Just for fun Cory had him repeat back a few lines from Raging Bull.

"Say this, 'Did you fuck my wife, Joey?'" Stephan didn't understand. "It's a line from a movie starring Robert DeNiro."

"Oh, yes. I know Robert DeNiro. I like him very much."

"So say the line. 'Did you fuck my wife, Joey?'"

Stephan drew the deep breath of the Final Jeopardy contestant. "Did you fuck my wife, Joey?" Not even close. He might as well have been ordering French fries. But it did give them both occasion to laugh.

Cory finished the dialogue for Stephan, doing both parts. "'I heard some things, Joey. I heard some things.'

'What things?'

'Some things; I heard some things.'

'You're fuckin' crazy. Look at you, you fat fuck. I can't even see the TV your fat stomach is so fuckin' big.'

'I'm aksin' ya. Did you fuck my wife?'

'Yah. I fucked her. We all fucked her. Salvy, Eddie, me, we all fucked her. You crazy fuck...'"

Cory was into it. Stephan stared intently. Passersby on the streets looked at him as if he were mad. Cory had loved this scene from the moment he saw it on screen. It was easy to memorize, seething with familiar tension. It delineated a violence he learned from the inside out.

The girls giggled on their way back to the car, the bulk of their packages hiding everything below the neck and above the knee. Kookai, Et Vous, Chippies. They had executed a good run at these three stores; picked up shoes, blouses, jeans and sweaters, and a pair of black dresses for La Scala that evening that would put five years on them - the necessary five years to be taken seriously on the club scene.

In the next three days, they would procure lingerie from Chantel-Thomas, customized perfume from Anouck-Gouton, have their hair cut and nails manicured at Erte, been saunaed, massaged, and facialed at the spa in the ornate basement of the Hotel Ritz, and eaten at some of the world's finest restaurants, including Chez Ami Louis and Natacha. And in the process, out of the window of a car or the corner of an eye, they would catch a glimpse of an historic sight or two - who could miss the Eiffel Tower or the spires of Notre Dame, or the Arc d' Triomphe and the Etoile when driving down the Champs Elysee? And all because the next four months they would spend in Krakow, Poland. And nobody had any idea what was in store for them there. For these bulimics of hedonism, the days in Paris were the binge of pleasure before the purge of the post-communist east.

Cory, too, was indulging himself. For the first time in months, he allowed himself dessert at dinner. French patisseries were unparalleled. And cheese. Camembert, Reblochon, Pont-l'Eveque. Complimented by delectable glasses of red wine from Bordeaux and Burgundy. Falling asleep every night under the frescoed ceiling sixteen feet above his king-sized bed, counting the golden cherub's huddled in the corner cornices as if they were sheep, he felt utterly Napoleonic in this palatial suite that wanted for no ostentatious detail. Only a Josephine would complete the scene.

And yet, the most loamy harvest of his brief stay in Paris came not from luxuries he had been afforded but from the telephone. Georgia's Sunday morning call.

"Hello." Cory rolled over to answer it.

The voice on the other end was mollifying music

from ancient evenings, a secret of mystics whispered into the ear of the uninitiated. Georgia spoke to him as if she were in no hurry. "Cory? It's Georgia. How are you?"

He rolled back over into the cocoon of his eiderdown quilt, soft against the naked length of his body. "Hey, it's good to hear your voice. A link to the homeland."

"You too. How's everything going? No problems, I hope?"

"None. Paris may never recover." She laughed at the other end. She knew exactly what he was talking about.

"And they're not giving you any trouble?"

"What trouble? You've already told them they could do anything they wanted. I'm just along for the ride."

"Should I have been less generous?" Georgia asked, sincerely.

Cory laughed. "What do I know about raising a daughter?"

"Sometimes an unbiased outsider, at least a smart one like yourself, can see things wrong that an intimate is blind to."

This was not the conversation he expected when the phone rang, and he was hardly going to get into it with a parent about their kid's behavior. But he loved listening to her. It seemed as if they had all the time in the world. Just talking. Her voice tumbling over the wire likes waves into the eddy of his soul.

"Lani's all right. She just wants for nothing. At

least materially. I don't know about the rest. I don't know if she'll tell you but I know she misses you. If that's what you want to know."

"No, I wasn't fishing for that but it's nice to know." A gap in the conversation; each waiting for the other to begin again.

"And you?" Cory asked.

"Me? You mean how am I doing?"

"Yeah. Anything."

"You mean I could tell you anything right now and you'd just listen?"

"Sure. You have such a great voice, so soothing. It's like a bathrobe for my ear, just makes me want to sit back, relax and listen to you."

Georgia spit out a laugh. "Bathrobe for your ear. Interesting metaphor."

Cory couldn't help himself. Her intonation stirred his heart, a loving calliope of crests and troughs. It was as if he could feel the whispers of air formed in the back of her throat then spun through her vocal chords, picking up vibrations and pauses then tripping down her tongue, out through her mouth to a leap off her lips until they softly parachuted onto the drum of his ear. The end result; they made him feel so...so...peaceful.

Georgia's giggling tapered off. She was amused but after a few moments of silence she tried to deflect the praise. "Oh, it's the actress thing. All that training."

"No, it's not pretentious. It's just nice to talk to you." It was much more than that but Cory thought it best to put it simply. If he had to go into detail about the supplicant buzz in his head, or the thousands of tiny fuzzy fingers marching warmly across his skin, or the blood rushing to his genitals and swelling his prick along the inside of his thigh, he would never find the words to express much less justify what was unconsciously happening to him. All he could think about in that moment was what she was wearing, where she was standing, or was she sitting, or lying down like himself? Where did all this come from? A voice? He certainly wasn't meditating on it before the phone rang. He had been trying to think of the best power forwards in the NBA that the Lakers should go after to fill the void left by James Worthy's departure. How did that lead to the rototiller in his stomach now?

"Yes. I know what you mean." Georgia drew a big sigh.

Cory recognized that sigh. He threw back the quilt and stared at his erection but he dared not touch it as long as Georgia's breath filled his ear. For a male accustomed to grabbing his genitals, it was an exercise in restraint. She did not speak, as if she were in the room quietly watching him.

Finally, "Well, you better put Lani on the phone."

"Sure." He'd have loved to have been greedy and begged for more words, more spaces between words, more breathing in his titillated ear. But he stood. "I'll go get her."

Cory threw the phone on the bed and gazed at it - a lover sleeping in white. He waited for the blood to subside, wrapped the complimentary bathrobe around his body and traipsed across the suite to the girls' door and knocked. "Lani, your mom's on the phone. Line one."

A faint murmur that resembled, "Okay." Cory waited until he heard conversation then returned to his room. He cradled the receiver in his hand, listened for a moment more, to refresh his mind, to load another syringe with her voice, heard something about the Paris cafes, then hung up. He thought about jacking off in front of the full-length mirror encased in mahogany. But something about its purfled edges sweeping up to the lancet arch made it to regal for such a vulgar dissipation. Instead, Cory settled into his cozy bed and let the ooze of infatuation flow through his veins.

So this was Paris.

CHAPTER TEN

Georgia Hart hung up the phone, her insides turning over - a tempest in the lower drawer of her stomach. She hadn't felt this way since, since, well maybe never. Not exactly. The last time she had been so queasy was in the months that followed the tragic stillbirth of her son, whom she intended to call David. She and Andrew had the name picked out way beforehand, after his long-deceased father. Georgia insisted on referring to the fetus as David even though it never drew one breath from the world in which she had imagined him as a boy and a man. So many plans considered but never this one. But that was nearly two years ago and seemed longer; she had taken on so much business in an effort to put some ground between them.

Perhaps the reaction was physical. She had passed on breakfast, spent the morning out in the sun reading the newest draft of Pillar of Salt which restored the original ending, one the producers had considered too gruesome to allow. But the story was a true one, and it had been decided that shying away from the real ending would be a disservice to the audience. The disturbing scenes would stay; the challenge for her as an actress was swelling like a marsh in flood. A role for the ages. Would this one put her in the ranks of Streep, Hunter, Foster, and Pfieffer? Or even Davis and Hepburn? That alone was enough to make the bile rise. No, this wasn't about the script. Somehow, this was different. This was oddly pleasurable, like a chocolate compliment or the silence that follows a marksman's gunshot through the bulls-eye.

A wealthy, wealthy woman, heading in a direction she could not afford. That's what she was thinking as she entered the hallway. The screenplay she held loosely in her fingers dropped to the marble floor; the slap reverberated through the house. Its vibration seemed to circle her, bent at the knees like an Indian tracker.

What she realized at that moment were two things: how absolutely alone she was in her extravagant manor and how a young trainer named Cory Sonne could change the chemistry of her body.

CHAPTER ELEVEN

Why does a woman stay with a man she no longer loves? It was the only thing on Cory's mind as he stared out over the wing of yet another airplane. This time, a Hawker 800 jet that belonged to Lynton Aviation out of London. A hired gun while Andrew waited for his new, stream-lined Falcon 2000, sans yellow stripe. Lani and Niki flipped through Vogue, Elle, and Mirabella, bellowing out the single epithet "anger" every time they came upon what was, in their opinion, a perfect looking woman. Cory had made a comment to them early on, "There are no perfect bodies; trust me. They're only perfect in photographs." They heard him, even nodded as if in agreement, but continued drawing secret comparisons between their young, maturing physiques and those the media chose to hold up to society as if they were the wicked witch's veracious mirror in the Legend of Snow White.

Were they related? The girls' desire to be desired and the reasons a woman stays with a man she doesn't love?

There was his mother. A beautiful woman, even against the magazines' standards. Constantly deflecting wolf calls from construction workers, wearing over-sized blouses and sweaters to hide her voluptuousness, traveling her eyes along the ground to avoid the inevitable engagements with men whose conversations began with their dicks. A banquet of attention on the streets, while shopping, at social functions yet under her own roof, she starved. There were engraved champagne glasses tucked away on her kitchen's upper shelf that had not kissed the grape since her honeymoon. There were places on her body that had not been touched by any hands in as many years. When Cory came upon this knowledge in his early teens, a portion of his heart severed and drifted towards his mother's custodial lament like some arctic flow of ice.

And then there was Georgia. Cory kept thinking of the comment Lani had made when they had just finished buckling in and were awaiting takeoff. Reading out loud from some sex survey, their way of inviting comments from Cory, they emphasized this question: "Should age make a difference in your enjoyment of a partner?"

Lani blurted out, "Yeah, unless you're into making

love with your father."

Cory couldn't let it pass. "With Andrew?"

"No, not me. My mom. You know she only married him because he represented a father figure she never had?"

"No. I didn't know that. Sounds like you're simplifying the situation." Cory responded.

"Am I? She doesn't love him. Do you think a woman as sexy and as sexual as my mom could really get turned on by Andrew's hairline? His soft body? His old skin?"

"You're so young. Who knows what turns anyone on? I guess Andrew's too busy being a genius and a legend to worry about pumping iron." He didn't know why but he felt Andrew needed defending. Would the idea of trying to impress these young girls even matter to Andrew? Would he have told Cory not to bother? He was, after all, a virile and energetic man despite his age.

"All I know is I'm going to marry someone my own age and with a 'rad' body." Niki added.

"No Supreme Court? No multi-national corporation? No award winning journalist for CNN in your future? Just want to marry some rich, 'rad' guy?"

"He's going to have to be able to afford me." Lani said; Niki nodded her approval.

The jet turned into takeoff position, barreled down the runway, and the conversation was lost. Somewhere back on the tarmac.

But Cory wouldn't let go of its relevance to his own fantasies. He saw himself sitting in tousled bed sheets with Georgia on her stomach, locking into a cold plum with her tired jaw, the length of her body still trembling from satisfaction, her pointed toe arcing up and back from mattress to buttocks like a toppled metronome. She, a pre-serpent Eve enjoying the forbidden tree in the Eden of Cory's youth.

"Can I get you something to drink, Mr. Sonne?" The flight attendant asked. Gale, a freckled redhead, proper and poised, straight out of an E.M. Forester novel. Mr. Sonne. Very rarely had he been called that; a bank teller once in awhile, that was it. To him Mr. Sonne was his father; he shivered to compare himself.

Gale pulled open a sliding drawer. Tiny bottles of Cognac, Glenfiddich, Royal Crown, Makers Mark, bracketed by slim, six ounce cans of Coke and Seven-Up. "Additionally, champagne and white wine in the refrigerator." Behind her was a tray of smoked salmon, decorated deviled eggs, sourdough rolls, and an assortment of cheeses.

Why does a woman stay with a man she has fallen out of love with, maybe never loved? Cory was only guessing about Georgia. Little hints dropped like bread crumbs - the way she and Andrew never touched in the times he had seen them together, her keeping her hair dyed blonde when Andrew had a professed attraction to brunettes, Lani's remarks. Though she'd never confessed it, there was something about the way Georgia looked at Cory that pleaded for him to dive in, to lift up a corner of the shroud draped over her inner pedestal.

Why? A lifestyle like this - champagne, elegant cuisine, sterling service, Mr. Sonne, Mrs. Goldman. Could one really let it go so easily once it had seeped into the blood? Cory could only guess. But these were merely trappings. There had to be other reasons, other mirages that would excite his eyes but never quench his thirst. That's what he was thinking in this Hawker 800, on his way to Poland with two girls who, if you placed the fabric of your life in their hands, would only check the label and could never even conceive of the idea of trying it on.

CHAPTER TWELVE

The house on Decker street screamed out to Cory, shimmering in his dream, heat off a desert highway. A turn of the century frame parched and peeling, a front porch still standing despite the soil erosion. Desiccation. The hot wind of abandonment. Orchards surrounding it, with concentric, unkempt rings of rotten plums whose putrefying smell kept strangers away. Plums. The eyes of a young Cory's thought. Even now he could recall the expression on his mother's face. Question. "Did dropped fruit rot in Adam and Eve's paradise?"

Jagged daggers of anger; canyon leopards dancing with their spots then carrying them away to sacred places.

But here. The house - a prison of mixed messages.

The ancient plumbing was where it all began. It, being the final stand. Eli. The Prophet of the Bare Knuckle. The scintilla in the singing kulak's down-swinging scythe. Slashing and Slashing. Taking him by the collar and, with a flashlight in the other hand, demanding Cory lead the way as they walked with a stoop through the storage space. Under the house. It had been his older brother Ray who'd stuffed too much paper down the toilet bowl, causing it to stop up and overflow. Under the house. Cory always got tagged for service when it came to anything there. He knew it like the back of his hand. A road map. He had always dreamed about those intersecting colored lines in the window of the Texaco station and where those roads lead. Now he just watched the pulsating veins on the back of his hand. He had built the workbench, laid down the pine for the flooring, organized the boxes and cabinets, sorted through the junk, flotsam of foolish consumption, a mosaic of outdated years.

In space, asteroids collided, knocking planets out of alignment. Imagine.

Temples swelling. Eli's frustration grew as he grappled with a rusted pipe. It would come. His Temper. It was like the tide, predictable, unrelenting. They would be unable to solve the problem on their own, and a plumber would have to be called. And payment? When there was barely enough for tomato soup and tuna fish casserole? Fury. Eli provoked. Gall, bile, choler, spleen. The rise that rivals a busted radiator spewing acrid steam.

The flashlight in Cory's hand began to shake. The wrench in Eli's slipped; his thumb took a small gash. Calling on the Almighty! Calling in an aria of expletives whose rhythm Cory would carry with him the rest of his life - the primordial lullaby. Persistent, like the freezing man who's sighted distant fires. Eli yanked the light away from Cory. Fresh blood on the blackened hand with a rich glint. Laceration. A split second later, the beam of light swiveled around; moving behind him Cory thought, until - WHACK! - the head of the the light impacted across his skull. Knees buckled; the slow, thick trickle of blood down the outside of his cheek. A taffy-pulling world, a carousel's pinion hum. He wanted to go out but the thought of what his father might do to him next kept him conscious.

Even now, worms were crawling through the skulls of history's greatest warriors.

Cory didn't hear the first words, regaining his senses only when Eli's footsteps landed on the wooden slats in front of the workbench. The door slammed. Locked. A murmur, an obscene caller stammering about "...straighten up and fly right!" Again, Cory had been locked in. So many times. Stewing in the basement below the floorboards when Eli couldn't stand the sight of him.

Hours followed; kingdoms fell. A California Angels T-shirt balled up against the side of his head to stop the blood. Approbation. Through a small opening Cory watched a heavy half-moon traverse the dark sky - his only light.

Out of the corner of his good eye, he caught it. Then heard it. A slithering snake with a venomous rattle. He would not move. Could not. Not with a mouse, not in a house, not in a box, not with a fox, no snake allowed green eggs and ham, he would not move, no Sam I Am.

In the middle of the dungeon, standing. The heart stops when the snake's slow abrasion tests the anchor of your heel. You have said you will not move and you don't. You are stone. You are scared, sweating igneous rock that needs a glacier and a billion years to displace you. And all the time you think about being bitten, bleeding down from your head and poisoned from the shin up. Mortification. There will be no more marshmallow roasts, no cross country trips, no wet as-yet-untasted pussy, no more home runs, or naked dives at Little Falls, or Oreos, or Eskimo pies, or cold apples in hot summers. Just snakes that float you away on their undulating backs from the levee of your unirrigated dreams. Cory flashed. Was the rattle really moving away from him?

Where was the choir of small-testicled boys rejoicing in God's cruel sense of humor?

Finally, after Eli had fallen asleep, Becky had come down to free him. The snake. The musty bowels of the house. His stone fear. Temporarily left behind. A quick trip down the road to Dr. Bettencourt's home and a few stitches later, the incident had passed. Prevarication. He had to make his story consistent with his mother's. He had bumped his head on a low-hanging pipe under the house. Just another of the many lies Cory would have to remember to tell about himself and about his family.

This time, however, was different. In that hollow darkness of the basement, an unimpeachable resolve galloped up, an armored knight. A glove had been thrown down, a gauntlet laid. Cory would never again be trapped by snakes. The next time their eyes met, Eli Sonne, Eli of the Jackals, Eli the Blood-lover, would be introduced to something unfamiliar - an opponent, not a victim.

Incubation. Fulmination.

CHAPTER THIRTEEN

The jet dropped out of the clouds and seemed to skim the last twenty kilometers of frozen Polish farmland before touching down on the cracked runway. This had always been Cory's favorite part of flying. The low altitude glide. No longer topography but a headlong cleaving of the passing terrain. Details visible. A slanted fence, haphazard shack, the craning neck of a bundled wagon driver whose mud-caked wheels stripped new lines in fresh snow. In the belly of this metal bird he waited for the kiss of the wheels thinking of Jonah swallowed by a whale and praying for forgiveness.

Krakow, at last.

The welcoming party cut a path to the jet rolling out customs carts for the luggage. A petite redhead named Carolyn Mann, who had worked with the Goldman's before, recognized Lani immediately, and they shared the hugs of sisters reuniting after the spring term. The cold of the eastern European winter was made stiff by the buffer of the Carpathian mountains to the south and compressed by the constant cloud cover that would shield the sun for weeks on end.

"Oh my god, Lani, you are such a...woman." Carolyn shrieked looking up at the girl she hadn't seen in years.

"This is my friend, Niki." Carolyn was not shy about hugs.

"Yes, I know. We spoke on the phone." Carolyn turned to Cory. "And you must be Cory."

Cory stuck out his hand; Carolyn slid right past it and wrapped her mittens around his torso. They made it only three-quarters around. "Nice to meet you." He mumbled.

"My, my…so, solid. Don't let me make a habit of this; I won't be held responsible for what I might do." She turned to the girls. They shared a laugh. Cory's face turned red. Embarrassment was one way to keep his face warm.

Behind them stood three men of varying ages. Carolyn introduced them. "This is Waldek and Andrzej." The two polite Poles, hands folded in front of them like altar boys, tipped there heads. "And this is Jerzy. He's my counterpart here in Krakow. We are in charge of running the Goldman house and arranging personal transportation for you guys."

Jerzy, a soft-spoken, elongated man with a thick peppered mustache and a face that reminded Cory of Peter Sellers stepped forward. "Welcome to Krakov."

It was Cory's first Polish lesson. Krakow was Krakov. By sound. W would be V. The beginning of a language orientation that might as well have been from the, well, the orient it would prove so far beyond him.

The Polish drivers, Andrzej and Waldek worked fast with the bags. They were young and fit, Andrzej the obvious athlete of the two.

In front of the terminal they piled the luggage into a white Ford Aerostar, a status car by Polish standards. Carolyn and the girls went with Andrzej in the green Audi; Cory and Jerzy in the brown Mercedes Sedan.

The house was not far from the airport. Ten kilometers of sloping white hummocks and hibernal meadows, barren trees and muddy roadsides until they reached the upper crust community known as "starszy ranga" - which means superior rank. The Beverly Hills of Krakow. Halfway around the world to end up in a different version of the same place, Cory thought.

But it wasn't the same.

All the way in from the airport Cory could not shake

the notion. He was now behind the Iron Curtain. He was breathing the air of freshly dispelled Communism, watching former "comrades" shuffle along the icy sidewalks, rolling past barbed wire fences that could have been from any farm in Minnesota. But here they possessed such different meaning. Millions had been imprisoned by this same barbed wire then slaughtered by the fascist butchers of both the Third Reich then the Supreme Soviet. The fences caged in more than a slate of frozen turnip fields. And Cory Sonne was here. Not reading about it in some boring high school history class but seeing it, feeling it press up against his chilled face, living in it now.

Wow, so this is the land of the Cold War Enemy was all he could think.

The Goldman residence lay behind a half mile perimeter of wrought iron bars, its cubed, austere, gray exterior broken by the red and white and the stars and stripes of the Polish and American flags posted at the entrance. And, in a nice touch from the Bel Air designers who had converted it for Andrew, a brown plaque near the door with four golden stars and the burnished appellation - HOTEL HOLLYWOOD. You wouldn't find it in any Michelin guide but the service would be beyond premium.

Andrzej transferred Cory's bags into the Mercedes. Jerzy lead him inside. The foyer was spacious with bleached wood paneling and a deep shag area rug with a gypsy pattern. Beyond it, through modified French doors were the family, music and living room areas and the dining area off to the left through another set of double doors. The kitchen, laundry and storage were below.

Two sets of stairs in the foyer ascended in opposite directions leading to the twelve bedrooms of the second floor - two of which had been converted. One into an editing room, the other into the gym. All those restless moments of wondering whether or not it would be adequate were now behind him. Cory inspected the equipment; it was sub-par but he figured it would be about the best one could expect out of Eastern Europe.

The only deluxe item was the treadmill, a Kettler. German. Cory had never used one but was assured of its quality. The multi-station machine had uncased metal cables that laid much too loosely over plastic pulleys and a plastic weight stack that tilted at odd angles when it was being raised and lowered. This annoyed him. Top of the list of things to miss about America – state of the art fitness equipment. He turned to Jerzy.

"I'm going to need some tools to tighten these bolts and shorten the cables."

"You will have them tomorrow." Jerzy nodded as if it had been done the moment of his request. But Cory was soon to learn that, like everything else in Poland, tomorrow could mean anything from tomorrow to two weeks from tomorrow. "Will this be sufficient for Mr. Goldman?" Jerzy asked, referring to the gym.

Cory heard the reverence in the voice. It was the verbal red carpet rolling off the tongue before the name - Mr. Goldman. It sounded almost practiced, cultist. "Yeah, I think so." Cory replied, not wanting to offend.

On the way down the stairs, Cory watched as two of the security guards, Leyt and Dante, dragged the girls' luggage in. His eye caught something that startled him. When Dante bent down to place a small hand bag on the carpet, his jacket hung open, and there against his chest in a tanned holster, was a shiny, black nine millimeter pistol.

Suddenly, Gabe's words sling-shot back into Cory's brain. "Andrew Goldman, our Super Jew, rubbing it in their faces by making a Holocaust movie in Eastern Europe." There was no way of knowing how safe this whole production would be. The Cold War had sewn a harvest of silent terrorism among these farmer-apparatchiks and their opposition. Even at this Krakow home, the security guards were not taking anything lightly.

A gun. The Great Equalizer. Cory had known his share of violence but never fired a weapon, never even touched one. He would have been the worst soldier had he been eighteen in 1968 and drafted. Something about the bullet exploding out of the phallic barrel. The sexual correlation had always fascinated him. One ejaculation to create life, bring such pleasure; the other to take a life and, perhaps the sickest notion of all, bring pleasure as well to the aggressor pulling the trigger. He shrugged it off but its significance would not be lost on him.

"Andrzej will take you to your hotel; you must be tired." Jerzy indicated the door where Andrzej was bundling up to face the cold once again.

"Thank you. What do I do about returning here in the morning to work with the girls before school?"

"Here is a list of all the telephone numbers. This is the Hotel Hollywood office number here. You must simply call and we will send a driver for you." Jerzy handed him the paper and smiled; he had no upper lip.

"How long have you had that mustache?" Cory asked.

"Since I was a very young boy."

It did not surprise Cory. He said goodnight.

The Hotel Orbis was an Iron Curtain Ramada Inn - a double winged, eight story structure on the bank of the Vistula across from the famed Wawel Castle.

"Welcome to Krakow." The speaker, Martin, was a young man with a thinning, natural tonsure and the thickest pair of horn-rimmed glasses Cory had ever seen.

"My name is Cory Sonne. I'm with the Movie Production." Both women on either side of Martin wore gray jackets and skirts. Cory noticed their thick hips and large calves. He wondered if the stereotypes of Eastern European would prove to be true.

"Yes, of course. You would be, now wouldn't you."

He was trying very hard to sound out the English.

"Not likely I'd chose this spot for a leisurely vacation." Martin's vapid look distracted him for a moment. He had not deciphered the remark. Cory prodded him. "My room."

"Yes, of course."

From the far end of the lobby, at the hotel bar, the sounds of laughter and muffled English could be heard. Most likely part of the film crew that had already arrived. The porter waited with the baggage cart, whistling a familiar tune. He stepped in quickly to take the key from Martin. "Room 662, Mr. Sonne. I hope you enjoy your stay in Poland."

"Dzienkwia." Cory tried out his first Polish word. Thank you.

Martin nodded. "Prosze." It would be about the only Polish he would be able to remember correctly over the ensuing months.

On the elevator, the gap-toothed porter continued whistling the tune. When the doors opened to the sixth floor, Cory finally recognized it. The theme from Hawaii Five-O. Was the fat, little man deriding him or making a subtle effort to connect? At that moment Cory realized the labor of even the simplest mundane behaviors, common courtesies, comings and goings, would be layered with doubt and misapprehension. In short, there was no way around being a stranger in a strange land. Yet again, he thought.

Down a long, long hallway marked by dark brown doors between orange and rust striped wallpaper, they strode. A workman in white overalls stepped out with his arms wrapped around a toilet bowl. Cory looked in through doorway. The ceiling-high windows had been blown out and the walls sheathed in ashen black. The porter urged Cory past the disheveled room.

"What happened there?" He asked.

The porter looked back over his shoulder then rubbed his thumb and forefinger together, indicating money, as he whispered conspiratorially, "Big, big zloty. Klejnot." He pointed to his watch then went back and forth from the money gesture to the watch. "Boom." Growing more animated at the thought of a dirty deal gone sour, he spread his arms wide and high. The buttons on his tight jacket strained against their holes. Then he dragged a finger across his neck. Every language, even sign language, shares universal elements. In this case, death.

Five doors down. 662. Cory wasn't thrilled with being so close to the bombed out suite. Not only because the energy was bad but the sounds of renovation all day long could prove unnerving.

The room was not attractive. Two single beds separated by a small night stand with an antediluvian phone and a broken built-in radio. Luckily, Cory had brought his own boombox and compact discs. Two chairs up against the large window, similar to the one that had been blown out down the hall. An old TV on an ostentatious mahogany chest of drawers. The whole color scheme diminished him - muddy browns, faded yellows, gold brocade on the walls like pureed canaries. Surely, the Hotel Hollywood could spare a few bedspreads with some color he thought.

The porter dropped the heavy bags on one of the beds. Cory slapped a 10,000 zloty note in his hand. It was part of the money that had come in the initial starter kit that Miranda had put together for him. He was told 10,000 was a generous tip though it was a mere seventy-five cents U.S. She must have been right; the porter seemed pleased.

A cold Polish beer, Zdiewicz, from the mini-bar, and a feet-up gaze at the winter-shrouded panorama of old Krakow, for some reason, calmed him. One hour passed, and well into the next, Cory was still sitting, staring. The canvass of the medieval city, once known as the gateway to Asia, narcotized him. He could see beyond the begrimed Vistula, past the catholic spires and anemic treetops. He could see into his own past as if it were a foreign country of which he was now a resolute ex-patriot. Somehow, here in Krakow, with its architectural magnificence, its atmosphere of fin-de-siècle stateliness, its cavalcade of churches and aristocratic palaces, all of which spread before him from the sixth floor window of the Orbis Hotel, in some way Cory found perspective. He should truly put it behind him, the horrible event that continued to plague him, even tried to follow him half way around the world to rest on his lap while he pondered the languid city. Maybe, just maybe, with the help of this legendary province whose soil had been tramped with the most resplendent of royalty and the most despicable of murderers, Cory could find release.

CHAPTER FOURTEEN

The sickle moon hung in the dark East German sky as if waiting to swipe down across the night. The glow of torches dappled the red bricks of an abandoned chemical factory in the desolate, industrial town of Eberswalde, notorious for its manufacture of Zyklon B tablets used in the WWII extermination camps.

In the February cold of this witching hour, a dozen neo-Nazi skinheads marched towards the Richterplatz pub that had just turned out its last drunken customers, three Mozambique slaughterhouse workers earning and spending Bundesbank backed marks from the government work exchange program.

The Mozambicans had only one path back to the

relatively safe haven of the hostel where two hundred of their countrymen also housed. Twelve swastika emblazoned radicals cut across that path, brandishing tire irons, lead pipes and brass knuckles polished in anticipation of this face-off.

"You, black boy, we're curious to know why you think you can come into this country, take one of our jobs, take our money, then have the motherfucking nerve to shack one of our women?" Steffen, the apparent leader, tall and awkward with a mouthful of criss-crossed teeth, shouted in German. This last comment incensed the flock, already inching forward and flanking the three scared foreigners.

"Please. We give you no trouble." Amassi Nedal pleaded. He knew the resentment. It had not been the first hassle he had endured. He and Krystina, his pregnant Bavarian girlfriend had been at the wrong end of a knife twice already. But something about this encounter, the late hour, the planned engagement, the torches, signaled an escalation. His mind flashed on his unborn child. Boy or girl? It was the last mundane thought he would have. Everything that followed would be notions about how to get out of this alive.

"You're nothing <u>but</u> trouble; you're a harvest-infesting insect, and we're here to stamp you out."

What followed was a macabre attack that bordered on organized athleticism as the bludgeoners would advance, strike, then retreat to make way for the next wave of assailants. All in very methodical, clockwork, primal precision until the victims lay bloodied and subdued on the wet, icy pavement. Three black bodies, bones crushed, lungs perforated, heads stomped, prone on the crimson and white snow, two barely breathing, one in the anti-dream, the soulless parade of the sub-atomic dissolve.

Fifty meters away, with the engine of his BMW M3 still running, Lars Rostock, a gray-haired, angular man in his early fifties, had looked on from the driver's seat. When an overheated Steffen finally turned to him after the beatings and smiled, Lars put the car into reverse and spun out of sight. Less than a kilometer down the road, two police cars in full siren screamed by them. A waitress from the Richterplatz had seen the fracas from afar and called in. But they did not alarm Lars, for everything had gone exactly as planned. The police, the civil-rights groups, the judges, the "good" people of the newly unified Germany would all have their atrocious murder to rail against, and it would make headlines for months to come. But it was only the preliminary step towards a much greater recognition. For the leader of the clandestine terrorist arm of the extremist body known as the German Alternative, there was such pleasure in stirring the cauldron of hate.

CHAPTER FIFTEEN

Just off Szewska street, in a tiny courtyard across from St. Anne's Church, the Collegium Novum arts building braced its fifteenth century columniation for the arrival of the Angelino teenagers, Lani and Niki, in their Guess sweaters and Doc Martin pseudo-military black boots.

Andrzej had been waiting in the Orbis hotel lobby for Cory at half past seven and taken both he and the girls to meet their teacher and orientate themselves to their new school. Day two in Krakow and the sun had yet to make an appearance. A gray and white stampede of clouds wrestled for the lower regions of the southern skies. There were few pedestrians on the sullied streets cut by cable car tracks diverging unaesthetically. And, of course, there was the cold. It was the coldest that the California native had ever been in his life. Thank God Georgia had given him that Patagonia catalogue and a thousand dollar allowance.

Inside the school, Judy Breslau waited. "Mrs. Breslau, I'm Cory Sonne and these lovely young ladies are Lani Goldman and Niki Gaspari." The girls shook hands with the diminutive woman whose flat head and matted black hair parted down the middle gave her the appearance of a Prohibition flapper hit on the head with an anvil.

"Welcome to Krakow and the Collegium Novum. Today, my darlings, we are going to talk about the curriculum and pass out books and study guides. If you'll follow me to the library." Judy moved to the hallway; Cory interrupted.

"Mrs. Breslau? I'll leave the girls with you. What time should I have the driver pick them up?"

"Oh, yes, fine, fine. I shouldn't keep them more than two hours today." Mrs. Breslau's crisp English betrayed her Cambridge education. The syllables may have reflected the Queen's but the rhythm of her speech, like a throat overfilled with whispered secrets, was definitely Slavic.

As Cory took his leave, Lani turned to him with one last plea of rescue. She was not looking forward to knuckling under her studies fresh off the excitement of Paris and Europe for the first time. And yet she knew there was nothing he could do, nothing he would tell her in that moment that would salve her wound of academiosis. Cory figured that, like a child faced with a new injury, she just wanted to show him where it hurt. That was the look, so convincingly demure and alluringly guileless; there was no doubt that acting was in her DNA.

As he stepped from the courtyard to the street, Cory watched a bundled man rise from the bus bench across the way. It was snowing now, and he could not make out the features to be sure but the drab green hunter's cap with the wool ear flaps was the same. He had seen the man get out of the taxi behind them when they first pulled up to the college. He remembered the hat. His father would wear one just like it when he'd disappear with his drinking buddies on long weekend trips. Nothing about his old man escaped Cory's attention he was so intent in those early years on not provoking him. One had to learn the signs and avoid the detonation buttons. They were so many and so varied.

Yes, he remembered the hat. And now the stranger across the way stood, too suddenly Cory thought, when he spotted him, the deliberateness of a nervous action. For some stupid reason Cory decided to follow him, all the while fixated on the image of the 9mm pistol in the holster under Dante's jacket at the Hotel Hollywood. It was as if that one brief glimpse had set the wheel of suspicion in motion. Cory snickered to himself thinking of how Gabe would laugh if he knew what was running through his mind. Not even in the country twenty-four hours and already on the trail of a suspected bad guy.

He waved off Andrzej who stepped out of the van parked half way up the sidewalk. Was he crazy? He didn't know the first thing about this kind of work. And what would he do if the man just suddenly turned on him and pulled a knife, or worse, a gun? Run? Or what if the man simply turned and asked him why he was following him in garbled Polish? What would Cory say, "I thought you were following me." And in English no less. No, it made no sense at all. And still he followed him down the narrow Ul Wislana. What did curiosity actually do to the cat?

Past one old stone building after another, buttressed up against each other. The shoe repair shop, the pizza shop, the jewelry shop with its window display of hand-crafted silver and amber pieces, past the tobacco shop, the hostel, St. Adalbert's, the oldest church in Krakow originally founded in 995. All the while quickening the pace as the man realized he was being followed.

The snow dove down harder; his quarry disappeared around the corner up ahead and when Cory turned it himself he faced his first view of the Rynek Glowny, the square. The man in the hunter's cap was gone. Or at least absorbed among the many dark-coated bodies scuttling across the frozen cobble stones kicking up fresh powder and slush.

That was the end of the pursuit. But Cory stood and immersed himself in the majesty of the grand plaza he had read about in his guide to Krakow. The history was undeniable. The largest square in medieval Europe. A slight jog of the imagination and one could easily see the lords and ladies, maids and squires, merchants and vendors hawking their wares across the flagstones centuries ago. It must be the size of six football fields packed together, Cory thought. Cut through down the middle by the Sukiennice, the medieval cloth hall which divided the square into east and west and contained booths packed with everything from produce to hand-carved chess sets.

Cory kept himself warm by pacing off the perimeter, attempting to verify his estimate of its size. But the many fascinating structures lining the sides prevented him from keeping an accurate count on his strides. He stopped half way through his task at the Town Hall Tower near the southwest corner. A woman and a man exited the building from a small door around the back. Cory went over, opened it, and stepped inside.

It was a relief to get warm. A young man coming up the stairs bumped into him from behind. "Excuse me." Cory said; he had been blocking the way.

"American?" The youth inquired.

"Yes. And you?" Cory noticed how very thin the young man was, collar bones prominently displayed at their articulation point along the manubrium.

"Polish. But I lived in New York for a while. You here for the Goldman picture?"

"Yeah. Are we that obtrusive?" Cory asked.

"No, you're the best thing to happen to this part of the country since Solidarity."

"That's nice to here, I guess." The man was nearly bundled now, readying himself to face the weather.

"What is this place?" Cory craned his neck to see to the top of the tower.

"All that remains of the original town hall built in the fourteenth century."

"Wow, that's old."

"Everything's old in Krakow, even the ideas. You'll get bored of that soon enough."

"Are you a guide?" He had the austere look of knowledge about him.

"No, I'm an actor. I run the Teatr Satyry. It's a satirical cabaret. It's quite good, best in Poland they say. But then it's all relative; isn't it. We perform in the Gothic vaults below on Friday nights. You should come see us. It's in Polish but the comedy's broad enough that you could follow, maybe even laugh, without knowing the language."

"Thanks for the invite." The young man passed by Cory and opened the door.

"Maybe I'll see you on the set." He turned. "I've got a small part in the film. I get shot in the head or something. It's good money. That's the thing about Goldman coming here. It should single-handedly revive the economy in this region - for awhile."

Cory didn't know what to say. He didn't feel like explaining why he wouldn't see him on the set. Would a starving eastern European actor understand the concept of a legendary director hiring a private trainer for three thousand dollars a week and flying him by Concorde then private jet half way around the world simply so he could supervise the scientific sweating of his movie-star wife? Probably not. Would anyone understand that, even in L.A.?

There was only one more thing he could think of to ask. "Did you see a man come in here with a dark coat and green hunting cap with wool flaps?"

The actor laughed. "No, sorry. But then I didn't pay much attention. God's bi." The door swung heavily open against the brisk wind outside and the young man disappeared into the shredded blanket of white. It was really snowing out there.

What was he doing there? Cory knew he'd be better off touring the sites with someone who could explain what he was seeing. And on a more comfortable day. The man in the faded green hat was gone, for now.

CHAPTER FIFTEEN

An oppressive heat strangled the plum orchard. The rotting smell seemed the incense of a fetid offering to the rain gods for some relief. Thirst. Thirst drove eleven year old Cory to the hose for water. The weeding around the porch steps was grueling work in this July swelter. Sizzle.

From the faucet, Cory could see the glint of sunlight reflecting from the aluminum ladder his father mounted in the grove. Like some splintery Morse code the signal changed. The message became clearer in its wavering. Warning. Warning. Eli Sonne was coming towards him, angrily carrying the ladder over his shoulder. Cory picked up his triangle hoe quickly and resumed work. There was a passion to his weeding necessary to avoid comment from his enraged father. How he hoped that Eli would simply pass him by on the way to the shed. He struck the clumps of limp sour grass hard. Incise. Scrape. Lift.

A rock. Smack onto the hard rock with the tip of the hoe. So hard, in fact, that the head of the tool snapped just at the point of attachment to the long wooden handle. Shit. He picked it up quickly. But too late. Eli had seen him with the two separate pieces in opposite hands. Broken. The only thing to do, Cory thought, was tell him quickly. If he tried to hide it, Eli would only have more cause to send his Navy-ringed backhand across Cory's face. Again.

"Daddy, the hoe busted. I was digging hard at the weeds and hit a rock. It must have been old."

Crash. The ladder dropped to the dust. Eli swiped the pieces from Cory's hands, inspected them for a moment then bellowed, "You're not supposed to whack at them, you dig them up for chrissake."

Just then his mother's voice swelled from the house. "Cory. Cory." She called. He thought he might have been saved from a sure beating as she stepped out onto the porch in time to cut Eli's attention from the hoe.

But he was wrong. As Cory turned to face Becky. Slam. The backhand. The ring striking just below the cheek, sending Cory to the dirt, oddly parallel to the ladder. Becky stood silent.

"Cory. What kind of fucking name is Cory. Your son's stinking name. It's a sissy name. I never should have let you have your way."

"Eli." She yelled at him but did not move to intervene. She knew there was nothing she could do about the beating that Eli would or would not administer to the boy but she knew how to protect herself. Becky Sonne was going to stay on that porch and plead with her voice that one blow to Cory's head was enough punishment for Eli's plum crop having gone bad. She would not put her body between them; she knew all to well that they'd both end up worse for the effort.

Eli bent to one knee. He grabbed Cory's chin, turned his face and examined the cheek. "He don't look like no movie star now." He laughed, a husky snigger interrupted by a spasm of coughs. "You're mamma wanted you to be Cory. Some fucking Cory fucking movie star that gets her all wet between the legs. But you ain't no fucking movie star, are you boy? Just a no good lazy slacker who busts up good garden tools so he don't have to work the rest of the day. "

Eli straightened himself. The broken metal triangle in his left hand, the handle in his right. He looked to Becky at the front porch, hesitating as if deciding whether or not to strike Cory again. Becky knew if she spoke he most certainly would. She bit her lip and urged him with all her mind to retreat to the cool of the work shed. Eli scrutinized the pieces of the hoe once more then took his first step away from Cory. Becky let out a deep sigh after the second step.

She wasn't sure if Eli had heard her or not but for some reason he spun on his boot heel and took one, clean hard whack at the back of Cory's legs with the wooden handle. Only one. Then the brisk strides stabbing through the dispassionate dust. Cory watched him from the ground walking off as if Eli were sideways to the world. He had learned to love the sight of Eli's body moving away from him, fading away, growing small, diminishing. He had hoped that one day it would just disappear altogether.

He got back to his feet. If he stayed down too long, it might only invite Eli back. As he turned to where Becky watched from the porch. He nodded that he was okay. He knew she could not come to him. She had done that once before and Eli had gone ballistic. It was up to him to clean his own wounds; to heal himself.

Becky watched her brave son limping towards the faucet. The rake was moving through her heart again, clearing away another pile of deserted, dead blossoms.

CHAPTER SIXTEEN

The next week was spent falling into a routine. Early morning wake-up call, breakfast at the buffet downstairs in the Orbis dining room, usually a bowl of grain cereal, some fresh fruit with plain, nonfat yogurt, four hard-boiled egg whites, and herbateh - tea in Polish, one of the six words Cory could remember. These were the only edible things on a three-table spread that included jellied meats, cardboard textured rolls and pastries, greasy eggs and heart-attack kielbasa. Cory didn't mind the funny looks he'd get from the waiters and waitresses who filled his cups. They'd just have to get used to the leftover egg yolks on his otherwise clean plate.

Andrzej or Waldek would be waiting for him at half

past seven in the lobby, and they'd make their way through the slushy, drab streets on yet another sunless day. Half the time it snowed; never was it anything but "butt-ass" cold as Niki called it.

Cory would sit with Jerzy in the Hotel Hollywood office sending up intercom communiqués to roust the girls. Only once had he mentioned the incident involving the man in the hunting cap. To eschew suspicion, he simply asked, "Is there any additional security for the girls when they're out and about?"

"No, I do not think this will be necessary. Why do you ask?"

"Just curious if there was anyone who might be watching over us, you know, some of your people."

An unsettled look captured Jerzy's face. "Is there something wrong, Cory?" He was giving Cory an opening. But it was probably all a mistake. Probably Cory's imagination running off. Diarrhea of the mind Gabe would say. Fuck that Gabe for making him so suspicious. He said nothing. Didn't want Jerzy to think he operated from a platform of fear.

Three long days at school for the girls while Cory forced himself to play the tourist, even in this inclement weather. He familiarized himself with the streets, the little shops, the many museums whose names he could never remember. But he knew the lay of the land and could refresh his having been there by finding it on one of the labyrinthine maps. Sometimes he even invented his own nicknames. The Arabic looking defense building known as the Barbakan was the "Kan". The Kosciuszko Monument became "the Mound"; it was a three hundred meter hill in the woods behind Hotel Hollywood, built and named in 1820 for Tadeusz Kosciuszko, Poland's most famous revolutionary hero. A veteran of the American War of Independence, Kosciuszko returned to Poland in 1794 to lead the revolt against the Partitions. The uprising failed and he was jailed then exiled to France. To the Poles, he exemplified the popular insurrectionary tradition that involved peasants rather than intellectuals. The view from the Mound was spectacular, three hundred and sixty degrees of southern countryside, the Malopolska and Tyniec. The lookout monument in honor of the prole Pole, not unlike his contemporary counterpart - Lech Walesa. The working class trainer, Cory Sonne, used this hill occasionally as a workout for the girls. Two miles of hiking in the deep snow uphill got their hearts started in the morning.

The late afternoons found them all down at the studio. Although most of the filming was going to be done on location, there were fifteen scheduled days of shooting on a soundstage. Plus, there had to be a central locale for wardrobe, props, crew meetings, etc. And that place was the Kombinat Film Studio, a converted mental institution that the Polish crew often joked commissioned its artists from the former inmates. Carolyn Mann had accompanied Cory, Lani, and Niki to the cold madhouse - few places had central heat even though the coal dust hung in the air all over the city. The whole ride over in the back of Waldek's Audi, she regaled them with the account of her recent separation from her boyfriend of seven years, Blake, a bronc rider one fall away from a permanent paralysis to hear Carolyn tell it.

"If I can give you one piece of advice about men, girls..." she covered Cory's ears with her slender, mittened hands. "...don't fall in love with what happens between the sheets. I'm not saying don't ride them 'til their buns burn. Oh no, that's not to be missed. Just find one that hugs you and tells you how wonderful you are before he buries his nose in the sports page at the breakfast table."

"Oh, for sure." Niki intoned, as if "sure" were a wave washing up on the sand. They all smiled at Cory when Carolyn removed her hands; he pretended not to have heard from his shotgun seat in the front of the car.

Five seconds later he turned and asked, "Anyone save this morning's sports section?"

"Ewwwwww!" Lani and Niki squealed at the same time. Carolyn landed a mock slap on his stubbled cheek. The funny thing was that Cory had given Gabe explicit instructions to save and send the LA Times sports pages directly to his Hotel Orbis address. If they only knew. He could compare the habit to their lust for Vogue, Cosmo,

Elle, etc. They wouldn't agree. Cory had learned enough about the difference between the sexes and their subsequent perceptions to know there was seldom anything they would agree upon. He had often noted that if he ever spent a wild night fucking a girl who flipped to the sports section first thing next morning, he'd drop to a knee and propose on the spot. He had a number of little tests like that for women, a secret agenda, a mental tabulation. Occasionally a female would slip into his life, pass one or two but then begin failing miserably. It never occurred to him that there might be anything wrong with the tests themselves.

A portly young man named Martin, son of the Unit Production Manager, clicked into his portable radio as he walked ahead of the group, looking back over his shoulder to address them. "I've got the director's daughter and her friend and they're supposed to do some p.a. work this afternoon."

A female voice squeaked back. "Yes, yes. Bring them down to wardrobe."

Martin looked to Carolyn for approval. "Wardrobe it will probably be for the rest of the week. We're putting together over a thousand uniforms for the scenes of the camp. Scenes of the camp, yes?"

"Are we actually going to film at Auschwitz?" Lani asked Martin, shuddering even before the reply.

"For three days. Have you been yet?"

"No, they've been getting accustomed to the

surroundings. Didn't want to overwhelm them the first week." Carolyn interjected.

"Yes, yes. I see. Probably a good idea. A good idea?" Martin had a habit of repeating himself, contorting the end of his exclamations into questions.

They had been heading down a long corridor lit by intermittent single light bulb fixtures, giving the walls a dirty eggshell color, cracked walls, oppressive walls. Stopping at a solid door, cut with a tiny window at eye level, Martin motioned them inside.

A Japanese girl bowed awkwardly then spoke in stilted Polish to Martin before switching to English.

"This is Yoshi, one of the wardrobe assistants, yes?"

"Pleased to make you." Another series of bows.

Carolyn introduced the girls. Cory scanned the room. Scores of military A&P style industrial racks five shelves high and aluminum. The newest item he'd scene in this half-dilapidated monster of a building. They'd walked a quarter of a mile already and only been on the western wing. Two other workers were going through piles of striped shirts, prisoners' shirts, worn and yellowing. Cory smiled to himself. Lani and Niki were going to spend a week of their internship folding and putting away clothes - a service for which each of their mothers paid an immigrant woman two hundred and fifty dollars a week to perform at their lavish California homes. The irony of it. He knew that Georgia demanded they labor on the production in some capacity since the studio was footing the bill for the whole family joining Andrew. It was a token gesture but a necessary one in Georgia's opinion for more reasons than one. Cory hadn't ever considered that to be one of his mental tests for the measure of a woman but he gave her high marks for it.

Standing there in that cavern of costumes, watching Lani and Niki sulk and skulk at the vast tables of dirty laundry, a severe pang descended his torso. It seemed to pull the back of his throat towards his diaphragm. He tried deep breathing but it stayed with him. He was missing a woman he barely knew, who probably didn't give two shakes of a rat's ass about him, and was somebody else's wife. No, no. He couldn't let this happen. So much of his life, his pain, came from not having control, being weak. Not now. Like the gospel song decried, he had overcome. He had taken control of his life; he had suffered for his armor, paid the wicked price. She would not get to him this way, this way that left him susceptible, open, unaware of a strange emotion. Cory Sonne was strong, a specimen, a warrior who had defeated his past. He would not miss his mother. He would not let the image of his father mask his future like some tattoo of the soul. And, warm and sweetly soothing though they were, he would not tread the waters where Mrs. Andrew Goldman's siren song stealthily enticed him.

On Friday, a blistering storm rampaged over the city

dumping two feet of snow on the already blanketed region, as if a clean white sheet had been laid over a soiled one. Cory spent most of the day watching old movies, or movies on videocassette he had never seen - Double Indemnity, Big, Zebrahead. The girls stayed home from school where Carolyn nearly had to resort to physical force for them to do their homework. Eventually, they joined Cory to watch "Big" though they both confessed to having seen it at least three times. "Tom Hanks is such a doll." Lani spurted out.

Cory's body had finally adjusted to the time change; he no longer dragged through the days, the seductive notion of lying down to sleep every noon hour had subsided. Instead, he'd pumped iron in the Hotel Hollywood gym, going through the motions on every body part for exercises he planned to use with Georgia. Though his duties seemed to have expanded into chaperone/bodyguard for the girls, his main purpose still remained to train Georgia Hart so that she could physically transform herself, into a character suffering from malnutrition in the grievous conditions of wartime Krakow.

Funny thing how much Cory had ruminated about the characters in Pillar of Salt, the screenplay, now that he was actually there in Poland, where it all took place. In his mind, Georgia was Anna Kamenski, the Jagellonian literature professor who caught the eye of Hans Frank, SS Governor of Krakow during the war and for whom he lusted until discovering, to his dismay, that she was a Jew.

Cory had set foot in the quad of the Collegium, traced the very steps that the real Anna must have paced a thousand times. How deep did her footprints sink in snow like this fifty winters ago? Did she dine in the underground restaurants of the Rynek Glowny? Or marvel from The Mound at Orion balanced on the night's southernmost edge? Anna most certainly was here or the ghost of Anna. And soon the body of Georgia Hart would step onto this same frozen ground and slip into that ghost like a second skin. Of that, Cory was sure.

Friday had finally brought the repairman from the only athletic equipment company in the region. He cut and clamped new cable lengths to the multi-station high-low pulley machine. The result was an improved performance but nothing to write home about. The window of the gym looked out over the back yard, a two acre spread replete with an octagonal shaped gazebo and a grove of stark poplars.

"In the springtime, you will not believe how lush and green this all will be." Jerzy stepped up next to Cory as he surveyed the bleak landscape.

"Haven't seen anything but a hundred different shades of gray since I've been here."

"This is winter in Poland."

The repairman fumbled with his tools, hiking his pants up again and again as if there were no such thing as a belt.

"So, Jerz, how did you get roped into this job?"

"This job is very prestigious. I was honored when the government requested to interview me. I had been the special liaison for the beloved John Paul II when he returned last year. You know, of course, that Krakow is his home parish?"

Cory had heard something of that. He wasn't much on religion. The only thing he knew of the Pope really was that he now traveled around in a glass booth on a flatbed truck when he went among the big crowds at parades. The "Popemobile" someone had called it. Apparently, a madman had taken a shot at him. Just another desperate act in a world whose so called progress towards peace was a thin veil over a violent face.

"So Catholicism is pretty popular?"

"It is the backbone of Poland. When the Soviets tried to stamp it out during the communist times, they could not. And now, with a Polish Pope, you see, these are a proud and devoted people."

"And you?" Cory asked sensing Jerzy was talking only statistics.

"Of course, I was raised that way. But my father was shot by the Nazis when I was an infant, and my brother was executed by the Soviets as a spy when his only crime was smuggling penicillin into rural hospitals. Then my wife, a woman full of love and faith, died a horrible, agonizing death of cancer. I am sorry to say that I am not one who can still believe, in the face of all this suffering. Perhaps it was my education that finally did me in."

"What do you mean?"

"I studied philosophy at the Sorbonne in Paris as a young man. That's enough to leave you a doubter for the rest of your life." Though he stared straight ahead through the window at the grove of naked trees, Jerzy seemed by his stillness to be moving straight into Cory's heart.

Suffering.

If there is a God, as twenty million Polish Catholics believed, how could he permit all of this? A man who suffers too much, the six million, Bosnian rape victims, African girls and their genital mutilation, Cambodian sex slaves, Armenian, Native-American, and Gypsy genocides, the gulag, and on and on, like a perpetual teletype of pain. Cory had the feeling that this question and others like it were what Jerzy had studied in school and then spent his life returning to.

Jerzy's gaze did not abate. Somehow, he was still coming at Cory. Almost as if he expected to find something similar. A story that would confirm his beliefs, exonerate him from having fallen so far from the altar. Jerzy carried death with him. And the question of death. That was what floated in his eyes. Was that what the Polish Cultural Affairs administrators saw when they recommended him to Andrew Goldman? Could Andrew be that manipulative to hire a key man with those same eyes to pierce him with a constant reminder? To keep the spirit of the picture, or rather the despair of the picture, staring him in the face, even in the countenance of the man who ran his Krakow home?

Too much conjecture. Cory had to appease the eyes that begged an answer. "I know what you mean." It was all Cory chose to say; all he could say. Jerzy heard the vibration of pain in Cory's voice. He knew.

A loud thud. The lid of the repairman's tool box closed with a definitive burst. He beamed, proud to have been of service to the great Andrew Goldman, come to Krakow to make the big Hollywood picture. Cory was getting used to that look. It was always there to greet him when doors graciously opened, food was served or workers did their little but important part in keeping the Pillar of Salt express rolling.

Cory tested the machine. Fine. So why did he suddenly feel nervous when he slipped out from the pec-deck pads? Tomorrow or the next day perhaps, he would be putting Georgia on that same seat.

CHAPTER SEVENTEEN

Andrzej returned Cory to the Orbis, playing a pirated Oingo Boingo tape as they drove. Cory deliberately commended his choice. "Boingo, I like these guys." Andrzej cranked the volume. "Dead Man's Party" bleated from the cracked dash. The last words Cory heard before stepping out and shutting the passenger door were, "...who could ask for more; everybody's coming, leave your body and soul at the door."

It was evening and still cold. The snow had stopped. The wind, too, had subsided. Instead of going in right away Cory walked the footpath to the bridge. The black Vistula mirrored the hotel, diffusing its shimmering lights into cloudy apparitions. Cory's mind jumped from Jerzy's tragedies, to the gun in Dante's holster, to the urn filled with the ashes of his mother. He remembered standing over the Kern river, river of her childhood, with his uncle Dustin, Becky's half-wit brother. They had all floated there as children. On inner-tubes and rafts. It was one of Becky's most peaceful places, the place she asked her ashes to be spread. Cory had been surprised by Dustin's elucidating remark, "It is only in silence, leaning over a river in winter, that one can really think about death."

The words came back to him now in his coldest winter and over the dirtiest river he had ever known.

In the elevator on the way up to his room Cory couldn't take his eyes off a high cheek-boned woman opposite him - the first genuinely attractive one he'd seen since his arrival. He pressed for the sixth floor and noticed the lit seven. The woman smiled at him then spoke in English with a heavy Italian accent.

"Are you with the film?"

"Well, yes. I work with Andrew Goldman." He didn't want to launch into an explanation with his floor approaching.

"I'm Claudia. I'm one of the actresses." The doors opened. His floor.

"I'm Cory. It's nice to meet you." He stepped out.

The doors began to close and he saw Claudia scan the control panel with a pointed finger, swearing in staccato

Italian as she missed the “door open” button. They closed. He heard in loud English, "Come down to the bar..." And something else which he could not make out. An invitation? Too him? He supposed so.

Down the hallway, he passed door 650, the bombed out room. A deal gone sour? A murder? A terrorist act? Did the porter really have any idea?

Come down to the bar. Why not. Claudia was a welcome sight for eyes weary of the sullen and the gray. He found himself thinking about sex. It had been over a week since he'd last been laid. Francesca. A little dose of that would go a long way in this climate. Though he had never found himself craving any one woman, he craved “the thing”. The act itself. The release. Cory seldom went long periods without pressing the flesh. There always seemed to be somebody around, somebody willing to get lost in a sea of sweat and tongues and orgasms. This Claudia was forcing it to the surface, the urge.

After dropping his hat, coat, and gloves in his room, Cory visited the Orbis Bar at the far end of the lobby. A crimson Naugahyde chair swallowed his relaxed form. Claudia introduced her recently acquired friends, Erica, the wardrobe coordinator, and Hiam, an Israeli actor playing Anna Kamenski's father. They offered him long pretzels from a jar and ordered red wine.

"They sell a red Sophia here very cheap. I know it's hard to believe a Bulgarian wine could be any good but it is, trust me." Claudia informed Cory.

"Ten minutes you know her, and she asks you to trust her. Cory, have we learned nothing in all our years and dealings with women?" Hiam joked. He gripped Cory's hard shoulder with his bony hand and would repeat the gesture often.

"When did you all arrive?"

"Yesterday and today." Erica offered. She had a round face and wavy blonde hair that practically touched the floor when she was seated. She was American - Chicago. "Pretty much everybody is here or will be by Sunday night's party."

"Party?" Cory asked.

"Opening reception, my boy." Hiam was the self-absorbed father he would play in the film. "They're going to give Andrew an award for making the film here."

"The first of many awards I predict if things go as well as they should." Erica added.

"You really think so?" Cory asked, taking his glass of red Sophia from Claudia who kept vigilant watch over three things - the waiter, her cigarette, and the entrances and exits of the other patrons.

"No doubt. If Andrew can stay away from the kitsch which punctuates so many of his more commercial ventures, this could be the big one, the one that makes them take note of him as a serious filmmaker."

Cory sipped the wine. Claudia was right. "Good

choice." Cory lifted his glass to her across the table. She returned the gesture then threw back her remaining portion.

After two bottles, fifteen cigarettes by Cory's nauseated estimate, and a jar of pretzels, and after listening to Hiam's complete analysis of the crisis in the middle east, Claudia and Cory got up to leave. They had silently exchanged signals to exit together.

"Well, the goodnight, goodnight. Parting, as they say, is the work of Moses." Hiam laughed at his own joke, one he had most certainly used a thousand times before, and watched the two of them leaving together with the expression of a man who knows storytelling is no match for the silent mouth of a thirty year old athlete with the easy power of a crouched jaguar.

"Seven?" Cory asked as they stepped into the elevator.

"Seven. Six. Wherever you want to go."

Even the glaze of red wine could not be blamed for the glint in Claudia's eyes. If they were lips, she'd have been licking them. She seemed to be relishing the role of seductress, the older woman, though in reality they were close to the same age. A decade of this type of living had put more wear and tear on Claudia than she would have liked. Cory, on the other hand, was ripe. A mango in her eyes succulent and ready to be split open.

It went the way it always went. Her head pressed

into his hard chest, admiring it with her cheek as they stood in the middle of her ugly brown hotel room, undressing each other slowly, sloppily. The deliberate trail of the woman's hand along his contours; he squeezing her with a small hint of his strength.

The particulars, in this case, were nice for Cory. He found himself reveling in her smells, the hair, the exotic perfume, her skin cream - all the scents of a woman who adorns her body. Except the smoky taste of her mouth. It made the kissing inglorious. So he took pleasure in the fucking.

There was always that excellent bit of excitement that comes from the body revealed. A new body. The form of another woman dappled with shadow and light. He would enter and possess. He made his living shaping bodies; and he defined himself by the cache of bodies he took for himself, played with, satisfied, fucked. Yes, fucked. In the end that was what he always seemed to be telling himself. When they heaved and undulated beneath him, it was the only place he could find refuge, in the house of the hard cock, the one on which they danced so rhythmically, under which they squirmed, moving as if trying to get away but arms wrapped around his broad torso like a vice. And he would drive it into them, hard, brutal. Not to harm them but only because he heard the words in his head as they were coming, as he was coming. "I'm fucking you now. How do you like being fucked? I love fucking you." He controlled the pace, the thrusts. It was most certainly a voice in his head. But whose? His? He often felt he did not recognize the voice but if not from him, from where? It never seemed to matter because the voice was eventually and always drowned out by the sounds of climaxes, his or hers or both. And then the heavy breathing and the rolling off. And the voice was gone.

Cory had taken Claudia where she wanted to go. No better or no worse than any that had come before her. For him, at least. He had no way of knowing what she felt. And even if she had told him; he doubted whether he'd have believed her. Claudia Colnago, the actress, was accustomed to red wine nights like these.

It didn't matter that he was trying to dress quietly. She wouldn't have stirred if he'd been chopping wood. She was that far gone. The faint music of a lilting violin seeped through the heavily fogged window. Cory noticed it, taking one last look at the smooth sweep of Claudia's buttocks and thigh, draped over the white sheet. But he could think of only one thing. Georgia Hart arrived tomorrow. The woman in front of him had taken long pulls on his cock; the woman he would see tomorrow had been taking long pulls on his heart.

On the way back to his room, at the glass window near the elevator, he spotted the source of the sorrowful music. In two feet of snow under the window of room 650, the bombed out hotel room, a diminutive young woman bowed sweetly on her violin. A magenta scarf curled around her neck and hung down past the left side of her waist. It swayed with her composed movements. The Vistula flowed black behind her.

Cory watched her for a long time. It seemed such an irrational thing. Solo violinist standing in the freezing cold, deep into the night, playing, no crying out a melody for no one. Then it struck him. This wasn't practice or performance. This was mourning. Playing for the dead.

Cory Sonne collapsed into an exhausted sleep that night to the sound of a violin and, like so many who lived in this part of the world, thinking about love and the dead.

CHAPTER EIGHTEEN

The jet was to arrive at noon. Cory had spent the morning bundled up and running along the eastern edge of the Vistula. Just past the turnaround point, a rusted barge in a watery, steel grave near the railroad bridge, a motley dog had made sport of him, nipping at his heels. Cory spent a hundred yards running backwards, feigning a lunge now and then to stop the German Shepherd's advance. He'd snapped a branch off a local tree to use in his defense. With the advent of a strict headwind accompanied by snow flurries and the sweat under his jacket freezing up, twenty degrees seemed like zero. What finally saved him from the menacing distraction was another hungry dog bent on a canine face-off.

Andrzej had picked Cory up late. He tapped his thumbs along the inside of the steering wheel the whole way to the airport. His car had stalled out at a stoplight in town, and he had flooded the engine in his impatience to restart it. Somehow, Cory had understood this explanation even though it came littered with half Polish phrases. Andrzej was visibly relieved when they arrived and found Jerzy, Carolyn, and the girls still waiting near the customs counter. The plane had not yet landed. He gave a quick account to Jerzy of the delay and took his upbraiding deferentially. The incident had the air of catastrophe avoided. Tensions were tightly wound. The stoic Poles were such a contrast to the giddy Americans anxious for the reunion.

Lani and Niki, as was their habit, waited till the last minute to wrestle with loading their cameras. One small tantrum later Jerzy had solved the problem. The customs officials motioned them through.

Carolyn nudged Cory who had been staring out the window at the spinning propellers of an old cargo plane, a fixture from a distant past.

On his way down to breakfast that morning, Cory had noticed for the first time the chalkboard in the hall directly facing the elevator doors. Across the top was stenciled the name of the production: PILLAR OF SALT - Call Sheet and Noteboard. On a plain white page dated Sunday 2/11 it read simply - Reception. Grand Ballroom. 7 p.m.

It wasn't the announcement that stuck in his mind but the quote in chalk on the bottom of the black board. "No one believes it is happening now."

What is "it"? Cory thought to himself. The party? The production? The phrase portended more. That stubborn notion wedged in his mind when Carolyn broke his reverie and escorted him to the tarmac. He was nervous now and his feet heavy.

The Lynton Aviation jet eased to a halt, the sole bird on the airfield. The familiar flight attendant, redheaded Gale, propped open the door.

The first body out belonged to Jack Grady, a white-haired bear of a man who paused at the entrance, surveying the welcoming party. Cory was pierced with immediate intrigue at the way the man made eye contact with every one of them, sizing the group up one by one in a split second, then turning back to the cabin, "Everything's Jake. Welcome to Krakow."

Jack lighted down the steps with an athleticism befitting a man twenty years his junior. At fifty-eight, the ex-homicide detective turned personal security wizard considered himself well within his prime. Hell, he'd yet to purchase his first pair of glasses. As a young man he'd made his living spotting for announcers at football games. For certain he was hawk-like in more ways than one.

She arrived with the grace of a Jackie O clone. The woman who owned more Armani and Fortuny than Gloria

Vanderbilt, and had equal measures of chic without the blue blood, appeared in a purple Patagonia pullover and made it look like Givenchy. The first thing Cory noticed, however, was the face. Beautiful. Narrow. Possessed of divination. The same configuration of pulchritude that he remembered but drawn tighter to the bone. In a second he knew she had followed the diet he'd left behind to the "t." T for transformed. For that's what she had done. Georgia Hart had transformed her physical self from voluptuous ingénue to vulnerable victim, she would be Andrew's believable prison camp Venus with her seemly but sunken face.

Andrew followed close behind her but Cory couldn't take his eyes off Georgia. It had been just over a week. Suns and moons had risen and fallen. Snows swept the shire; winds whistled shrill symphonies. The waiting had lengthened that week into a separate lifetime.

Throwing composure to the wind, Georgia and the girls converged into a group hug punctuated by shrieking and squeezing. Andrew got his share but with no where near the conviction. Jack introduced himself to Cory and Jerzy and shook the hands of the drivers before orchestrating the collection of luggage.

"I missed you guys so much." Georgia canted in the language of women removed. "Are you just dying here or is it bearable?"

"Oh, mom, the school is so hard and the math teacher is Polish with this thick accent that sounds like he's talking through peanut butter." Lani complained.

"Yeah. You have to help us out, Georgia, or we'll be ruined." Niki added.

"Has it been this cold the whole time?"

"I guess this is typical. They say it won't let up for a month." Carolyn took Georgia's carry-on and started them moving towards the terminal. Georgia veered slightly to greet Cory who had been hanging back with Jerzy.

"Look at you all bundled up. It's a long way from the beach; isn't it surfer boy?"

"Hey, Georgia. You look great." She kissed his frozen cheek with a slightly parted mouth. The wetness would be ice in seconds.

"No, I don't look great but I look the way Andrew wants me to look. It'll be good for the picture." She spoke Andrew's name as if it were a musket being filled with gunpowder.

"You look great." Cory reiterated. "You're getting to the lean physique you need, and that's making me look like I'm worth the coin that you're paying me."

"And I'm dying for a piece of cheesecake or some fried chicken from the Ivy."

"Not in this man's army." She rubbed his back with her naked hand then practically whispered.

"It's good to see you."

Then she was gone from him for the rest of the day. Lost in the whirlpool of her hungry daughters, for now it would be as if they were both hers, and lost in the abridged education she was sponging up from Carolyn about the agenda.

As Cory followed with a luggage cart, he felt a slap on his shoulder from behind. "As far as I'm concerned, Cory, my boy, you've already earned your entire pay. Georgia looks dead right for the role. When that woman puts her mind to something, there's no stopping her."

"Thank you, Andrew. But there's still a lot of rough sailing ahead trying to keep her that way. These people have no concept of low fat."

"You'll do it. She's put her faith in you, and I'm glad for it. Just one thing." Andrew looked serious as he leaned in.

"Yes?"

"Don't either of you ever suggest that kind of diet for me." Andrew slapped his own, round belly. "I'd just assume die with a sausage on my plate and a crate of Haagen-Dazs in the freezer."

"But you should at least be concerned about your health..."

Andrew put a finger to his lip. "Ah, Ah, Ah. My father lived to be ninety. Ate everything in sight and never did one sit up."

Cory smiled. "No one does sit ups anymore. Bad for the lower spine. We call the abdominal work crunches."

“Whatever it’s called, I’m not a subscriber. I’ve got

my father's genes."

"Sounds like he was blessed; hope you are too."

"Oh, I'm blessed all right. Wouldn't be here now if it weren't so."

They were waved through customs with wide, side-stepping smiles. The Pillar of Salt express was turning over its engines.

CHAPTER NINETEEN

The excitement seemed to carom off the lobby walls of the Hotel Orbis. Americans, Croats, Israelis, Poles and a sampling of other proto-European nationalities converged on the grand ballroom for the welcoming reception. It reminded Cory of Caesar's Palace in Las Vegas before the Bowe vs. Holyfield World Heavyweight Championship boxing match. He'd been invited by one of his clients and sat at ringside next to Magic Johnson. Bigger than life, the whole show. Hyper-real. Just like this party. There were many kind words directed at people who had not yet earned them and much over-zealous embracing by co-workers well aware that they were embarking on some great adventure. In the end it would all prove auspicious but in the pumped-in heat of this dark paneled conclave, these players were gambling strictly with the currency of good intention.

Cory had spent his Sunday braving the cold in the Rynek Glowny, the square, looking for an American newspaper with a thorough update on the NCAA basketball scene. He had been called in by a close friend of Jim Harrick's in the off season to develop a specific strength program to improve the leaping ability of UCLA center Cornell Washington. The combination of plyometrics, sportcord sprints and power shoes had added six inches to Cornell's vertical jump. Before Cory left the states, Cornell had been the leading rebounder in the Pac 10. It was driving him crazy that he couldn't keep track of the Bruin cagers. Gabe had yet to come through with one L.A. Times sports section. No luck for Cory in Krakow either.

The fortunate thing for him was running into Yuri Jaworki, the Polish cinematographer and his bald assistant cameraman, Mikola. The cold didn't seem to bother Mikola's bare head though the skin was quilted pink and red. Yuri, a rail thin scarecrow in the habit of chewing on his own lip, wore a Cleveland Indians baseball cap smashed down practically to his eyebrows.

They took him to a subterranean Italian pizzeria called Da Pietro. There may have been no sportspage but a welcome slice of home came in a tomatoey wedge of thick crust.

"Just remember one thing, Cory," Yuri said

through a mouthful of pasta, "The Polish are a very stupid people. They've never been able to agree on anything; even their damn country has been wiped off the face of the map numerous times throughout their history."

"Pretty ruthless about your native country." Cory had added.

"I live in America now. I only came back here because Andrew asked me. I left this place as a young man and never looked back. Stupid people I tell you. Stupid. Everyone blames the Nazi's for slaughtering the Jews but the Poles were handing them over first thing when the Germans crossed the border. They will never live down the shame of it if you ask me. And today they still do the same stupid things. For example, there is still tremendous anti-Semitism even though there are no Jews left. The Polish are paranoid. Catholicism has brainwashed them; they behave like sheep, stupid sheep. And politically, they were the First to break free from Soviet domination and still they have not efficiently privatized. Czech, Slovakia, Ukraine are already farther along. Stupid people."

Stupid people. He uttered the phrase so black and white. Cory would forever associate it with Yuri, the brilliant cinematographer who made his living creating shadows.

Yuri was the first to shake Andrew's hand as he entered the ballroom. It wasn't long before all the head's turned and glimpsed their cinematic king. Andrew and

Yuri made the rounds, Georgia tucked neatly between them in a bulky gold sweater and black leather pants. Lani and Niki trailed behind with Carolyn, conspiring to locate the dashing Sean McDonough.

From every place Cory stood he found himself always looking for the same view. A table of sliced cold cuts and cheeses, deviled eggs and tiny breads, the same unsavory fare on the breakfast buffet table every morning, separated the captivated trainer from his seemingly fragile client. There were a hundred people or more passing between them but he managed to draw a bead on her every time he looked up from his bottled water. He thought of how spindly she had become from the restricted diet and how he might crush her with his two hundred pounds of muscled frame. He would have to hover over her like a bear protecting its cub. Oh, and what hovering. He loved to think about it again and again, the repeated pleasure, like licking an all-day sucker.

Sean McDonough, all six foot two of him, leaned down to kiss her cheek. Then he shook Andrew's hand. The intimacy that would be required from these two to make the picture work demanded some chemistry. Cory knew this and watched closely to see the story that their bodies together would tell. Instinct told him they were well matched, though it was Lani who seemed enraptured as she immersed herself in Sean, his pouting lips, his sorrowful stare, from underneath her mother's protective wing.

Cory's own insecurities may have retarded his open-mindedness but, that aside, he could not grasp the concept that Andrew was going to orchestrate his wife's emotional and sexual slavery in the character of Anna Kamenski. And for the entire world to see.

Cory had overheard Andrew once explaining why he hired Sean, not a solid A-list actor in Hollywood but a theater-nurtured Dubliner. "Though Hans Frank was by all accounts a ruthless and evil man, I didn't hire Sean because he personified villainy; on the contrary, I wanted him vulnerable, attractive. I wanted people to see not only the horror but the mechanics of a man arriving at the horror, the flicker behind the eyes that convinces a man that what he's doing, no matter how abominable, is right. After all, these Nazis must have, at some level felt that what they were doing was right. Though he is the antagonist, I want to portray the man as well as the monster; the empathy and the evil. And Sean has that capability. He can seduce men and women with that face."

Cory stood at a distance. They all laughed out loud at something Niki had said. Sean towered above the pack like Gulliver's little brother. They were a short lot, these movie people.

Cory endeavored to spot that seductiveness in Sean that Andrew found so universally appealing. He'd never personally known any bi-sexuals. If he had heard the rumors, surely they had. Perhaps Andrew didn't mind.

Perhaps this was common among movie people, people in the arts in general. So this strapping star had an appetite for young men, too. His sexual orientation didn't even seem an issue as across the ballroom, he certainly had them all charmed. The way Georgia exposed her throat when she feigned embarrassment made him think of Nazi Draculas biting into her flesh. For only the second time in his life, he fantasized about what it might be like to be somebody else. In this case, Sean McDonough. Not because he was curious about making love to another man but because soon enough he'd have her undivided attention day in and day out. And that was something to treasure from this ultra-busy woman.

The microphone squealed as Andrew grabbed it with his left hand, the commemorative plaque in his right. The mayor of Krakow had just thanked him for bringing the film to their home and wished "the greatest filmmaker in the world" much success. Andrew followed with a heartfelt thanks, reminding everyone that they were doing something that really mattered. Cory had lost sight of Georgia until her long fingers cupped his inter-locked palms.

"I'd like to start working out tomorrow morning." She nearly startled him. "My call is eight a.m. so I'll send the driver for you at six. Is that all right?" Georgia smiled at him. As if she had to ask.

"Whatever you say, boss. It'll be nice finally training someone who's motivated."

"Are the girls that lazy?" Georgia was fumbling through her purse, half-listening.

"Not lazy, just wimpy. The development of a fitness mentality is the last thing on the mind of a girl whose glutes still defy gravity. I try to impress upon them that they'll thank me later for the education but..."

"But they're just smart-mouthed, high-spirited vixens with ideas of their own."

"Exactly."

"Yes, that's exactly what they are. Just accept it. They know they have to do some P.E. They'll show up but don't expect them to actually listen to you - they're teenagers." Georgia pulled out a tiny package wrapped in brown paper. "I brought you a little gift. Do you read?" She handed it to him.

"Fitness journals mostly. Some magazines."

"Well, this will force you to flex your imagination."

"Should I open it now?" Cory asked.

"Later." Georgia answered then began her retreat to the podium.

"Thank you." Cory uttered.

"See you in the morning." And she was gone, swallowed in the shoulders of the rapt crowd applauding her legendary husband, flanked by Yuri, Zygmunt Kosa, the Polish producer, and a dithering gaggle of local gentry.

Cory zeroed in on Jack Grady. He had been fascinated by Jack from the moment he stepped out of the jet. A man who was hyper-aware of his surroundings. He was part eagle, part panther, part protective mother and part Big Brother. In fact, the way he looked out for Andrew reminded him very much of his own brother, Ray, at least when he was young and the difference in their ages made Ray the physical superior. It stirred his heart now, half way around the world, thinking of his brother for the first time in a long while. Memories from a time when they had cared for each other, when they shared a mutual enemy in their father, when pain and confusion had not put an ocean of blood between them. Cory remembered what Sidney Poitier, a long time client of his, had once told him. "It's hard to fight the cynicism and despair as you get older but equally as hard not to wrench a cry for the sentimental."

From the freezing cold of southern Poland, Cory's heart warmed for Ray. He made a mental note to locate him when he returned to the states.

CHAPTER TWENTY

"What you tryin' to do nappy head?"

A broad shouldered black kid with a glistening afro turned on Cory in the shallow end of Nuss Pool. The summer had sweltered to record heat; Cory and Ray brought their laceless tennis shoes, their Oakland Raiders towels, their quarters and sought refuge in the crowded municipal pool.

Cory had been showing Ray his underwater handstands when he accidentally fell sideways and kicked the black kid on the funny bone.

"I'm sorry. I didn't mean it." Cory replied with the bigger boy directly in his face before he even got his eyes opened. The black kid, shaking out his right arm, backhanded Cory upside his head, not hard, just a territorial smack.

"Hey, he said he was sorry." Ray swaggered through the waist high water over to them.

"Don' mean nothin' what he said; Joy Boy rapped me good."

"He accidentally kicks you so that gives you the right to hit him in the head?" Ray's nostrils flared; Cory knew what was coming.

"I'll hit you, too, you don't back off." Their chins converged on each other.

"I'll save you the trouble." A lightning quick Ray threw a fist across the kid's face. His head snapped back but he wasn't hurt. The kid lunged at Ray, and before he knew it he was in a headlock and submerged. Cory jumped on the shoulders of the black kid but was immediately pulled off by one of his buddies.

A gasping Ray sucked in some air as the black kid raised him up for only a second to scream in his ear, "You's one stupid motherfucker, white boy." Then back under the water. Cory, pinned back by the beefy friend, watched Ray's arms yanking in vain at the thick forearms of the black kid. After three more dunks, Cory could see Ray's face turning blue. Each time up, the black kid seemed to grow more and more violent, his words nastier, as if the thought of inflicting some real hurt on Ray grew more enticing. Luckily for the both of them, the lifeguard, a sizable college kid, intervened.

Both Ray and the black kid were suspended from the pool for the summer. No matter, school was starting in two weeks and they'd be in the orchards working most of the rest of August anyway. For years following the incident Cory lived in fear of running into that same kid somewhere when Ray wouldn't be there, and that would be the end. It never happened.

As if nearly being choked to death weren't enough, when Eli found out, and he did though they never figured out how, Ray got a beating for not letting Cory fight his own battles. The remark was, "That boy doesn't learn to fight back, he'll either be dead before he's twenty or turn into a fag."

From then on Ray never stepped in again. Cory spent many fearful years and a few tense situations hoping he would until the days of iron. By the end of his fifteenth year, Cory no longer needed Ray. Nature, Joe Weider, bar and dumb bells had bulked him up. He didn't need anybody. He could bench press the fattest black kid in Ventura county twenty times over.

CHAPTER TWENTY-ONE

Cory untied the string. With his Swiss Army knife he sliced the scotch tape and meticulously unfolded the brown wrapping paper; he was saving both and savoring Georgia's package that had come all the way from Los Angeles in her purse. In a small way, by bringing him this gift, she carried him with her the whole trip. He liked to think of it that way.

A slim book. A collection of poems by the Polish Nobel Prize winner Czeslaw Milosz. The cover photo depicted a small boy crouched in the middle of a muddy street in occupied Krakow contemplating a trampled dandelion. In the background, slightly out of focus on the hill, was Wawel Castle, a flapping Nazi flag frozen in time on its high pole. Cory opened the book to the orange Dutton's marker. Half way down the page of a poem called "Artificer" he read what was underlined:

"He wonders at his brother's skull shaped like an egg,
every day he shoves back his black hair from his brow,
then one day he plants a big load of dynamite
and is surprised that afterward
everything spouts up in the explosion.
Agape, he observes the clouds and what is hanging in them:
globes, penal codes, dead cats floating on their backs, locomotives.
They turn in the skeins of white clouds like trash in a puddle.
While below on the earth a banner, the color of a
romantic rose, flutters, and a long row of military trains
crawls on the weed-covered tracks."

In the margins Georgia had written in red ink, "It is feeling that shapes beauty."

Cory read from cover to cover. There weren't a lot of pages but still the little he read was not easy to understand. He hadn't much experience with poetry. Lots of images. Scores of things out of sequence, ideas and descriptions that didn't seem to belong next to each other in sentences. In short, very different from his own reading experience. And yet, an undercurrent of resplendence and tragedy flowed through the stanzas.

He remembered that much from high school English classes. Poems were divided into stanzas, and they didn't necessarily have to rhyme. They did in the olden days but contemporary works seemed to have been released from the shackles of form. They had a freedom all their own.

This Polish poet, this Milosz, he didn't rhyme at the end of his lines but an internal rhythm flourished. And there was no doubt in Cory's mind that this was poetry. Great poetry. The Nobel Prize for chrissake; it said so on the cover. Instinctively, Cory knew that Georgia read this to get into character, to become Anna Kamenski the literature professor who would most certainly have had a kinship with this Milosz, the chronicler of the time. He felt flattered that she had made an effort to include him.

Cory fell asleep with this image in his mind: Georgia Hart as client and Georgia Hart as Anna Kamenski, wartime heroine, seesawing up and down on a giant book wrapped in brown paper and string, straddling a gigantic dumb bell. Up and down went the opposing, smiling Georgias. Things were beginning to look different, even to him.

CHAPTER TWENTY-TWO

Cory and Eric ate entirely different breakfasts at six a.m. Cory's requisite egg whites, white roll and "herbateh" with lemon was joined by a rare and generous slice of cantaloupe, shriveled from its overland journey out of Bergamo in northern Italy. The Oglio river valley boasted the best produce for that time of year. The Hotel Orbis went to great lengths to procure this anemic cache of fruit for its Hollywood guests.

Opposite him Eric Reifenstahl feasted on the fare of the region - an offal beef hash crowned with two sloppy fried eggs, four triangles of waxed Swiss cheese and black coffee. Cory imagined this ritual, leaden breakfast couched in his stomach while Eric pored over an editing table all morning - thus the prodigious gut. That was his job. Editing. He had learned from his aunt Leni as a boy in Cologne. Leni Reifenstahl, whose pro-Nazi documentary Triumph of the Will was perhaps the most incendiary piece of propaganda the twentieth century had produced. It was, in essence, Hitler's calling card at the doorstep of Aryan Supremacy. Eric escaped the specter of this masterwork, studied at Jagellonian in Krakow, spoke fluent Polish, and went on to become a mouthpiece against fascism in his homeland as well as a brilliant editor. Andrew Goldman understood the value of attaching such a controversial man to the film. In reference to the media criticizing Andrews's fraternizing with individuals so closely tied to the Nazi party, Cory had once heard him say, "What better way to know your enemy than over a glass of port and a cigar with one of its offspring."

A suffocating darkness compressed the early morning; a sun threatened to rise behind the curtain of fog. Jack Grady was already up and dressed when Cory entered the Hotel Hollywood. He'd been walking the grounds since 5:00 a.m. and his mustache mottled with the unfreezing drops of his captured breaths. It took only a minute for him to explain the battery changing procedure of the hand-held radios to a rapt Dante. They exchanged good mornings as Cory headed to the gym.

The long gray T-shirt nearly hung down to the

hem of her plaid shorts. It read: IGNOTUM PER IGNOTIUS. The muscles in her lean thighs twitched as she walked; she wore Reebok cross-trainers without socks. Cory laughed to himself. He must have been twitterpated, blinded by a burgeoning love. For even with tousled hair, bleary eyes, and no make up, he still believed her beautiful. She would only belly laugh if he told her so.

"What does your shirt say?" He asked, indicating the treadmill for a warm up.

The neck of the T-shirt was cut low, by hand. Georgia pulled it away from her breasts and read it upside down. "It's the favorite saying of one of my dear friends. He even named a sidewalk cafe after it. It means something like, 'an explanation even more obscure than the thing it explains'. It's too early in the morning to be translating Latin, Cory."

As the stationary meters rolled by, the fog dissipated and shards of sunlight combed the blanket of snow in the backyard; Georgia began to wake up. They stretched. They did four different sets of one hundred abdominal crunches, punctuating their silences with mundane conversation until Cory remarked. "Thank you for the book. I read every poem last night before I fell asleep."

"Oh, you're welcome. What did you think?" Georgia's eyes found their imperial light.

"Well, I'm not sure I understood most of it."

"That's where you're wrong, Cory. Whatever you get from the poem, whatever you feel after reading it, that's right. That's what the poem means to you. Sure the poet has one thing in mind and you may have another. They may even be close to the same thing but they are both valid." Cory thought Georgia would make a good teacher. She inspired confidence at the same time she could explain.

"So even if I don't know who the 'he' is in the poem, I should be able to understand it?" Cory handed Georgia a set of ten pound dumbbells. "Flat bench flyes. Hug the barrel, remember." Cory demonstrated.

Georgia stretched then contracted while Cory observed, ready to spot her if the weight got too heavy.

"When you read 'he', you get some sense of who it is, that's what you bring to the poem." Her breathing was heavy; the striations in her chest more prominent now than ever. She had really gotten lean. Lost some muscle but mostly bodyfat over the last month.

"But he must intend something. I mean the poem is dated 1931, Wilno."

"Well, Milosz is probably talking about the impending rise of the Third Reich. Remember the lines about the 'banner, the color of a romantic rose, flutters, and a long row of military trains crawls on the weed-covered tracks'?"

"Yes. That was the end of the passage."

"Well, the banner could be the Nazi flag with its passionate red background. And the military trains. It wasn't difficult if you were an intellectual at the time to feel what was coming out of Germany with the rise of the Third Reich and the post WWI fallout. Milosz gives us the feeling of these things in his poem. The irony of calling the flag the color of a romantic rose versus the idea of military trains on a weed-covered track. It's ominous, and frankly quite frightening when you consider what we already know about what happened."

"I see. How do you know all this?" He handed her the dumbbells for a second set.

"I do a lot of reading when I take on a role. Especially this one."

"As you know, I read the script. It seems such a depressing thing to make a movie on. Who's going to see this movie anyway?"

"Let me tell you a story."

Cory interrupted. "Do your set first. Then tell me the story when I put you back on the treadmill for a six minute interval. Can you tell me the story in six minutes?"

"Yes, Andrew. God, you men are all alike. You sounded just like him when you said that. You've got that same 'director' thing."

"Sorry. I mean, I didn't mean anything by it."

"Give me the weights," she barked.

Georgia cranked out twenty-five reps, five more than he required of her, then popped up off the bench, catching a glimpse of herself in the mirror on the way over to the treadmill. "God, I look like something out of 'Night of the Living Dead'." She messed with her hair; it didn't help.

"Get over here. I'm not taking pictures, I'm keeping you lean." She blew him a head-cocked, mock kiss. "Now, tell me the story."

He brought the treadmill speed up to seven and a half kilometers per hour.

"It's easy to say, well, Andrew is making the film so that people never forget the Holocaust. And you'll hear the reply, 'Who can forget the Holocaust.' But it's happening. On the flight over here, Andrew handed me an article from last month's Vanity Fair magazine. It described in detail how a large percentage of the German youth were actively setting about denying that the event ever happened. Part of the article talked about this extremely popular computer game called "The Master Plan" that puts the user in charge of orchestrating the entire genocide of the Jews. A video game whose objective is to build the ultimate network of death camps and annihilate an entire race. This is happening now. And that's scary."

Cory thought of the saying at the bottom of the

Noteboard near the elevators in the Orbis lobby, the schedule board. It said the same thing.

He shook his head, "Unbelievable."

"Damn right. So you can see the urgency for a man like Andrew, who has the talent, the resources, the will to make this kind of movie. When a nation or a generation amuses itself with the idea of piling up corpses that represent real people in the form of an electronic game and ignores the grave misstep of its fathers', denies its own history, someone has to shed some light on that dark path. It's almost as if to say, can he afford not to make this movie. Can we?"

Tiny streams of sweat coursed the margin of Georgia's neck. Seeking her breast. On their way to her heart, Cory thought. God, what was it about her that drove him so mad? She oozed passion. About this movie. About working out. About life, it seemed. His palms tingled; his eyes burned as he imagined his cheek flush against hers. It struck him for the first time that everyone must feel these things for her. Men must fall in love with her by the hour. The province of his secret infatuation was, perhaps, nothing more than a spot in the cafeteria line of hungry admirers all futilely banging empty trays and spoons, begging for a hand out. It depressed him suddenly. His fantasy diminished. His perceived intimacy evaporating in the heat of this scorching revelation. Nonetheless, he wanted her to keep talking, for in her words, in the way her mouth divulged those words, Cory could bathe in phonemes and vigorous breaths. A famished wolf so near the carcass, he would eat her with his eyes and ears. The urge to kiss her was so great that holding back very nearly brought tears to his eyes. Even while he missed her during the past ten days, he hadn't realized how much. He tried to keep his composure by asking a question. "But here's the thing. I don't understand how this particular story, 'Pillar of Salt', accomplishes all that. Isn't it sort of a perverse love story between a big time Nazi and a female literature professor who, unforgivably for him, happens to be a Jew?"

"It's the story of a man who chooses power over love out of fear." It sounded suspiciously like a tag line from a Coming Attraction but Cory let her proceed. "It's the story of discovering love then being unwilling to make the changes necessary for that love to come to fruition. If you show an audience a situation where a man has choices to seek a higher moral ground, even if that character faces the conflict and fails, the audience, subconsciously, knows the way to that better place. As they watch the movie and put themselves in his, or her, position vicariously, they know the choice they would make, the right choice. Because the consequences that befall the character, who makes the so called 'wrong' choice, end up so dire. Therefore, the film, despite its truthful and horrific outcome, remains a useful tool, educating and enlightening the audience at the same time it entertains."

Georgia sighed. Cory stopped the treadmill. "Holy donuts, Batman. Sounds like you've got it down."

"I better; I'm the one who has to make Anna Kamenski believable."

Cory laid her down on the mat and stretched her lower back, cross torso. The gym door opened. A half-asleep Lani wandered in, followed by her sidekick. Georgia spoke from the mat, craning her head back towards the door. "Hi, baby. Both my babies."

"Mom," Lani whined. "It's snowing - again. I want to go to Cabo."

"How about a hug from your mother?" Lani rolled alongside Georgia on the floor.

"Ewww. You're all wet."

"It happens when you work out hard. Though, I guess the idea might be foreign to you." Cory chimed in.

"Ha. Ha." Lani shot back. Georgia cradled her daughter, pound for pound and body part for body part her physical equal now.

"What do you have planned for the girls this morning, Mr. Sonne?" Georgia asked. Niki joined the fray on the mat. The mother feline and her kittens. Cory stood and clapped his hands together.

"This morning I thought a hike following the

railroad tracks would be nice. You can see what corn fields look like in the dead of winter."

"Dead, I'd imagine." Lani moaned.

"I have to get going anyway, girls. You know how nervous Andrew gets on the first day of shooting. Wouldn't want to be the one holding him up, especially not today. I'll see you on the set a little later, right?"

Georgia Hart wiped the sweat from her forehead, down the side of her face, under her chin, and all the way through the cleavage of her glistening chest. And she did it with the end of a towel still draped around Cory's neck. A shot of electricity surged between his legs; he was hard in an instant. That she had done this to him on purpose there was no doubt, then she merely said "thanks, Cory" and walked out with her girls. It was the single most erotic erection he had ever known, and he had to get rid of it quickly in order to start the morning hike. Lani or Niki getting a glimpse of his distended sweat pants, cock straining to poke through, would not do. Why was the distraction of his physical desire so much a part of his relationship with Georgia? He was thinking cold thoughts. Would Anchorage, Alaska ever get an NFL franchise?

CHAPTER TWENTY-THREE

"Let's start with the basics. Built from Jurassic limestone, this particular structure we see today was erected in the beginning of the sixteenth century by King Alexander and his brother Sigismund. In 1905 the task of renovation of the edifice fell into the hands of Stanislaw Wyspianski who envisioned a new 'Acropolis' for Wawel Hill but was soon undone by the ravages of the first world war and economic considerations." Judy Breslau's breath clouded the air. The diminutive teacher had all the facts and couldn't get them off her tongue fast enough. Lani and Niki heard only the rubbing of their mittens together, scratching for warmth.

The tour was Georgia's idea. They didn't need her

back on the set until late in the afternoon and for only one shot. The morning provided the perfect opportunity to see the place where Anna Kamenski spent many an indentured night.

This was Wawel Castle. A magnificent embodiment of Polish history and culture and ranked among the few monuments in the world which were so deeply connected with the past of a people and so deeply engraved on its consciousness. Andrew Goldman loved icons. They were so cinematic. This wasn't the castle of Dr. Frankenstein, the wicked witch, Uther Ben Dragon; nor was it Versailles, Camelot, or Windsor. This Krakow Jewel was the Lincoln, Washington, Manassas, Mt. Rushmore, Viet Nam Memorials, and then some, all rolled into one for the Poles. He knew that to capture the story of the Nazi Governor who usurped it and ordered the destruction of the nation from its hilltop boardrooms, was to strike deep into the desecration of this proud but ill-starred people's history. Andrew knew how to move audiences and Wawel was his image.

That is why it topped Georgia's list only her second day in the city. She wanted desperately to see it before the film crews began manipulating it for their own ends. Pristine, undefiled by shotmakers. And Cory joined them.

The group had walked up from Grodzka Street along the cobbled rampart on the slippery southern slope. The chilled air and the difficult incline left them winded at the Armorial Gate to the courtyard. Georgia looked to

Cory. "Even you're out of breath."

"Not out, just short."

"Some jock you are."

Judy interrupted them. "The angle tower to your right, over here, is called the cock's foot. It greets the sun every morning, and by both its form and its name, it evokes associations with popular legends and proverbs reaching back to the Middle Ages in which the motif of a cock occurs."

"Mrs. Breslau?" Niki asked.

"Yes, Miss Gaspari?" Judy was in the habit of addressing all her students by their surname.

"Are we going to have to know all this?"

Cory rolled his eyes. The universal bleating of high school students around the world. How many times had he heard that very phrase in his secondary years at Thousand Oaks high school?

"We will review everything once we get back in the classroom, Miss Gaspari. What would delight me would be for you to enjoy the beauty and the significance of the place."

Georgia put a reassuring hand on both their backs as she urged them forward.

"In 1921 this monument to Tadeusz Kosciuszko was erected. The original statue was destroyed in 1940 by the Nazis. But the preserved casts were located and the present statue derived from them as a gift from the city of Dresden."

Cory leaned between the girls. "That's the guy from 'the mound'."

"What?" Lani quipped, irascibly.

"Kosciuszko is the guy who they built our mound for. The one we hike up to for a workout? The revolutionary guy?"

"What are you now, Mr. historian?" The cold did not wear well on Lani. Cory pulled her into a headlock and gave her a set of two-knuckled noogies.

"Maybe this will warm you up." Cory rubbed along the part in her hair then quickly let her go.

When Lani pulled away Georgia leaned in and whispered, "Me next." Cory swung his right arm around her shoulder and feigned the same treatment. He noticed how perfectly her head fit the indentation between his neck and upper shoulder. She hesitated then moved away from him sharply - a lioness sensing trouble at the mouth of her lair. What did not escape Cory was the first affectionate contact the two of them had shared. Not a hello or goodbye hug. Not stretching in the gym or palpating a muscle contraction. The first spontaneous contact. The gesture of friends. The familiarity that took them past the trainer/client relationship; fun not formal. Easy, outside the realm of their business together. A new plateau where smiles sparkled, unmistakably delightful to the senses.

Georgia had felt this before in her life. A return to the movement in the lower drawer of her stomach but not so queasy this time. Palliative. An erotic laxative against the hardened years of her marriage. Only a few times, across from charismatic male leads, had she let herself fall into this kind of…trance. Yes, that's what it was. A trance. It felt so good, and in the past she had felt justified. At least in her mind. "Good for the picture," she would reconcile back then. A sanctioned flirtation in the name of method acting.

Now, however, she had no excuse. He was so young and her personal trainer for chrissake. She should know better.

For Cory Sonne, waging his own private war against deep emotion, this was something completely new.

"This gate, called the Vasa Gateway was formerly protected by defenses of round bastions such as this one on your right and towers, demolished now, in the days of Sigismund III in 1595. This was the only entrance to the castle until the mid-19th century. This portal and shield are decorated with the Polish eagle, much like the coat of arms of the United States and that sheaf, there, which comes from the Vasa family arms."

Lani turned and whispered to Cory and Georgia. "Can you imagine what it's like having her for three classes a day? I think I'm going to lose my mind. Help me, mom!" The demonstrative daughter of the actress emoted.

Georgia turned her around and pointed her in the direction of her teacher. "You will remember every detail."

She returned.

They were inside the Royal Castle within minutes but not much warmer. Lani's post-cherubic, pre-Rubinesque face was the color of a bad pearl. She wasn't joking about freezing. Niki huddled close to her and they took turns breathing on each other's cheeks and trying not to bust a gut - they could laugh they were so cold. Through these cavernous rooms, even the impulse to chortle had its own echo.

Judy continued on, the disaffected tour guide. Only Georgia asked questions, in part, Cory thought, to keep this poor woman from feeling unappreciated. Georgia had a way with that sort of thing; always made the hired help feel esteemed, down to the unsavory sewage inspector. "That Mrs. Hart," they would say, "she's a kind woman" or "a pretty lady" or "she's got a sweet spot as big as the Queen Mary." Truth be told, she knew a very simple secret. People wanted to feel good about themselves no matter what they did for a buck.

"I think this is the room." Georgia pronounced. "Isn't this the bedroom where Hans Frank slept during his stay?" She looked to Judy.

"I believe so. It is the bedchamber of Sigismund the Old who ruled from 1506 to 1548. He was one of the most controversial monarchs, with ties to the Hapsburgs of Austria. And, I believe, Hans Frank was also closely associated with that lineage. In addition, Sigismund was a keen connoisseur of the arts, and his refined tastes established the Krakow Castle with some of its most resplendent years. Again, Frank, too, fancied himself a man of impeccable taste. There must have been some assumed kinship with the old Polish ruler, who was in fact more Swedish than Polish."

The five of them stood in silence. Through a momentary crease in the clouds outside, a sheet of sunlight wedged into the wood and stone bedroom taking the shape of the Renaissance portals on the eastern wall. The two Florentine paintings across it emerged from the dark shadow. Cory stepped over to them and read the subtitled English inscriptions. "Madonna and Child" and "Madonna Adoring the Child". From what he'd read of the Pillar of Salt script, and what he'd learned of Hans Frank, whose nickname was the "Jew Butcher of Krakow", Cory couldn't imagine these paintings staring down at the Nazi General in the night. He shot a look to Georgia. They shared the same thought.

She spoke the words, "I can't imagine he'd have left those on the wall."

"Yes. Many things were removed and sent to Canada, which was the name the Nazis gave their vast storage facility for pillaged artifacts and treasures. But these remained. They have been there since the restoration of 1905."

"What's this about Canada?" Niki asked. Stepping

in place to keep her toes from freezing. "My uncle lives in Toronto."

"No, not Canada the country. If you'd been reading, you'd know that when the Nazis required the Jews to register and purchase tickets to the relocation camps, they deceitfully informed them that they were buying passage to Canada. Making them purchase their own tickets had the effect of placating them against the rumors of death camps. All of their belongings were appropriately marked for shipment to Canada and when they separated the people from their possessions, part of the goods were placed in storehouses at the camp and the remainder were loaded on trains to Romania. These series of storehouses were called 'Canada.' The possessions went to Canada and the Jews went to any number of labor or death camps. And Hans Frank shipped much of the valuables from Wawel to Romania and Berlin. But these two paintings, for some odd reason, stayed."

Cory could not help but notice the Madonna looking down on the child. He had seen that thin smile and extended hand from his own mother so many times, nursing his wounds in private, wounds incurred from a frustrated father gone ferociously mad.

Judy continued. "Of course, my favorite irony is this tapestry on the opposing wall. One must wonder what Frank thought while gazing on this scene from 'Combat of Hercules with Cacus', a Brussels work of Geraert van

Strecken. Do you think he saw himself as Hercules, mighty, powerful, a vanquisher of foes? Or as Cacus, son of the flame god Vulcan in Roman mythology? A monstrous fire-breathing brigand who terrorized the countryside."

"This one here is Cacus?" Suddenly, Lani was interested. Maybe it was the muscular male physiques. Or the violent story. Either way, she'd snapped to attention.

"Yes, Cacus had stolen some of Hercules' cattle and hid them in a cave on the Aventine Hill; but a lowing cow betrayed Cacus, and Hercules killed him in retribution."

"How do you know all this?" Niki asked in amazement. Judy blushed.

Georgia answered for her. "She paid attention in class."

"Very funny." Lani returned. "It would be a heck of a lot easier to listen if we weren't freezing to death."

"Yes, yes. It is getting cold. Perhaps a warm coffee at the souvenir shop is in order."

The girls nodded their heads eagerly. "Just one more thing." Georgia stepped over the velvet rope partitioning off the bedroom furnishings and moved to the four poster bed. She gazed up at the headboard underneath the tester. Looking for something. "It's not here."

"What would that be, Mrs. Goldman?" Judy asked.

"Have you read the book from which this movie is being made? 'Pillar of Salt'?"

"I'm afraid I haven't."

"No?" Lani and Niki snickered. Georgia admonished them with a look. "Well, the story has it that Anna Kamenski, my character in the movie, a literature professor at Jagellonian University, had her first encounter with Frank when he summoned her to the castle to translate an old literary quotation in Polish that was carved in the headboard. The line apparently came from an ancient Italian Aria and said something like, 'My love is a deep flame that hides beneath the darkest waters.'

"Yes, I remember something about that. I think it was the influence of the Italian baroque architects that Sigismund III brought in to restore the castle after the disastrous fire in 1595. Giovanni Trevano and Tomasso Dolabella. Perhaps it was some other room or some other bed? But the Italian quotation makes sense, does it not?"

"My love is a deep flame that hides beneath the darkest waters." Georgia repeated it to herself, fixed on the blank headboard. There were no words. And no way of knowing whether the scene of Anna and Frank's first encounter was historically accurate. In any case, she would play it like reality. She was burning the words onto that wood with the heat of her imagination.

CHAPTER TWENTY-FOUR

The blood squirted out from the little man's forehead in a pristine, crimson arc, and he convulsed violently backwards before falling into the snow. Long, flowing liquid fingers spilled and steamed over the frozen ground beneath the augured cranium of "just another Jew." Three pair of shimmering black Nazi boots just kept walking.

Except for the trickle of death, everything was still.

"Cut!" Andrew yelled.

"Cut!" The first A.D. echoed through the megaphone.

In the background, the tiny Remu'h Synagogue burned black against the gray sky; ul. Szeroka was a street transformed to its WWII ambiance. Black coated extras in thick-brimmed hats scuttled in the background. Faux gates and facades from the period blended in with the actual remaining structures in this Kazimierz district.

"I don't know, David. The squib didn't look real on the monitor. Looked more like a red water fountain than a bullet-pierced brain. Can we get more splatter?" A bundled up Andrew shuffled into the middle of the street where crew members replaced the stained snow with fresh shovelfuls. The little man who had been shot was immediately escorted off to the effects trailer to have his exploding forehead replaced.

"I can do that. Is that more realistic?" David responded, accordantly.

"I don't know. Ever see a man shot in the head? I haven't. But if I'm looking at it on screen, I don't want to be distracted by the beauty of the blood's clean, curved line. You know what I mean? A little messier calls less attention to the wound and more to the act. Let's try it that way."

The A.D. spoke again through the megaphone "Everybody reset for the shot. Back to one."

Jack Grady surveyed the crowd gathered behind the crew's line. No fewer than three production assistants, P.A.'s they were called, worked at keeping them from creeping closer to the action and in the way of everyone trying to get this done before the last and most difficult take of the day - the long tracking shot.

All in all, for a first day, things had gone smoothly. Except for the blood on this take, everything had exceeded expectation. The weather had cooperated and been sufficiently overcast with only a slight dusting in the early afternoon. The mixed crew, Croat, Pole and American alike, had proved they could work both fast and effectively despite the language barriers, and the choice of Hans Frank's random execution in the street for the first set-up provided the gravity that the production needed out of the gate. There was no doubt in anyone's mind that they were making a serious picture.

Sean McDonough had come out swinging with a wide-eyed evil in his steely countenance that had Andrew tingling with delight. Early on, he had turned to Rory Cohn, his longtime cameraman, and said, "At last, I'm surrounded by real acting genius. This guy is amazing." Rory nodded. They both knew this would be the one.

Jack didn't know a damn thing about making movies. Homicide. That was his specialty. And that fabulously unreal dying man represented nothing but make believe. He'd seen men gunned down before and pulled the trigger more than he'd like to recall in his career to do it. Even the most gifted director in the world could do nothing to approximate it. Sean's revolver to the old man's head was about as close to murder as spit to champagne. But murder wasn't the gig anymore. Protection. That put bread on the table, now.

Up until he spied the man in the hunting cap, there had been nothing out of the ordinary. He didn't know why this guy should be any different than the other gelid onlookers but he was. In thirty-five years of police work, he'd honed his instincts like a micro-laser. And something had flipped his switch. The square-jawed man in the drab green hunter's cap with the wool ear flaps was now the object of his intense scrutiny. It wasn't so much his appearance that unsettled Jack as the way his eyes moved from one location to another and never once looked at the action of the movie scene. Almost as if he were counting. Jack new that counting stare. In Viet Nam he'd watched men counting off yards for mortar fire, counting trees for possible snipers, counting men out for tactical maneuvers, and worst of all, counting bodies. His bodies. That's how he always thought of those fresh-faced, square-shouldered mini-John Wayne's in Nam. Being in charge weighed so heavily on his soul all those years he'd wondered if he hadn't worn a hole in it clear through to the other side.

Then it happened. He'd so hoped to avoid it because he knew it would only make his job tougher. But their eyes met. In an instant they recognized each other. The sentry and the stalker. Cop and criminal. Hired shield and hired gun. Theirs was a game that went on deep in the mind, so deep that the light coming through thinly, as if from another nebula, could be recognized only by one of its own. While most of the minds around them worried about mortgages, sick children, the rising price of coffee, these two men contemplated terror and terror avoided. They turned it over like malleable dough, kneaded it, waiting for the radical oven's liturgy of fire.

The man in the hunting cap identified his adversary. Not his mark but the man who would stand between him and his target. The upturned corner of his lip confirmed Jack's suspicions. It was the only friendly gesture he would receive. Jack Grady could only watch as his newly distinguished foe slipped into the crowd like mud before the flood. The idea of an easy security assignment died aborning. His worst fears had commenced. The game was on.

CHAPTER TWENTY-FIVE

Three weeks he had been in Krakow. A city he was quite familiar with as a double agent for the Stasi, the German secret police, and the Soviets in the days of the old regime. The lax Polish security, thick in the head and lazy, made this an easy city to hide in. Now he was simply a soldier for hire. A field operative who knew reconnaissance, terrorism, and assassination. The man in the drab green hunting cap with wool flap ears named Bernard Zweig.

Criss-crossing the icy streets on his retreat had warmed him some but made him ferociously hungry. Before he could eat, he'd have to make the call. Though it wouldn't please his superiors, he had to let them know what had happened. That he suspected someone might have made him. Someone connected with the movie; he would find out who from his technical wizards in Berlin.

"Berlin Hospice Center." A young male voice answered in German. It was the amusing cover name of the German Alternative, an unfriendly faction at best.

"The coal becomes the diamond." Bernard uttered cryptically. Instantly, he was connected.

"Yeah." The low gravely voice still recovering from a bout of strep rushed into the phone.

"Zweig. They're off to the races. I'm gathering precise information. May have been made."

"So soon?" The question came like a dart. Lars Rostock could never hide his displeasure. It had cost him two wives. He hated what he hated and liked what he liked, which wasn't much. Bratwurst from Leipzig and Belarusian vodka topped a short list.

"Gray-haired bear of a man. Salt and pepper mustache. Looks to be Goldman's personal security. He's a hawk. Ex-C.I.A. maybe. Have Griest detail him out for me." Bernard finished the report; his instinct was to simply hang up. There was nothing left for him to say and the only thing left to hear would be reproach. But he waited.

"Go underground for a few days. We will proceed as planned." Click. Nothing more to be said at this time. Bernard had been unfortunate but there had been no mistakes made and the team would move forward. The only thing that had been lost was Rostock's complete confidence in him. When the party was over, it would be the prize Lars would return.

Bernard Zweig could eat now. He was in the mood for a nice, bloody steak.

CHAPTER TWENTY-SIX

Four cappuccinos and a hot tea. Cory never could acquire the taste for coffee or any of its derivatives. At last the wimpy tourists were warm. It didn't stop Lani from leaning in to Cory, pretending to be innocently absorbing his body heat. Georgia looked on, smiling at Cory when he rolled his eyes.

"You see, Walesa was the man to lead the solidarity movement, the revolution so to speak, but he is not the one to run the country in peacetime and towards economic prosperity." Judy lectured.

"So who is?" Cory asked. He started this line of questioning, eager to know more about this resurrected country.

"Unfortunately, no one can agree on that. The united labor parties of solidarity have splintered into over two hundred different groups. No one can agree on anything except the fact that relying on coal is wrong. Both environmentally and economically. The supply is shrinking. And the next biggest industries are also mining. The transition time is now and everyone's bickering." Judy's tone had switched from educational to personal. The political side of her was creeping out between sips from her paper cup.

Niki braided her hair. The machinations of any politics, let alone those of an iron curtain country, might as well have been mountain ranges on Mars. Lani, too, had the glazed over look. They just don't want to know, Cory thought. Was he so disinterested at that age?

"Nothing is moving forward. One car plant in the whole country and it's licensed from Fiat. They make tiny, inefficient cars."

"Are those the square looking cracker boxes we're always overtaking on the road?" Cory asked.

"Yes."

"What a menace. They'd never make it in L.A. Could you imagine those things putting along down Sunset boulevard during rush hour, all the Mercedes and BMW's honking to get by?" He addressed the table but no one seemed interested. Except Georgia. Good old Georgia. Sweet to the core. She shook her head.

"And women's rights have taken a giant step backwards." That got the girls' attention. "Just last year they passed a very strict anti-abortion law. I tell you sometimes I look at this damn castle on the hill and think we're heading back down the path to the middle ages."

"That must be attributable to the power of the Catholic Church?" Georgia commented.

"Indeed."

A gust of wind blew open the cafe door. It cracked against the wall. The elfin shopkeeper in a hand-knit shawl and a dull babushka the color of over-steamed shrimp waddled over to close it. She mumbled something in Polish that caused Judy to turn. Looking back to the table, Judy wore the expression of someone apologizing for a flatulent uncle.

"The thing that always seems to come up when I talk to the employees over at Hotel Hollywood is that you can't change the minds of the older generations. Is that true?" Cory picked up the ball.

"There's an old communist saying, 'We pretend to work and they pretend to pay us.' The standard of living is low, the infrastructure is in dire need of an overhaul, and people need to learn that their own motivation will merit them better lives with the housing, health care, and the amenities that they want."

"Can Poland make the switch?" Georgia tapped the table with two fingers, side by side. It struck Cory that they resembled the legs of a pin-up girl on some blue-tiled pool deck. He suddenly wanted them in his mouth.

"They used to get an inferior version of all these things without having to work. Can they work hard enough now to afford the improvements? Decades of laziness and sloth are not easily undone. In answer to your question, Mr. Cory, we are torn by generation and by philosophy. And, as in other parts of the world, fear still rules the lives of this people. Not so much fear of the government now, but of the economy. It's a mixed bag. I have my own opinions."

Lani let out a big sigh. "Boy would I love a nap, right now."

Georgia laughed. She looked down at her watch. "Oh, shit. I have to get to the set." She stood. "Judy, would you like to come to the set with us?" Judy blushed, unused to such familial kindness from her employers.

"Well, I've never been to a movie set. For that matter, I've never been to a movie."

Lani's eyes nearly popped out of her head. "You've never been to a movie?"

Georgia pulled the girls chairs out to rattle them from their lethargy. "Come on. Let's hustle."

"No, I prefer books and museums." Judy answered.

"Not once? Never in your whole life?" Niki couldn't believe it either.

"No. I've seen movies on television of course. But I've never paid for one or seen them at the theater."

"You're kidding?" Lani couldn't comprehend the idea.

"No, I'm quite serious."

"Then you're in for a whole new education." Georgia added as they braced for the chill beyond the cafe door.

The woman in the babushka decided to change her opinion of the Americans after Georgia left a fifty thousand zloty gratuity. One of the few things Carolyn had forgotten to mention was the no tip policy in this country.

"That's incredible. Never been to a movie," The girls kept saying to Judy and to each other. It was the most startling thing they had heard and the only thing they would remember about their day at Wawel. Except, of course, that it was 'butt ass cold.'

CHAPTER TWENTY-SEVEN

Thirty feet of aluminum dolly tracks lay in the snow. Rory screamed out, "Back to one," after finalizing the details of the long, complicated shot. He would be following as Sean McDonough walked and inspected his weapon, wiping the blood from the barrel. Blood splattered from the head of the old Jew whom his character had just eliminated in the name of disease control. His gloved hand would discard the stained handkerchief which would land at the feet of Anna Kamenski who had walked curiously in the direction of the gunshot.

Pull back and pan up to reveal the ominously beautiful face of the leading lady who would come to haunt the Nazi exterminator more than the tally of corpses he created.

Andrew threw his shoulders back. The tension in his upper torso knifed through his cold body. He was nervous about this shot. He had to get it right. The protagonist's introduction to Frank's evil ways was pivotal to the audience's ability to identify with the character. Will they invest in her emotionally? That first impression, the first subliminal visage of the character's whole being, will carry significant weight in assuring that connection, and thus the success of the movie. How to pull it off occupied the mind of the hulking director.

Out of the make-up trailer came the blandly dressed and pale faced version of Georgia Hart that would be Anna Kamenski. Peg, her assistant, a stocky New England girl in Sorrel's and oddly checked trousers, carried a heavy coat. Something to throw over her shoulders in between takes.

Andrew took her gently by the elbow and turned her back to the crew, stepping off across the intersection of ul. Szeroka and ul. Middowa. He whispered something in her ear; she nodded. Then he left her, cueing the A.D. on the way back to the monitor.

"Places everyone," came the bullhorn.

Georgia moved to her mark. Sean and the other Nazi Officers hovered near the dead old man in the blood-soaked snow.

Cory watched between the heads of Andrew and Lani, who leaned into her father, not unlike the way she had sought warmth from Cory back at the castle. This young girl was either very cold or very starved for male contact. In assessing the situation, Cory couldn't rule out either.

Yuri Jaworki, the director of photography, stared at the cloud cover. Not only were they losing light but the storm clouds rolling in were dark, absorbing what little was left. He chewed nervously on the corner of his lower lip, mumbling to himself.

"Don't worry, Yuri. We'll get the shot." Andrew reassured him.

"Yes, yes. Those bastard clouds. This is why I never liked southern Poland. Much too unpredictable."

"Rory?" Andrew yelled.

"Ready!"

"Let's go." Andrew called.

"Rolling!"

"Speed." Yelled the sound man.

Taking a quick glance at his actors and seeing them poised, Andrew called it out. "Action!"

Sean as Hans Frank, the tall, menacing Nazi in the dark overcoat, marched through the snow wiping down his weapon and talking of Schopenhauer, "'The will periodically withdraws itself entirely from the guidance of the intellect, and consequently of the motives. In this way it then appears as a blind, impetuous and destructive force of nature, and accordingly manifests itself as the mania to annihilate everything that comes in its way.' You must have the <u>will</u>, lieutenant. You should read Schopenhauer."

Rory had perfectly captured the walk and the speech with his lens. As the handkerchief floated down to the icy path, the camera racked its focus to Anna's fettered winter shoes coming into the frame. The camera then pulled back to reveal her finding the bloody rag in the snow. Andrew watched her expression. Terror and compassion. Pride and futility. Sorrow and pity. In the pit of his stomach he felt the ooze of inspiration like an open wound. It took only this first shot, this one instant to convince him that he was destined to make the greatest film of his life. Georgia Hart was wearing history, human and cinematic, on the canvass of her luminous face.

CHAPTER TWENTY-EIGHT

It was in a convention room of the Orbis Hotel, or half a room to be technical, that Cory viewed his first "dailies." He'd been involved with so many movies as the trainer of their stars, been around movie people most of his adult life and lived in the movie town of L.A but here in this small conference room of Krakow's answer to the Holiday Inn, he had finally been invited to see the footage from the day by day shoots - the dailies. From the heavy 35mm camera magazines, into the hard cases with the foam padding, by van over to the film lab, processed, copied, then repackaged and sent off to the editors for a rough assemblage. That was the birthing odyssey of the captured images on film. In little more than a twenty-four hour turnaround, in the late evening hours, the entire crew had the opportunity of viewing the filming of the day before. It was the editor/breakfast companion, Eric Riefenstahl, who had extended the invitation to Cory though he himself was seldom there. Cory was grateful and felt privileged to be included.

The crew - production assistants, electricians, grips, make-up and hair stylists, set decorators, and Yuri's cinematography team lounged around in a loose arrangement of thin cushioned chairs with straight wooden backs. Cory hid in the corner trying to be as inconspicuous as possible while still getting a clean look. He noted that very few of the actors were present. Eric mentioned later that for the most part they were a superstitious lot and avoided anything that might jinx their performance - dailies being top on the list.

Superstition didn't seem to stop Sean McDonough, however. He always entered with a loud pronouncement of his arrival and often carried on conversations with the characters and about the events on screen. More than once, Cory heard him comment, "What a handsome devil that Hans Frank is, evil incarnate though he be."

Black and white footage. That, too, was unique. Eric reminded Cory what a rare opportunity it was to be watching dailies in black and white. Most films were shot in color simply for the reason that it was predominantly all that theaters were equipped to handle. The co-op of "artists" on this production was thrilled to work in the medium, and Yuri was considered the finest cinematographer around when it came to the colorless light and shadow game.

All Cory knew was that it looked spectacular. From what he'd seen in documentary footage of WWII and other events of the time period, this film, shot only yesterday, easily looked from that era. If he did nothing else worth noting in Pillar of Salt, Andrew Goldman would have at least accurately recreated the Krakow of the Nazi occupation.

Rollo, one of Yuri's underlings, ran the projector night after night from his stool in the back of the room. Cory would watch with fascination as he expertly pinned, threaded, clipped and flipped gates, gauges, and film stock with the precision of a watchmaker. And never once did he lose the long ash that dangled from his lip-hugging cigarette.

On screen, Sean as Hans Frank was dominant. He had the stateliness and the posture of a powerful man. The black Nazi cross seemed his birthmark not just a pin on his lapel or an insignia on his cap. And his eyes were the scourge of a private hell which he built to rival the good works of every temple and every rabbi in Poland.

The scenes were riveting, poignant. Then there was Anna Kamenski. She looked so fragile up there on the screen, sometimes tiny and reduced, sometimes fourteen feet tall. This woman was not the Georgia Hart he had come to know, not the firebrand that complained about the intensity of the workouts just before attacking them with unequaled resolve, not the pixie smile that could turn to the bewitching leer. Certainly the make-up helped, the lighting, the black and white. But there was something else.

Could it be that she was too thin too early on? As her trainer, the guide to her physical condition, had he overdone it? For the first time, he was worried. She had listened to him closely, done everything he had asked of her, and it had worked. Too well, perhaps. No one had complained to him, not even Andrew. And Cory had the feeling that if Andrew were not happy he would know about it right away. There in the dark, with her sunken but ravishing face painted on screen, Cory realized he had to say something to her the next morning. He knew he was setting himself up for misery, for he had learned long ago that telling a woman there was something wrong with her looks was about as smart as stepping loudly behind a mule. But the dailies had given him a picture of Georgia, or Anna as the case would be, that might have been more objective than the one he saw when he looked into her eyes in person. He owed it to her to at least bring it up. Her looking the part was, after all, why he had been hired.

CHAPTER TWENTY-NINE

The Polonaise Film Lab at 18 ul Karmelicka, next to the tiny Carmelite church, had all the modern film developing technology available anywhere else in Europe. The owner, Jan Toranska, split his time between this new shop and the one in Milan, which he had opened after selling his "reel carrier" patent to Eastman-Kodak. Dual citizenship and an equal facility in Italian, English and Polish made the double life palatable. But in his older years, without children and after the death of his wife of forty-three years, the sentimental lure of his home land of southern Poland tugged at his heart strings. He knew it would be a rough go at first with so little production being done in the area. The Goldman film was a boon, and he had been personally honored when Andrew had visited his lab and given his approval. It was a vanguard contract that would hopefully pave the way for not only his business but future film production in the country as well.

A proud man with noble intentions, Jan Toranska, like so many of the new breed of entrepreneurs emerging in the democratic Poland, wanted desperately to be the capitalist trailblazer on the path to privatization. Perhaps this is what accounted for his short-sighted hiring practices. For, certainly, if he had done a thorough background check on one of his new lab technicians, Nysa Malbork, Jan would never have hired him. Though he had proficient lab skills from his stint as a chemistry student in Warsaw the only job Nysa had ever held for any length of time was as a developer for the Bureau of Tourism, and it was common knowledge that the Bureau was filled with spies, double agents, and agitators using the legitimacy of the government post as a shield for much shakier operations.

Nevertheless, Nysa's work ethic flourished and Jan relished the fact that he never once had to remind Nysa about chemical viability or workplace integrity. Putting Nysa in charge of duplication of the "Pillar" dailies had seemed the logical choice. Not one scratched negative or botched process in the first full week on the job that included long hours and longer reels. Those Americans were prodigious shooters and printers. How was Jan to know that every third duplicate was going straight onto a take-up reel meant not for the "Pillar" production offices but for an unmarked gray film-carrier that found its way to the Skala Shipping Service then onto a train for the Berlin Hostel Center?

For a man who exercised caution his entire life, dodging the policy knives of the many political circus regimes he'd served as a successful businessman, living a life that bounced between two countries, this one oversight, the unscrupulous Nysa pocketing two million zloty a week for his underhanded act, would be the blight on his career.

CHAPTER THIRTY

The sign read: Berlin Hostel Center. All were welcome inside. At least as far as the reception desk where any traveler could receive a wealth of information about low cost hostelry and inns in the city of Berlin and its surrounding provinces. Beyond that, however, were a series of small, clandestine rooms where few wandered. And unless one knew that Schickelgruber was Hitler's real last name and asked for a piece of Schickelgruber pie in perfect German, he ran the risk of an Uzi jammed up under the chin the moment he passed the skinny, Marlboro-smoking receptionist with the Pippi Longstocking curls.

In one of those back rooms, Lars Rostock sat comfortably in a high back leather chair reading the latest essay on anti-terrorism in the February, 22, 1994 issue of the International Tribune and snickering to himself. The myopia with which these journalists often viewed the specter of professional political agitation never failed to amuse him. All things were proceeding as planned. Soon enough this columnist and a host of others would have fodder for their op-ed pieces. The beauty of his unfolding plan would unfold in the early Monday morning hours of the upcoming week.

Lars had just spent an informative half hour on the phone with Bernard Zweig, his operative in Krakow. Although Zweig had been laying low, as ordered, he still maintained his evening and early morning vigil outside the Hotel Hollywood and felt confident that he had safely learned the terrain and the coming and going habits of filmmaker Andrew Goldman, his security, and his family. All of which could prove very useful down the road.

"What about the salt and pepper haired man - Goldman's bodyguard?" Zweig asked Lars. He was certain the look that had passed between them that day on the location of the shoot was one of identification, two veterans of the same war, smelling of the same gunpowder and savvy enough to know one of their own kind.

"Retired Los Angeles Policeman. Now specializes in personal security. But no dummy. Assisted Gunter Strauss in Vienna on two Interpol cases during has last years on the force. Exercise extreme caution." Lars felt certain Zweig would not be outmatched. After all, Bernard had been trained by the Stasi, and comparing one of its ranks against a lowly homicide detective from the cesspool of Southern California where the only significant violence was lethal, gang-related capture the flag, jealous husbands with itchy fingers, or robberies gone wrong, was unfair at best. Perhaps when their murders resounded with the siren of political change then he might deign to think of Los Angeles' law enforcement as equipped to handle true madmen with a purpose. For as well as he knew human beings, he knew himself better, and that was what he was. Pure, unadulterated madman with a purpose. He had never forgotten the words of his Nazi father, "Dying is merely a worthless and pathetic necessity unless you die for your beliefs."

A knock at the door. "Yeah?"

A young but reverential voice leaked through. "Herr Rostock, the film is ready."

Lars seated himself in the folding chair between the projectionist and the gray film container against the wall. The flicker of light on the silver screen revealed the celluloid product for which the head of the German Alternative had agreed to pay two million zloty a week. Now, with the blood money of his neo-fascist terrorist organization, he could keep tabs on just what kind of propaganda Andrew Goldman and his brainwashed Hollywood sycophants would be spreading about his biological father - Hans

Frank.

CHAPTER THIRTY-ONE

It was snowing, again. Cory could already imagine the complaints from Niki and Lani when they rolled out of bed. He watched the large flakes falling outside while Georgia warmed up on the treadmill. They reminded him of feathers, a pillow fight in heaven among legions of hard-hitting angels.

How should he tell her? Normally, he waited on these things until general conversation provided an opening. But Georgia wasn't talking much this morning, just concentrating on her breathing. Hell, he had to say something.

"Do you ever watch yourself in dailies?"

"Not anymore. I tried it when I first started.

Thought I could be objective about it, you know. But I don't think you can. You learn the hard way that how you see yourself has very little to do with how everyone else does." Georgia took a deep breath. Cory was silent.

"So I gather."

"Have you seen them?"

Cory nodded. "They run them after dinner every night at the Orbis, in one of the conference rooms."

"And?"

"What? You want me to tell you how spectacular you are?"

"Of course."

"Well, you are. You know it. In fact, I think I've heard you say so yourself."

"I've also said you were good-looking. You don't believe that for a minute do you?" She laughed.

"No, never believed I was good looking. I'm fit, I know that. But good looking? Not mine to say. But you, well, you are good looking and you know it."

"Yes, I do. And you'll know it, too, when you're my age - about yourself. Right now, it's just a naïve humility you have. It's charming." Cory brought her speed down, it was time to stretch but he brought her over to the mirror first.

"Flex your chest, like this." Cory demonstrated a posture that brought his pecs into prominent display, then assisted Georgia in striking the same pose. "Look at you.

You are so lean. See this?" He pointed to the striations in her chest and the muscles along her neck. "This is a serious absence of bodyfat."

"Isn't that what I'm supposed to have? That's what my trainer's been telling me."

"Yes, but I'm a little worried that it's too severe, too soon."

"Ah, now I see what you're getting at. You didn't like the way I looked on screen in the dailies, and you're trying to tell me this in a roundabout way. Is that it?"

"Yes. It is. I can't lie. Never was very good at it."

"You're right; you're turning red." Georgia brushed the back of her hand across his cheek. There was still silence for a moment.

"There's a fine line between getting lean and doing damage to your body. You look like you might be losing too much lean body mass. I'm beginning to worry about the sunken look your cheeks have and the boniness in your upper torso. I'd like to have a blood and urine test done, just for safety's sake. Make sure you're not deficient any of the essentials."

Georgia turned away abruptly. "No way." She sat down on the bench to begin her lat pull-downs.

"There's nothing wrong with being cautious."

"I won't do it. End of story. Now, can we continue here?" What had he done to upset her so? He had never seen her turn on him so quickly.

"I'm sorry that I upset you, Georgia, but I'm trying to do my job in the best way I know how. This information would be helpful to me." She reached for the bar to begin the set herself. Cory held it away from her, preventing it. Something was going on; he was taking tremendous heat form her, and he wanted to know what it was that he had done wrong.

"Look, it's not your fault. I understand what you're saying. It's just that…" She couldn't bring herself to speak the words. Her chin dropped. Why had his request for a blood test brought her to the brink of tears?

"What? What is it, Georgia?" His voice was nearly a whisper. "You can tell me." He dropped to a knee, next to her on the bench. She leaned her head into his shoulder, bit her lip and sobbed.

"I try so hard not to think about this but every once in awhile it creeps up on me and attacks me by surprise. And then, I get like this, all flustered."

"What creeps up on you?" Cory stroked her hair.

"David." There was a long pause. Cory waited. "Andrew and I had decided to try for another child. He had gotten it into his head that he wanted a son, someone to carry on the name, progeny and all that. We argued back and forth for years about it until finally he wore me down. We went to specialists and took all the precautions necessary to ensure it was a boy. Monitoring my menstrual cycle, body temperature, progesterone levels, blah, blah, blah.

You need to know the exact hour of ovulation and that's when you make love, giving the male sperm, the faster swimmers, the chance to get there first and penetrate the egg. It was all pretty scientific and laborious but it ended up working. I became pregnant with a son three winters ago. David - that was the name we had picked out for him. Things were going fine for the first four months except I had a little trouble keeping food down. Then, after a routine blood test, the doctor called the two of us into his office to explain that I had a rare tissue disorder that was preventing the proper nutrition from crossing the placenta wall, and…" Georgia stared straight out the window at the snow, as if the shimmering white veil could obscure the pain of remembering.

"You don't have to tell me all this." Cory knew all too well the pain of remembering and wanted to spare her the suffering.

"No, I want to tell you. Perhaps it's important that you know this about me. I was under constant supervision, taking all kinds of medication, still sick to my stomach most of the time, all in an effort not to lose this baby. But it happened. One night, I woke from a terrible dream in agony and found myself lying in a pool of my own blood. I was rushed to the hospital but by the time I arrived, the baby had miscarried. It was the end of a long ordeal, and, truth be told, the end of Andrew's and my intimacy."

"Was it possible to try again?" Cory asked, naïvely.

"No, no." Georgia stood. "I think I've had enough for today."

Cory understood. Instinctively, he moved in and put his arms around her. She held him tightly for a few moments. "I probably shouldn't have told you all this. But I wanted you to understand the problems I have with my blood. No need to alarm some local doctor about a potentially dangerous situation of which I am already aware. I hope you understand. And, as for my look, don't worry. It's all going to work out perfectly for the movie, and I'll be fine. Trust me."

Georgia left the room. Cory moved back to the window, gazing at a foot of new snow on the ground and seeing in his mind a fragile woman wrapped in the sheets of her bed in a pool of her own blood.

CHAPTER THIRTY-TWO

The largely unrestored ul. Kanonicza still retained all of its gothic charm though the stone facades of its three story buildings along the east side had not faired well against the ravages of coal dust and carbon monoxide, which, along with a paltry amount of oxygen seemed to comprise most of the air in this winter-wrapped city. Up at the north end of the street, equipment trucks kept their motors running, their heated cabs the refuge of many a frozen crew member. Two huge Simson generators powered up the lights and cameras set to record the progress of the black Duisenberg, the Nazi limousine that would transport Anna Kamenski from the Collegium Maius district up Wawel Hill.

As late as ten o'clock last night, the day was scheduled for the soundstage at Kombinat Studio, the initial dinner scene. But when Andrew looked outside and saw the size of the falling snowflakes, something had told him this weather was not to be wasted. He phoned Erasmus who phoned Mykael, the Unit Production Manager, who started the phone web spreading out until everyone down to the last truck driver knew they were going on location with the Duisenberg throughout the snow-covered streets of the old city.

Cory felt exceedingly grateful for his Sorrels and sorry for the poor slobs in conventional work boots whose toes must have been half way to frost-bitten by noon. He stood inside the empty office building doubling as a staging area by a tall, first floor window and looked out over the street through the glass' yellowed film. The canopy covered the stationary A camera where Rory, Yuri and Andrew assessed the shot. Earlier he had seen the three of them walk into a foot of fresh snow and gaze through the framing lens around Andrew's neck deciding that this was the place for the long approaching shot. Cory watched now as they checked the lighting.

Much of the crew huddled together trying to generate some heat while still maintaining socially acceptable distances. Cory spotted Georgia coming from the make-up room in her modest dress and long, somber coat, her hair pulled back into a tidy, braided bun. As she approached him, he noticed how dense her make-up was. The hollow cheeks of the black and white dailies were precisely placed patches of ashen brown face paint, and the brackish concavity around her eyes gave her an exaggerated, sunken look as if her eyes had retreated from the very thing they'd seen.

"You look…different." Cory offered, still standing at the window.

"It's my embraceable, intellectual peasant look. Do you find it irresistible?" Cory laughed. 'Yes' would have been his answer but he'd already stepped over the line once this morning and she seemed in much better spirits now. He'd stick with the laugh.

"You picked a boring day to come on location." Georgia commented, wiping the remaining dusting of snow off the back of his Patagonia jacket.

"Well, Lani and Niki are safely off to school…"

"Exasperated with Judy by this time no doubt."

"No doubt. Besides, Waldek had to come down here from Hotel Hollywood with an extra pair of Andrew's special, Chilean wool socks, so I hitched a ride. That okay?"

"Sure. Just not much to see." Georgia leaned into the window and caught a glimpse of Andrew under the canopy. Cory watched her watching him, his eyes fixed on the flank of her neck, stretching as she turned to the window pane, a vampirish invite of the first order. In a flash he imagined himself bearing down on it with icicle-like incisors melting as they sunk into the warm blood of her carotid artery.

"Do you know what Waldek asked me on the way over here?" Cory said.

"If you knew Julia Roberts?" Georgia guessed.

"No, but close. I do by the way."

"Oh, don't name drop with me. What did Waldek ask you?"

"He asked me if I surfed."

"Logical question. You're a Californian, broad-shouldered, tan, blonde, athletic. Doesn't that about cover it?"

"Yes, and I have tried it. And when I told him that he began singing to me. 'Surfin' USA'."

"No?" The idea tickled Georgia as much as it surprised her.

Cory imitated the thick Polish accent as he sang, "…catch 'em surfin' at Rincon, and down Doheny way, San Onofre sundown and …bay, all over La Jolla …tell the teacher we're surfin', surfin USA."

Georgia's throat danced with laughter as she covered her mouth, trying to stifle it. She caught Cory off guard as she slapped him on the side of the arm and pulled at his jacket like a schoolgirl. One verse was enough. The crew was beginning to stare.

Outside, Andrew stepped into the street, on his way

over to the building to get warm. He looked up into the window and squinted at the picture of Georgia, in the guise of the dour Anna, laughing her pretty head off and smacking her trainer on his prodigious chest. It did not please him. Up until that moment he had put it out of his head, dismissed it as inconsequential, the change that had come over Georgia since their arrival. For the week prior to their journey she had been quiet, introspective, nary a smile crossing her lips, and yet nervous. Not in her usual way, the bitchy tantrums that normally preceded her tackling a lead role. No, she seemed distracted, melancholy and with a tendency towards long, protracted exhalations. A different kind of worry than the one he was used to. An reluctant prom date, a mother in the lobby of an emergency room, a wartime bride watching the wheels of an approaching telegram messenger. For the most part, he thought he knew why but now he was not so sure. With the filming commenced, she was losing her edge, so carefully cultivated in the years since her miscarriage, the edge he felt was necessary for Georgia's ultimate success as Anna, and Andrew wasn't sure that her relationship to this personal trainer didn't have something to do with it. At any rate, the sight of her laughing with him up in that window did little to convince him that she was ready for the scene where she was about to be escorted into a hell of Hans Frank's making.

If things proceeded down this path, he would have to

do something about it. That's what he was thinking as the Duisenberg pulled up into position. Time to get Anna into place.

CHAPTER THIRTY-THREE

Cory stopped at the reception desk in the lobby for his key. He had made a habit of leaving it there for safekeeping, and it gave him an opportunity to be social with the desk staff who all seemed more than willing to assist him with his Polish pronunciation. Distinguishing between the "s", the "sz", the "cz", the "dz", and the "z" itself was driving him batty. There was so much "shushing" going on when they spoke it sounded like their tongues were tiny feet dragging through wet gravel. His Langenscheidt pocket Polish dictionary offered little help. And yet, most of the staff members spoke and understood English well enough to carry on at least a minimal conversation.

It was 7:30 when the crew wrapped shooting for the

day. All the assigned drivers were busy shuttling Georgia, Andrew, Lani and Niki, who had stopped by after school to catch the last two set-ups and flirt with Chuck, the Soundman. They had met him at the opening reception and run into him the following day with Carolyn in the square when they were perusing some of the local jewelry shops. Chuck had just purchased an "official" Soviet Special Forces watch and agreeably escorted them to the joints he'd scoped out.

No available drivers. No problem. The Hotel Orbis was just across the river from Wawel castle and Cory didn't mind the walk. As ugly as the Vistula was, polluted and black, it was still a river, and rivers had always held something special for him. Though he'd never had the opportunity in his life, he knew he'd have made a great rower. The sport required powerful, long legs, a strong, broad back, immense discipline, and the VO2 Max of a distance athlete - all of which he possessed. Secretly, he had a dream of owning a rustic cabin on a deserted lake somewhere in the northern U.S. or Canada and rising at the crack of dawn, steam coming off the lake, turning over his single shell boat, dropping the oars quietly into the water and stroking into the morning sun. He could almost here the hypnotic sound of the repetitive dipping, pulling, retrieving of the blades as their displacement of the water propelled him across the lake. Solitude, sweetness, his body consumed with exertion for the Zen of it. Those were the kinds of pleasant dreams that could carry him away.

Martin handed Cory his key and a small package from Georgia. By the size and shape of it he guessed another book, and he was right.

In the brown and orange lair of his room, where he was now quite comfortable thanks to the addition of a dark blue bedspread and two movie posters from the Hotel Hollywood, "Cinema Paradiso" and Louis Malle's "The Lovers", neither of which Cory had seen, he sat at the window.

The book was a paperback, the Dover Thrift Edition of Elizabeth Barrett Browning's "Sonnets from the Portuguese and Other Poems". Cory read the preface. "Elizabeth Barrett born 1806; died 1861. Married the poet Robert Browning. Best known for her remarkable sequence of 44 love poems "Sonnets from the Portuguese" which were completely original, but her husband, to whom they were addressed, suggested the whimsical artifice."

Turning page after page in the thin book, Cory found himself immersed in the fabric of words whose weave was nothing short of sensational. He could hear the children playing, the women weeping, the angels entreating the author to experience life to its fullest. There were flowers rooted in the soul, light leaping in the flame of love's fire, lute and song, a dauntless, voiceless fortitude, pale cheeks and trembling knees, antidotes of medicated music answering for mankind's forlornest uses, and an exchange of a near sweet view of Heaven for earth with thee. At any other time of his life, Cory Sonne wouldn't have made it past the first few lines. But this book, these poems came from Georgia Hart; they were a gift, valued enough by the giver so as to command the respect of the recipient. For the first time, he was not scared to read about love, not ready at the drop of a "beloved" to turn and run, willing to listen to a sylvan voice speak about feelings in the dense wood of the relationship between a man and woman. Elizabeth Barrett Browning was right to express "...how that great work of Love enhances Nature's."

Cory gazed across the Krakow skyline from his sixth floor window, and reverently placed the book of sonnets on top of his boombox, a place of honor. It was a little past 8:30. He'd read all forty-four sonnets, and he was hungry. Carolyn invited him earlier to join her and some of the crew at Da Pietro. Italian restaurants could always be counted on to serve at least one reasonably healthy dish - pasta. But could he manage to wrangle it from the kitchen before it was drenched in oil or some saturated, fattening sauce? He'd give it a try.

The taxi from the hotel to the square took only seven minutes and cost a mere 20,000 zloty - two bucks. But they could only go so far as ul Wislana. From there it was two blocks of foot traffic which, in this kind of weather, was no small jaunt. Cory braced against a brisk wind and turned the corner into the Rynek Glowny just in time to see the face of the assistant director, Peter, as he pulled open the door of the restaurant. Though he had been there once already with Yuri and Mikola, he was not sure he would remember where it was. The entrance was nothing but a hole in the wall. Cory followed Peter in.

A slim blonde girl whose nametag read Oskubac took his coat. She looked like a Susan or a Shelly to him; maybe that was the translation.

The restaurant was down a double set of stairs and gave the appearance of being converted from a catacomb. Though the ceilings were high, they, like the walls, were solid dolomite. Their jagged contours made Cory think each room had been dug out by hand over the centuries, boulder after dislodged boulder. Underground rooms like these must have been used as hiding places from invading forces during the crusades, the middle ages, and later on for bomb shelters.

Carolyn waved Cory over into the next room. He floated through on an aromatic trail of garlic and pizza bread and took the seat next to her. She kissed him firmly on the lips, smelling of rosemary and red wine "Glad you could make it."

Introductions all around were cut short as everyone's attention turned to Sean McDonough who showed up with two six packs of Guinness and dropped them on the table, "Dig in, brothers and sisters of the hops and barley." Cory noticed there weren't too many takers.

Guinness was a dark, thick beer, an acquired taste for anyone not raised on the stuff. Cory nudged Carolyn who passed him one. The idea of a beer seemed much keener than the act of drinking it as it turned out. The only other taker was Chuck, across the table from Cory. Everyone else seemed content with liters of the house red.

Sean took the seat at the head of the table, two tables actually, end to end, and assumed the paternal patter that such a position often dictates. He controlled things for the rest of the night, something, no doubt, he was probably used to as a Tony, Emmy, and Ace award winning actor. "Is it me or was it fuckin' cold out there today?"

Everyone laughed. Not a one of them escaped the bone chilling cold. "Colder than a witch's tit." Chuck added.

"Colder than a Plutonian witches tit," added Yuri seated on the corner at Sean's left.

"Is plutonium cold? I thought they used it in making nuclear explosions?" Carolyn asked.

"Not plutonium. Plutonian. As in from the planet Pluto, the farthest planet from the sun and therefore the coldest."

"Oh, I get it."

"That's too bad Carolyn, my dear, because I'm looking for a woman that doesn't get it, at least not often. They make the most lively lovers." Sean's Irish accent was getting thicker as the Guinness drained.

The waitress patiently took their orders, dodging Yuri and Sean's leering looks and completely oblivious to their innuendo. Cory and Carolyn kept most of the conversation at their own end of the table with Chuck and Peg, Georgia's assistant seated next to him. They talked of the long shoot ahead of them and things they missed most about home. Peg had a pure breed Sharpei named Kazak, after some ancient Chinese warrior, that she had to leave with her sister. Owing to the fact that the dog came up in conversation three different times, he guessed she had quite an attachment.

Betty, Andrew's assistant, seated at Sean's right, reminded Cory of a Doberman Pincher. Perhaps why she and Peg always hung out together, some kind of subconscious canine connection. As Cory listened to her, he thought it odd that she, too, was telling a dog story.

"She was my high school English teacher and her name was Miss Calcetas." Betty spoke methodically with a heavy Texas accent that made her seem dull and easygoing. Nothing could be further from the truth. She was a Harvard grad with a perfect SAT score who spent every waking hour serving Andrew Goldman.

"Calcetas, what is that Indian?" Yuri asked.

"No, Filipino. Anyway, the summer between my junior and senior year, she was living on the outskirts of Denton, that's where I'm from, Denton, Texas, and it's a blistering hot summer and all. Well, the principal's callin' and callin' to make sure she shows up at the teacher's orientation but there's no answer. Now this woman was a real dog lover, had six of 'em runnin' around on her property, a half acre of saw grass and fig trees complete with the rusted truck up on blocks in the side yard. Well, local police head out to pay a visit, seein' as she ain't answered her phone for anyone in over a week at the beginnin' of August, and you know what they found when they busted inside?" She looks around the table but no one's guessing.

"No, but I imagine you're gonna tell us." Sean intoned in his best southern accent, albeit not good enough.

"I ain't from Georgia, McDonough." Betty corrected him. "But nice try."

"What did they find?" Peg asked, genuinely curious.

"A carcass, with nothin' but a few scraps of meat left on its bones. The skeleton of what used to be my English teacher. She'd died of a heart attack, or heat exhaustion, or somethin', and the dogs had plain eatin' her. Can you imagine?" The salads arrived.

"I'm hungry now." Chuck punctuated the end of the story.

"Don't you see the irony?' Betty asked a silent table.

"Yeah, the dog lover was eaten by her own dogs." Carolyn said.

"Not just that. She was Filipino. They eat dogs in the Philippines. It was a clear cut case of a dog's revenge."

"A dog's revenge. Sounds like a good title for a book." Chuck mentioned between chomping bites of his poor excuse for a salad.

It continued like this all the way through dinner. Blustery story swapping, affectation and incredulity. Cory listened and soaked it all in. His pasta and marinara was relatively clean tasting and a generous portion. He ate a little more than half and sipped his Guinness slowly. When Sean offered another, Cory politely shook his head. He passed it down the table anyway then pointed a long bony finger at Cory.

"People, people. Quiet down. I don't believe we've heard this one down here speak a word."

All eyes turned to Cory. "Who, me?"

"Yes, you, Mr. Bronze Blonde Adonis nursing your Guinness like a schoolgirl." Sean was well on his way to ripped.

"What? I'm a much better listener than talker."

"Surely you have somethin' to add. Tell us a story about your school days, like Betty here." Sean implored him.

A wash of memories burst into Cory's brain. School buses, suspenders, freckled face girls eating fifty-fifty bars, blue and gold steps, clapping out erasers after class, piñatas in Spanish class, "Blood on the Highway" in Driver's Ed., homecoming football games, the exhilaration at taking the mile relay baton on the track, sitting on the low stone wall and watching the girls tennis team practice in their short white skirts with their muscular, tan legs, and on and on. But none of these was a story. They were images, and he was not adroit at putting them together in an interesting fashion. This was one gift he was sure he did not possess, much like his inability to remember jokes. Two guys walk into a bar…that's all that ever stuck with him, and the occasional punch line, 'Why do you ask two-dogs-fucking?' "Really, I can't. Somebody else go ahead."

Sean picked up the remaining beers in the six-pack. "If you don't tell us about some significant fact in your life, my friend, will we never come to know and love you."

Cory relented and searched the back trail of his mind for the right anecdote. He found one and hoped he would not embarrass himself in the telling. "Well, all the way through eighth grade I attended a private Catholic school. My mother insisted. And although we had a religion class every day and were always attending mass as a class, I never had much of a belief in God. I could take him or leave him. Until one Sunday when the parish was sponsoring a pancake breakfast to raise money for the class field trip to the San Diego Zoo…"

Sean interrupted. "Naturally, to see the chimpanzees and apes from which the good priests and nuns taught you we all evolved?"

"Of course, just like it says in the bible," Cory replied. The table broke out into a huge laugh. A new phenomenon for him, making people laugh.

"'Inherit The Wind'. I saw that movie." Peg jumped in.

Cory continued. He was pleased to see he had their attention. "As luck would have it, I was also the quartermaster for the Boy Scout troop, troop 303, which held its meetings in the very same Veteran's Hall that the pancake breakfast was being served in. The whole thing was a real cooperative effort with parents helping out serving and all that. One kid's father, William Quackenbush, even owned the local chicken farm. He donated all the eggs for breakfast and cooked them to order in the kitchen alongside the local butcher who'd given the school the sausage at below wholesale, etc. etc. You get the picture - big community thing. So me and Pat Anderson sneak into the storage closets, grab a scout flashlight, and climb up a wall mounted ladder into the attic that runs over the whole building. We walk along these very thin one by eight planks, half laughing, half frightened to death, in the direction of the breakfast hall. We were gonna spy on everyone from above when Pat loses his balance and slips off the plank. His right foot crashes through the ceiling, dislodging one of the tiles that dropped, I found out later, directly onto the Monsignor's plate of pancakes, splattering syrup all over him. It took a few moments to retract his foot, but all the room had seen that foot sticking out of the ceiling and held its breath hoping, I imagine, that the rest of the boy didn't fall through with it."

"Extraordinary." Sean exclaimed, somewhat disingenuously Cory thought.

"Don't tell me, they nailed him by I.D.ing the shoe?"

"That's what good old sister Francis was attempting to do. Remember, we still had to go back inside that hall and work the second shift of breakfast. Lucky for us there was a stash of old hiking boots in that Boy Scout store room. She must have suspected us though because she took an extra amount of time giving both him and me the twice-over."

"You said earlier that this story was what convinced you to believe in God; how so?" Carolyn asked. With the entrees arriving, the story had seemed to lose its momentum and she remained the only true listener, except for Sean.

"I don't find it any mere coincidence that the one tile of the thousands he happen to step through would be the exact one directly over the Monsignor's plate. Out of two hundred people dining on eggs, sausage and pancakes, it lands in his plate? I believe that was a message. A sign that we'd better mind our behavior."

"A true believer, eh? Well, Cory, the moral I see in the story is just the opposite. They trusted you with the keys to the kingdom and you thumbed your nose back at them by ruinin' the Monsignor's breakfast. And got away with it to boot. Cheers, my friend." Sean raised his Guinness. Cory, not one to argue with a movie star in his element at the head of a dinner table, acquiesced and joined him in a salute of warm beer.

CHAPTER THIRTY-FOUR

Sufficiently fed and entertained at Da Pietro, Cory thanked Carolyn for the invite and walked her to the taxi stand where one full-bearded bald-headed driver slumped over the wheel of his '68 Mercedes 200 diesel. Cory tapped the window, knocking off the light dusting of snow the wind had deposited. Carolyn insisted he share the ride. But she was headed in the opposite direction, and it was already very late for someone who had to get Andrew Goldman rolling in the morning and be up with the socialist chickens next door. Besides, he liked the walk home along ul Podzamcze.

A trio of bats darted through the skeletal trees along the rampart at the riverbank. Not another body moved along the castle concourse. One set of headlights cut across his path on the street ahead as he approached the churchyard, St. Peter and Paul's or St. Andrew's, he could never remember which was which. The idea of so many churches packed within the confines of this old city still baffled Cory.

The car stopped in the middle of the road. Cory couldn't make out anyone inside but they seemed to be waiting for him. When he was close enough to hear the idle of the engine, Sean McDonough threw the passenger back door open. "What are you? Part Eskimo? Get in."

Cory dropped into the taxi. "Nothing wrong with a brisk walk; good for the circulation," he offered.

"Shiatsu, caffeine, sex, these are good for the circulation and a lot more enjoyable." Cory noticed the driver was smoking the same long cigarette as Sean, a Dunhill. A verse of Italian Opera squealed from the radio, some woman with a crystal shattering voice. Sean's filter tip became his baton. "This isn't one of my favorites but there are some nice solos."

"What are we listening to?" What Cory knew about opera could fit onto a matchbook cover.

"'Rigoletto', Verdi. Don't get me wrong. I adore Verdi but this one is so damned stiff and structured."

"I'm sure you're right. I've never seen an opera."

"Never?"

"Never. I can't even name one opera. Mozart

wrote a couple; didn't he?"

"My friend, you have not lived until you've felt the thunder of 'Don Giovanni' or wept at the tender affection of 'Romeo and Juliet'."

"I take it you're a big fan?"

Sean's huddled posture unbent as he launched into a bellowing verse that amused the driver and drowned out the radio.

"'Where art thou, Venus?
Venus, where art thou?
The flowers open to the sun.
The birds renew their song.
It is spring. The bridal couch is prepared.
Come quickly, beloved, and we
Will celebrate the holy rites of love.'"

Clearly, the man had opera training. His sonorous, alto exhortations practically rattled the frayed flaps on the taxi driver's sun visors.

"'Holla! Achilles, Helen, Euridice
Orpheus, Persephone, all my courtiers, Holla!
Where is my Venus?
Why have you stolen her while I slept?
Madmen, where have you hidden her?'"

He stopped only briefly then in a lower, basso voice, began singing in reply to his own melodious questions.

"'Venus? Stolen? Hidden? Where?
Madman! No one has been here.'"

Again Sean's voice pleaded as the desperate protagonist.

"'My heart breaks.
I feel the chill of death's approaching wing.
Orpheus, strike from the lyre a swanlike music,
And weep, ye nymphs and shepherds
Of the Stygian fields,
Weep for Adonis, the beautiful, the young;
Weep for Adonis, whom Venus loved.'"

Sean's voice trailed off into the frozen night, he shrank back into the cracked leather of the seat, melodramatically feigning death.

"Bravo!" screamed the taxi driver. "Bravo!" Cory clapped obligingly. Sean dropped his chin in a slight bow before taking a long drag on his cigarette, holding it then expelling the smoke in a dragon-like stream. One thing was for sure. A person may not agree with everything or even anything that Sean McDonough said or did but the man had energy. There could be no denying his appetite for life and work. And from what Cory had seen in the dailies, he was making even the malicious villainy of Hans Frank charismatic and captivating. Sitting in that seat, watching the man after his back seat mini-opera, Cory suddenly got a glimpse of the future, of Sean McDonough being feted as the budding genius, the new hot leading man, the cover boy who'd take his place alongside the Mel Gibsons and Tom Cruises of the entertainment world. It was all coming

together for Andrew's Pillar of Salt express. This must have been how he envisioned it. There was most definitely a bright future ahead for Sean but on this night, the merry actor was thinking ahead to only one thing - how to get this trainer Adonis, Cory Sonne, up to his hotel room.

CHAPTER THIRTY-FIVE

Sean had started telling Cory the story of the opera he had been singing, "The Rake's Progress" by Stravinsky, before the taxi dropped them off at the Orbis. Through the vacant lobby with the lone janitor in his soiled red vest and rolled up white sleeves, polishing away at the marble floor with his buffing machine, then at the reception desk where they got their keys and messages, even into the elevators, Sean continued expelling the details.

"Tom Rakewell and his true love Anne plan their marriage much to the chagrin of the father who thinks him a bum. Tom, believing that fortune is the ruler of human destiny, makes a wish - to have money - when suddenly a man appears, Nick Shadow, bearing the news of some heretofore unknown uncle dying and leaving Tom an inheritance. He coaxes Tom into coming with him into London to tidy up the affairs, and he stays on with him as Tom's personal servant, agreeing to take payment only after a years time has passed. Tom promises to send for Anne when the time is right.

"Summer comes and the resplendent Tom is very much the heir, frequenting the brothel and abandoning himself to the loose life of the city. Though he has been seduced by Shadow's lessons, he remembers Anne and is distracted away from uniting with her by Shadow's magic gesture to "suspend time" so that he might indulge. The forgotten and sorrowful Anne decides to go to London feeling something that compels her to Tom.

"Sated with a life of pleasure, Tom makes his second wish - to be happy. Shadow convinces him that the only true path to happiness is to be free from everything. In a twisted logic he coaxes him into marrying Baba the Turk, a circus prodigy of nature. He will be ignoring both passion and reason by not being attracted or obligated to her, achieving true freedom and therefore happiness by the completely unemotional and irrational act of marrying this oddity."

The elevator doors opened to Cory's floor, Sean placed a gentle hand on his wrist as he started out the door. "Come with me, I've got a CD of the opera in my room, you can take it."

Cory hesitated. Though he was well aware of Sean's notorious bi-sexuality and, admittedly, somewhat apprehensive of all this sudden attention, there was no way this tall, skinny Irishman could force him to do anything he didn't want to. He let the doors close and they went up a floor.

"Meanwhile, Anne shows up in London. In the midst of some hoopla Tom sees her and implores her to return to the country and forget about him. Anne firmly refuses until she finds out Tom has just married this mysterious veiled woman. Anne leaves and Tom uncovers his bride only to discover that she possesses a full black beard.

"The forlorn Tom is now miserable. He throws a wig over the face of the haranguing Baba, putting her in a trance which she remains in through the next act. Tom then dreams of redeeming himself to Anne by solving the world's hunger problem with a fantastic bread-making machine. He tells Shadow of this and makes his third wish - that his dream be true. Shadow appears with a "false bottom" machine that Tom believes will do just that. He throws all his money into the failed enterprise of manufacturing them and becomes a bust. Now he's unhappy, broke, and with no prospects for regaining Anne's favor."

Sean placed a CD's into his stereo. His suite stretched twice the width of Cory's and though it, too, possessed the same dreadful decor the abundance of furniture, a trio of colored lamps, and potted plants all combined to give it considerably more vitality. The king sized bed with a flimsy, gilded headboard sported a thick ivory comforter. Stacks of books and CD's lay scattered across the divan, and a half a dozen framed photos angled across the desktop surrounding a sculpted golden apple. Cory picked it up, surprised by its heaviness. Sean came out of the bathroom and saw him with the apple.

"I take that with me everywhere. Sort of a talisman. Reminds me of the eternal temptations."

"It's beautiful." Cory replaced the apple then leaned a shoulder into the doorway near the bathroom, listening to Sean finish the story as the opera bubbled in the background.

"A crowd gathers in the now dilapidated house for an auction of all Tom and Baba's things and gets whipped into a frenzy when "an unknown object" is sold to the highest bidder, only to find that that object was Baba herself who emerges from her trance too late. A drunken Tom and Shadow take to the street and Anne returns to the house where she encounters Baba packing to leave. Baba exhorts Anne to find Tom and save him.

"The year has passed and Shadow now confronts Tom about his payment, revealing that he is in fact the devil and payment shall be in the form of Tom's soul - at midnight he must kill himself. As the clock begins to chime midnight, Shadow again tampers with time by stopping it long enough to engage Tom in a card game for his soul to be played in this magic period of grace."

Cory watched as Sean became swept up in the music and mimicked dealing cards. Outside the window behind him, the snow descended in unflagging diagonal sheets. For the briefest moment Cory wondered whether Georgia was warm enough. At this hour, she probably lay peacefully in her bed next to Andrew. A jealous pang shot straight to his heart; he reminded himself not to feel this way.

Sean moved closer to him holding up an imaginary card. "Shadow will cut three cards and Tom must guess what they are. The first he does easily with the help of Shadow's hints. The second he gets with a lucky guess as fortune intervenes. As the third card is drawn he hears the voice of Anne and sings about his regrets. He knows that the card must be the Queen of Hearts, and he is right. His soul is spared; Shadow is defeated but not before he deprives Tom of his reason. This all leads to the final scene which I sang in the taxi where he becomes a madman and believes Venus will come to him. And when Anne does come and realizes this torment, she takes on the role of the Goddess consoling the repentant rake. Her father comes to fetch her and Tom is left alone. He falls back into lifelessness."

Sean fell onto the bed, arms spread, a long exhale rising to the ceiling. From the CD the voice of Anne cried, "Although the heart for love dare everything, the hand draws back and finds no spring of courage…" Sean rolled up onto an elbow.

"Pretty depressing stuff," Cory remarked.

"Depressing? I think tragic. But its beauty prevents it from being depressing. It should invigorate you, illuminate a path for you."

"That's what Georgia says about 'Pillar'."

"And she's right. Good girl." Something about the way Cory said her name made Sean sense a delightful attraction. "You fancy her; don't you?"

"Who wouldn't?" Cory responded, perhaps too quickly and too defensively.

"Right, who wouldn't? She's a spectacular gal, gorgeous and talented like nobody's business. You see yourself with someone like her, Cory?"

"Ah, no, well I don't know…" He hesitated. She was thirty-seven and the truth was he had never been with a woman that much older than himself. His proclivity for firmness, rounded hips, for carnal appetites and trampoline bellies had always steered him towards young women, easy and knowable. He'd worked with other trainers who walked the thin line of the quasi-gigolo with their penchant for older women, and he scrupulously avoided that association. And Georgia was his client, after all. Something inside him warned him to stay away from that line, far enough away that he couldn't even accidentally fall over it.

Cory found himself staring at his boots, trying to find a way to finish his reply. When he looked up, Sean was right there in front of him, closer than a man waiting for a response to a question would stand to a man unable to answer. In the way Sean's eyes bore into his own, the way his hand reached for Cory's shoulder, the small parting of his lips, Cory knew what was coming. He froze. It occurred to him then that his ceasing to move was not out of fear or confusion; he knew well enough what would follow. In his younger years he'd have put a clenched fist through the man's abdomen and out the other side. But now, he did not move. His legs stiffened; the soft hairs of his body brushed to attention with a dermal, electric charge, his face felt flushed and hot. Cory ceased to act because something in his mind demanded that he experience this. For a man who had done all the seducing in his life, for once he wanted to be acted upon. At that moment it didn't seem to matter that the seducer was a man. The last thought that went through his mind as he watched Sean's beguiling face close in on him was - this is what it must be like to be a woman, this is what it must look like to see a man closing in with unbridled desire.

The kiss was gentle. Sean's scent, Chanel or Polo or something haute couture mixed with Guinness, preceded him, and though his shave was close the coarse feel of his upper lip distracted Cory into analyzing the kiss instead of feeling it. He broke it down in his mind: firm lips, tender application, hands roaming the pecs and tracing their sternal attachment, head tilted slightly to the left and the narrow nose imprinting the right cheek with its square point. Though he did not resist the force of Sean's mouth, he was hardly an active participant.

Sean pulled away, said nothing, and looked for a reaction. But Cory simply waited, silent and curious. Was he playing a game? Was Sean? The room filled with the voices of the operatic Anne and Tom slinging inflamed and pitiable phrases at each other.

Across the border of Cory's shoulder and down the line of his akimbo limb, Sean slid his hand until it gripped Cory's. He arced it around the front of his hip and rested it firmly on the seam of his khakis. The long bulge fit neatly into Cory's palm, he fondled it through the fabric, and while he did, Sean leaned into him for another kiss at the same time he undid his own pants. Cory removed his hand just long enough for Sean to unzip the fly. Without the benefit of underwear, Sean's erection fell out against Cory's fingers. The weight of it, the heat, the smooth texture of the taught skin surprised him. He'd spent so much time stroking his own cock, he thought he would recognize the feel of another but this was remarkably different. As simple as it may have sounded, the fact that it belonged to someone else made a huge difference. When one grabbed one's own hard-on, there was no distinction between the feel of the hand wrapping around the stiffened appendage and the feel of the appendage being compressed by that hand. The two sensations went hand in hand, or hand on cock as it were. The totality of that experience was a whole other animal than holding another man's erection. And for this first time in his life, Cory had been able to satisfy this overwhelming curiosity. Sean McDonough's engorged prick lay trapped in his hand, and he, Cory Sonne, was comfortable with it. That was all that was happening and all he needed to know. He had been labeled homophobic by more than one girlfriend over the years. Such was not the case, and he had proved it to himself. Cory let go and walked past Sean to the window.

"Cory, you tease." Sean breathed the sigh of thwarted arousal.

"I'm sorry. It's just not my thing. I thought maybe I could convince myself to give it a try but it's just not in my nature. What can I say? I'm a pussy hound born and bred."

"Maybe you haven't given it a fair shake?"

Cory looked at his hand then at Sean's cock. "I gave it a fair enough shake."

"Well, I'm not going to beg, Cory. I don't do that?"

"I'll bet you do if the mood is right."

"True." Sean was playing with him now.

"Sean, I like you. I just don't have the inclination."

"How can you be sure?"

Cory could see a pair of lights in a low rent

apartment building across the river down by the railroad bridge. "When I was fourteen, I grew about six inches and gained thirty pounds, mostly muscle. It seemed like overnight I was suddenly the biggest, toughest kid in school. One night after a frat party in Oxnard me and my crew, stumbled onto a faggot blowing his buddy in a back alley. Needless to say we were all overcome with that tremendous desire to deal with our fear of homosexuality by beating the shit out of the two of them. Despite my size and strength I had never been called upon to fight before. And, of course, at that time, liquored up and on the prowl, my boys expected me to rise to the occasion and deliver some serious punishment, which I did."

Sean responded sardonically, "If your friends could see you now."

"Two of them are dead. One's in prison. Not many of the guys I grew up with amounted to much. But that's not the point. The point is, I respect your right to chose your sexual orientation. I don't have a problem with it. I'm just not one of you, homosexual, bi-sexual whatever it is."

"I guess I should be grateful that you spared me the beating."

"I'm through with violence. All that stuff is ancient history."

Cory listened as Tom Rakewell sang the verses he had heard Sean belt out in the taxi. Sean smiled. "We're all rakes; aren't we? Knowing what's good for us, what the right and noble choices are and rarely following through?"

"Maybe." Cory thought of Georgia. What kind of a rake would he be if he were allowed to fulfill his fantasy of having her? It would go against everything he had been working to avoid - the deceit, the breach of etiquette, the intentional harming of others. Though he felt she harbored some fondness for him, that was all it could ever be and he knew that. So why did this fantasy about her recur with the weight of undeniability? He asked Sean, "If the temptation to act a certain way has such irresistible force, isn't there some validity to it? If we want to go there or do that thing, isn't it for a reason?"

"Yes, yes. But the reason is self-serving. And often hurtful to someone else. That's the devil. That's sin. That's the moral universe they've been trying to sell us throughout the centuries. And we've been resisting en masse in a boffo way."

"Human nature?"

"Pleasure principle. It's Freud. Maximizing pleasure and minimizing pain. Problem is we can't always distinguish between the two. And it's religion that historically has tried to make that distinction for us in a way that usurps all self-reliance."

"Back to religion, huh? Didn't get enough at dinner?"

"I have as much interest in religion as any devout practitioner. I was born into it. Had it crammed down my throat in catechism. But the more I read, the more I realize that religion is personal, not institutional. Your relationship with God is your own business. Hell, organized religion was only started so that our ancestors who invented agriculture, who conceived of the beginning of man's domination over nature, could pass on information about agricultural practices from generation to generation. They created this complex mythology about understanding Mother Nature. It was all rudimentary storytelling that got way too complex over the eons."

"It's getting a little deep in here, Sean. You don't really expect me to make sense of that at two in the morning?"

Sean laughed to himself. How often had simple conversation conveniently mutated into a soapbox sessions. It was a habit he disliked about himself but couldn't seem to prevent. "You're right. At any rate, make your own rules, your own laws, your own belief system. That's what I always say and what I do. And mine just happens to be run through with hedonism, to get back to the topic of sexual appetites. This is the reason that I drink, I fornicate, I devour - art, travel, culture. The gospel according to Sean McDonough."

"Were you always like this?" Cory asked, picking up the golden apple and polishing it with the tail of his shirt.

"I retreated into art; that's how I shaped this world view. My advice to you - be careful not to be seduced by it,

Cory. It can whisper things into your ear that can make life awful hard to look at."

"I've heard those whispers."

"Brave boy. Brave and beautiful boy."

The echoes of Eli's voice came shuddering back to him. Brave boy. That's what he always used to say when Cory would try to stand up to the punishment. It only infuriated Eli who would strike him with the force of a titan, with the intent to oppress for a lifetime. Brave boy. Even his compliments wielded spikes of derision.

In the voice of a speaker bent on being clearly understood, Cory responded. "Man."

CHAPTER THIRTY-SIX

The ground before him lay strewn with a sea of rotten plums. As he walked, he felt like Jesus floating across the water to St. Peter. There was no putrescence only the squish of slippery decay under his feet. The rows and rows of trees to the left and right of him wavered like leafy mirages. He paid no attention to them on his periphery only to the two directly in front of him near the stump of an old hickory where he used to take his lunch. Even though the crabgrass had grown thick there, he could still detect the unevenness of the dirt beside it, a small hump on an otherwise smooth patch of orchard ground.

The orchard dream always began the same way, with him packing Eli's old leather suitcase. He had removed it from the top shelf of the closet in his parents' bedroom while his mother wept on the front porch, her sobs lilting in through the fractured upstairs window. He didn't even bother wiping the dust off of it. Just opened it on the bed and scrambled to pack some essential things - a shaving kit, a pair of worn shoes, a warm coat, a Mackinaw that once served a true purpose in Chicago before his father moved out to California in the late fifties, a button down white oxford with a ripped collar, pants, two changes of undergarments. Then there was the belt. He hesitated at the belt, wondering if there were still streaks of his own dried blood on the leather edges. He wrapped it around his hand then made a fist, squeezing it. A great pain coursed his arm, as though the tiny bones below his knuckles had all been shattered, a web of torment that spun up into his head and heart. As the intensity grew, he realized he could no longer hold the belt; it seemed to be electrifying him, and he tossed it into the valise and strapped its buckles shut.

The familiar dream. Cory was going on a trip, trying to run away, with a suitcase full of his father's things, down through the plum orchards where he had slaved in labor and escaped as a boy. But try as he might only one direction emerged where this path of rotten fruit pointed, and more than anything in his life he did not want to go there. Never. Never. Never. He had been there once in the most horrifying of ways and once was enough for an eternity. He had spent the rest of his life trying to get away from it but the dream persisted, bringing him again and again to those fateful trees near the hickory stump. Only this time he could see Sean's sculpted golden apple resting on top. It shone in the noon sun and looked so out of place, so formal and inorganic. As Cory got closer he noticed a tiny black worm wriggling its way out of the metallic coating. He watched as the worm got longer and longer. Again his hand, clutching the handle of the suitcase, resonated with a pain so agonizing it shut down the dream and tore Cory from his sleep. He had traveled half way around the planet and that fetid orchard had found him again. Why couldn't he put it out of his mind? Was there no salvation for a boy who had no alternatives?

He awoke with a start and saw nothing but his bland hotel room and the long yaw of yet another winter storm outside his Krakow window.

CHAPTER THIRTY-SEVEN

It happened in the night. While Cory struggled with his nightmare, while Andrew worried about the look in Georgia's eyes when she gazed at Cory, while Georgia dreamed about laying her body down on top of her trainer, while Lani and Niki imagined themselves on the summer hot sands of Malibu beach, while Sean lamented his conquest denied, and while Jack Grady sat awake in his bed knowing that terrible things lurked around the corner. While all of these Los Angelinos occupied their minds, Lars Rostock was out in the night coordinating the simultaneous bombings of nine different German towns.

In Munster, Salzgitter and Dessau, in Dillenburg,

Schmalkalden and Gera, in Karlsruhe, Dinkelsbuhl and Regensburg. All small, provincial towns, peaceful and out of the way. Families with small businesses and farms, the German heartland that boasted no glaring political tempests. Why should nine separate package bombs explode in nine separate post offices, killing one indigent rummaging through the trash and partially destroying all nine government buildings? Who was behind it? Why these locations? These were among the many questions the news agencies would be asking all morning, attempting to put the pieces of the puzzle together.

Lars Rostock stood high on the hill at the center of Regensburg and watched the flames of the firebomb climb into the night from the federal building. There would be no mail tomorrow, perhaps for weeks. All those checks, catalogs, letters and packages that would have brought happiness or solace or commerce were gone. But that meant nothing to him. What he ruminated on as he imagined the same explosion happening in the eight other cities was one simple fact. He had spent his life in pursuit of this goal and he was now satisfied that he had reached it. He had become a living weapon. A knife against the throat of the social democratic ruling class of the newly unified Germany, the fuse that threatened to ignite a neo-fascist combustion that would reshape the greatest nation on earth and advance the true, hidden agenda of every German citizen who secretly knew they were the superior embodiment of the human race. Lars knew the fabric of the German soul. Twice this century they had tried and failed to subjugate the world, and as the turn of the millennium approached he would make it his personal quest to put his people back on the path to world domination. This explosion of a small post office in an out-of-the-way city and the others that he had coordinated with it were merely a calling card for the New German Alternative. There was so much more to come.

Lars Rostock had been labeled a "terrorist" his whole life. It was their convenient term for him. He killed for the GDR; now he was inciting violence for his own political agenda, following in the footsteps of his father without the benefit of the Reich. If all went according to plan, he would gain the favor of those who could make the re-emergence of the Reich possible. That is what drove him to devise this widespread bombing scheme to get their attention as well as that of the authorities. Looking into the starry sky between the head of the constellation Draco, the Dragon, and the outstretched arms of the constellation Hercules, Lars spotted his constellation, the group of stars that took the shape of the Nazi cross and which he named Pater, in honor of his father. Someday, when the power from all factions would coalesce, he would mandate that astronomical change. For now, it satisfied him to know

Hans was up there, watching over him, the son practicing the murderous art of the father, forging his own identity in the process.

A black Audi sedan came up the dirt road and parked next to him. A thin blonde woman in a black jacket and black leather skirt walked towards him with the purposeful stride of a soldier. Vera Gosler had joined the New German Alternative last winter when she had been discharged from the regular army for forging signatures on munitions acquisitions requests. Though her superiors suspected something subversive, they had no proof. Fact was she had been stockpiling plastic explosives, timers, detonators, fuses, cases, dangerous chemical compounds and the manuals for their usage ever since she was introduced to Lars Rostock at a German Expressionism exhibition sponsored by a mutual friend. The two of them had hit it off intellectually, philosophically but more importantly, sexually, from the start.

Returning from the Regensburg post office where she watched the result of her handiwork, Vera knew what the protocol would be. She had removed her pants in a public restroom, slipped into this tight leather skirt and not bothered with panties. As she approached Lars, she prepared herself mentally for what would follow; reminding herself that sacrifice was necessary for the success of their objective.

He grabbed her around the waist with one hand and by the back of the neck with the other. They kissed ferociously for a moment then he pulled harshly at her hair and jerked her head back. Her skin stretched tightly across her face.

"You are magnificent." Lars remarked, looking deep into her reverential eyes.

"Thank you, my darling."

He turned her body towards his car and slammed her torso over the hood, still controlling her by the fistful of her silky hair as if it were a rein. With his free hand, he lashed at his belt buckle, quickly undoing it and opening his pants. He hiked her skirt up the remainder of the way, exposing the spread of her buttocks then jammed his cock inside her and rode her as if were Alexander the Great galloping into battle.

Down in the town, he could hear the sirens and see the flashing lights of the fire trucks working furiously to limit the damage. High in the sky over it all the Nazi constellation between Hercules and the Dragon shone brighter than he'd ever seen, glinting with the prospect of legitimacy. While he thrust himself into Vera, slamming her bony knees into the front panel of his BMW he could see the image of his father flashing before him, the image he had seen as a young student from the archival film footage of Hans' execution. He had never seen the face of the man in real life only photographs and film. But he felt most certain that if he had been able to look into his eyes he would have known what he believed deep in his heart, that the courageous mission his father and the founders of the Reich had embarked upon, the annihilation of the Jewish race and the establishment of Aryan supremacy, had been a just and worthwhile one. "The Germans are not 'a people' but *Das Volk*, 'the people'," was his father's famous quote. Of this, there could be no doubt. He would take up the gauntlet now and would not be stopped by the establishment, by the chattel of common civilians, not even by the propaganda of a Hollywood filmmaker defaming the memory of his father.

Vera shrieked in the pain of Lars' pulverizing orgasm, relieved to know she had served her genius once again.

CHAPTER THIRTY-EIGHT

It was morning on the bookstore set in the Rynek Glowny when Cory passed by Sean; he gave him a stilted smile and received a smirk and a knowing look in return that told him everything was cool. No heartbreak, no guilty feelings, just the understanding that even though sex did not take place between them, they could still be friends.

Cory arrived shortly after nine. Georgia had left word with Carolyn that she would not be working out in the morning. Cory spent the free hour with Dante in the security guards' front station getting yet another lesson in the art of chess. He had gone down to defeat quickly time and time again but Dante modestly pointed out along the way why his moves were or were not good. He could think ahead four or five moves and that was it. Dante told him that real experts could think ahead thirty or more moves and dozens of different scenarios. It did not take him long to realize he would never be good at the game but he liked playing.

Lani and Niki had managed forty minutes of circuit training between the treadmill and the free weight stations Cory had set up and complained very little about it, perhaps because they were listening to the new Cranberries CD that had come in a care package from one of their girlfriends back home. Cory accompanied them with Waldek to school. From there he had gone to the square to watch the morning's proceedings.

An armful of rejected, period coats piled high to her chin, Peg exited Georgia's trailer. She caught sight of Cory discussing with Chuck what to do about his sore knee when she informed him that Georgia wanted to see him if he had a minute. If he had a minute. He had to contain his excitement long enough to finish advising Chuck about alternating hot and cold packs and utilizing certain towel exercises to improve his flexibility.

He knocked on her door.

"It's open." Cory shook the snow off his boots. "Oh don't worry about the snow. It's indoor outdoor carpet in here."

"Peg said you wanted to see me?" He had missed

her this morning. The small piece of her he had absorbed was her voice outside the security room as she spoke to Carolyn on her way to Andrej's waiting car. Shortly thereafter, his bishop and queen had been captured and Dante had checkmated him with a head-shaking smile.

"I wasn't sure I would see you today so I left a message at your hotel. But I wanted to invite you with us tonight to the café Ariel. It's a small spot in the Kazimierz district where they have music and poetry readings, etc. Tonight they're featuring a klezmer quartet and Andrew's looking for a local violinist for a small part in the film. Anyway, it should be very culturally satisfying. Lani and Niki are coming; would you like to join us?"

"Yes, I'd love to. Thank you very much for the invitation."

"Don't mention it. You must be getting bored in your down time."

"No, not at all. Please don't ever think that. I've been meeting some very interesting people, reading the things you've been giving me, learning how to play chess. Plus, I've got my own workouts. I use the gym in the afternoons sometimes when I can find a driver to shuttle me back and forth."

"Well, good." She smiled at Cory, imagining for just a moment the sweat beading on his chest as he pressed a pair of dumbbells and wondered if he could possibly know the re-emerging heat he brought to her loins. Of course not. Look at him standing there, so humble and infatuated. There's no doubt he could fuck, she thought, but what did Cory Sonne know about making love? This was something she could not afford to think about with a ten minute call for the scene.

Cory waited near the door. "By the way, thanks for the Elizabeth Barrett Browning book." He searched his brain for the passage he had taken great pains to memorize, "'What I do and what I dream include the as the wine must taste of its own grape.' It sounds good, sounds romantic; but I'm afraid you'll have to explain to me sometime."

Georgia smiled then turned away for a moment then back to him. He was her student it seemed. She thrilled at the prospect of introducing him to the beauty of verse then let out a deep sigh. "Out, out. I've got work to do."

"Yes, I'm sorry. Good luck…I mean, I didn't mean that, that's actually a bad luck thing to say; isn't that right? You're supposed to say break a leg or something aren't you? But then, as your trainer, it doesn't sound like good advice; it certainly doesn't sound like something I should be wishing for you…"

"Goodbye, Cory."

"Right. I'll see you later."

Collapsing onto her vanity table, Georgia expelled

an even bigger sigh. That boy. That beautiful boy.

As he stepped out of Georgia's trailer, he stopped. In the corner of the southwest sky he could see a long patch of blue. Real Blue. Nearly three weeks in Krakow and this was, as far as he knew, the first clearing in the dismal gray cloud cover. Experiencing that sliver of radiant color hovering over the steeples of the Mariaki Church, Cory realized how much he had taken southern California weather for granted. Quite often when Lani and Niki whined about wanting to be back home on the beach, he secretly agreed with them. But he could never say so. He knew better than to usurp their territorial, youthful rebellion. Georgia's invitation was all the sun Cory needed today. No complaints.

A film crew of more than forty workers attended to the particulars of their jobs outside the Zakladka Bookstore. A dozen cables ran from the truck generators across the stone floor of the arcade and into the high-ceilinged shop. The mobile trailers for the cast paralleled the Sukiennice in the center of the square. A military style lunch tent stretched from the Pamiatkowy Gallery on the northeast corner half way down to the Town Hall Tower. The smell of beef stew and pirogues - small pastry turnovers stuffed with mashed potatoes and cheese - cut through the cold air. Cory ducked in to say good morning to Dibac, the head chef for the production and brother of Machek, the chef at Hotel Hollywood. Peg and Betty sat at the first table with Jack Grady who appeared to be lecturing them about something serious. Peter's voice barked over the radio on the table between them. "On the bell, people." It was followed by a blaring bell that let everyone know the camera and sound were rolling on the set.

Cory whispered to Dibac, "Do you know the café Ariel?"

Dibac nodded, stirring a huge cauldron on the stove of his catering truck. His must be the warmest job on the picture, Cory thought. "Is nice place. Small but very popular."

"Is it dressy? Should I wear a jacket?"

"People in Krakow sometime wear jacket to market and then wear sweatshirt to church. You do what you want to do with your clothes." Dibac knew his way around a kitchen but he was little help with etiquette.

After the establishing shot inside the bookstore, Andrew consulted with Peter and Yuri about where to position the extras in the scene. He did not want anything to distract from the revealing shot of Anna who the camera had been following from the back - Hans' point of view as he entered the room. The discussion surrounded the use of a natural "wipe", a person cutting across the camera's line of sight. Cory watched from behind Mikola in the doorway of the side entrance. They decided to give it a try. Peter instructed one of the extras on where his mark would be and the signal to walk by.

Sean, in a long dark coat with the collar turned up, methodically smoked his cigarette maintaining a careful distance from the other actors. Georgia stood with Damon Weil, the Austrian actor playing Janusz, her professorial screen husband. Cory had never met him and had only seen him once in the lobby of the Orbis talking with a few of the Croatian crew members.

Yuri called for a second scrim to cover the windows. He wanted even less light shining through, keeping the faces of the "hunter and prey" heavily shadowed. For the most part, they were using the natural light and adjusting only the lenses to keep the subjects illuminated.

The Zakladka Bookstore. The fateful place where Hans Frank first laid eyes on Anna Kamenski. She was browsing through the shelves with her scholar husband when Frank fixed his gaze upon her, noting the strong profile, the ponytail of hair the color of summer straw, the regal nod she exerted at the turning of a page. Waiting for her to catch his eye, it was there and then that that inexplicable something passed between them, that jolt of electricity that knows no morality or circumstance other than its own creation, the chemical combination that has more to do with biology than psychology, the inescapable attraction that comes before a man or women has the opportunity to analyze that attraction and make a “rational” decision about how to handle it. *Anima Mundi* Frank had referred to it in the script in the scene where he tries to elicit a confession from Anna.

Janusz was oblivious while she watched the stranger over a copy of St. Thomas Aquinas’ essays. She had never seen Frank before but detected a magnetic power in him. He had just recently arrived in Krakow and was practicing a favorite exercise of his, dressing in civilian clothes and milling about the city, attempting to gain a feel for how the average citizen lived, worked, behaved - the tasks that kept them busy, the thoughts with which they were preoccupied, the shoptalk. Though married and with a son, the discovery of a beautiful and perhaps consenting woman was never unwelcome.

On the day he first encountered Anna Kamenski, after she had fled his presence, he had a feeling that they would meet again but he could not have surmised that she would be the undoing of his soul and force him to confront everything about his identity as a man, a soldier, an arbiter of power and a seeker of love.

Anna, on the other hand, could sense the self-serving pomposity in the man, attractive though he seemed. Following instincts that would prove deadly accurate, she would take the unsuspecting Janusz by the arm and escort him out of the bookstore, hoping never to see the stranger again.

That's how it read in the script.

Andrew needed to get that "look" in her eye. The one that recognized in the first moment that she was unquestioningly taken by this stranger and, conversely, realized in the following moment that nothing good could possibly come from it. Georgia had to give him all of this in one look, one expression that the camera would seize upon as it moved in on her turning face and uplifting eyes.

Silence fell all around them. Sean placed himself behind the right side of the camera to give Georgia a line of sight for the shot; she was supposed to be looking into his eyes after all. The swarming pack of crew members and bystanders stood frozen as the scene was slated and Andrew watched his talented wife. "Action!" The command came. She took her time, absorbed in the book between her hands. The camera dollied in very slowly. Andrew began whispering the directions to her. "You sense something behind you. Someone is watching you over your shoulder. You know it. You don't want to turn around but something compels you to confirm your instincts, your curiosity is getting the best of you, slowly, nonchalantly, you turn to see if you are right."

Although Sean, dressed as Frank, stood between Cory and Georgia, when she turned, her eyes did not fix on Sean but continued past his right shoulder and locked on the doorway of the second entrance, onto the eyes of the riveted observer Cory Sonne. In that instant of elongated time, the kind of second that seemed to last an hour and would stay tattooed to his memory for a lifetime, Cory felt his own soul burning as though the core of his being had been struck like a match and every vein carried the flame like a fuse heading towards his heart where it was destined to explode. What saved him in that trance-like state was Andrew's pile driver voice bellowing, "Cut! Beautiful. Beautiful. Print that. But let's cover it."

Georgia turned from Cory's gaze and did not look back but dropped her lips toward her hands, folded, as if in prayer. She paced near the bookshelves but never once glanced over at him. Was he mistaken? Did she mean nothing by it? Did anyone else feel what he felt? Apparently not. The entire crew immediately went about their business of preparing the shot again. No one said a word to him. This kind of emotional display was common place, old hat, ordinary. No one would have believed Georgia was directing her eyes towards him and meaning it. But she had; hadn't she? Now, only minutes later, he, too, began to doubt it. The roiling of his insides told him something had happened but maybe it was predicated entirely on his wishful thinking. Maybe Cory's fantasies were encroaching on his rationality.

Maybe he so desperately wanted it to be so that he'd misinterpreted the action of the scene. His thoughts were interrupted by the calling of his name.

"Cory, come over here." Andrew, standing next to the video monitor with Yuri, waved him over.

"I hope I'm not interrupting," Cory said. Although he'd been on the set since the beginning, he never felt as if he belonged and often thought that most of the crew, who seemed to benignly tolerate him, secretly resented his close association with the heavies.

"Nonsense. I just thought you might like to get a look on the monitor of the last shot. Get an idea of what things are going to look like." Andrew obviously didn't realize Cory had been watching the dailies. Perhaps he wasn't supposed to be. Maybe Eric Riefenstahl had overstepped his bounds when he proffered the permission. Cory wasn't about to confess to anything; nor was he about to stop going to the dailies at night.

Dave the video guy cued the tape - that seemed to be his name, not just Dave but Dave-the-video-guy. Cory watched as the radiant countenance of Anna Kamenski turned to the camera and filled the frame with a glow of passion and terror that not only rocked her being but filled the viewer with wonder about who or what it was she had seen.

"Now that is an actress, my friend. There aren't but a half dozen women working in film today that can even give you that, much less on the first take. I'm telling you her whole professional life has been building towards this role. She's going to rank right up there with Hepburn, Davis, Bergman and history will kiss her feet."

Cory smiled. He was in no position to know whether Andrew was right but instinctively he agreed. Becoming involved with movie people as clients had prompted him to pay more attention to the industry itself. Weekly outings to the movies, a thorough review of the daily L.A. Times Calendar section and an assortment of movie magazines, and participation in the gossip that inevitably made its way into conversation had all become habit for him. Although he was, for the most part, unqualified to make a proclamation like that, he was far enough inside the circle to agree with confidence.

Wearing the same worried look he'd had in the mess tent, Jack Grady interrupted them. He was about to tell them something they weren't going to like. He'd been on the phone with Gunter Strauss earlier that morning, the department head at Interpol in Frankfurt. The two were longtime friends from the LAPD homicide days when Jack came to rely on a steady stream of information from Gunter in an effort to solve the infamous Necktie Strangler case. After three years and two dozen dead prostitutes in both Los Angeles and Vienna, Jack had finally hauled down Harlan Klingover, a prominent Austrian businessman with homes in both cities. The case had made international headlines because of the bizarre nature of the serial murders and the subsequent confession of a rich and driven entrepreneur who'd spent his childhood in an urban brothel. A literate and riveting autobiography he'd penned on death row gave him a second dash of celebrity and a certain cult status over the years. Through it all, Grady and Strauss had cooperated to bring this cold hearted killer to justice. Jack had contacted Gunter before he left the States and planned on visiting him before his stay in Europe ended. He had never expected to hear what Gunter had told him that morning.

"Nine cities all over Germany, all attacked at the same time?" Andrew was trying to get the details straight.

"Not attacked really, just bombed in some type of coordinated effort." Jack added.

"And does your man Strauss have any idea who's responsible?" Andrew asked.

"Though no one has claimed responsibility publicly, he follows the trail of a few select terrorist organizations, mostly neo-Nazi, neo-fascist stuff, and he thinks one in particular known as the New German Alternative might have been behind this."

"It's devastating and scary but exactly how does this involve us?"

"It may not involve us at all but by coincidence

they had pulled in a man at the German border on what they thought to be a completely unrelated incident, some arms smuggling charges, and after a thorough search of his property found a VHS videocassette copy of the 'Pillar of Salt' dailies."

"What?" The connection began to dawn on all three of them, Andrew, Yuri and Cory. They shared astonished looks, each wondering if the other were imagining a similar worse case scenario. They didn't speak.

"Gunter personally reviewed the tape. He recognized Georgia and described to me on the phone what he had seen. It was the scene on the street where Frank shoots the old Jew."

"But how?" Andrew asked, still reeling from the incredulity.

"I think we should find out. I've mentioned this to both Peg and Betty so that they can stay on their toes should anything out of the ordinary happen but I don't think it wise to dwell on the event. Don't want to raise any panic though I'm sure this means nothing."

"Are you?"

"Let's just say I'm optimistic. First thing I would do would be to switch labs. My guess is that wherever they're developing the dailies, someone's making a copy and sending it off. Could be the projectionist."

"Rollo? No way." Yuri demanded. "He's been

with me for many years. And he's Jewish."

"All right. If you say so. At any rate. Let me do some investigating and see what I can come up with. In the meantime, keep half an eye peeled for anything suspicious." Jack looked addressed Cory. "You especially. You're with Georgia, Lani and Niki at off hours."

Andrew was steaming mad. Cory sensed something. He felt Andrew Goldman's hear bearing down on him in a look, as if he had lowered the veil that was his public good nature and for the first time given Cory a glimpse of the real man, a soul-bearing slice of himself. Cory could do without a second helping of that. He looked away from Andrew and followed Jack out of the bookstore. Something had changed between him and Hollywood's most successful director - for good.

CHAPTER THIRTY-NINE

Fifty years ago the Kazimierz district bustled with a robust Jewish community, one fifth of the greater Krakow population. The city itself was a microcosm for Poland as a whole where twenty percent of the people were Jewish and that minority kept pretty much to themselves, establishing a thriving environment among the "gentiles" where informal business dealings allowed a free-flow of economy, a freedom of worship and education, and for the most part freedom from overt institutional persecution. Hatred and racism may have been subversive and grist for the mill of ongoing ethnic tensions but it was still a better life for this post WWI generation than those that went before it.

Cory waited in the quadrangle of what used to be a merchant's center, leaning against a granite pedestal of what must have once been a giant statue. All that remained were a man's sandaled feet in stone cut off at the ankle. He watched through the facade of arches near the entrance of the plaza recently constructed for "Pillar" scenes involving Anna Kamenski's family home. The place had the feel of a ghost town - abandoned buildings, busted out windows, rubble on the sidewalks and in the doorways. A colorless, lifeless, turn of the century industrial park laid out in an unlucky horseshoe shape where the hawking of sellers and inquisitive voices of clinging children echoed only in the idea of what once had been.

Café Ariel was the lone exception, the one seed of song and social connection struggling to sprout from the rocky soil. The brown Mercedes Sedan, driven by Jerzy, pulled up. Cory watched Andrew open the door for Georgia, Lani, and Niki and wondered if he'd done the right thing by showing up. He had labored over the decision all afternoon. Andrew's eyes had been a clear warning. Of that he was sure. But the refusal of Georgia's invitation would have sent an equally disturbing message: that Cory did not want to be around her. And nothing could have been further from the truth. The reward was worth the risk every time Cory weighed the two. So there he was.

"We could have picked you up," Georgia commented as they converged on the entrance.

"No, it's just a walk across the bridge for me. Good exercise."

"Oh, please." Lani added with a whine. The girls greeted Cory with an unusually warm camaraderie perhaps owing to the fact that he was not there to put them through their paces. "What do you think?" Lani flashed an amber bracelet.

"Gorgeous."

Niki displayed hers in response. "Look."

"And they weren't expensive at all. Amber is so cheap here. We bought some for all our friends."

"Two popular girls like you, is there any left in the city?"

"Funny." Lani reached up and pinched his cheek like a bantam auntie with a fetish. At the door Jerzy introduced Andrew and Georgia to the Café Ariel owner, Marisa - a plump middle-aged woman in a chartreuse caftan and bauble earrings that resembled fishing bobbers. As was always the case with Andrew Goldman, she was honored by his presence in her establishment. It was a visit she would be able to milk for the rest of her life. Yet another legacy of Andrew's tremendous success.

Ushered inside by Marisa, they were seated at the front table while all eyes in the room surveyed them. The café wasn't much bigger than a parochial school house with wooden floors, dark stained chairs, tables and no windows. A cappuccino machine hissed on the railroad-car bar in the back corner, manned by a skinny, long-nosed college girl with too much hair framing her rutabaga face. Marisa whispered to her in tintype Polish as she nervously prepared drinks for Andrew's table.

Cory took the seat at the front corner of the table which would leave Andrew, Jerzy and Georgia behind him and Lani and Niki lateral to him when viewing the musician's corner - a meager podium with no amplification system.

The band appeared shortly after the guests of honor had been seated. They required little preparation, a traditional klezmer quartet comprised of an upright bass, two violinists, and a percussionist/vocalist.

Cory sat there, stunned. One of the violinists was the blonde woman with the long scarf he had watched from his hotel window. As she warmed up, running the bow across the strings in a series of fragmented moves, Cory remembered the sad melodies she played underneath the bombed out window. The inclination to share this information with the table overcame him but he wondered how Andrew would react. With this most recent disturbance in Germany and the possible connection with the radical neo-Nazi group Jack had suggested, Cory thought it best not to even mention the sixth floor carnage.

Marisa stood in front of the group and announced facts about their recent Eastern European tour that had been capped with top honors at an international festival in St. Petersburg. They called themselves the Tatry Quartet in honor of the mountain range where their mentor had lived and where they had made their start playing in small resort bars for tourists who came to ski in winter and hike in summer. The vocalist, a sort of gypsy Mama Cass Eliot, started the band off with a rousing rendition of "Leopold's Siege," a gypsy standard.

Cory listened with keen ears and eyes glued to the delicate, facile fingers of the female violinist. She played with speed and precision but more impressive was her identification with the dramatic thrust of the music. Her body swayed like a windblown reed on the riverbank, her feet rooted and unmoving, her chin pressed firmly into the cup at the instrument's base where her head and the violin seemed to bob and weave as one. Although the music filled the tiny café, she seemed to be somewhere else, gathering her buds for the bouquet that would be their song. Cory knew that exercise in mind travel. He'd used it many times in his life to escape the pain of being beaten by his father and, later, the pain of remembering. Deep inside he knew that she, too, had mastered this behavior but what she did with her violin was bring something back from that adventure - music, beautiful music that provided a window to her aching heart. One

could not help but be moved by her passion.

Turning only once, in the course of the set, to witness Andrew and Georgia's reaction, Cory saw how they had recognized it, too. There was no denying the power of this music and these musicians.

Georgia's eyes met Cory's. As if the melody were a soundtrack to the movie in her mind, the moment played real and poignant. She had become accustomed to looking at him and liking it, and she had invited him because his company made her smile, made her somehow comfortable in this cold and taxing environment. With violinists feverishly sawing away in this cramped café, Georgia was suddenly transported back to that first day when they had met, the walk across the eyebeam in the foyer of Chateau Rosebud. The instant realization that a mathematician must have when the final piece of a formula reveals itself. The numbers in her heart tumbled then and the tumblers of her soul had fallen into place as the mere presence of Cory Sonne was evidence of a key she had never known existed. Or perhaps she had buried any hope of such a feeling existing. She'd work hard at denying all of it but here she was, a month later, half way around the world, performing the greatest role of her life, sitting in a café with her husband and daughter of seventeen years, getting swept away in the distinctive music of the region, and staring into those eyes once again that brought her, in a flash, all the way back to

their beginning. And what was present at the beginning was there now, only worse. All her efforts at denial had failed. Secretly, she must have known this would happen, and maybe she had invited Cory to the café that night for just that reason. And maybe she had wanted to place him right alongside Andrew to aid her in dismissing this infatuation once and for all.

None of it worked. She wanted to fall into those eyes more than ever, to nestle in those strong, sculpted arms for real and exhale the hot breaths that such an embrace would generate. But she knew she could do nothing about it. She could say nothing. Andrew's hand suddenly on her thigh sent all her speculation spinning away. She smiled at him.

"He's amazing, isn't he?" Andrew whispered. It took Georgia a moment to realize he was referring to the violinist and not Cory. "I think he's just what I need for the Nazi party scene."

"Yes." She stroked the top of his hand. "He's perfect." When she looked back at Cory, there was only the back of his head and the music. The sweet, ethnic mellifluence. Why was this music suddenly making her long to hold Cory? It was neither hers nor his but they were both completely absorbed in it.

For their encore, the quartet barreled through a rousing rendition of "Hava Nagila" that had the entire room clapping in unison. Once again Cory studied the female violinist who delivered this spirited ballad but whose own facial expression was stone. The instrument and the hands working it told the whole story; her countenance betrayed nothing.

When the performance ended and the applause subsided, Marisa introduced the musicians to the Goldman group in the front room of the café. She and Jerzy took turns interpreting when necessary. The young male violinist, Poldek, humbly bowed again and again during the conversation and eagerly consented to join the picture. Cory watched the reactions of the woman, Agnieska, who stood well away from the three men in the group and fiddled with her instrument case. Sensing her exclusion, Georgia moved over to her and placed a hand on her forearm.

"You played magnificently."

In clear English she responded, "Thank you."

"You speak English?" Georgia asked. Jerzy moved over to the two women thinking he might be needed.

"Yes, I studied many languages at the university and played in London for a year."

"Is that a hint of German I hear in your accent?"

"Yes, I lived there as a young woman and with my husband for many years."

"And you're married? Any children?" Georgia seemed truly interested.

"I have a beautiful daughter, Maria. But we are two; my husband died last year."

"Oh, I'm sorry." There was silence. Then Georgia squeezed her hand.

Andrew had finished with Poldek and turned toward the others. "Well, shall we?" He motioned for them to leave and they headed out the door again thanking Marisa for the evening.

Jerzy pulled the Mercedes up to the door. "Do you need a ride, Cory?" Andrew asked with an indifference in his voice that belied the look in his eyes during the evening.

"No, just a short jaunt over the river. I'm fine."

"Suit yourself." Andrew got in the passenger seat. Lani and Niki filed into the back.

"I'll see you girls tomorrow morning." Georgia stood in front of him. "And you? Working out early?"

"Yes. I'll have Carolyn send a car for you at six thirty." She smiled. "That was fun wasn't it?"

"Yes, thank you again. Very much." He watched her disappear into the back seat.

"Goodnight," she said as Jerzy closed the door.

"Bye." He patted Jerzy on the back. "Night, Jerz."

"I'll see you tomorrow, Cory. Sleep well."

Cory watched the sedan drive away, back through the facade at the entrance to the quad. The temperature

was well below freezing at this hour but he felt no chill. Georgia Hart. He could barely bring himself to hold her gaze any more he felt so sure she could read his mind. He had just spent most of the night at café Ariel not looking at her but man did he know she was there.

CHAPTER FORTY

Out of the corner of his eye Cory found Agnieska. She had just said goodnight to the other players and walked off in a different direction than the men. For some reason, he decided to follow her. He remembered how foolish he felt following the man in the green hunting cap but he felt sure he could trail Agnieska without putting himself at risk. He told himself it was only curiosity getting the better of him and figured if she were walking on this cold night and carrying her violin that she must live close by. Besides, she was headed in the general direction of the Orbis; perhaps for her ritual, vigil recital underneath bombed out room 654. He kept his distance and she never once looked back.

Had Cory known how far Agnieska's trek home would be, he might never have given in to the whimsy of following her. They had trudged through the city proper, past the square, past the National Museum, and along the footpath of the public park before turning down a street of broken asphalt and shoddy houses. At the end of the block, she entered a small yard bordered by a makeshift fence of planting stakes and chicken wire.

Half shielding himself from sight behind a scarred birch tree, he observed the front window, hoping to get a glimpse of Agnieska or her daughter, wondering if there was anyone else in the house. Moments later, she walked out the front door, still dressed in her long coat but having replaced the violin case in her right hand with a double barrel shotgun which she bootlegged and kept out of sight until she was right up at the fence. She raised it at Cory.

"Come out from behind that tree," she shouted.

Cory raised his hands like a prisoner. "No, don't shoot. I'm not armed and I don't mean any harm."

"Then why are you following me?"

"I don't know. I was just curious. It's me, from the café. I was at your performance tonight."

"I saw you there, watching me. You were thinking more than just about the music. What do you want from me?"

Cory stepped towards her. "I assure you. I don't

want anything. I was just surprised to see you at the café because I had seen you before at the Hotel Orbis, playing under the window of room 654." Agnieska's stance softened. She lowered the rifle; Cory lowered his hands.

"If I did not open my heart and pour out the notes, I think it would explode from the pressure."

"That's what it sounds like to me and why I'm so curious. I've heard rumors."

"Of course. As the story gets repeated it takes on new shapes until finally it is not recognizable any more. Most don't know the true story to begin with so what can you expect but rumors?"

"Telephone." Cory added, laughing.

"Pardon?" Agnieska asked.

"It's a game we play in the U.S. as children. You sit in a circle and make up a story and tell the person next to you and they pass it on to the person next to them and on around the circle until the last person has to repeat the story and it's funny because it never ends up close to the original. That's called telephone."

"I see." A rift of silence between them in the yard was broken by a dog's deep throated bark. Cory turned. A mangy German Shepherd with one ear pinned back and half-bitten commandeered the road. "Don't worry about him, he only eats communists."

Cory mustered a chuckle. Agnieska opened the gate and motioned with her head for him to come inside.

"Come. I'll fix us some tea."

"Herbateh." Cory remarked.

"Yes, herbateh. Very good."

"It's one of the ten words I know. Don't expect anything else in Polish except please and thank you."

"Well you can add 'podkradac' to the list."

"What does it mean?"

"Stalker." She motioned him inside with the rifle.

The tiny house was sparsely furnished but neat. A brick fireplace with a chest high stack of wood, copper kettles with dried flower arrangements in the corners, a sunken tweed couch the bluish color of advanced frostbite in the middle of the front room and a three legged dining table with matching chairs. An old phonograph on a sideboard, a cupboard filled with record albums. A tattered, oval shaped rug with concentric red and navy rings separated the living room from the kitchen. Agnieska replaced the rifle in the back of the closet and hung up her coat. Cory removed his and laid it across the back of the chair.

"Ojczyzna…" came a little voice from the hall followed by an elfin girl with rope-like pigtails, not more than four years old, in a pink nightgown.

Agnieska hurried the teapot onto the stove then swooped up her little girl with both arms and a simultaneous kiss to the cheek. She spoke to her in Polish and told her not to be alarmed by this strange man stoking their dying fire. The beauty of an adoring mother and sleepwalking daughter by the light of kerosene lamps was not lost on Cory. The hands that wrenched out such passionate music from the strings of her violin now found their way along the contours of the little girl's face; she was playing it for all the maternal love it could absorb.

"She thought you were her cousin Leopold who visits every so often and brings her black licorice." Agnieska said.

"I'm sorry, Maria. Perhaps next time." Cory intoned.

Agnieska shot him a frightened look. "How did you know her name?"

"I heard you mention it to Georgia at the café."

Relief. She had forgotten about the conversation. "Yes, that's right." She turned to Maria. "Say goodnight to the nice man, dumpling."

In measured but honeyed English Maria chimed, "Goodnight, nice man."

The tea hit the spot. It had been over five hours since Cory had eaten and the hunger pains crept up on him the moment he saw the bread and cheese painting hanging in Agnieska's hallway. The power of persuasion in a single frame.

It was some time before Agnieska, sipping methodically from her own mug, managed to relate the story of her husband's death. But Cory listened intently to a series of choice and enlightened words that formed not only an explanation but a framework for her and her former husband's political ideology as well.

"I met Johann in Berlin in 1980 when I was a music student and he was teaching language, Croatian and Slovenian, and Hegelian philosophy at the university. He was from Zagreb, Yugoslavia and had narrowly escaped a life's sentence under Tito's regime for political activism. He was very bright but had little patience for scholarship. The world needed changing after all, too many children were starving and citizens dying unnecessarily.

"We fell in love instantly when we were separately lured into a local music hall where a rare Mahler work was being performed by a Rwandan Tutu quintet. The hollow drums managed to capture a sort of simmering anger that was not the composer's trademark. It was unique and Johann impressed me with his understanding of music though he himself was never a musician. For a layman, he had a burning passion for classical music.

"We spent a few carefree years studying, working, making love all over the city in summer and under a well worn down quilt that his mother gave us as a wedding present. She made the trip all the way up from Sarajevo in a boot maker's truck and back with an antique dealer. But Johann was becoming deeply involved with militant subversive groups whose aim it was to overthrow the socialist party. When the unification came about, his tiny band of agitators were no longer valid. By this time I had a promising career with the symphony developing and he wanted to return to Yugoslavia, to get involved with the growing political unrest of that tumultuous country. We spent months apart, I got lost in my music, he in his activism. Our bimonthly rendezvous' were always intense, intimate but ultimately not enough to sustain us. I got pregnant with Maria shortly into his work in Yugoslavia."

Cory listened intently. It was like watching a foreign movie right before his eyes. He'd never been a big fan of them until Francesca - sweet, saucy, sex-crazed Francesca, could she be any more different than this woman in front of him now? The subtitles had always bothered him until she cajoled him by the promise of a blow job in a public theater into Fellini's "Amarcord". This time the sound of the Italian language and the gorgeous photography allowed him to follow the movie without concentrating so much on the written words. And then the scene where the young kid gets smothered in the mammoth breasts of the lady from the tobacco shop. A shot to the gonads. Just recalling it could get him hard instantly for months after that. Cory got so lost in the film in fact that he didn't even remember about the blow job. Francesca reminded him on the way home and he received it in the front seat of his car parked in the Fidelity Savings lot next to Francesca's apartment building. Agnieska's story was every bit as captivating as a Fellini film.

"It was a very hard time for the both of us. The baby fairly eliminated my career as a virtuoso on the violin, and if it hadn't been for the kindness of my good neighbors in Berlin, I don't know how I would have made it through. I was not resentful of Johann. What he was doing was very important and he had a way about him that made people want to believe in his ideas, want to follow him. The collective presidency of the Yugoslavs was failing miserably and he was rallying for reforms and a new socialism that again fell on deaf ears, for, as we know the rallying cry of ethnic solidarity and a new Tribalism drowned out all the cries of the mistreated and pleas for sanity. Johann again became an enemy of the power elite and escaped here to Krakow where I joined him three years ago. I had been gone from Poland for so long though I was always aware of Lech Walesa's Solidarity reforms that were reshaping my home country. Secretly, I think Johann was jealous of Walesa's success. He always envisioned himself a savior of the people but he was all theory, he didn't understand the average worker in the factory or the shipyards like Walesa did."

"But by that time, you would have thought Poland would have been a safe place for him." Cory remarked.

"For awhile it was. He spoke fluent Polish and he returned to teaching again, all the while his heart was breaking for the tragedy that was to become the former Yugoslavia. Also, even though this country is no longer communist and tiptoes its way into social democracy, the corruption runs very deep. And Johann loved nothing better than to root out fat bureaucrats skimming the cream from the urns of the state."

"And they took him out before he exposed them?" Cory asked.

Agnieska looked at him quizzically. "Why is it that you want to get to the end so fast? Such an American thing, I find. You are always wanting to know what happens next, so impatient. This is why I cannot watch your movies, they very much telegraph everything that is to come. I often think it is simply to reassure their audience that what they subconsciously think is going to happen, indeed happens. That doesn't speak well for the audience's interest in more complex issues." A tear came to Agnieska's face.

"I'm sorry. I didn't mean to offend you." Cory moved to offer her his napkin but she rebuffed him and stood by the fireplace, caressing a small silver frame with a picture of Johann in it.

"No, it's not you. I was just remembering that this was Johann's constant complaint about the Americans who would not get involved in the Bosnian conflict. He felt they had no desire to understand the complexity of the issues facing both sides and hurt the chances for an early end to the aggression that ruined millions of lives. Millions. Here in Krakow we are only a short drive away from the extermination camp, another place where millions were senselessly annihilated. The evidence is all there right in front of us and yet it happened again to those poor victims in Yugoslavia. Johann fought for understanding his whole life, for ideas and governments that would put the people first."

The fire began to die down again. Cory was two seconds away from getting up to throw another log on when Agnieska beat him to it.

Agnieska continued, "The world is filled with men, and I do mean men, for if you look at all government historically you will see nothing but the hard, fat faces of men of power invoking their will, men who, for whatever reason, are consumed with the overwhelming need to oppress. This is what I loved about the man that was my husband. Being a man himself he understood this. It was his position in the late years of his life that perhaps we could break the chain of oppression once and for all by leaping free from the mode of imitative rebellion."

Agnieska was moving from the personal to the sociological. Her speech, the forward movement of her body towards Cory, her gestures all indicated a fervent lecturer. It was as if Johann had been reincarnated; he could see and hear the man in the words and contours of his beloved wife.

"You see, the humiliation of being oppressed informs every aspect of a person's suffering, the humiliation that one's behavior is entirely dictated by the oppressor. But then the revolutionary behavior itself, as a response, is also dictated by the oppressor. Shortly before his death, Johann was gaining widespread support for a whole new idea for sharing power in government.

"After working as an in-house revolutionary for most of his young life, Johann finally came to realize that justifying the actions of the revolution, which most often mirror those of the State against which it is positioned, was nothing more than fancy footwork. The Generals and Experts of the State use the same justification for violence as a means of maintaining the status quo that the revolutionary uses as to uphold his militant ideals of 'overthrowing' that very State. Only the state calls it necessary 'force' when it oppresses, as opposed to the 'violence' of the rebellion.

"Johann allied himself with Sergio Panunzio on this point. Mainly that normative, material or coercive force manifests itself via socially sanctioned, or legitimate, instrumentalities: the communications media, the schools, rule-governed codes of conduct, entrance criteria into the professions, the legal system, the armed forces of public security, and the institutions of detentions and punishment. Positive Law holds all this together. Violence, in turn, is the perfect analogue of force except that its activities do not possess established social sanction and its behaviors do not represent Positive but Potential Law. Force represents the interest of the present social system while violence is the cutting edge of an alternative system."

Cory listened in rapt silence while she steamrolled.

"What would one do without the other as its rationale for existing? This is the justification for the acts of savagery that often come from the members of the State-that-would-be in order to wrest attention from a State-that-is already using despicable force. The kind of violence we shake our head in disbelief at, completely unable to put ourselves in the position of the revolutionaries who have resorted to those means only in order to conform to this ideologue. What Johann proposed was a drastic shift away from the vicious cycle of protest, this polarization approach, these acts against the State that supposedly served to mobilize the workers. Here is where he was running similarly, at least in broad scope, to Walesa, and why he so admired him.

"But if those masses don't rise up in response to this type of leadership, the State certainly will, in order to crush it. Then the revolution finds itself in a desperate position they justify even more violence. Or, as Hegel wrote, 'Die and become what you are.' And Martyrdom works so well in perpetuating this cycle. It's all circular reasoning. The word revolution means exactly that: a turning of the wheel. Problem is - the wheel that spins is always the same wheel."

Agnieska paused, taking stock of Cory's interest. Was he following her; was he even this interested?

His eyes were glued on her. He watched as the flicker of the kerosene lamp danced across her inflamed face. A plain looking woman that was suddenly becoming immensely attractive to Cory. An old string of words came back to him in that charged pause between her paragraphs, "Men become aroused with their eyes, women with their brains!" Even though Georgia had often provoked his desire with the utterances from her mouth, they were never separate from the complete visual surrender that would overcome him when he laid eyes on her. Agnieska, on the other hand, was nothing to look at. But listening to her play the violin, listening to her speak about revolution and philosophical orientation, and he now understood how intellect, too, could move the blood.

"It's all a slew of words and reasons to justify holding on to power no matter which side you're talking about," Cory added.

"Yes, and the strange and terrifying growth of the modern State gave birth to the revolutionary spirit of our era and has conjured up either a rational or irrational State which, in both cases, is founded on terror.

"To break this pattern, Johann proposed that the revolutionary abandon his most basic idea of what power is and what humanity is, to create a model for being without being like the oppressor. As long as the oppressed live in the duality in which 'to be' is 'to be like', and 'to be like' is 'to be like the oppressor', then true transformation was impossible. Johann rallied for men to enter into a dialogical communion with one another, he preached, a secular religion that all peoples could identify with, for men to risk the act of love for one another and thus create a new model. My glorious husband, a true revolutionary ended up a terrorist of love. And for this he was killed, lured into a hotel room with a rigged briefcase full of money for his Croatian brothers that exploded and eliminated both enemies of the State."

Cory didn't know what to say. It was a lot more complicated than a deal gone sour. How could he begin to explain it to the Polish porter who sensationalized it like some bad TV? He couldn't. He knew he couldn't. In fact, trying to explain to that very man the brilliant ideas Agnieska had just brought to light in his mind, ideas that were so dangerous they had brought about the death of their originator, would have been as daunting a task as Johann himself must have faced every day of his life.

Agnieska could see that Cory understood. She stood in front of him, turned to the fire, and watched the flames lick the oxygen right out of the dry wood and light up yellow-orange. For the life of her she didn't know why she had just put him, put herself, through that. But it felt good. For a few moments, during the telling of the story, it almost felt as if she was the listener and Johann's warm breath was again upon her cheek, half spouting off, half begging for her to agree. She was warm all over.

"What will you do now, Agnieska?" Cory felt a need to break the silence.

"I play with the quartet and hope to save enough money to go back to Berlin. I will resume my dream to become a virtuoso. You see, music never disappoints. I have no more faith in men's ideas, in humanity. To me, only God matters, and music is God's ideas."

Cory thought about the money. The per diem Carolyn had given him that morning was still in his pocket, still in its envelope, two million zloty. "How much money do you need?"

"What do you mean?" Agnieska didn't understand the question at all.

"To get back to Berlin and chase your dream? How much money would it take?"

Agnieska laughed. That was the question all right. She thought she hadn't heard him right the first time. She had done the calculations before but she was so

far away from her goal and with Maria's recent trips to the doctor and her traveling expenses she hadn't given it much consideration as of late. She blurted out, "Twenty million more zloty than I've got."

"Twenty million. Twenty million." Cory mulled it over. The idea that struck him was a crazy one but it just might work, he thought. "Agnieska, come with me."

CHAPTER FORTY-ONE

Agnieska had used the public telephone outside the corner market to call the taxi. When they slid in and Cory ordered the driver to take them to the Hotel Orbis, she crawled over him and clawed at the door handle in an effort to get out. Cory had only mentioned that he had an idea that might help them get the money she needed; she was unaware it entailed going to that most dreadful of places. Without her violin for security, she would feel unarmed, a naked and useless soldier approaching the enemy trench begging to be overrun with a barrage of grief.

Cory held both her thin wrists with one hand and wrapped his arm around her torso while she whimpered into his chest. "I know I'm a complete stranger but and I know what you're feeling but you have to trust me on this."

No answer from Agnieska. A strange pulling sensation overcame her. The notion that she would be forced to confront that awful site washed up against her heart like a harsh tide. But against her face the hard chest of this man, this patient listener, bathed her in a warmth and security. Since Johann's death no man had ever come this close to her. Polite, condoling embraces, yes, kisses on the cheek from her friends, yes, but this young American, Cory Sonne, held her the way Romeo must have held the dying Mercutio or Jupiter comforting the grief-stricken Orpheus. Her head was filled with grand compositions that rendered these classic stories - music in her mind that battled the anguish of remembering Johann. It felt so good just to be held, and for this gift alone, Agnieska would go along with whatever plan Cory devised.

Never once looking up at room 654 they entered through the hotel's double doors and strode through the lobby. As far as she was concerned now, there was no room 654, no reason to come back. Somehow, she knew this would be the last time she would ever see the Orbis.

As they headed towards the bar, Cory thanked his lucky stars that Sean McDonough occupied his regular spot at the corner table. He wondered as he approached with Agnieska if he could count on him for a favor. Sean was busy regaling Yuri and Mikola with a story about Martin Short making Robin Williams laugh so hard he nearly choked to death. They all stood when Cory introduced Agnieska.

"I have a proposition for you." Cory stated. Sean gave him a quick lift of the eyebrow. "Will you join me in the casino?"

"Gentlemen?" Sean waved his arm inquisitively at Yuri and Mikola.

"Sure, why not. It helps out the local economy." Yuri said.

"Actually, it's a bunch of Brits that run the thing." Mikola added.

"No?" Sean blurted out. "Then by all means let's take those limies for every zloty they've got."

The troupe headed to the elevators. Cory felt suddenly excited and somewhat proud that he'd organized a plan that these movie luminaries had backed with a stamp of approval.

On the way up to the Penthouse, Cory explained Agnieska's plight, though very superficially, and his plan for turning his per diem into a twenty million zloty bootie. He'd have tried it on his own but felt instinctively that if Sean the star and Yuri the native-made-good were gambling with him they might be more inclined to let them win.

Sean not only liked Cory's thinking but Agnieska's violin playing as well. He, too, had drifted off to sleep on more than one night, listening to the somber sadness of her strings. They had all thrown some money into the pot and found themselves with nearly four million zloty as a starting bankroll. All but Mikola, he intended to park himself at the blackjack tables and attempt a leg up on his recent losses.

The elevator doors opened onto the tenth story view of the snow-covered city. To the left was the disco; to the right the casino.

Two craps tables, two roulette wheels, four black jack tables, slot machines along three walls and a bar along the fourth, all "manned" by busty Polish Barbies with stiff cotton candy hair, Otto Dix make-up, and red sequined vests over low cut white blouses that made them look like "Hee-Haw" pin-ups. A trio of tuxedoed managers floated in and out of the tables with hawk-like expressions.

A vixen named Virginia ran the roulette table where they finally settled in. Cory kept looking at her nametag and thinking of Virginia - the State. It didn't jibe with this Polish cutie with elegant fingers but dog-like incisors on an otherwise ingratiating smile. Sean powered through the Chivas and as the game progressed kept insisting to Virginia, "There is a Santa Claus. I tell you, there is." She smiled politely though she had no idea what he meant.

Agnieska, who had never been in a casino in her life, wedged between Sean and Cory, the stranger and the movie star. A surreal wave of exuberance washed over her. Nothing of hers was at risk. This was pure gamesmanship, pure celebration with a possible huge upside. Two handsome men where tempting fortune for her and spinning the portentous wheel for her future.

Cory, Sean and Agnieska huddled conspiratorially. Cory's whispering mouth against Sean's ear gave him goose bumps. The thrill of the bronzed boy had certainly not dissipated. Sean laid down the four million zloty, one of the tuxedoed goons inspected the money, shoved it down into the cash box and nodded his approval. Virginia slid eight stacks of blue and gold chips across the stenciled green felt towards him and wished him good luck.

"Dzieki." They all three thanked her in Polish at the same time. She smiled.

As agreed, Sean placed small bets on the 4, 5, and 6 for the fated numbers of room 654, then placed a column bet on the layout space above the left hand side group of twelve numbers that included the four, then a big bet on the black, thinking there could be no blacker reason for this morbid betting scheme. 35 to 1 payoff odds on the number bets, 3 to 1 on the column, and 2 to 1 on the black. This would be their strategy for the night and they would hold fast to it, winning big or losing it all.

Virginia placed the ball in its track and whipped it around the lip of the spinning wheel in the opposite direction with a flick of the wrist.

Giggling and watching, rolling and humming, rolling and rolling, the ball finally losing speed and dropping in, bouncing and bouncing and settling in on black 26. Virginia called it out, “Twenty-six, black.” She quickly removed all losing bets with a swipe of her arm.

Agnieska moaned. “No, it’s okay, the bet on black was big enough to more than offset the others, we lost up here but won over here. We’re ahead.”

“You’ve done this before, Cory, eh?” Sean asked.

“Used to drive to Vegas on Sunday mornings, Church of the Open Road. My buddy Vince’s convertible Dodge Dart, pull all-niters at the five dollar tables, get plastered on free drinks, then drive back for class Monday morning. Good thing it was only junior college.”

Virginia paid off the bet and cleared the board. Other than one semi-conscious career loser in a polyester suit one size too small, the table was theirs. Sean laid down the bet again only this time he dropped two chips onto the 26 as well. “That’s my superstition. You watch, that number will come up again real soon.”

“It better be within the next thirty four rolls are it’s a losing proposition.” Sean reached over and, shocking the hell out of Cory, stuck his middle and index fingers into Cory's nostrils.

"I know that, Mr. Bigshot." Cory grabbed his wrist and removed the fingers, laughing. Not just because it was so unexpected but because he recognized the gesture from a scene Sean did in Marked By Blood - an Irish mob movie from a few years back that made big noise from the critics but was probably too stylized for the general public.

"Place your bets, please." Virginia droned for probably the eleven thousandth time. The ball spun again.

"This is going to take some time, Agnieska. We have to chip away at them. We may go up for a while and back down but if the fates are with us, we'll pull it off." Sean and Yuri looked at Cory. They liked this kid. Using his per diem to help out a woman whose talent on the violin probably equaled theirs, artistically, but who happened to have chosen a pursuit that paid a bricklayer's wages.

Roll, hum, bounce, bounce and drop. "Ten, black."

"All right." Cory clapped his hands, clearly the most excited of the group. He'd always possessed a keen interest in the Fates, why an ace might come up when it did or a pair of dice show a seven or an ivory ball skip across a frictionless wheel and rest in a specifically numbered canoe. Random? Ordered? Entropy? Destiny? It fascinated him, and the roulette wheel seemed an entertaining manifestation of the question. After what she'd been through and the way she played her violin, Agnieska "deserved" to make enough to return to Berlin; did the Fates agree?

Virginia slid their winning chips towards them. Cory loved the surf-like sound of chips coming toward him across the velvety baize. So different from the scudding noise of chips being whisked away. When he mentioned the difference Sean only shook his head and noted, "You're so full of it you could knock a buzzard off a shit wagon."

"Nuances. You have to be aware of the nuances. I'd think, as an actor, you'd know about things like that." Cory's vodka and tonics expunged the brazen underside of his normally reserved self.

"Place your bets please." The always dutiful Virginia barked.

Rolling, rolling. The loser at the end of the table had placed all of his purple and green chips on the two number split between the 31 and 34. Rolling, rolling. Sean laid out the team strategy upping the small bets just a tad and reducing the amount of the black bet. Cory decided to let this deviation from the plan go. So long as he played the correct spaces.

Rolling, rolling, bounce, bounce, bounce.

"Twenty-six black." Virginia called out. The three of them shrieked. They had hit it big.

"Ha! I told you, so, my friend." Sean bellowed then took one step back from the table and announced to the room in his most Shakespearean voice, "I do not suffer fools gladly!"

The room drew a breath and everything came to a stop. The loser at the end of their table picked up his cigarettes and stormed out of the casino, cursing under his breath, most likely blaming the Americans for his bad luck.

Shushhhhh! The piles and piles of chips washed towards them. "Yes, yes. I do believe I hear that difference you were speaking of, my friend. Yes, I do believe I hear it now." They all laughed, except Virginia. She knew all too well how the management frowned on lucky gamblers on a croupier's shift. Three more numbers came and went and still the house had yet to take money from this Hollywood quartet with the superstitious strategy that seemed to be paying off handsomely. Virginia was quickly replaced by the blunt-faced Danika but to no avail. As the hours went on, the blue and gold chips piled up under the leaning bodies of this jovial bunch.

In between a series of loses they managed to find big wins. The black hit more often than the red, the first column hit nearly fifty percent of the time, the 5 hit,

Sean's 26 hit twice more, then came the 6. Danika gave way to Cecilia then the 6 hit again. The four amateurs were beside themselves with elation.

Agnieska got suddenly serious. "Cory, perhaps this enough. Perhaps it is time to quit."

Cory knew she was right; things were bound to turn. He made a quick calculation of the chip piles. They had amassed nearly fifteen million zloty. Before he could say anything, out of the corner of his eye, he caught the tuxedoed Goon nodding to Cecilia. "Place your bets, please."

Sean divvied out the familiar six bets. Without turning his head, Cory watched with his eyes as the Goon moved over to the far corner of the bar where a short, pugnacious man in a double breasted suit sat spewing a huge, nervous chaos of smoke. When the man opened his hand to gesture at the Goon, Cory noticed he had no thumb, only a slight ridge, the size of a Rollo. This absence of a thumb gave his hand a spatula-like look as he waved off the Goon with a few mumbled words.

Bounce, bounce, bounce. Their eyes swiveled to the wheel. "Thirty-four, black." Cecilia intoned.

"Holy shit. It's a good thing that guy down at the end left. He'd be pissed right now." They tried not to laugh at his misfortune for they knew all too well it could easily be their own but they did anyway as the familiar "Shushhhhh" of their winning black bet came towards them.

It was then that Cory saw the Goon settle in at Cecilia's left, a position he hadn't occupied during the whole night. Cory tried to read the expression on his face but he was stone. Assassins, lifetime politicians, expert philanderers must have this same ability to give nothing away with their eyes, something Cory knew he would never be able to do.

8 red was followed by 36 red then by 20 red. Three rolls in a row with zero payoff since their last big hit, since the Goon's conversation with the four-fingered man, since the new sentry position at their table. The frustration of the other three was mounting; the bets had been getting bigger as their lucky streak dashed onward.

"We couldn't possibly be shut out four times in a row. I feel it; this one is going to be lucky." He set out half a million zloty bets on the four numbers, another half on the column and five million on the black. Over seven million zloty on the table at one time.

Agnieska opened her mouth to speak but no words came, only the release of non-syllabic air like the burping of a Tupperware lid.

"Prosze." Cecilia excused herself momentarily and turned to the Goon. A simple nod of his head indicated for her to proceed and take the bets. She whipped the ball around the separator for her only patrons. Sean, Yuri, Agnieska all watched the wheel.

Cory looked up at Cecilia; she stared back. Her chin seemed a notch or two lower than before so that she had to roll her eyes up a little to see him. Cory looked over to the Goon. Still unmoving, arms crossed, a tetanus of the soul setting in to lock him to his post.

Rolling, rolling, rolling and humming, rolling. Cory looked at the table. The idea that had been formulating in his mind suddenly fell into place. As Cecilia drew a breath to speak the words that would end the betting period, Cory reached down with one crane-like hand and cupped a million zloty stack of chips then leaned over the table and slapped them directly on the green space numbered 0.

"No more bets, please." Cecilia cried but too late. Cory's bet was legally down. Her eyes pulled to the wheel by the bounce, bounce, bounce, bounce of the ball.

A wide-eyed silence from every player, from Cecilia and the strictly from the Goon.

There it was. The ivory ball resting in the spinning green canoe of the number 0. His overwhelming instinct had been right. Cecilia looked to the Goon, showing the first sign of cracking with a resigned nod of his head. As she cleared the table of the strategic seven million zloty Sean had laid, the Goon uncrossed his arms and walked away. Seemed he didn't want to see those special, black and red million zloty chips doled out to the winners, thirty-five to be precise, counted out methodically by Cecilia in seven stacks of five then stacked on top of each other into three stacks of ten plus five on top, then shushhhhhed across the baize.

They stared down at the pile. They had more than quadrupled their money. They each knew they had just done something spectacular. Rarely does "luck" so clearly coincide with ones "plans." It was an accident of good fortune that was as karmically rewarding to them all as it was fiscally.

"Now, do we quit?" Agnieska meekly suggested.

The biggest laugh of the night followed her tender voice. Sean hugged Yuri then turned and hugged Cory with little Agnieska sandwiched between them.

Mikola finally joined them, having busted out in blackjack. Sean deposited a million zloty chip in his shirt pocket and declared, "Nobody I know is going to leave here a loser tonight."

They cashed out. And after a million zloty tip to Cecilia for her troubles, they folded their forty million zloty bills in half, pocketed the loot then blew kisses to the casino and retired downstairs to the lobby bar to imbibe cocktails for which they didn't mind paying.

It was well after midnight. They were all high, drinking and laughing and reliving the thrilling moments that would be fodder for bar-talk in years to come. But although Maria was a brave and independent girl, Agnieska seldom left her alone at home, and she wanted to get back as soon as possible. The idea of Agnieska going home alone with a wad of money like that was unsettling to Cory. A taxi was called, and he decided to accompany her against her urging.

Heartfelt good-byes were traded between Agnieska, Sean, and Yuri. They realized only all too well that they would probably never see each other again even though Sean insisted he would keep a close eye for her London premiere as a soloist. As was the case with so many things attached to this movie, another episode of pure magic had been theirs to savor. With only a per diem and some spare change and a table full of good intentions, they had changed this woman's life for the better. At least that is what they hoped. And holding on to this hope would allow them to think of a violin that might now produce an outstanding "Ode to Joy."

Trusting no one, and well aware that the cab driver might have somehow consorted with the casino owners, Cory had the man drop them a good half mile from Agnieska's home and waited until he drove off to turn and walk in the proper direction.

They giggled and talked on the short walk home, warmed by the mirth of the evening and the idea of things to come. They didn't even mind that it started snowing.

They stopped at Agnieska's gate. This was where he would take his leave. She turned back to him, threw her arms around him as he leaned over for an embrace, and whispered in his ears, “You can stay the night with me. It’s the least I can do.”

Cory pulled slowly away. “I’m sure it would be lovely, Agnieska. But I must go.”

“How will I ever thank you?” The musician with a backbone of steel began to cry.

“Remember the happiness we shared tonight, the laughter and celebration. Put it right there in your memory next to Johann – for balance. Let’s just call it one of God’s ideas.”

She hugged him again. “Thank you, Cory. Thank you, thank you, thank you. I will never forget you.”

“Oh, there is one thing you can do for me.”

“Yes?”

“Buy Maria a big bag of black licorice and tell her it was from the ‘nice man’ who is sorry he woke her up tonight.”

Pope Julius’ smile upon seeing Michelangelo’s finished Sistine Chapel could not have been any bigger than Agnieska’s. The fortunate fresco of her future had been painted that evening on the roulette table by this man in front of her and for what reason she could not divine. But there was forty thousand zloty in her pocket. It had happened, and she knew, in all likelihood that she would never see him again. On his cold lips she placed a long, firm kiss while holding his face between her hands. "Goodbye, Cory."

"Do Widzenia, Agnieska."

She watched him walk down the street dodging the ice and broken asphalt then ducked inside. As she pulled out the wad of cash and remembered the faces of the men who laid out the chips, she fell to her knees and wept, for herself and Maria, for room 654 unbridled from her memory, for terror subsided, for happiness.

That night, Cory fell into a rare, undisturbed sleep. He could not wait to tell Georgia the next morning about the evening's spectacular adventure. She would surely get a kick out of it. In his dreams there were no plums, no Eli, just red and black numbers and bouncing ivory balls, nervous anticipation followed by celebratory laughter, smoking violins, colored music spewing from the mind of God, and a little girl in pigtails enjoying a big bag of black licorice.

CHAPTER FORTY-TWO

What distinguished this gray Wednesday morning from every other morning so far was the prodigious amount of snow that had fallen the night before. It wouldn't be long before the traffic, the coal dust, the wood ash from the city's chimneys would soil what was at that moment an undefiled surplice over the cassock of the land. With so few cars on the road just after dawn, Cory enjoyed an uninterrupted view that amazed him, a southern California surfer wholly unfamiliar with snow.

With a proud expression on his face, Waldek popped a tape into the car stereo -Live's "Throwing Copper." Cory had always loved this hard rock CD, especially "Lightning Crashes". The simple guitar chords, the singer's soulful voice, the passive drum beat that rolled in like a wave and broke onto the chorus. He sang under his breath, galloping with his head in time to the song: "Lightning crashes, a new mother cries, her placenta falls to the floor, the angel opens her eyes, the confusion sets in before the doctor even closes the door." Slowly the bass joined in. "Lightning crashes, an old mother dies, her intentions fall to the floor, the angel closes her eyes, that confusion that was hers, belongs now to the baby down the hall."

Drums kicking in, the song crested. Waldek joined in on the chorus. They smiled and sang together. Cory wondered if he knew what it meant. "Oh, now feel it, comin' back again, like a rollin' thunder chasin' the wind, forces pullin' from the center of the earth again, I can feel it…"

The rolling white hills lolled by. Live. Van Morrison. Coltrane. Agnieska. Cory had always been envious of musicians. They could do so readily and so nakedly what he could not, get in touch with their feelings and express them. Actors, too, for the most part. And yet, he had known enough of both to understand the curse. That kind of connectedness came with a price; it could not be turned on and off. Like a stuck faucet. The artist's flow of feelings, when it wasn't running creative or productive, could very often run miserable and desperate. Still, he admired those who could comfortably, intrepidly dwell in the territory of the heart, a region he often felt, for himself, lay just over the next ridge, a scary trek he dared not make.

Georgia was not up when he arrived. Cory joined Dante in the security room in the midst of examining an Interpol Report on the bombings in Germany. He looked over Dante's shoulder at the photocopied map of the country. There were red X's over the nine cities.

"They look pretty evenly spread out. Those Germans. So methodical." Cory remarked as he hung up his coat.

"Yes, I was noting that. May I show you something?" Dante asked, picking up a pencil.

"Sure."

He drew a straight line on the map connecting Munster to Dillenburg then another straight through the middle of the country to Schmalkalden and continuing over to Gera then straight down to Regensburg. Cory could see where he was going with this. His pencil then moved in an equivalent way from Karlsruhe over to Dillenburg straight up through the center of Germany, through Schmalkalden up to Salzgitter and over to Dessau. The two of them stared at the image these lines had created. Spread across the span of the German map was a penciled swastika.

The red light under the video monitors flashed on. Someone was at the front door. They looked up to see

Jack, slapping off the snow from his pant legs and boots. Cory grabbed the map off the desk and they went to the foyer.

"Cory. I'm glad you're here. Is Georgia up yet?"

"No." Cory held up the map. "Jack, take a look at this. Dante figured it out."

Jack held the map in his hand. "Son of a bitch. So simple and no one picked it up. Dante, you're a genius. I don't know if it will add anything to the investigation, though. What time is it?" They all looked at their watches. "Six fifteen. Too early to call Vienna. That will have to wait." He handed the map back to Dante then indicated Cory. "Right now I want you to grab your coat and come with me."

"Do you think that Dante's right?" Cory asked Jack as they bundled up.

"Yes. You have to understand something, Cory. Right now is a very troubled time in Europe. There are historical precedents at work here. The resurgence of old hatreds, the shrinking economy, the drop in the standard of living for a majority of the population. It is precisely those kinds of conditions that have twice given rise to a tyrannical German State, and both those times the aggressors virtually started out as grass roots terrorist parties. The people in power are trying to be watchdogs but it's hard to control everything in a 'free' society without being tyrannical yourself. It's a fine line, and unfortunately it makes it difficult to cross over and stop these neo-fascist groups," Jack explained as they exited the compound.

"But they blew up buildings in nine different cities."

"Who? Without any clear cut evidence anybody could claim responsibility and avoid prosecution. As far as I know they have very little to go on and only some speculation as to which activist group is truly responsible. There are a few dozen of them, you know. What worries me is what they could possibly want from us."

With over a foot of fresh snow the path around the perimeter of the Hotel Hollywood compound was tough going. At the edge of the hill that butted up against the backyard, Jack made a sharp left leaving the trail cut into the woods and following the line of trees along the back fence.

Jack indicated one of the beech woods. "Take a close inspection of this tree trunk."

Though he had no idea what he was looking for, Cory studied the tree. Nothing out of the ordinary. He turned to Jack, "Yeah, so?"

"Now come over here." They moved to the next tree in the line. "See anything unusual?"

Small slices had been made about two feet apart all the way up the trunk to the fork of the main branches eight or nine feet off the ground. "Toeholds?" Cory asked.

"Probably, made with a small pocket knife it appears."

"Somebody's been climbing this tree."

"Give it a go." Jack interlocked his fingers and offered his hands to Cory for a boost. With the lift up he was just able to grab the first branch and pull himself up into the cross section where he settled in easily. Jack pulled out a tiny pair of collapsible binoculars, opened them, and tossed them up to Cory. "Here. Tell me what you see."

From this vantage point, Cory could see over the gazebo and the backyard vegetation of the Hotel Hollywood directly into all the back windows of the building. The curtains in the gym were open and Cory could see the top half of the treadmill and the multi-station machine. The curtains were drawn on the next two rooms but below them he could clearly see the dining room table where they took all their meals. It was empty. He scanned all the way over to the east side of the building, to the corner, Andrew and Georgia's bedroom. Their curtains were sloppily drawn so that through a small gap he could see the portion of the room where the large armoire, the bureau and the closet doors were. A body slinked by the opening then out of view. Georgia. No doubt about it. A moment later she appeared again, pausing in front of the bureau as she pulled on her sweats then stood there, naked from the waist up. Cory realized that moment that he had never seen her torso in anything other than a leotard. He knew her shoulders were well defined, and of course, he knew the outline of her neck and upper chest all too well. He'd watched so much sweat descend towards her cleavage; it was one of his most revered indulgences. But he had never seen the flesh of her ribcage and abdomen. She wasn't just flat stomached, she was ripped. A firm belly with small lines of definition. Wearing a crop top in any health club, she'd be the envy of most of the men as well as the women with abs like that. Sure she had the genetics, for there would be no accomplishing a look like that without them, the fascia have to adhere in certain ways after all, but he had done damn well with her to bring out that washboard aesthetic. And then, there were those gorgeous breasts.

It was only a split second. But it burned itself in. Cory dropped the binoculars to Jack. The guilt of voyeurism set in. How did the song go? "A taste of honey is worse than none at all."

"See anything?" Jack asked.

"No, no." Cory said, flustered. "I mean, yes. I see what you're getting at. You can see into every room on the back side of the house when the curtains are open."

"And they are almost always open on this back

side."

Cory hung from the low branch then fumbled for the hand-carved notches, clutching at the trunk of the beech wood and shimmying down quickly. He jumped the last five feet down to the snow and righted himself in front of Jack. "You think somebody's been watching?"

Jack pulled out a plastic bag with a number of crumpled gum wrappers. "Found these in the snow right here at the base of the tree. Going to send them off to Gunter at Interpol in Vienna and see if we can't get a fingerprint."

"This is serious; isn't it, Jack?"

"Somebody is watching Andrew and taking a keen interest in not only the making of this film but the movements of Andrew and his family on a daily basis. This is reconnaissance, pure and simple. It may just be for information purposes and it may not. But we can't take any chances. I know you came over here as a trainer, my boy, but from now on you're a bodyguard as well."

"Holy shit, Jack, I don't have a lick of training for that." Cory responded.

"At this point, it's just a matter of keeping an eye out and trusting your instincts. You're in the personal service business. You probably have a good idea about how to read people, right?"

"I suppose so."

"If you're really paying attention, you'll know. You spotted the marks on the tree and even deduced what they might represent. Deduction. It's all about keeping your senses sharp and using your powers of intuition and deduction."

Jack grabbed a broken fan of branches from up the hillside and raked it along his tracks on the way down. Then he went over to the base of the tree and furiously raked at the snow, filling in the depressed spaces and trying to erase all sign of their having been there.

"What are you doing that for?" Cory asked.

"You tell me." Jack answered.

"If our guy…"

"More than likely, it's a male but don't assume it."

"Okay, if our lookout returns and sees our footprints, he or she will know we've discovered his spot, then he'll retreat." Jack nodded.

"Very good. See. You're deputized. And the more our suspect retreats, the harder it is for us to draw him out until it's too late."

Cory didn't like the "until it's too late" part. Jack seemed to say it with a finality that bordered on "in-all-likelihood." Nevertheless, he would follow orders and instead of every face on the street belonging to a former communist-turned-social-democrat they would now

strike him as a possible subversive or spy. He chuckled to himself. If Gabe could see him now. Bodyguard/detective/anti-terrorist agent. What the hell did he know about such things?

CHAPTER FORTY-THREE

Georgia was already warming up on the treadmill when Cory got to the gym. Although she wore a sweatshirt and bike pants, the image of that resplendent, athletic torso he had seen through the binoculars kept slamming into his mind.

"I thought I heard you pull up a while ago." She mentioned, wondering where he had been.

"Yes, I was outside with Jack, talking security."

"Then you know about the tape of the dailies that was found?" She seemed surprised.

"Yes, obviously you do, too."

"Of course, you think Andrew's going to keep something like that from me?" She was not in a good mood. Cory sensed her simmering anger was not meant entirely for him.

"No, no. That's not it at all. It's just that the last I heard, Jack had wanted to keep it under wraps. I wasn't sure who or what that meant." He checked her pulse. "Pretty high for seven kilometers per hour at zero incline."

Georgia blew out a deep breath. "I'm sorry. Andrew and I had a hard night. You have to understand something. When you live this life, and you live it with Andrew, it just seems like there's always someone who wants to mess with you, disrupt any chance at normalcy or peace and quiet. Most of the time it's just phone calls and unsolicited interruptions. But a thing like this, well, it's chilling. And it's not the first time."

"No?" Somehow this didn't really surprise Cory.

"Years ago, when Lani was just a little girl, we had a few occasions that were tantamount to extortion and a near kidnapping attempt."

"Holy shit."

"There hasn't been anything like that in years, though. This thing now, it comes at a bad time."

"I'll say. In a foreign country where you don't speak the language and you're really at the mercy of others."

"It's more than that," Georgia stopped. Whatever she was thinking she just shook it adamantly out of her mind. "Are we ready to lift?"

Cory had been setting up a circuit for her. Just the thing to distract her today. She would move from the dreaded pull-up bar, to push-ups, to single arm dumbbell rows, to the pec-deck, over to the bench for a pullover then in front of the mirror for upright rows with the twenty pound E-Z-curl bar that would go right into standing bicep curls then finish with tricep press downs on the high-pulley. Twenty reps at each station in the circuit, except the pull-ups where she would struggle to knock out three or four on her own; Cory would spot her generously to complete eight. Three times through the circuit with eight minutes of high intensity interval in between. Cory loved this workout himself. Could work up a real sweat and a pounding heart rate. Today it would be a difficult and painful enough scheme for Georgia to keep her mind off the prospective troubles.

There was so much he wanted to talk to her about. He was dying to tell her about the adventure with Agnieska at the casino but this was not the type of workout that was conducive to chit chat, and it seemed she was not in the most receptive mood. He'd tell her later.

After a second go round on the circuit, Cory put her back on the treadmill. She stared out the window for a long spell then turned to him abruptly. "Do you ski?" she asked.

The question caught him off guard. "Well, I haven't skied too much in my life but I do like it. I dated a girl for awhile who skied for UCLA. She was quite insistent that I learn, and she was a pretty good instructor. Went on to be some type of geophysicist. Interesting girl."

"Is that a yes?"

"Yes. Why?"

"Andrew and I had a tense discussion last night," Georgia spoke through heavy breaths. "You see, my very best girlfriend, Donna Nyall, is in Geneva this week for a conference. She's an international finance consultant. Since Andrew is shooting only Sean's castle scenes on Friday and Saturday, I was planning on taking the girls and going to Zermat to meet Donna and ski. None of us has ever skied the Alps, and Lani is quite good, really."

"Leaving tomorrow evening?"

"No, Friday morning."

"Were you planning on skiing?" Cory had to ask.

"Well," the answer was obviously yes but she didn't want to admit it.

"I can see why Andrew was upset. What if something happened? It is a high-risk sport. I know. I've rehabilitated a few knees."

"I know, I know. But I'm still going, and we're meeting Donna in Zermat. I've already had Carolyn make reservations. I'll make the decision about skiing later."

Cory took her off the treadmill and towards the pull-up bar for another circuit. "Hey, it's your life. And you know Andrew better than anybody. Do what you gotta do."

"I plan on it. But he wanted me to take Jack with me. I told him that it was he who needed the close security. It's Andrew and the film that are vulnerable, not me."

"Maybe so. But you're a big part of it; you can't deny it. I think he's right to be so concerned."

"I understand. That's why I recommended that you come with us for the weekend." Georgia stood under the pull-up bar. Cory didn't know what to say. Of course he would go but what he did know was that he was now being put in the middle of them. There was no mistaking the look in Andrew's eyes yesterday on the set and last night at the café. Although he ached to be near her, Cory had promised himself to keep the lowest profile possible and steer clear of interfering in either the making of the film or the relationship of the film director and his superstar wife.

"Do a set." Cory pointed to the bar. Georgia jumped up, grabbed it overhand, crossed her feet underneath her, and without a spot from Cory, cranked out eight full repetitions on her own. She dropped off and turned to him.

"Pretty strong, huh?"

"Of that there is little doubt." Cory agreed.

"So I need you to talk to Carolyn today and help her with the plans for the trip. I'm going to put you in charge of the girls, make sure they're packed on time and properly, etc. And when we get there, if you could rent the ski equipment and hire instructors. Is that okay?"

"Sure." Who was he to argue against a free trip to Switzerland? He pointed to the mat. "Push-ups. This is a circuit remember. No rest between sets, I don't care how impressive your pull-ups were."

"You're such a bully." Georgia punched him in the chest with a solid fist and caught him off guard.

"Ouch. You know what your problem is?"

"Pick one. I have many. Is it my abusive trainer?"

"No, too much testosterone. You're really a man trapped in the body of a goddess."

"Is that why you like me? Maybe you're really gay," she replied as she dropped to the mat and assumed the push-up position. With a back as straight as a sideboard, she dropped her body towards the floor and pressed it up in a military tempo, hands a little wider than shoulders, hips, chest and chin coming an inch from the floor then forced back up with a violent firing of the pec muscles. Textbook form and Cory knew it. He had taught it to her and she had eagerly learned.

“Look at you. You even do your push-ups like a man and better than most.” Cory dropped to one knee beside Georgia to make sure her chin and chest were coming all the way down and whispered in her ear as she neared the end of her set, “Besides, what makes you think I like you?”

Georgia collapsed onto the mat and expelled an exhausted laugh. “That was the funniest thing I’ve ever heard you say.” A laugh. She needed that.

CHAPTER FORTY-FOUR

The crew parked the trailers up along ul. Podwale next to the public common piled high in snow and a block and a half from the main buildings of Jagellonian University. They spent the morning shooting exteriors and were moving equipment inside when Cory arrived on the set with Andrzej after seeing the girls off to school. There was no doubt that rumors of connection to the neo-Nazi group had circulated among the production. A solemn pall had fallen over the cheerless, workman-like grips and electricians lighting the scene inside the library. Their eyes addressed him with a certain suspicion; he was still not immediately recognizable to them as a functioning part of the film.

At least today Cory had a reason to be there. He had spent a terse twenty minutes with Carolyn after his workout with Georgia in which she laid out the jet's arrival and departure times into Sion, Switzerland. She gave him a list of pre-screened restaurants, ski shops, and contact numbers in Zermat, and handed him an American Express gold card with Andrew's name on it and a small three compartment wallet stuffed with zloty, Swiss francs, and U.S. dollars. Whenever possible he was to pay with cash. Not that Andrew's credit was anything less than sterling. They simply didn't want his name being flashed around any more than necessary.

The library was a dour, stone building on the eastern flank of the Byly Quad. Vaulted ceilings and daunting gargoyles at the capitals of every granite column that anchored the mantle of antiquity and guarded the cumulative knowledge of nearly three millennia. Cory stood on the far side of the cavernous room. Near the information desk, Andrew gave instruction to Marek Linz, the hump-backed actor playing the librarian.

Georgia sat quietly at a long, polished table accompanied by a bevy of thick books. Although the crew was between takes, her interest in the pages in front of her did not wane. Cory knew the scene they were shooting, and by the concentration on her face he could tell it was not Georgia Hart at the end of that table but

Anna Kamenski.

"Roll film!"

Lieutenant Schlesinger, Hans Frank's right hand man and an SS Officer pounded on the library door demanding admittance. Inside, Anna Kamenski's heart skipped a bit. She exchanged a frightened look with the librarian then hustled to remove the stacks of books from the end of the table, shielding every hint of her presence. The pounding came again, more insistent. The librarian shuffled over to the door but waited until she was out of sight before opening it.

The heavy oak door had barely cracked open when the SS Officer thrust his forearm into it, sending it and the librarian flying backwards as if it were mounted on well-greased bushings instead of creaking old hinges.

Schlesinger, ever the arrogant German, spoke perfect Polish addressing the librarian. "When I give an order, dog shit, I expect it executed immediately." He struck the nervous old man with the back of his hand. "When you keep me waiting, you keep the Commandant waiting, and he suffers delays far less patiently than I." Again he struck the librarian. "Do you understand me?"

"Yes, yes. I'm sorry. But I am an old man and do not move well."

"You will move less well with two broken legs." Again he struck him, this time hard enough to draw blood from the old man's prominent nose. A small gleeful smile crossed Schlesinger's lips. He so enjoyed this part of his job. Coming into buildings, sometimes uninvited and unannounced and assaulting whomever the citizens posted at the doorways as lookouts. He wanted to make sure every one of them knew it was a position not to be envied. In fact, in some kind of twisted logic he surmised that if he beat every lookout and doorman to a pulp, soon no one would desire the post and make his task of troubleshooting potential enemies to the Reich that much easier. It was necessary to create fear at the very beginning, right at the door, with the first man. This kind of terror traveled in waves over any building and signified that the representative of power had arrived, and power in the Reich, in Poland at this time in history, usually meant being able to make decisions that affected life or death. It was this addiction to power that fed his need to abuse and transformed his fist into an Aryan trumpet.

The two Nazi's surveyed the empty library. Schlesinger's eyes fell onto the reception desk where the old man's book remained open on top, then over to the table where Georgia had been sitting. A small pamphlet lay open, face down on one of the chairs.

"Are you the only one here?" Schlesinger asked in as friendly a tone as the henchman ever used.

"Yes. As you are well aware, I'm sure, your Commandant has closed the university and imprisoned all the intellectuals. Me, I am just a custodian. Bless the Commandant for keeping me here to watch over the books."

Schlesinger's eyes returned to the pamphlet as he spoke. "Yes, it's unfortunate that the linguists are urinating all over each other in the barracks at Birkenau at this moment for the Commandant is in need of a language expert to interpret an inscription on an antique piece up at the castle. Do you speak Italian, French, Spanish?"

The librarian feverishly shook his head. "No, sir. I understand some German, beautiful language. I must make an effort to learn more."

Unsure whether the man was lying or not, Schlesinger began speaking at him in bulleted phrases of Italian, then French, then Spanish, asking in each language if he were a liar and would enjoy having his balls cut off. With no visible reaction to any of this other than confusion, Schlesinger gave him reprieve.

"You make my order very difficult." Again his eyes fell onto the pamphlet. He walked over and picked it up. "Have you a problem with your blood, old man?"

Clearly, he had no idea what the Lieutenant was asking, "I'm sure I don't understand, sir. Certainly not."

"Do you consider yourself a thorough man, a fine custodian?"

"Yes, sir. I have worked here for thirty-nine

years."

"Yes. I expected as much." Schlesinger's level voice turned accusatory. "Then answer me. Why would a man who has had weeks alone in the library by himself not have bothered to return this simple pamphlet to its proper place. It would drive a faithful employee like you mad would it not? Unless someone had been reading it up until the moment we arrived and made off in a hurry. Could that be the case, old man?"

The librarian tried to turn and run as Schlesinger approached again. The second Officer grabbed him by the collar and prevented that retreat, thrusting him towards his superior. Schlesinger rolled the pamphlet up, placed it under the chin of the old man, and whispered. "Come straight with me. There is someone else here, isn't there?"

The petrified hunchback shook his head. "No, no. I am the custodian."

"Liar!" Schlesinger shouted and struck him on the top of the head with the heel of his fist, sending him to the ground. "I'll give you one last chance. Is there someone else here?"

Concerned with the blood that trickled down the side of his face, the wheezing old librarian gave no answer.

"You'll have much more to worry about than that blood if you don't answer me now." Schlesinger didn't even wait but kicked him in the ribs again, forcing the bile that had accumulated in his stomach to spatter onto the marble tiles. The floor and the librarian's fluids were strikingly similar in color.

As Schlesinger readied his boot for yet another kick, a female voice boomed in Italian, "Fermarsi!"

Anna emerged from the labyrinthine shelves commanding the Officers to stop beating the old man. As she drew near, Anna continued her conversation with Schlesinger in Italian then switched to French and even threw him a curve by using some Russian, of which he could speak little. She implored him to let the old man alone; she would go with them to the castle and interpret the inscriptions.

As she bent down to tend to the old man, the SS Officer pulled her away by the arm. Schlesinger stood over the librarian and spit on him. "Do you think she has saved your life old man? There is still the treason of having lied to an Officer of the Reich." Schlesinger pulled the gun from his belt, cocked it, and pointed it at the librarian's head. Strangely enough, the old man showed little sign of terror, perhaps expecting that this was his fate, to die at the hands of this brutal German thug. He looked to Anna. Between them a notion of love, loyalty and goodness passed briefly - a pinhole eye of calm in a Nazi storm.

Schlesinger hesitated. There would be no killing.

He lowered the weapon. “If I kill you then I make more work for myself replacing you with someone to watch over this library. You are lucky old man that I am saddled with such pressing orders.” He kicked the whimpering old man in the ribs one last time before escorting Anna Kamenski to the Duisenberg waiting outside.

End of scene.

The onlookers and crew had been so mesmerized by the performances they stood frozen, momentarily transported back to the Krakow of the 1940’s. That is until Andrew bellowed out, “Again.”

CHAPTER FORTY-FIVE

At four thirty in the afternoon the sky was already dark, and darker still the Curate's house on Wawel hill. Szania Lipski had given only one tour of the castle that day. at noon, the warmest part of a day that, if they were lucky, broke the twenty degree mark. He had spent the rest of the afternoon replacing the valve on the gas intake line of the second story apartment he occupied on the grounds as the only live-in official of the state museum. To his satisfaction he was now able to move freely about his room without shivering and able to offer his guest a fresh pot of tea.

Bernard Zweig was not a tea drinker but in this bitter cold anything warm was welcome. Zweig had been keeping a low profile over the last two weeks since being made by the retried L.A. cop, Jack Grady. He'd been given the order from Berlin to back off and had spent the time reading at the local library and browsing the antique shops for WWI paraphernalia of which he was an avid collector. Good fortune had smiled on him, in fact, as he'd stumbled upon a munitions shop carrying a model 1918 Schmeisser with an authentic 32-shot Lugar magazine, a 20 centimeter barrel, blowback operated and still very clean. It was the granddaddy of the sub-machine gun and developed by Louis Schmeisser, a true German weapons genius.

The discussion turned from Zweig's unique find to the business at hand. Lipski was going to be Zweig's eyes and ears when the Pillar of Salt production ascended the hill for three weeks of filming on Monday.

The position of Curate at Wawel was one Szania had occupied for over seven years, since the death of his father. He had been relatively young when he was awarded the post but was more than qualified, having been raised on the grounds as a boy and having endured both the Nazi occupation and the Soviet whimsy which vacillated between desecration and veneration of this historical landmark. After the overthrow of communism, he had returned from running a boarding house in Wadowice to the duties his father had so loyally attended. But with privatization came the unpleasant reduction of both his salary and privileges on Wawel Hill. He'd been forced into the apartment upstairs as the bottom floor of the Curate's house was renovated as a gift shop, and the prospect of buying a small country farm for retirement had all but disappeared. Until Andrew Goldman had decided to make a film in Krakow and Bernard Zweig had arrived with cash for Szania to make a report. What Zweig didn't know was how deep the anti-Semitic fault ran in Lipski's soul and that he'd probably have done the job for free.

An envelope choked with zloty hit the tiny glass table in front of them.

"As we agreed." Bernard said. "To be matched weekly, providing the information is accurate and worth the price."

"My end of the deal is simply to let you know where they are and what they are filming. That, I can assure you will be handled. But let me remind you, I am a historian, not an agitator. Anything outside of information is all your responsibility."

"And my pleasure, should it come to that. But right now, we're in a wait-and-see situation. And you are my eyes and ears."

Szania brought out a bottle of cognac, twisted off the lid and poured into the cups, "Then let us drink. To sound vision." Szania chuckled to himself while Zweig remained stoic.

"The vision, my friend, is of a new order. You should be honored to play a small part in the complex plans of its visionaries."

"I am, Mr. Zweig. I am. Are you forgetting that my father served the Nazi governor, Hans Frank, right here fifty years ago. The man who rid us of the Jewish plague."

"Yes, and now they have returned to film a movie to evoke sympathy against this heroic act. I wake each morning in the most eager hope for the order to prevent this damnable film from happening. That is what I will drink to. To the order to disrupt."

The two men touched mugs, clutching the tepid contours of the enamel to warm their hands; their hearts already ablaze with the notion of violent chaos.

CHAPTER FORTY-SIX

Jessica brought Cory's water on a silver tray to his seat at the back of the jet. Inside the glass was over-priced, French carbonated water. Outside the window, the over-priced Swiss Alps.

"Anything else, Mister…Cory?" It was against her habit to call her adult passengers by their first name but Cory had insisted on it. He never wanted to think of himself as Mr. Sonne.

"No, that'll be it. Thanks." What he would have loved to say, 'Yes, there's something else. Could you tell that gorgeous, rich, world-famous actress up there chatting with her financier friend that I'd die for just one chance to remove her panties and that I'd take an entire weekend to do it? That's how hypnotic the seduction would be. But he didn't. He just smiled at the perky redhead who probably could have guessed by the way he kept looking over at Georgia.

Cory could hear very little of the conversation between the women in the two front seats. Lani and Niki exchanged a portable Gameboy between them at the table in the middle of the jet that seemed more like something to pass the time than a serious competition. When Niki's little Mario died by banana asphyxiation, she dropped the player on the couch.

"Oh, I hate you. Why do I let you talk me into these stupid video games?"

"Because you need to improve your hand-eye coordination," Lani replied.

"I'm not the one who hits tennis balls over the fence and into the swimming pools."

"I did that on purpose." Lani smiled.

"Now, girls, if you can't play nice," Cory interrupted.

"I'm going to the bathroom." Niki huffed her way to the back of the plane. Lani came over and sat on the arm of the couch across from Cory.

"Why do you want to be one of many?" A cryptic question from a girl that had seemed bent on detesting him this week for no other reason than a change of pace.

"Excuse me?" Cory asked.

“I see the way you look at my mom. They way you act around her. You’re only the ten thousandth guy to be smitten with her.”

“Hey, I have a job that requires me to pay close attention to Georgia. Let’s make no mistakes. That’s all I’m doing, and I don’t have to justify myself to you.”

“Then why are you getting so defensive?”

“That’s not defensive; that’s informative.”

“Oh, I see.” Lani paused, pulling an imaginary thread on the cuff of her sleeve. “She doesn’t fool around, you know.”

“I should expect not.” Cory confirmed.

“Seems a lot of the men in her life get that impression. Andrew’s age and all. The sexy roles she’s played.”

“Well, it must be tough on you having such a beautiful, together, famous and loyal mother. Not the usual complaints of a teenage daughter.”

“No, I have no complaints. Just didn’t want you to get your hopes up.” Niki came out of the bathroom and Lani’s confiding demeanor snapped suddenly back into its schoolgirl counterpart. She addressed Niki, “You want to watch a movie?”

The hidden twenty-seven inch Sony Television automatically emerged from the opposite end of the conference table console. The girls donned their headphones and were quickly engrossed by the video

"Heavenly Creatures", a story about two girls their age who plot to kill one of their mothers.

Cory shook his head. No matter how emphatically or nonchalantly he denied it, she was perceiving the truth about the situation. He knew she was a smart girl but she now proved herself a master linguist of the non-verbal language of the body. He hated her for her keenness and her veracity. Of all the "truths" she had yet to discover in her life, and there were many, why had this one come so early on and so clearly?

Between Andrew's and Lani's warnings, Cory was going to have to watch himself, guard his words and actions for both their sakes. But even the self-reproach could not quell the rebellion in his heart as he watched the profile of Georgia, leaning over the arm of her leather airplane seat, whispering secrets to her close friend. As her head turned on the axis of its exquisite neck and her lambent eye caught Cory's, Georgia fixed him against his chair like a knife thrower with a smile as pointed as it was deadly. The tall trainer with the body built from rock divined only one thing from that look, and that was that if Georgia gave him an opening, he would fall like a stone. Cory closed his eyes and prayed to whatever god it was that orchestrated the colliding of atoms, prayed not to lose the control he had so carefully cultivated from a chaotic past, prayed not to trip a land mine on the road ahead which seemed inextricably headed through the

country of Georgia's heart.

CHAPTER FORTY-SEVEN

Zermat lay nestled at the base of the famed Matterhorn in the Swiss Alps, an hour's drive from Sion by private limo followed by a quaint fifteen minute sleigh ride to the front door of the Zermatterhoffer. Nineteenth century charm that cost big time twentieth century money. Chocolate shops, creperies, watch store after watch store, clothing boutiques from Hermes to Tyrolean Children's, souvenir stands and ski equipment rentals, cozy bars and elegantly undersized restaurants all lined the narrow cobble-stoned street - the one main thruway of the town. In the middle of the plaza, along the canal whose spring time melt off amounted to the origin of the Visp river, stood the majestic Zermatterhoffer, the first

hotel built at the resort over a hundred and fifty years ago.

Cory handled all of the checking in while porters carted bags from the sleigh and tagged them for the appropriate suites. Things perked up pretty quickly behind that desk when the name Georgia Hart came off his lips. Two clerks from a back room suddenly appeared, almost as if they had been lying in wait for a five-star-service ambush. In a matter of minutes, Roland, the bell captain was personally escorting the women to the top floor. Georgia and Donna shared the premiere suite and Lani and Niki were opposite them just down the hall. Cory's room was a floor below on the corner.

Cory tipped the porter and before unpacking scanned his to-do list. The concierge had already informed him downstairs that the two ski instructors, Paolo and Dieter, would meet them at eight thirty the following morning on the front steps. Skis had to be rented. Cory picked up the phone and dialed Georgia's room.

"Yes?" She answered as if she knew the question already.

"It's Cory."

"I know."

"I guess so. I'm the only one around here without an accent."

"Not to them."

Cory laughed. Everything was about perception. He knew it instinctively but enjoyed the idea that Georgia constantly chided him about it. "I'm going to reserve some skis at Maximillians directly across the way. Am I doing this with just the girls or are the big girls planning on skiing as well?

"You'll have all the women to yourself, Sheik Sonne."

"You mean me…and Dieter and Paolo."

"Dieter and Paolo?" Georgia almost laughed.

"Yep. Meeting us tomorrow at eight thirty on the front steps."

"Oh, this should be fun." Cory couldn't tell if she was being serious or cynical.

"The shop closes at five. That's forty minutes from now. I'm going over now to do some reconnaissance. Can you meet me there with the girls in twenty minutes?"

"We'll pick them up along the way."

"Thank you. I'll see you in twenty. That's Maximillians and it's just across the street and down two doors. Are we cool?"

"We're cool. Donna was right about you."

"Donna? I just met the woman what could she possibly know about me?" Georgia pictured his face turning firehouse red. She was doing this to him on purpose.

“She’s a brilliant and insightful woman and can draw a bead on a man in a matter of minutes. She’s rarely wrong.” Georgia goaded him.

Three seconds of silence.

“And?” Cory implored her to continue.

“And what?” Georgia feigned innocence.

“Are you going to tell me what she said about me?”

“No. I’ll see you at Maximillians.” She hung up the phone.

Cory stared at the receiver. What was the handle supposed to say in response to his stupefied incredulity? Deny it. Deny it. Deny it. He tried but couldn’t. Goddamn her; she was flirting with him. If the weekend continued on like this, it would be hell.

There was no Maximillian at Maximillians, only Sasha, a seventeen year old French version of River Phoenix making an all out effort in his off hours to become a ski instructor himself. For the time being, he fitted and tuned skis for the tourists, and worked very patiently with Cory and his brood in trying to find the right skis for the icy conditions and the right boots for foot comfort.

It was Paris all over again. Only this time there were four of them. ‘Isn’t this suit adorable?’ ‘Isn’t that hat too cool?’ ‘Aren’t those gaiters rad?’ ‘I’ve got to have this; I've got to have that.' Put it all together and seemed a perverse Dr. Seuss rhyme from his niece, Suzy Seuss, valley-girl on a Snapple high.

Georgia tried to rein them in but not really. She was more conspirator than monitor, and Donna didn't help as she had no ski gear with her. She was desperate not to be without in light of Sasha's prediction that the mountain would probably be very cold tomorrow. Cory tried to be the facilitator, fetching different sizes, returning the rejects, keeping people's piles separate. More than once Georgia told him to relax. He always responded, "I am relaxed, just organizing."

After three quarters of an hour of renting and buying and a prolonged dallying by both Lani and Niki towards Sasha, they were finally set. The overwhelmed French youth didn't seem to mind too much that it was well past closing. All that attention and a big tip easily made up for his late start on the ski patrol's ritual cocktail hour up the street at the Spindle.

The women took their boots with them back to the hotel and Cory made three separate trips across the plaza with skis and poles until everything was in order at the ski lockers in the basement.

The ladies had long since retired to their suites. The Concierge flagged down Cory with a message from Georgia. "Dinner is at seven, correct? We'll see you in the lobby at 6:50. Georgia. P.S. I've been reading the

German poet Rainer Maria Rilke. I have to get you a copy of this anthology. You'd love it. Just wanted to pass on this quote - '...where can you find a place to keep her, with all the huge strange thoughts coming and going and often staying all night.'"

Cory reread the quote three times before looking up. How much did Georgia really know about him? Was the 'her' in the poem his mother? Was it Georgia? Was it the feminine form of Nature? Did Georgia know how he struggled every night with thoughts of death, of Eli, with nightmares from his childhood, floating, sacred and profane images of his mother, images from the orchard?

The Concierge stood next to him with the look of a carnival barker offering another ring for the toss. "Everything all right, sir?"

He wanted to respond, 'Has everything ever been all right? I should think not in the entire history of civilization. As long as there are those who have and those who want, as long as the powerless fight against their conditions, and abusers flail at loved ones perceived to be enemies, as long as evil has a home and destruction has a suitor, nothing will ever be all right.' But he didn't. He simply quipped as he always did, as everyone always seemed to do, "Fine." 'Despite the dead body I stepped over to answer this phone or make this meeting or attend this party, everything's fine. Don't mind the vomit; it's just God puking all over the cage of our incarcerating lies.' "Everything's just fine," Cory repeated.

Tucked in the corner booth at the back of Chez Helene, the group had merited more than a few curious looks from the elite clientele that could afford to dine at an exclusive restaurant where the menu had no prices. "If you have to ask the price; you're not rich," his mother Becky had once told him. Perhaps this was what Georgia had wanted for herself all along. Perhaps she had settled for a lifestyle where she never had to ask the price - for anything. And in the process was unaware of the great price she was paying to maintain it.

Lani caught Cory staring at Georgia and shot him a conspiratorial look. He had been somewhat surprised when the four women had shown up in the lobby at six fifty-three. They must have been famished; that could be the only explanation for being almost on time. Cory was careful not to mistake the promptness for respect. The restaurant was just up the walk from the Zermatterhoffer, and their table was waiting.

The maitre d' brought the bottle of Firestone Vineyards 1992 Chardonnay Donna had ordered. She had yelped with glee when spotting it on the wine list. They were half way around the world and drinking from a vintage made just up the road from their California homes in the Santa Ynez Valley. Cory found it somewhat odd but enjoyed the way Georgia put up no protest.

Among other strong characteristics of the woman, Donna Nyall knew what she wanted and wanted what she wanted when she wanted it. Regardless of where she was and how inappropriate it may seem to others. Georgia told the story of her friend once returning an entree at a restaurant because it clashed with the perfume of the waitress who was serving her.

Between their being seated and the arrival of the salads, Lani and Niki had managed to name ten reasons why snowboarding was superior to skiing, three of which were really the same reasons worded differently. "Why do you insist in going on and on?" Georgia asked. "You know snowboarding isn't allowed in Zermat; you knew it all along. You should be happy to be out of Krakow for a little while. That was the point." She charged.

"I am. It's just that I miss..." Lani stopped. Whatever the thought was it had vaporized.

"What? What do you miss?" Georgia prodded her.

"I don't know. Daddy." Not the real answer to be sure.

"Oh, sweetie. That's nice. I'd like to know what your first answer was but that was a good recovery." They all laughed. Georgia certainly new her daughter.

"I know what you miss." Niki intoned. She spoke

freely, owing perhaps to her and Lani's frequent and undeterred sipping from Georgia's wine glass. "Sean McDonough's buns." A collective sigh from the four of them, Georgia included.

"He's a hunk, you can bet your bottom dollar. On his bottom." Donna added.

"You think so, Cory?" Georgia asked him from the other side of the booth.

"What, that Sean's a hunk? I suppose." He had to hold himself back. Wouldn't it just shock the skin off their bones to know that only a few nights ago he had kissed the man, held his stiff cock in his own hand? Most likely they wouldn't believe him, accuse him of making it up just to mock them. But oh how true it was. The bi-sexual star on the rise. Cory had a feeling that if Sean were with him at the table, he would have fucked any one of the four, or any two, or any combination. And the following morning, he wouldn't have felt the slightest bit of remorse about doing it, about the consequences of a daughter doing a twosome in a drunken melee with her mother, or how best friends might no longer be best friends having shared the same man, or how a married woman might feel after succumbing in a moment of weakness and then having her moment of passion trivialized by a lecher's insensitivity. That was Sean all right. But these women wouldn't want to have anything to do with that guy. They'd just continue to romanticize this handsome, charismatic actor and revel in the swill of their Cinderella complex, thinking it to be the nectar of the dream come true.

Sean McDonough. A fascinating man worth knocking back a beer with but beyond that? Entropy in the flesh. A three-legged cat trying to bury shit on a frozen pond. Should he warn them? Destroy their fantasy? No, he just smiled and remarked, "Let me put it this way. He has as many intriguing passions as notches on his bedpost. Does this make him more or less interesting?"

The waiter, a short, cue-ball-of-a-man arrived with two hands full of five plates.

Madams, Monsieur, I'm sorry. The Firestone Chardonnay was the last bottle from that vintner. May I suggest something from the Stags Leap Winery, also from California in the Napa Valley?"

"Stags Leap? No thank you. Their vineyards are too far east in the valley where the soil is chalkier and the vintages compensate by leaning far too heavily on the 'berry' side. Georgia, what do you think? French?"

Georgia leaned over and kissed her friend on the cheek. "Donna. I've missed you."

"Oh, dearest. I've missed you, too."

The waiter cleared his throat. Donna returned her attention to him. "Play the sommelier, my good man. We've given you are entrée choices. We shall live by your selection."

The waiter bowed at the waist. "Very good."

When he was out of earshot Donna whispered to the table. "Or die by it." Snobbery like this never ceased to amuse Georgia. Innocent enough from a woman with a true heart of gold. Forgiving these peccadilloes was easy when one considered that she'd personally raised over two million dollars for Aids Project Los Angeles and was on the board of director's at Cedars Sinai hospital.

"I'm sure you're right about Sean, Cory. But he is marvelous at what he does. I'm really impressed by his craft and the performance he's turning out in this movie. Andrew's beside himself with delight at how well it's going." Georgia said.

"Always so diplomatic, G." Donna added. "Cory, seeing as you're surrounded by women and do not run the risk of embarrassment by any of your own tribe, specifically - men, I wonder if you might give me an honest answer to a probing question?"

"As long as refusing to answer is also an option."

"Fair enough. Though it's not about you, per se. It's about men in general. Why is it that the typical, inexorably predictable behavior of a male is that no matter how much or how good he is getting it in a relationship, he will inevitably stray?" As if bracing for a harsh answer to her question, Donna took a long, last swig of her Firestone Chardonnay. "Goodbye Santa

Ynez Valley; hello, who knows."

Cory took a long pause. He could not look at Georgia, and Lani's eyes always seemed to possess something akin to a sinister glow. This was going to be a difficult answer but something compelled him to speak. A feeling of liberation washed over him as if this were confession and the four women at the table a sort of voluptuous priesthood

"This is the truth. I'm not trying to rationalize anything by saying this but you have to understand what happens to us physiologically. I can almost guarantee it's a Y chromosome thing. A man sees a good looking woman, a great pair of tits, a tight ass, and sees it with his eyes which are directly linked with an instinctive part of his brain that thinks 'procreate' or 'genetically desirable female' or whatever you want to call it but it is 'sex.' This reaction happens before the rational part of his brain can chime in with the analytical information such as: I've forsworn sex with any females other than my mate, I made a vow, I don't want to get the shit kicked out of me by her gorilla boyfriend, etc. These are all the thinking reactions. And then there are all sorts of sociological considerations that get heaped on top of that: having her would require social contact, do I have the money to date her, would she even go out with me? All this analytical strategy eventually leads you to the course of action or inaction. For men who've developed the strategy for coping with the reaction it's not so difficult. Those that are less adept at coping give in. But you've got to remember that the libido is being bombarded by this stimulus all day, all night - TV, ads, girls in shorts and halter tops on hot summer days, which in California is all year long, probably why we lead the nation in infidelity according to the reports."

"Ah, the old 'We just can't help ourselves' explanation." Cory's comments seemed to have hit Donna's soft spot.

"I could have summed it up like that but I tried to be more thorough. The reaction is unavoidable. It's there. It's real. It makes the blood rush, the gonads tingle. That's human nature. But what matters is how men deal with the reaction. That's where the trouble starts, with the brain, not the penis."

"So what you're saying is that every man is going to have this response, we just have to accept it and hope that he values his relationship more than acting upon his instincts?" Donna asked.

"Yes. I suppose."

The waiter arrived with the wine and turned the label to Donna for inspection. "Chateau Carbonneau. Very fine. I think you'll find it very reminiscent of the Firestone, madam."

Donna raised her glass for the tasting and gave a mock toast, "To men. Can't live with them; can't skin 'em for a handbag either." Her cheeks collapsed as she chewed the wine and gave it a thorough swish across her tongue before swallowing. "Oooh, that's very nice. You done good, Jacko. Pour away."

Any delight the waiter had found in being allowed to choose the wine disappeared after being addressed as Jacko. Nevertheless, he filled the glasses expertly.

Cory's headshake and internal smirk converged with Georgia's steely gaze. Her lips did not move; they betrayed no syllables. And yet, in her stillness, in her galvanized glance, she was telling him something.

CHAPTER FORTY-EIGHT

Something about the sound of a ski carving a long s-turn in the snow pacified Cory. It was one of the first things he fell in love with when he had taken up the sport as an adult. No fan of the cold, he had to overcome a few pet peeves before he could give in to the smooth seduction of the rhythm and the surrender to gravity that made skiing so exhilarating. He'd gotten pretty good at it in a naturally athletic sort of way. But nothing like Dieter and Paolo.

The two instructors would take turns at the front and back of the line, advising, chatting, cracking unfunny jokes they'd probably told a thousand time, skiing backwards just to show off. The clear skies and the relative warmth of this middle winter day made the experience all that much more pleasurable.

Capping a spine of jagged mountains separated by over twelve miles of glacier was the mighty Matterhorn. One side of the ridge slid down into Switzerland the other into Italy. Eggs and bratwurst for breakfast in Zermat; calzone and Chianti for lunch in Monte Rosa.

The American, by way of Krakow, quintet spent the better part of the morning skiing the bottom third of the glacier on the Swiss side and getting the rust out. Hardly a group Dieter could take back to the steep moguls of Rifflehap Ridge but nobody was hugging the hill or riding their tails either. All in all a high intermediate level group, nobody much better or worse than the next.

Lani and Niki, bent on impressing the suave mountain guides constantly displayed their daring and waited with feigned impatience at the end of the runs for the adults to catch up. Cory didn't mind hanging back with Georgia. Donna, clearly the best skier of their group, cruised along giggling and grateful to be away from the boardroom.

A gondola up to Promontory Point spilled them out onto a steeper face. Paolo split the group in two. From what he'd seen, Lani and Cory were the two most aggressive, vigorous skiers. He left them to Dieter while having Niki, Georgia and Donna follow him down the groomed face of Sassy Feel.

After a small traverse, Dieter pointed out the three prominent ridges of Tasch's Stairs, jumping off points caused by natural folds in the mountainside. "If you stay to the right, it's much smoother but you can get much air under yours skis along the left side as you can see."

"Are you a jumper?" Cory asked Lani.

"Are you?"

"Maybe when I was your age. Taken too many falls since then." Cory returned.

"Well, I am my age." Lani pivoted quickly on her Rossignol 4S's and dropped over the lip onto the run. Dieter looked at Cory and motioned for him to follow.

"Why did I know she would do this?" And he was gone. Dieter brought up the rear, staying more to the middle of the run and making fewer turns to facilitate his speed. He may have started after them but he would most likely be at the bottom when they finished.

Lani took a few quick turns to slow herself down before hitting the first of the three launching pads. Cory could see her ahead of him. She spread her arms to her side and got mildly airborne before disappearing back down onto Tasch's second stair. Cory followed, instantly reminded of the exhilaration of weightlessness that came from speed and trajectory. "Whatever you do, don't lean back." He could still hear Theresa, the sexy and tenacious UCLA collegiate champ, saying before she'd

bolt off. And he didn't; he stayed right over his skis and landed cleanly.

Seemed he and Lani had the same idea. They'd enjoyed their first jump so much they decided to carry their speed a little more into the second lip. This time, she sailed over the edge, her long blonde hair trailing her like a paper Chinese banner, held back from her face by a thick, magenta Bogner headband.

Dieter sped by him on the second slope, tucked like a downhill racer. He hit the ridge in the middle at what must have been fifty miles an hour and sailed out, not up. Cory caught this out of the corner of his eye as he prepared to jettison himself from the icy hillside again.

Flying. It was like flying. Even though he was probably less than three feet off the ground and for less than four seconds, he still fancied himself a gortex-feathered bird with imaginary wings that spread from the sides of his body out to the shaft of his ski poles. He could definitely get into this.

The steepness of the shorter third face leading to the last lip was more severe. When Cory landed, fear set in. This could get gnarly. He looked down at Lani. He could tell from her quick, carving turns, almost as severe as hockey stops, that all this newly acquired speed was a little too much for her as well, and as she launched herself over the last ridge he saw her flail with her arms as her skis spread and her body careened left. No way she'd get

a smooth landing out of that.

Cory cut his speed drastically and eased himself over the crest. Lani had wiped out all right. A yard sale in skiing terminology - poles and skies spread to all points of the compass, and her body was just sliding to a stop as she came into view. Dieter had stopped fifty meters down the hill and looked up just in time to see Cory stop next to Lani.

"Are you all right?" Cory asked, concerned.

Lani hesitated, taking stock of her bones. "I think so. I landed hard on my left knee but nothing's agonizing."

"Except watching you."

"Oh, shut up. Okay, I bailed."

Cory reached behind him for one of her poles and a ski. Dieter watched from down the hill and yelled up. "Do you need some help?"

"No!" Lani bellowed back quickly, wounded pride sprawled out on crunchy snow. She looked up at Cory, breathing over her, setting her pole and ski down at her side.

"I'll get the other one." Cory slid his skis down the slope ten feet then sidestepped back up the mountain with her second ski and pole. Lani made an attempt at getting up.

"Ahh!" She fell back to the snow and grabbed her left knee.

"No, don't be grabbing your knee. That's not a good sign."

"It's not excruciating but I definitely banged it." Lani tried to stand again, this time shoving hard off the snow. Cory held out his pole and she grabbed it to steady herself upright.

"There we go. Can you put any pressure on it?"

Lani drover her boot heel into the snow. "A little."

Dieter had been sidestepping his way up the hill and was half way to them. "Everything okay here or no?"

Cory shouted back. "A little trouble with her left knee." He turned to Lani. "Want me to help you on with your skis?"

Lani nodded. Cory placed them parallel in the snow uphill from her. She leaned on his shoulder and snapped her right boot into the binding. "There's one." Cory said.

He whacked the snow off her left boot as she prepared to insert it into the other ski. She was leaning heavily on him nearly hyperventilating in her efforts to lock in. "Keep taking deep breaths, Lani."

"Always with the breathing with you. You should have that tattooed to you forehead."

"Hey, just because you can't ski don't blame it on me." Finally the left boot snapped in.

“Ouch!” There was definitely trauma in the joint somewhere. She slugged Cory’s shoulder. “I can too ski.”

Dieter had arrived. “You think you can ski?” He asked.

Cory laughed. “All evidence to the contrary.”

Lani grabbed her poles, slipped her hands through the straps and pushed off for a turn down the slope. She hadn’t swished five feet from them when she fell again. This time the skis stayed on. “Owww!” This time the cry was more from frustration than searing pain. Dieter pulled her up with his pole.

“I think we should get you down to the gondola house and take a look at your knee. I’ll ski you down.”

Dieter swung around to her downhill leg, a little in front, then spread his skis wide, placing his right ski on the outside of her right ski and his left outside of her left. “Hand me your poles and scoot in to my back. Grab me around the waist and see if you can glide with me down the hill, you don’t have to put any pressure on your skis, just try to keep them in line with mine as we snowplow.”

Down the mountain they went, two bodies pressed together, two sets of skis wedging long slow turns and criss-crossing the slope. Luckily there were no bumps and a straight shot to the gondola house.

After everybody met up at the lunch spot and the initial worry had subsided, Cory and Dieter set about examining the knee. Cory had learned years ago how to manipulate a knee to search for signs of anterior cruciate ligament, collateral ligament or meniscus damage. Lani removed her boot and set her knee at a ninety degree angle on the bench. Cory sat on the top of her foot, grabbed the back portion of her calve, stabilized her joint then pulled towards him. The "drawer" test, Dr. Mandelbaum had called it, and he'd shown it to him over and over until he felt confident that Cory grasped the feel of the procedure.

"The joint's solid. Probably just a contusion or some soft tissue damage. But, if your smart, it's the end of your skiing for today."

"Are you in a lot of pain, honey?" Georgia asked.

"No. It throbs a little." Lani answered.

"Probably best to elevate it, ice it and take an anti-inflammatory, right away."

"You can take this gondola all the way to the bottom; it is only a hundred meters up from the Zermatterhoffer." Paolo informed them.

"Maybe we should just call it a day." Donna offered.

"No, no. You guys keep going. Donna, it's your vacation. You should ski. And, Niki, this will probably be our only chance to ski this season. I'll be all right." Lani turned to Cory and flashed him her best doe-eyed look. He recognized the familiar plea, the one where the

woman expects Time to roll back and where she waits for the chivalrous male to volunteer what is ethically required of him - assistance in a time of distress.

"I'll go back to the hotel with her. You gals go ahead and enjoy the rest of the day." Cory said.

"No, we can all go in."

"No, please, mom. You guys stay. It's the Alps, and the condition are awesome. Dieter, Paolo, back me up here."

"She's right. It's quite beautiful today, unusually warm and sunny for February." Paolo added.

"See. You must ski. If Cory will help me back to the hotel I'll be fine."

"Cory, is that okay with you?" Georgia asked.

"No problem."

"You can lock your skis and poles right here in the gondola house and just come up in your boots tomorrow if you're up to it." Dieter interjected enthusiastically.

"Okay. We'll see you somewhere around four of four thirty."

Georgia hugged her daughter.

Dieter returned after securing both their skis and poles and handed Cory the locker keys. "See you tomorrow, Lani, Cory."

Niki kissed her friend on the cheek. "Which one do you think is cuter?" she asked in a whisper.

Lani returned the kiss and the whisper, "They're

both 'hotties' but for a fling, I say go Italian." They giggled, true to the species of "animus teenagerous".

Georgia took Cory aside. "If you need anything…"

Cory cut her off. "She'll be fine."

"It's not her I'm worried about."

Cory cocked his head. "What?"

"Nothing. We'll see you later." Lani leaned on Cory for support as they hobbled to the gondola.

Donna leaned into Georgia's ear. "Reminds me of me in my younger days."

"What? Accident prone?" Georgia asked, knowing full well she meant something else.

"No, plotting for attention." Donna laughed.

Georgia watched her daughter in the arms of her trainer. Hers was a forced laugh measured to dilute the pang of jealousy that shot through her heart.

CHAPTER FORTY-NINE

They'd been in Zermat less than twenty-four hours yet Lani and Niki had managed to make this hotel room uniquely their own - clothes strewn recklessly, make-up and toilet cases emptied, their contents scattered across the bathroom counter, the night stand, a chair, bits and pieces of trash here and there, a Peanut M&M's wrapper, a USA today sectioned out, used tissues, mascara-blackened cotton swabs and more.

Cory put Lani on the edge of the bed then rummaged through the closet for a plastic laundry bag. "I'm going to get some ice. Do you have any Advil or Aleve?"

"In the bathroom."

“Good. Take three. I’ll be right back.”

Returning from the hallway with three handfuls of ice choked into the corner of the over-sized laundry bag, Cory had a sudden instinct that the closed bathroom door was about to reveal something unexpected.

Two seconds later he instantly regretted being right. Lani appeared, having shed her ski outfit and donned a thin white T-shirt with a USC Trojans inscription. She walked towards him with much less of a limp, the hem of her shirt pushed just high enough by her advancing thighs to display the tight blonde curls of her well groomed pubic hair. No underwear. Cory balked.

The ice bag dangled from his hand like a plucked chicken. “Tell me something?” Cory asked.

“Anything.” Lani sidled up to him and placed her hand between his pecs, feeling the indentation with her fingertips.

“Is your knee hurt at all?”

“A little.” Lani’s hand made its way down Cory’s torso, descending over the contours of his abdomen. She stared at the snap of his stretch pants; he stared at her. She was not stopping there.

Cory tugged gently on the back of her hair, craning her neck up towards his face. “You’re a bad girl; you know that?” As he moved in to kiss her, he swung the ice bag around pressing it firmly between her bare buns. She jumped back with a start.

"You bastard."

"You know you deserved it." He tossed the ice onto the bed and turned to leave. As if miraculously cured, Lani leaped on Cory's back, her momentum carrying the two of them onto the bed. She turned him over on his back and straddled him with her legs. Caught by such a wave of surprise, Cory resisted very little and found himself in a fit of laughter.

"Got you now." Lani had pinned his arms out to the side and began rubbing her pussy along the seam of his ski pants.

"What are you doing?" Cory looked down to her hips. The hanging T-shirt concealed his vision but there was no doubt about what he felt. He grew instantly hard.

"Waking you up. Somebody wants to play." She reached down and grabbed his cock through the fabric.

When he felt her hand on him, he knew in an instant what he should do. He should end this little tease right then and there. But he did not move, and every second that he remained still convinced Lani even more that she could indeed take what she had strategically planned to take. She slowed her movements down, reveling now in the thrill of riding his erection.

It felt so good, the swelling of his head. His rim flaring as each stroke of her luscious triangle sent shudders of pleasure into the center of his loins. Was there any greater feeling of concentration than the utter diligence of a cock teased hard? The walls could fall away, the sun break through and bake his naked form and still he would lay there, congealed to the sweating spot where a hot, wet and willing woman transfixed him. There was only one thing that could save him now - Reason. And it was knocking at the door.

Cory opened it.

Of course he could fuck her. Of course he would enjoy it and not just because it had been a while since he'd been laid. She was, after all, a sexy sixteen year old going on twenty-two with a baby Venus body and a tight box no doubt. No virgin, more than likely, but still fresh. A great place to explode.

But - and there were many "buts" - Cory knew as he heard the word in his head that there would be no overcoming the objections and that there would be no coitus.

But she's just a kid.

But she was not to be trusted in matters of birth control.

But she was his client, technically, and he swore off that behavior many years ago when Janet Velasquez flipped out and slashed his tires after he put an end to their training/sexual relationship.

But this would simply be about conquest, and although the idea of fucking the daughter of the mother whom he really desired presented some kind of perverse attraction for him, the grave possibility that it would turn Georgia against him was simply too much to bear.

But giving Lani the power of knowing her seduction had been successful would reduce him in her eyes and he'd never be able to recover the upper hand. Judging by her past behaviors she would laud it over him forever. The pussy was alluring…

…but the sacrifice far too great.

At any other time in his life, he would have succumbed, circumstances be damned. But now there was Georgia. Now, regardless of whether it was reciprocated or not, there was love. Yes, he could admit it to himself now. A nascent creature had emerged from the swamp of his heart, unrecognizable, malformed but bleating out one requisite refrain - Georgia Hart. He was in love with Georgia Hart.

All this went through Cory's head in a split second as Lani's hips continued to grind on his and her mouth began its descent toward his lips for the meal would never eat.

Whatever advantage Lani believed she held on Cory by straddling his body and continuing to pin his arms disappeared in a nanosecond. Cory's whole body bolted upright, throwing Lani onto her back with the ice bag spreading cold between her shoulder blades.

She rolled off the bed.

Cory was already standing by the door.

Her eyes dropped quickly to his distended pants; he made no move to hide his cock, so hard its tip emerged from the waistband of his stretch pants. Far from feeling embarrassed, Cory regained control of the sensation that so often accompanied his sexual encounters - his dominance. Her hunger for him and his denial of it put him right where he wanted to be. He had the thing, in all its swollen glory. The thing Lani wanted. But he did not have the inclination.

Cory's voice resonated low and steady. "If I were you, I'd fake a limp at dinner tonight."

"I might just tell her it happened anyway," Lani threatened.

"One of the things I like about your mother is that she's damn smart. She'd get to the truth eventually. But go ahead, open up that Pandora's box. I've got a gut feeling she's doubted your word before."

Lani picked up the ice bag and heaved it. With her aim wildly off to the right, it whizzed past an unmoving Cory who said nothing.

"I don't know what fantasies you have in your head concerning my mother but you're just fooling yourself." Cory walked silently to the door. "You will never be more than her employee. You work for her, remember? I don't care how good looking you are or if you're the best fucking trainer in the world."

Cory paused at the door and turned to address

her one last time. "I know what I am, Lani. Do you?"

The door shut firmly behind him. Lani dropped into a chair, the wetness on the bottom of her thighs sticking to the sportspage. "I had him," she whispered to herself then replayed the events in her mind, trying to figure out what she did wrong - for the next time.

CHAPTER FIFTY

All during dinner Georgia had see-sawed looks between a stoic Cory and an unusually reticent Lani. Donna had been keeping the conversational ball in play with amusing ski anecdotes, both hers and heard about, and Niki was still recovering from her breath-taking infatuation of Paolo.

They dined at Albion, the most exclusive and elegant restaurant in Zermat. Not a word about the shenanigans of the afternoon had seeped out of Lani's mouth and she had limped dutifully to the bistro. Pheasant, venison, duck pizza, gorgonzola gnocchi and pasta a la Siciliana, foie-gras and sliced garlic and rosemary baguettes, assorted greens with a raspberry red wine vinaigrette dressing, and a special treat, a favorite of Donna's, Veuve Clicquot champagne. The meal had been a feast. Georgia had only a nibble from the various entrees and a gigantic plate of fresh vegetables with balsamic vinegar. Still had those concentration camp scenes to shoot. She could rationalize taking the time off to ski but would never jeopardize her appearance on screen, even if just one little indiscretion at the dinner table would not set her back much.

By the time dessert came around, everyone was so full and so exhausted that by mutual consent the check was requested and not the world famous chocolate soufflé.

Donna picked up the bill. "Georgia, I know you have more money than God but I insist. I already feel like a parasite, a little tick bird if you will, feeding off the wealthy rhino who goes by the name of Andrew Goldman."

"Oh, please. Spare us your Masters in Fine Arts allusions." Georgia moaned.

Stuffed to the gills and slightly buzzed, they stumbled out of the Albion and up the cobbled stones toward the majestic Zermatterhoffer. Georgia walked with her subdued daughter, assisting her. "You okay, baby?"

Lani nodded. "Yeah, just tired."

They stopped at the front steps. "You girls can go

on up but I think I'd like to take a walk. Donna? Cory? Care to join me?"

Donna smiled. Not the bird that got the worm but the one that watched the cat creep up on an unsuspecting canary. "Not me. I'm going to soak in the tub."

"Cory?" Georgia asked, innocently.

"Sure. I didn't get quite the workout you guys did." A triple-layered, Mississippi molasses silence followed Cory's remark. It was clear everyone had suspected something was not quite on the up and up between Cory and Lani. He knew that somewhere along the line he'd have to set the record straight. If he brought it up, it would make him seem defensive and guilty. So he prayed for outside vindication.

They said their goodnights, and soon Cory and Georgia were hiking up the ten thousand steps out of the valley village to the cold and quiet mountainside.

A thousand words paraded through his head; their assembled questions were legion. But Cory did not speak. He was not going to be the first to break the silence. Unsure of exactly what her motivation could have been for inviting him, he would let her dictate their conversation or their quiet.

The higher they climbed, the darker it got until the light of the town was little more than a luminescent puddle skirting the hem of two steep, alpine sides. The steps became a baffle against which the vibrations of buzzing bars and the mumblings of street drunks all but vanished.

Only once were they passed. By a rapturous couple whose tender passions seemed to float them down the path. Cory could see their smiles in the half-moon light but not their feet which swept them along as if there were no ground.

At a waist high split rail laid out in half a hexagon, they stopped. Between long, visible exhales she finally spoke. “I already know what happened.”

Cory was stunned but not going to give anything up. “So many talents. A mind-reader as well?” The thoughts of how to address the Lani issue had been on his mind since they left the Zermatterhoffer.

“I know my daughter. But, you…Did you?” She asked a dangerous question with as little reproach as possible. But it was still there in the gravity of her syllables. In that one moment he was exceedingly grateful that he resisted for he knew that he could tell her the truth and that she would believe him.

“She made a full frontal assault, and I’m not used to saying no to such flattery but, no, I didn’t. I couldn’t do that to you, Georgia. That doesn’t mean you might hear differently from your daughter, however.”

“No, I’m sure she’s capable of that kind of treachery but I believe you.” She turned to the mountains and let out a burdened sigh.

"Something wrong?" Cory asked.

No answer.

"I'm no psychologist," Cory continued, "So forgive me if this is totally inappropriate but is it natural at this age for daughters to compete with their mothers like this?"

"I suppose, to a degree. But she's very underhanded, Lani, and very savvy."

"Oh, she's dangerous all right. I feel sorry for the bastards who'll fall head over heels for her then wage the bloody war of trying to keep her happy."

Georgia looked at Cory as if he'd just trampled her rosebushes. Then the look faded into one of complicity. "No, you're probably right."

"Hey, she's pretty, sexy even and smart as a whip, and she's got the two of you for parents. The road is going to be littered with corpses." They laughed. "It must be tough, you give birth to this person, try your damnedest to raise them right and then the day comes when it's really out of your hands. They're gonna sink or swim one way or the other without you. Nothing you can do about it."

"I just don't know if I'm ready to lose a daughter."

"Is that it or is it maybe you see in her the girl you were twenty years ago?" Cory regretted saying it as soon as it came out of his mouth but he had, in fact, been thinking about it and either the wine or the cold mountain air just stripped it from his tongue.

Georgia spoke forcefully, “No, she may look like me and share some of my traits but Lani is an entirely different creature on the inside. She feels so little remorse for her transgressions and operates with such a superior attitude. She knows how to manipulate and mold people to get what she wants, and she usually gets it. I was never like that. I may have had an air of superiority about me when I was young but it was only to mask my fragile ego. Lani’s ego is profoundly secure, to the core, but as a person, she’s gravely unsympathetic.”

It was at this point that Cory politely bowed out. Clearly, Georgia’s relationship with her daughter was troubling her, and he could offer no insight. His observations about her were culled from two month’s experience, and there seemed little he could tell her that she didn’t already know. He was merely thankful to have escaped her advances and avoided being a pawn in a twisted mother-daughter game.

He decided to change the subject. “Do you believe in God?”

“Yes,” she answered, grateful for the distraction. “I’m not religious but I believe in a Divine Being. And you?”

“Well, I got my Roman Catholic dose of it growing up but haven’t had much use for the notion as an adult.

But on a night like this, when I see the stars so brilliant and everything, it's hard not to wonder about it. I told you that I read a lot of periodicals, magazines, etc. And I find myself quite often actively seeking out articles, information on the origin of the universe and God as a scientific explanation. So something in me compels me to find out."

"I think that's just being human, you know, wondering about your place in the world, what meaning your life is supposed to have. Come up with any theories?" Georgia's Emmy-winning smile comforted him; he knew she wouldn't scoff at his ideas and so he offered them.

"All evidence points to the validity of the Big Bang as the beginning of the universe, and the beginning of Time. All life, all movement, all matter were generated from the Big Bang, right? That's when everything started changing at the most accelerated pace, and measuring change is the only way to know for sure what happened. But what about before the Big Bang? Everything was stasis, you know, the same. All things were the same - uniformity. All Hydrogen they tell us. An entire universe consisting of nothing but the simplest, elementary compound, the first atom with a nucleus consisting of a single proton with a positive electrical charge and a single electron bearing a negative electrical charge orbiting around it."

Cory's enthusiasm gained momentum the further into the explanation he got. Georgia watched with fascination as his hands made tiny gestures and tried to shape the ideas in the air in front of him. "That was it, the whole universe was these type of atoms, doing their atomic thing until suddenly, at one creative moment, one of those electrons broke away from its pattern and collided with the atom next to it to make helium from hydrogen. That set off a chain reaction that made the then static universe of hydrogen into an explosion of such magnitude we can't even grasp it. The chain reaction, the explosion, the wheels in motion of all change – Creation with a big 'C.' And it was all brought about in this most infinitesimal way, by this tiny little electron on an atom not doing what it was supposed to do to maintain stasis. I believe that that moment, the beginning of Time, that moment was God. God is the Decision-To-Be."

"You expect me to believe you came up with this all by yourself."

"Hey, I swear. This opinion's been forming for years in the back of my head."

"Well, it's certainly a fascinating notion, and I so loved the way you explained it, spittle and all."

"Sorry. I get carried away."

"God is the decision to be. Hmmm. Esoteric but I don't disagree."

"Now I'm no scholar but they did make me read Shakespeare when I was I high school, and every idiot knows old Willie is probably the most famous writer of all time. Do you think it's just coincidence that the most famous quote from the most famous writer of all time is, 'To Be or Not to Be? That is the question.'?"

"Now I think you're reaching, Cory." Georgia pulled her jacket collar tight around her neck.

"Maybe. Are you getting cold? Do you want to head back down?"

"No. This is nice. So peaceful. So punctuated with crazy notions about God." She poked his ribs as she moved closer to him. For warmth he thought, strictly for warmth.

"Well, I've run off at the mouth. You tell me something. Tell me what that quote meant on the note you gave me this evening."

"Rilke? Oh, Cory. I adore this man's writing. You've got to read it."

"I will."

"Apparently Rilke was Anna Kamenski's favorite poet but she was very conflicted about it because he was a German. But he wasn't her contemporary; he wrote at the turn of the century through the First World War."

"I can imagine that didn't go over well with her own people."

"From what I understand it wasn't any reason to

alienate her. Being a female professor was more alarming to them than anything else. One thing about the Jews, though, is they have a lot of respect for scholarship and they study even that which they despise in an effort to either better understand it or to undermine it."

Cory pulled the note from his pocket and read it back to her, "'Where can you find a place to keep her, with all the huge strange thoughts inside you going and coming and often staying all night?'"

"It's an amazing poem, from his 'Elegies.' It starts off talking about how the springtime needed you, a star waited for you to notice, a wave rolled toward you. All these beautiful images of Nature, with a capital 'N,' that when they are glimpsed touch off a deeper longing in us. Rilke brings us into such intimacy with that deeper hunger then peels off layers of the self and exposing us again to the core – a sort of poverty of raw longing. It's not important what the thoughts are, if you're even reading Rilke, you know what the thoughts are, they are the ones that continue to lead you towards answers, bringing more questions and more sorrow with them. In essence, they never go away at all, they stay all night. We all have them. I suppose all our life is really about is how we handle them."

"G, with all this around you, everything you have, you make life sound so depressing."

"Do you find life depressing?" She asked matter-of-factly.

"I suppose, sometimes. But I don't have what you have."

"Don't be fooled by the material. Worldly 'things' can be acquired but they seldom change the essential things inside. Look at me, I have everything, and yet still, I have this tremendous longing. What can it be? Why?"

"What does Rilke say?"

"I think what makes him extraordinary is that he doesn't speak from the middle of life. The poems seem to have been written from a great depth within himself and they whisper in our innermost ear, hypnotically, insinuating us towards the same depth in ourselves. I was reading in the biography notes that when Rilke was dying in 1926, he received a letter from the young Russian poet named Marina Tsvetayana in which she said that he was not the poet she loved most but that he <u>was</u> Poetry itself. I think that the voice of Rilke calling us to that deeper place within ourselves is what people mean by poetry."

"But how does this address the longing you were talking about? I mean when you read someone who is brilliant and taking you to that place, what purpose does it serve to go there? You seem to be saying it only depresses you."

"This is true. I have been tormented by this inner emptiness my whole life. The issue of abandonment as a child, of not belonging as a hauli girl raised among Hawaiians, I never had a sense of myself. Probably why I so desperately wanted to be an actress. When I study the emotional depths of these characters, I can get lost there, and I am closer, no, perhaps farther away from the inner emptiness, I don't know. When I am in the process, I am moving and doing and not sad and longing. This is why I have worked so much and so incessantly. I suppose it's the special gift that musicians have as well, as they play and play, the vibrations shudder them away from these longings, these realizations, the despair."

"It's hard, isn't it? You think back on your life or look out at the world and see so much pain and injustice and it just rakes through your heart; doesn't it?"

"True."

A muffled giggle came from up the darkened path. A pack of energetic youths tramped down the steps speaking demonstrative Italian. They huddled around a middle-aged priest whose white collar was barely visible under his winter coat and gave an ebullient "Buona notte" as they passed.

Cory spoke. "You think they were talking about God as well?"

"The whole world is talking about God and God's laws. Too bad more of them aren't following them. You know, getting back to your notion about God, Rilke was heavily influenced by the writing of Nietzsche. And it was Nietzsche who defined a whole era in philosophical thought, especially concerning spirituality. He called that yearning place that Rilke had already hollowed out in himself 'the death of God.' Interesting way of putting it; don't you think?"

"So the longing that you have, that we find in our deepest, darkest place inside us is really the longing for God?"

"Or the mourning of his death. I'm not sure I agree with Nietzsche but he makes some pretty persuasive arguments."

"I have a question for you?" Cory's schoolboy charm lit up his face.

"Yes?"

"Was this guy ever in love? Don't a lot of poets believe that love has the power to save us from these kinds of circumstances?"

"Good question. I think a lot of them do. But you'll find most poets write 'about' feelings. Rilke wanted to transcend that, and did, by making us feel what he felt. He wrote what he called his Object Poems, or Thing Poems, sometimes they are called. These poems throw the focus from the lyrical speaker of the poem and onto the thing seen. And, to answer your question, these poems came around the time that he fell in love with Lou

Andreas-Salome, who, ironically, spurned Nietzsche's marriage proposal which lead to his derangement later on. She was older and a very talented writer herself. She clearly shaped the young poet's life. They went on to become associates of Sigmund Freud. This woman had quite an influence on some of the most brilliant men of the early twentieth century."

"A woman after your own heart?" Cory interrupted.

"I wish. She was a gargantuan mind. I'm afforded the opportunity to meet all these great people because of being a movie star or because of Andrew. Not because I have anything real to contribute."

"Oh come on. Don't sell yourself short."

"Well, it's true." She turned away from him.

Cory grabbed her by both arms and turned her back to him. Her self-deprecating remarks made him angry, and he wanted to shake her to wake her up, let her know that she was to be admired not scorned. But before he could speak he noticed a single tear liberating itself from the corner of her left eye, and in that moment he wanted more than anything else in the world to kiss her. From where she stood, grasped in his hands at arms lengths, it seemed a continent divided their bodies. The ache to embrace her, to bridge the gap overwhelmed him.

Georgia looked into Cory's eyes. They were thinking the same thought, holding back the same flood.

Sandbags of the heart she had once read about moments like these. She understood it now more than ever. Her stomach dropped to her knees, and she felt the tear begin its descent along the inside of her cheek but she did not move her hand to wipe it. Instead, she lifted that hand towards Cory's face, fixed on hers, and caressed it with the back of her folded fingers.

This was not about sex, this desire that thundered him. It occurred to him in the millisecond it takes to register a thought that he would give up every fuck he'd ever had to hold this married woman in his arms and have her return the embrace with equal ardor, with no regrets. Cory knew he should not fall into her expectant mouth but reason deserted him and he could not stop himself. He moved his head forward, toward hers closing the gap between them by only inches every second, giving her plenty of time to resist, to stop him.

And she did. He had come half way through the cold air between them, half way around the world. The slightest pressure form her hand stopped the blissful arc downward into her lips. So gentle. So serene. So different from the way he had stopped Lani only hours before.

No words. Just the two of them, inches apart. Holding the moment, as if it were the last note from the turntable that faded now into tiny vibrations ebbing away. Each one of them waiting, not wanting to change their dangerous footing on a forbidden precipice. It would be so easy to fall. That mesmerizing fifteen inches that centers on the eyes, allows the face to become an entire landscape in which can be found the river, the wood, the mountain, and the blue sky. Cory was dying inside, as close to dying as he'd ever been, even counting the incident at the trestle bridge, even through the harshest of Eli's beatings. He was dying the death of the ball turret gunner who can see everything from his glass cage but with strict orders not to fire, impotent, able to protect nothing, unable to prevent anything.

Georgia had hovered long enough on the high wire of passion denied. She could endure the sweet torture no longer, removed her hand and left with brisk strides down the flagstones that slapped out a clear message, 'Please don't follow me.'

Cory's face reacquainted with the cold. He watched the back of her head shrink away from him. In one thieving second, thinking only of what was gone, he forgot about God, the universe, Rilke and Nietzsche, he forgot about the tear on Georgia's cheek and her hand on his face, and then, most horrible of all, with only her flowing hair throwing off light he forgot what she looked like. It was as if he could no longer see.

CHAPTER FIFTY-ONE

Fortunately, for the Pillar of Salt crew, a welcome reprieve from the Saturday morning snow allowed them to move equipment trucks up into the main quad of Wawel castle with very little misery. But there was still the a wind chill factor near zero degrees. At least work meant movement and movement meant warmth. In a way, this freezing day was perfect for intense manual labor.

Andrew stood with Yuri, admiring the dusting of fresh powder that would give their establishing shots of the castle courtyard a haunting beauty. "This is going to work beautifully, my friend," Andrew was beyond pleased, almost giddy.

"You know me, until it's on film it's still a sickening worry to me." Yuri remarked.

Andrew grabbed his brilliant director of photography by the shoulders. "I understand your worry but listen to me. Nothing can stop this film from making its mark in history. Do you hear me? Nothing. Every other film I have made means nothing to me now. This one, this horrifyingly brilliant tale will be the artistic exclamation point on my career. I will make it so."

Yuri smiled in agreement but deep inside he worried about such bravura. There was something else Andrew Goldman was telling him between the boundless optimism and the unchecked boasts. Something profoundly frightening in and of itself.

As Andrew paced the courtyard, his head buzzing with ideas about shot composition, he became consumed with the fight against his own tears. Over the past months, he had managed to keep himself so busy with the details of the movie that he hadn't the time to commiserate. Clearing his eyes and raising his lens to them, he focused on the exterior of the second floor residential wing and framed the image of Hans Frank's bedroom window. He could already envision the slow tracking shot from below of the bloodthirsty governor-who-would-be-king staring out at his domain through the wind-driven snowfall whose icy crystals formed no colder a bond than the blood that ran through his veins. He thought about Frank the man, about his blood, about the blood he had spilled on these very stones of the courtyard near the execution wall, about blood itself, the life-sustaining force, but what was really pumping through his mind were anxious thoughts about the sickness running through his own veins. The tears he staved off were for his own mortality. In a moment of weakness, of indulgent self-pity, he was discarding the suffering of the myriad that had died here in Krakow and crying for himself. For he was dying, and it would not be long before he too would join the souls of the deceased. Only one other person in this world new of his condition, Georgia, and he was losing her to a young, able-bodied trainer that he'd made the egregious mistake of hiring for his understanding yet cunning wife.

"Andrew? Andrew?" Yuri had called his name five times as he and Peter walked toward the director but Andrew had not heard. Yuri finally laid his hand upon Andrew's shoulder from behind and startled him from his reverie. "Andrew, are you all right?"

"I can see it now," Andrew had dropped back into the world of the present and barked the familiar refrain. He had found himself saying 'I can see it now' again and again on this picture. Never before on any production had he been so electrified by inspiration or had so clear a vision about how the scenes would turn out, their poignancy, their historicity, their spellbinding allure.

Perhaps because he knew inside that this would be his last picture. When the inevitability of Death is so close you can see your own shadow across its featureless face, the palpability of life is never so crystal clear and so delicious.

Peter began rattling off the list of exterior establishing shots they needed for the various winter scenes but Andrew's mind wandered off again.

"It's really all about blood; isn't it?"

Peter looked from Andrew to Yuri. He had no idea what his director was talking about. "Blood?"

"Yes, blood. The passing on of both love and evil in the lineage, in the blood. The lust for blood that makes a men murderous. The rush of blood that gives a man an erection to pass on life. The blood that nourishes the life in the womb. The heart that pumps the blood of life. Death, death that breaks the heart and poisons the blood. Don't you see. It's all about blood."

"Yes. Blood. I think I see. Blood on the snow." Yuri's mind was reaching out to lasso Andrew's imagination. Peter still had no idea what they were getting at.

"And on this shot right here," Andrew indicated with his hands, framing them against Frank's bedroom window, "I want us to slow zoom into Frank as he watches the sheets of snow beating against his castle, and as we zoom in, as we get closer to the man, going into his

mind, his psyche, the white snow…"

"…turns red." Yuri finished the sentence.

Andrew turned to him so excited he could barely contain himself. "Exactly."

Peter stood by, slack-jawed, and thought to himself that this was why he would never be a director. This was the pure creative muse that he lacked. There were many in the business who knew how to create technically perfect scenes but the province of such ideas as this belonged to the geniuses. And they were few and far between. He was watching one now.

Yuri echoed Andrew's thoughts. "The only moment of color in the whole film. All black and white except the blood red snow in this one long, intensely personal, revealing shot of Frank in the window looking out over the world he has created - external and internal. A world raining down bloody snow."

"Yes, but not the only moment. There will be one other. Can you think of what it will be?" Andrew asked - the test for his brilliant accomplice.

The look of concentration on Yuri's face surrendered to a concordant smile. "Yes. Oh, wonderful. It will be beautiful."

They said no more. Poor Peter was too embarrassed to ask what that moment would be. As if it were some long buried secret, Andrew and Yuri never mentioned it again. He wouldn't find out until the very

end when the fate of Anna Kamenski would be bound by that blood.

CHAPTER FIFTY-TWO

The runway lights of Krakow airport seemed to appear out of nowhere. Despite bad weather they were landing the Hawker Jet in Poland. It was a risky decision but not an uncommon one. A collective sigh of relief infused the plane's cabin with a healthy dose of carbon dioxide - the by product of breaths long held. They were home, at least home away from home.

For Cory, it could not have been any more welcome. The flight had been an emotionally devastating one. Less than twenty-four hours after his seemingly transcendent embrace of Georgia in the pristine Alps, he had been drained of every ounce of enchantment as if a giant leech had suffocated his heart and sucked the blood

right out of him.

What started with the back of her head galloping away from him had turned into a nightmare of indifference the following day as the seven of them, Georgia, Donna, Lani, Niki, Cory, Paolo and Dieter, rode the tram to the top of the ridge at the base of the Matterhorn. Lani's knee had made a miraculous recovery, and she was quickly back to her old self, flirting ferociously with Dieter.

Other than a polite "Good morning" and a "Thank you" when he handed out skis and poles, Georgia offered no other words to Cory. So strangely contrary to the night before when there were so many words and ideas and even words about words themselves. He did not need to be told why. The fantasy that they had coaxed at the top of the two thousandth step, leaning on the split-rail fence was impossible to fulfill. It had died with the receding view of Georgia, died absolutely and with repercussion.

As if the Fates agreed with Georgia, when they exited the gondola house at the top of the mountain and stepped outside, they were greeted by a fog so dense they could barely see ten feet in front of them.

"Stay very close to us and ski slowly. We don't get many days like this but they do happen, unfortunately. It should clear up a little farther down." Dieter said as he waited for everyone to snap into their

bindings.

Dieter peeled off down the ridge. Georgia and Donna followed quickly, then Niki and Lani. Paolo and Cory brought up the rear together with Paolo keeping off to the right, the steeper, downhill side of the slope.

They weren't thirty seconds into the first run of the morning when Cory began losing sight of Paolo and Niki, the only two he could make out in the fog. Cory could feel his speed picking up and carved harder with the edge of the ski, completing the turns more fully to slow himself down. He knew he must have been drifting to the steep side of the wide slope and corrected his course by veering left. At this point, he could see nothing, no one. He felt that at any moment one of them would come into view. But such was not the case. Then the thought occurred to him that maybe he was slowing down too much and a gap had opened up between them. He let his skis run a little. Still no one.

The fog surrounded him. He skied patiently, waiting for something to emerge from out of the blanket of billowy gray and white. But there were no voices, no swishing of skis, no shouts of peril or nervous laughs. He stopped, with no idea whether he was in the middle of the slope or whether someone might suddenly come edging out of the fog and barrel right over him. "Paolo? Niki? Lani?"

Nothing. The entire world had become invisible.

All he knew for sure was that there were two skis beneath his feet and snow underneath them. With his goggles on he could barely make out the texture of the snow right below him, and without any type of sight line he couldn't even tell the angle of the slope. It felt like an intermediate run to him, he wasn't leaning too severely into the hill to maintain his balance. This must be the main face of the slope. Again he shouted out. But no voice came in return.

The only thing to do was to keep on skiing down the mountain. With any luck he'd shoot right out of this blanket and see them waiting at a trailhead or along the side of a run.

He proceeded. Alone. Moving blindly in deliberate, long s-turns. It wasn't that he was scared. He knew that he was skiing a glacier and there were no trees to worry about; he was above the tree line for at least another three thousand feet. And surely he would hear if another skier was approaching and that would at least give him some relief of knowing there were others. No, this was not a frightening experience by any means but it was macabre - the cold, the sensation of controlled falling with no sense of the surroundings, no idea of when obstacles might jump out of nowhere and the prolonged agony of knowing the bottom was miles away.

A grueling twenty minutes later Cory broke through the thinning wisps of fog until the mid-mountain restaurant was visible off to the right. He had made it through but no familiar face remained. He spent the rest of the day looking for his group but never ran into them.

When he returned his skis to Maximillians at 3:30 Sasha had informed him that he had just missed Georgia and the girls.

A note slipped under his door from Georgia informed him that the taxi would be picking them up at 4:30 down in front.

A few superficial bits of conversation with practically no eye contact and nothing more. This was the sum total of his interaction with the woman who the night before had talked with him for hours, tucked up against him for warmth. It was nothing short of devastating, and Cory's stomach turned over and over the entire plane trip home. So many times in his life he had been scared to the point of nausea by fear, by impending violence, by failure. Only now did he realize that love, too, in one of its many incarnations, could inflict such pain. Just as the fog had disappeared and rendered the mountainside completely discernible to him in the Alps, a greater understanding about what Andrew was trying to accomplish with his film dawned on Cory as the jet set down on frozen Polish ground. The dark side of love had never been something he could conceive, in which he never invested much thought.

As they taxied toward the terminal, Cory could make out the figures of Carolyn and Jerzy trailed by Waldek and Andrzej and the baggage carts. He took one look to the front of the cabin, watching Georgia slip into her coat and flip the shining strands of her hair out over its synthetic fur collar.

Suddenly, everything was all wrong. The realization that he still had months on his contract there in Krakow stabbed into his heart. How could he do it? He couldn't.

The self-loathing hc had battled back as an adult, the unworthiness that had very nearly derailed him at UC Santa Barbara and then again when studying for his American College of Sports Medicine Certification was back and in spades. So quickly, so easily. How could this be? It seemed almost as if it was hiding behind a barrier in his soul, waiting, waiting for the right moment to leap out and bare its hideous fangs. Demons, demons everywhere and he lay there at their mercy, psychologically prostrate and unarmed. He needed to get out of this plane and away from all this, away from Georgia Hart.

Waldek depositing Cory at the Orbis Hotel could not have come a moment too soon. He dropped his bags on the floor, ripped off his coat and dove into the sheets. He tried breathing. He tried clenching his fist, his jaw, his abs. But none of it worked. A hydrant uncapped in

the summer streets, Cory's tears came in a torrent. For everything that had been and everything that was and everything that would be, Cory Sonne wept. He hadn't cried like that since…Eli. Horror of all horrors, it was just as if Eli had returned, or the ghost of Eli. How could he fight a ghost?

CHAPTER FIFTY-THREE

On the tall hills at the tip of Peacock Island, a privately owned forest of one hundred sixty acres in the middle of the Havel River at the southwest corner of Berlin, stood the 17th century baroque palace known as the Schaferberg Estate. Complete with a narrow jet strip, heli-pads, a natural harbor sporting two custom forty foot Scarabs as well as a one hundred and eighteen foot yacht, the island was a veritable kingdom for the German industrial giant Wilhelm Hauer.

Lars Rostock stared up at a towering canvass depicting a trio of austere blue horses stampeding through a multi-colored landscape when his host emerged from the elevator in the middle of the immense hallway.

“I see my stallions have drawn your attention?” The voice belonged to Herr Hauer himself, a circumspect, impeccably dressed man in his late sixties with a full and excellently coifed head of silver-white hair and the physique of a former gymnast.

“Herr Hauer, so good to see you once again.” Lars bowed slightly at the waist while shaking the hand of the much shorter man.

“There’s a certain natural mysticism to the paintings of Franz Marc. He was the founder of the Blau Reiter Der at the beginning of the century along with Kandinsky. They held in the highest esteem the notion that art should lay bare the spiritual essence of natural forms instead of copying their objective appearance with exact verisimilitude.”

“I’m not much of an art critic, Herr Hauer. Once a soldier, always a soldier.” Lars had been a scientist for most of his life and his familiarity with art and culture came primarily through popular avenues - movies, pulp fictions, an the occasional politically oriented play produced by leftist sympathizers.

“Pity. You have before you a priceless collection that delineates the entire history of German painting.” Lars swiveled his head around to take in the enormity of it all. From end to end and floor to vaunted ceiling the long hallway was a quilted puzzle of framed canvasses that gave the place a museum-like quality. No, different from a museum, overstuffed, garishly displayed, an embarrassment of riches, Lars thought. "And you will not find most of these paintings listed on any gallery register. As far as the free world is concerned they no longer exist. Because, my friend, they no longer belong to the free world. They belong to the Reich. And this genius here, Franz Marc, the true innovator of abstractionist painting, Picasso - that vulgar Spaniard - be damned, fought and died in the first WWI for the fatherland." Wilhelm kissed his own closed fist then opened it towards the majestic blue horses.

"You are a true patriot, Herr Hauer. No doubt why the organization has entrusted you with guiding it into the twenty-first century."

"Yes, no doubt. I'm sure. Come; they await." Wilhelm motioned for him to follow into the elevator where they ascended to the top floor and the most private boardroom of Schaferberg Castle.

Assembled in the dark paneled room with the oversized fireplace, inside which stood tall, fluted andirons supporting a blaze of thick logs, were a bevy of business heavyweights, some of whom Lars recognized and had dealt with before, others of whom he had heard and still others completely unfamiliar. If he had had to venture a guess at the collective wealth of the eleven men in the room it would have been somewhere in the neighborhood of thirty billion dollars - nice neighborhood he thought. And that was only book value. There were bank accounts, safe deposit boxes, vaults containing hidden wealth beyond any common man's comprehension. Of that he was sure. For these men were a direct connection to the treasury of the Third Reich during the war.

There were no introductions. Herr Hauer indicated for Lars to sit at the opposite end of the table in a comfortable black leather chair that despite its innocuous appearance still made him feel as if he were in the interrogation seat. He was Lars Rostock, former government virologist, master terrorist, political activist, and head of the New German Alternative, a puppet organization of a much larger, more sinister body known as the New Reich, whose proprietors were seated in front of him now. He was known to them quite well, and it mattered not whether he knew them in return.

"First order of business. Let us congratulate you on your latest assignment. I see from the front page yesterday that the media have finally succumbed to our innermost desires and printed a photographic map of the entire nation with an overlay of the swastika connecting the target cities. My sources tell me this photo made the front page and the news hour of virtually every major media market in the civilized world. And the rest we don't care about." The group laughed then pounded the table with one fist apiece in a sort of drumming applause.

They consisted mainly of hearty-looking men in their sixties and seventies, excepting two dashing Aryan playboys closest to Lars, one of whom he recognized as Thomas Macke, the microchip magnate.

"Thank you, Herr Hauer, gentlemen."

"We have much praise for your work, Lars. Between the Xavier Project and your revitalizing the New German Alternative, you have proven yourself to be a shining sentinel on which we may hang many of our greatest aspirations. However, there is a bit of business that has come to our attention that together we must address and rectify."

Lars braced himself. He knew what was coming but not the severity of the censure. There was no denying that these men could destroy him in the flick of an eyelash if they so desired. They had carried him on their shoulders throughout his storied and sordid career; they could crush him just as easily. He clutched the armrests, knuckles white, the raised tendons fanned out like rakes on the back of his hands. Never good at taking criticism, it had been his Achilles heel in the early days of the organization. Twenty five years later, having learned to breathe and to listen, he was poised to become one of the true insiders with access to the resources and the wealth of the New Reich. He didn't want to screw up now.
"What is it, Herr Hauer?"

"As you are aware of the American director

Andrew Goldman making the propaganda film in Poland, so are we. We also know about your man Bernard Zweig's presence in Krakow. And others, perhaps?" He did not wait for Lars' response. "It does not take a genius to deduce your particular preoccupation with the premise of the movie. I sympathize; we all sympathize. Mr. Goldman is a powerful man and his influence as a filmmaker would only be an obstacle to one of our goals, to erase the memory of the failed Holocaust or at the very least, relegate it to a historical footnote. Seems just as it fades from the public consciousness, someone comes along to fan the flames."

Thomas Macke nodded to Wilhelm Hauer who then conceded the floor to the young entrepreneur. "Herr Rostock. I deal with the Americans quite a bit in my business. To be sure, their fascination with the atrocities of the war exceeds any other country's. They do not understand the complexities of the constantly shifting map that has been Europe throughout history. Take their reluctance to step in on the Bosnia situation for example. They are a culture embroiled by violence and captivated with it, nonetheless. They will embrace this movie that their famous director is making, and it may even be a popular picture that generates a lot of interest for a short while but you must remember to keep your eye on the bigger picture. Thankfully, the masses have very short and very malleable memories. Especially for something as lightweight popular culture as a motion picture."

Lars understood their concern. Anything that jeopardized the greater mission would always come under close scrutiny by the leaders. But they could never understand his. They could never understand what it was to be tortured by the nightmares of wonder, the constant search of his psyche for the definition of the father. And he knew he could never explain it to them, could never make them understand.

Herr Hauer resumed his address. "Certainly you would agree, Herr Rostock, that your personal retribution should never get in the way of your commitment to the greater cause?"

"*Yah vol,* Herr Hauer." Lars new at that moment, when their confidence in him was ebbing, a stout response of total agreement was the only course of action. Although deep inside himself he doubted he could ever give up the fight to vindicate his father, first things first. 'Live to fight another day' had always been his credo. They couldn't possibly know of his plan - tightly sealed in the war chamber of his mind. Like any good intelligence agency, they were merely anticipating. He could easily sustain this slap on the wrist and placate them now with words and gestures. But the plan would remain.

"Good. Good. Your loyalty shall not go

unrewarded, Herr Rostock. Now, for our second piece of business." Herr Hauer spoke into the intercom, the only item on the polished onyx table around which they convened. "Bring in Miss Gosler."

Lars mouth dropped open. Vera. So this is where she had mysteriously disappeared after the bombings. He had tried to reach her to inform her of his trip to Schaferberg Castle. Now he could see there was no need. She had been called, too.

The door opened. A tall, gray-suited guard motioned for her to enter then shut the door behind her. Vera stood there in front of the men, her hair loosely about her shoulders, so casual, but she did not smile upon seeing him. That was not what baffled Lars, however. What he could not comprehend was why she was dressed in a plush red bathrobe.

CHAPTER FIFTY-FOUR

Three days had passed since Cory had seen Georgia. He had avoided the set at Wawel Castle not knowing how he would react or how he would be received. The scenes they were filming, her interpretation of the inscription above Frank's headboard, their first dinner together where he tells her that her family is still alive out at the Auschwitz labor camp, and the strange connection that the two of them will make as they work their way towards the dreadful bargain of love in exchange for life. No way Cory wanted to add to the tension.

Each morning he arrived at Hotel Hollywood he knew she was there. But when he would disappear into the gym, waiting for the girls to stumble in for their workout she would be gone by the time he finished. Lani seemed back to her old self, flirting, ganging up on him with Niki to complain, berate, bemoan. It occurred to him that secretly she must have known how Georgia had spurned him, how she consciously chose to remove herself from his presence. A small victory for Lani on the heels of her Zermat defeat. Much as the smile of the child hoarding the last cookie gives him away, Lani's smile expressed the fatuous joy of having gotten away with something. It was not easy for Cory to tolerate; in fact, it scorched him. But he'd be damned if he was going to show it. No way in hell, honey.

There was no sense in worrying about Lani or what she thought. It would make no difference either way in healing his relationship with Georgia. He had learned that much. But Jack Grady was another story.

When Cory stepped into the security room earlier that morning, Jack pulled him aside and delicately asked about what had occurred in Zermat.

"Cory, I've been around a long time. I know some things; I know people. I just want to reassure you that whatever you tell me is in the strictest confidence. I'm not accusing you of anything but I know something went down between you and Georgia in Zermat. You can tell me."

"I swear, Jack, nothing happened. I would tell

you, really. I trust you."

"Look, kid, the woman was a little sweet on you before. Probably just innocent flirting, self-flattery whatever. But you're a good looking kid and she didn't mind the attention. That was before. Now, she's going to great lengths to avoid you. That tells me that something happened. Now come clean. Because I gotta tell you, my job is this family's well being and protection, and things like this can lead to erratic behavior. And that makes my job much harder. Do you follow?" Jack put a reassuring hand on Cory's shoulder. It had the weight of a loving father's hand. Or at least what Cory thought a loving father's hand would feel like.

"I promise. All we did was talk. I mean there was a moment…" Cory hesitated.

"I had a feeling we were dealing with one of those." Jack knew the score before Cory even finished.

"…it was just, you know, maybe the wine, maybe the starry sky. We got close, you know, the kind of close where you think a kiss might be coming…but…but it was like nothing I'd felt before. You know, it wasn't about sex or nothing, it just felt good, electrifying. But that was it. Nothing happened, I swear to God. She just bolted, you know. Then we really didn't talk about it." A flustered Cory could barely find the words.

Jack shook his head. His gaze turned to the yellowed window.

Cory felt compelled to speak. "I didn't mean anything by it."

"No, kid. It's not your fault. Besides, like you said, nothing happened. You were only following your instincts; you're young that's what you're supposed to do when you're young. But these are some highly special circumstances here. And you're making my job a little tougher."

"How?"

"Because right now, you are more dangerous to Andrew Goldman than any neo-Nazi fanatic. If Georgia Hart falls hard for you, there's a possibility you'll destroy his film, his marriage, his life. It won't be good for any of us. I understand that you're here to keep her lean and looking the part but you gotta do that and only that. Distance yourself from everything else but your immediate objective. You have to. It's the only option. Anything else will only lead to disaster; you gotta believe me, kid. Do you follow?" Jack's voice was smoking serious.

"Yes. I hear you." Cory could do nothing but agree. The words and ideas he had been forced to confront deflated him now. How did it get to this? Things had been sailing along. There had been excitement, the intrigue of a completely foreign country, the buzz of a big movie, of contributing to something very special, something with a life of its own, a place in

history. He felt a part of the grand design, a player in the scheme of high art, an insider with a cherished sense of belonging. What was left for him now but bitter disappointment and alienation? He was too frightened to show his face on the set and even more apprehensive about confronting Georgia. The more time that went by between their speaking the greater the weight he put on those first words that would inevitably be spoken. He couldn't trust himself to come up with the right words, to say the right thing. Reserve, restraint, the implosion of the inward retreat, these were the old habits. They returned to him now in the wake of his misstep with Georgia. Cory could not escape the image of his own heart caving in on itself from the force of so much rejection and self-hatred.

Having finished with the girls in the morning and weathered the interrogation of Jack Grady, Cory left the Hotel Hollywood, eschewing the offer from Andrzej to drive him back to the Orbis and walking. Street after street, snowdrift after snowdrift skated away from him as he picked up the pace and found himself in full trot halfway home. It was as if he were trying to run from the pain or replace it with the physical duress of stinging lungs and aching legs. Run. Run, Cory, run. The mantra looped through his brain. How could you be so foolish as to put your faith in love? This world was made to crush the soul not to elevate it. Think about it. Think.

That is why Death is the great Icon, the great leitmotif. How foolish can you be, stupid boy, son of a plum farmer, and a failed one at that, son of a drunkard, an infidel, a punisher.

In the irony of the pure blanket of snow across the Krakow countryside came the blackest poison. Cory Sonne had descended back into the blackness that was his past, his inescapable nightmare, as if he had never left. The familiar rage flared through him; his blood boiled like lava from the lower depths. Falling into the snow could not cool him now, and so he ran, and ran, and ran. Until he collapsed on the bridge across the Vistula less than a quarter mile from the Orbis Hotel.

Having just picked up Carolyn at the hotel, Waldek's keen caught a glimpse of Cory, prostrate on the icy sidewalk as they drove by. He stopped the car. Together the two of them ushered him into the sedan then back to his room and tucked his frozen body into bed where he slept for the next twenty hours, too exhausted to even dream.

CHAPTER FIFTY-FIVE

Thursday morning, day 17 of filming, had been one of the most productive of the shoot. Sean shone brilliant in the scenes with Jurgen Pricht, the actor playing Rudolf Hoess, the commandant of the extermination camps at Auschwitz-Birkenau. Hoess had come to Wawel Castle for dinner with other SS Officers and commented about Frank having the best job in Poland and the best residence. "I must live with the smell of death over my garden wall. Here, my friend, you are above it all."

The shadows falling across the Nazi faces at just the right moments, the jagged stone backgrounds and monumental decor, the crisp dialogue coming off the tongue of superbly polished actors. In his most complete visions Cory never imagined these scenes could play so well. And the precision of the crew was astounding. They had nineteen set-ups in the first half of the day. More than any other film he'd ever shot Andrew commented. Not even so much as a blown klieg light or jammed camera. This day was colder than a witch's tit but smooth as silk.

The Wawel dailies had been magnificent.

The look on Frank's face when Schlesinger brings in Anna to interpret the inscription over Frank's bed riveted Andrew - a perfect compliment to the shocking but strangely intrigued look Anna gives Frank in the Zakladka book store when their eyes first meet. From this moment on the lives of the two characters are irrevocably intertwined. They both see this as Fate intervening but for very different reasons. Anna beseeches him for news of her husband. Frank promises to investigate. Anna accepts him at his word but knows there will be a price to pay. She'll cross that bridge when it comes.

The mating dance begins.

Frank instructs Schlesinger to take her home and verify her residence. She will be called again. Frank lays in bed that night staring up at the words carved into the wood but hearing them spoken in the voice of Anna Kamenski. Anna lies next to her sickly mother for the last time, remembering the parting words to her husband on a blustery February day, ordinary words, last words.

Black and white and beautiful.

Andrew leaned into Sean and gave him some final words before the shooting of his dinner scene with Georgia. “Although you are not going to tell her, at this moment, right here, you are making up your mind that you are going to kill her husband so that you may possess her completely.”

Sean’s eyes widened. Andrew’s words seared into his psyche. What brilliant direction.

“Roll cameras, now.” Andrew yelled.

“Cameras rolling.” Shouted Rory.

“Speed,” came the boom man’s voice.

The scene played out. Frank spoke with the imperturbable evil of a man envisioning the bullet piercing the skull of the husband even as he forced himself on the wife. He shivered with a delectable excitement.

“I find it fascinating, this perverse connection between us, Anna. Your husband is a Schopenhauer scholar. Schopenhauer is my guiding philosophical force. Rilke is one of your favorite poets; as a young lawyer I executed his estate and oversaw the financial aspects of his many translations. And I agree with you, a trumpeting voice that calls us deep into ourselves.”

"How can you sit there, pretending to understand Rilke, when you embody the very things rebelled against - oppression, fascist ideology, evil."

"You have the dramatic flair of a passionate teacher. I can just imagine the schoolboy crushes your male pupils must have had. Females, too, perhaps?"

"I was respected more than adored." Anna shot back at him in defiance.

"I'm sure you were. But you are wrong about Rilke being anti-fascist. I'm sure you'll agree that Rilke chose solitude and took the grief of his own loneliness as his teacher. He wrote that life was the enemy of art, that the world itself was the enemy of eternity. He wasn't anti-fascist, he was ant-life. A common trait among poets it seems."

Georgia wanted to retort. She had the ammunition to rebut him until she was blue in the face and he red with shame for having feigned comprehension of the poet. But she held her breath. For she knew this was exactly what he wanted, to draw out her passion, to get close to the fire that burned in her. There was no mistaking it from the languishing look in his eyes when she spoke. He must be denied, she thought. He must not be allowed to manipulate her. She had to keep her head about her. Calm. Calm and composed. The idea of choking him to death with her napkin, until his bloated tongue disappeared down his throat like a gopher, flashed across her mind.

A manila folder, a dossier, had been lying at his right elbow since they were seated. Frank slid it in front of him and opened it to a pair of typed pages.

"Since our last meeting, I have done as you requested. Despite the uniform and the position, I am after all, a man of my word. I have before me a paper with the names of Janusz Kamenski and Sarah Glaser, your husband and mother. They are both alive and temporarily housed in Auschwitz Block Seven. My good friend, Herr Hoess, has assured me they will be taken care of until he has heard from me. All that is required for their continued safe-keeping is my signature at the bottom of this page."

Anna stared at him from across the table. A waiter in a soldier's uniform appeared with a bottle of wine and two shiny silver goblets. His medals of valor clinked like a tiny wind chime as he bent to pour. A childhood image popped into her brain - galloping metal horses chasing each other around the tiny carousel that hung from her father's front porch. He had been dead these past nine years. Would they all be better of with him, dying rather than submitting to this Nazi horror?

As if sensing Anna's silent question, Frank addressed her muteness.

"There are many ways to die in the camp - starvation, beatings, hypothermia, diseases of all kinds.

But there is only one way to live, and that is if an order of special privilege is given. I have the power to give that order, Anna. That is what I bring to this bargain. I can keep them alive. But you must bring something to this deal as well. I only want to give one order; I cannot order you to enter into a relationship with me. You must choose to, of your own free will. If you do, the lives of your husband and mother will be spared."

"And cut!" Andrew yelled. "Brilliant, Sean, absolutely marvelous."

Sean McDonough smiled, "I know." Georgia Hart did not.

CHAPTER FIFTY-SIX

Jack Grady stood inside the window of the coffee hutch at the corner of ul Bastowa and ul Krynica sipping a dirt water java strictly for warmth. A black coffee man since the cattle drive days of his Montana youth, he never could abide the steamed milk and pretentiously tiny or over-sized cups of the cappuccino, espresso and café latte craze. Black as the alternating squares of a chessboard and in a paper cup if possible for a man ready to move at moment's notice. With a keen eye fixed on the newsstand across the street he prayed that his gut instinct would serve him well on this wildest of hunches.

The fax that Gunter Strauss had been trying to get through to him at Hotel Hollywood finally arrived.

He and Jerzy had pored over the contents from Interpol's forensic investigation in Vienna of the gum wrappers he had found by the lookout tree behind the compound. They had managed to lift a near full print off the foil wrapper and matched it to a Bernard Zweig out of Berlin.

With a record of political terrorism as long as an orangutan's arm and enough suspected involvement to course up the other side, it made perfect sense that he could be involved with the New German Alternative. Of Polish and German descent, Zweig was the former bagman for WAR, the White Aryan Resistance, and had spent time in the United States organizing paramilitary groups in Nebraska and Idaho where the free-flow of information about demolitions, terrorist tactics, and all supremacist racial philosophies was protected by law. More than half of all neo-Nazi propaganda actually originated from these American sources and made its way into Germany. His association with the New German Alternative seemed to be fairly recent although he was linked to its leader, Lars Rostock, in North Africa in the late seventies.

An 8 x 10 copy of a photo cinched it for Jack. This was definitely the man he had seen on the set that dreadful day when his assignment went from cakewalk to caution.

In addition to a positive I.D. on Zweig, the fax

stated that there were heavy traces of newsprint on both the individual wrapper and the top piece of the pack which he had sent as well. Gunter suggested the gum was probably purchased at a newsstand, an assumption with which Jack had run.

As it turned out, he and Jerzy had managed by phone and with a little help from Dante's knowledge of the city to locate the five newsstands within the city limits that sold Juicy Fruit. Of those five, only two were on corners, and a man constantly on his guard wants to have as much peripheral vision as possible when he's stopped and doing mundane business - a common trait among criminals. After two days of watching the newsstand on ul Karmelicka without a sighting, Jack had moved on to his next option, the second corner stand on Bastowa because it was closest to the center of town and the low rent apartments and hotels.

On this early Thursday morning he had left Dante and Leyt at the set and bestowed on them more responsibility for Andrew and Georgia's safeguarding than either of them had ever expected. They were young but sharp, and good soldiers always rise to the occasion. Jack had confidence in them. They sensed that and were ready to confirm it.

The indoor heat and the steam from the cappuccino machines coated the window with enough precipitation that Jack had to wipe the sleeve of his

Patagonia parka across it every few minutes. Outside, the chaotic gray skies threatened more snow. A battered blue streetcar rumbled by with fresh Coca-Cola advertisements on its side panels showing a gaggle of teenagers enjoying their sodas, dressed in grunge clothes with baseball caps whose bills pointed in every direction other than the one intended - forward and shading the sun. Perhaps it didn't matter in Krakow since, at least to Jack's observation, the sun never shined.

For nearly two hours customers had come and gone from the stand, buying newspapers, magazines, cigarettes and candy. None of them resembled Bernard Zweig. Jack was beginning to get restless. Too many years since he'd been on a stakeout. No patience for it anymore. He'd rather liked the habit he'd gotten into of being active, moving. He was a metabolic man, probably the reason for his early retirement. Didn't want a desk in a noisy precinct with snot-nosed greenies cutting their teeth on and wreaking havoc with his caseload.

Coming from the north, down Krynica towards the stand, Jack spotted him. The green hunting cap with the goofy earflaps, something out of "Field and Stream" Jack thought to himself. It had to be him. He watched the curly haired vendor take Zweig's money for the three newspapers Zweig had decisively plucked from the racks and new he had the right man when the vendor returned his change with a bright yellow package of, he could only

guess, Juicy Fruit gum. Bingo.

In a split second Grady was up from his stool. He made a half gesture towards his belt where he had strapped a two way radio for so many years to call for back-up. Here, out on a limb behind the Iron Curtain, he was all alone. If ever there were a time for him to follow the words he so often spoke into that radio - 'exercise extreme caution' - now was that time.

Jack exited the coffee shop into the frozen morning and covered his face against the headwind with his scarf as he made his way up ul Krynica fifty meters behind the professional killer Bernard Zweig.

The broken sidewalk was icy and sloped toward the street, making it more difficult than expected to hug the side of the building. Zweig turned the corner. As Jack approached it a sudden loud bang rang out, not unlike the sound of a sawed off shotgun. Jack flattened out against the granite stones of the Pierwszy Bank, drew his .45, and slowly edged his left eye around the corner.

A broad-shouldered man towered over his three-cylinder Fiat Avanti, reared up like a Grizzly and slammed his boot heel into the driver's side door which would not shut. It recoiled back at him; he growled and pulverized it again, swearing in a thumping, fist-inflected Polish.

Zweig had crossed over the street.

Jack replaced his gun and hurried along the

opposite sidewalk. Half way up the block, Zweig turned into an arched foyer between a leather goods shop and a currency exchange and disappeared.

The risk of being discovered increased tenfold as Jack stood at the entrance to the foyer and looked down the alley that led to the back apartments. He made his way across the wet cobblestones and emerged on the other end in a tiny, open courtyard looking up at two stories of flat windows on three sides.

A light flicked on in the second floor corner window of the eastern annex. Jack ducked back into the foyer as far as possible while maintaining a sight line. But from his vantage point, he could see only the jaundiced stucco ceiling. He noticed the fire escape on the north side of the building opposite the alley and made his way to it then quickly up to the rooftop.

Crouched along the thigh high wall and shin deep in snow, he moved at an angle to the window. As the room inside came into view, Jack could deduce very little. He would have to move further up the wall and risk being seen himself to get a better glimpse. As he did and the small, Formica dining table came into view, he could just make out a pile of newspapers and…a green hunting cap.

No sooner had he made this observation than the figure of a man emerged from the bathroom just beyond the table. Fully exposed on the opposite rooftop, Jack

had no choice but to drop to his belly in the snow. He was cold and getting wetter by the second but this did not faze him. He had his positive I.D. and his heart leapt with a certain sense of victory. The enemy was no longer a shadow emerging then retreating into the immense unknown of a foreign city. The enemy had a face and a fortress, untidy and ordinary as they were. Eliminating the uncertainties not only reduced the threat but the fear as well. Judging by what Gunter had told him about the way these splinter neo-fascist groups ran their activities, Jack had figured only one man on this mission. It appeared he was right. And now he knew where to find him.

It was a cold crawl on his belly back towards the fire escape ladder at the corner of the rooftop but when Jack figured he was well out of view, he stood, brushed himself off and walked to it.

About to step on the ladder, he heard the muffled slam of an apartment door and quick footsteps down stone stairs. He ducked back onto the roof, kneeling in the snow once again with an eye on the courtyard below. Sure enough, Zweig slipped his hands into his gloves and adjusted his cap as he hastened towards the foyer and disappeared back out into the streets.

A golden opportunity Jack thought to himself. He hustled down the ladder, across the courtyard, up the stairs and towards Zweig's flat. An easy lock to pick.

Once inside, he locked the door behind him. A pathetic, sparse interior with two ragged chairs in front of an outdated television and an end table with a ceramic fish ashtray stuffed with butts. A carton of Marlboro's next to a stack of newspapers on the table, the same one he had seen through the window. He had been right - Formica. Yellowed and pocked with burn marks. The place stunk of incessant cigarette smoking.

Jack followed the frayed carpet into the bedroom. A mattress thrown on the floor for a bed, a portable heater, turned off, a shadeless lamp with a naked bulb, turned off, a duffel bag with a pile of dirty laundry next to it. On the dresser, some loose change, a stack of books with German titles he could not decipher, and a laptop, a Toshiba T3300. He flipped up the lid and turned it on. He recognized the floating windows but not the German nomenclature. He shut it off.

He rummaged through the dresser drawers. Empty. The closet. Except for a dozen wire hangers, empty.

Jack went to the bathroom. Nothing remarkable. Basic hygiene stuff. He stared at himself in the oddly shaped cabinet mirror over the sink, a trapezoid straining to be a rectangle he thought. How did he get here? In the dingy apartment of a neo-Nazi sewer rat, an insidious hatemonger. He thought he'd put this kind of duty behind him when he'd hired on as Andrew

Goldman's director of security. No, wrong. He'd never had this kind of duty. Pimps, gang bangers, psychopaths and sociopaths, the dregs of urban oppression, disillusionment and delusion. That was his milieu. Archetypal European terrorism was new dye for the wool of this career detective. Was he in over his head? Why was he even in this apartment? If anything was going to happen, which was highly unlikely, (Did he really believe that?) he should let it come to him, react to it. No, no. Too many waiting throats had been slit in the dead of night. But what to do?

The question never got answered in his mind as the sound of footsteps in the hall yanked him back into the present. He shut the bathroom door and just as he was about to turn out the light, he caught a glimpse of himself in the mirror, tucked behind the door and in between the wall and the toilet. He reached over and pulled the cabinet mirror from its closed position about two inches so that it would reflect the wallpaper to anyone opening the door.

Outside, a key turned the lock and he could hear the door open. Breath. Breath. With any luck this whole thing would pass. Probably just forgot something. This curve ball would end up low and inside. He knew, even as he tried to convince himself of this, that it would not be the case, and he prepared for trouble.

Bernard Zweig had little to report to Berlin

during his phone call. Everything was status quo and, per orders, he would maintain his holding pattern and await further instructions. When he returned to his apartment and shut the door an unfamiliar smell hit him, redolent of coffee and musk. And then there was the bathroom door. He was almost certain he had left it open. He made his way to it slowly and listened but heard nothing. The handle turned and the door opened with little resistance. Flipping the light on, the first thing he saw was the reflection of the wall and the towel rack in the mirror. In a split second he knew something was wrong, and he reached for the gun in his belt behind his back as the door slammed into his right temple, knocking him to the bathroom floor.

There were no other options. Jack had to thrust the door at his quarry as hard as he possibly could and incapacitate him. Confrontation was his least preferred alternative but unavoidable. Fortunately, Zweig had started moving his head forward into the bathroom at the precise moment he had decided to smack the door with his full body weight. It knocked him clean on the side of his head and into the opposite wall and dropped him to the ground. But he was not out cold, and in his instinctive reaction to the blow, he kicked at the bottom of the door and sent it quickly back into Jack Grady as he sidestepped the toilet bowl and began to emerge from behind it, sending him backwards over the rim of the toilet. His right hand, brandishing his .45 smacked so hard against the porcelain tank it released the weapon and sent it across the tiles to rest underneath the sink.

The room spun wildly and Bernard's vision was too blurred to site the actual position of the man behind the door and so he brought his gun around and began squeezing off rounds in the direction of his best guess.

Without a weapon and pinned between the toilet and the door, Jack grabbed quickly for the plunger next to him and swung it around just in time to deflect a shot from Bernard's gun while at the same time advancing towards him on his knees.

With his left hand Jack managed to grab Zweig's wrist and point the gun away from him towards the living room. He leaped from his knees onto Bernard's dazed body and seized his throat with his right hand. Bernard grabbed violently at his wrist, trying to remove it while he sucked for air, still trying to recover his vision. But the hand was firmly around his windpipe; his best option was to go for the intruder's eyeballs.

With a claw-like swipe, Zweig went for the bobbing face in front of him but ended up with an ear and a patch of hair. He made the best of it and had enough leverage to pull the man's head to the left and loosen the grip on his own throat. The two men rolled over; Jack found himself on the bottom of the younger man.

This time it was his turn. To resume his chokehold was nearly impossible from his present position, especially while keeping the pistol at arms length. He returned the grasping of hair and yanked Zweig's head so hard across his torso, assisted by their extended arms grappling with the gun as they acted like a cantilever, that Zweig's head impacted with a dull but enfeebling thud on the porcelain base of the toilet. Bernard went out cold; his head dropped to the bathroom floor, his grip on Jack's hair and on his gun loosened at once.

It had been over twenty years since Jack had gone hand to hand with his life on the line and thirty since it was his job in the jungles off of Blood Alley and Da Nang. But the result was once again the same. Triumph. But then again the result would have to be the same. The dead are never afforded the opportunity to actually recognize their failed outcome.

Jack grabbed Zweig's gun - a Glock 9mm. Typical. German arrogance. A mean recoil. Perfect for assassinations but not good up close. What good were fifteen rounds if you were too slow to get them off or too stupid to send them in the right direction? Zweig found out the hard way.

Uncharacteristically for Jack, he felt no remorse for this scumbag in front of him. In fact, he wished the blow had killed him. There would be no compunction for

this sorry excuse for a human being had he been killed in self-defense. He took Zweig's pulse - still alive.

Straddling Bernard's body, Jack inspected both weapons. Bernard had fired five shots. The slugs were somewhere in the walls behind him. No way Jack could make it look like a suicide. Besides, even the Krakow police couldn't be so ditsy as to not make Zweig.

The idea rushed into his mind like a runaway train. He had to kill him. Twenty seven years on the Force he'd done the right thing, done the lawful thing. Even in the few circumstances where he could have dispensed swift and immediate justice he'd gone by the book. Sometimes his collars got what they deserved and the system worked; sometimes not and they walked the streets to torment the victims of their crimes. But here, if he let this man go, there would be vengeance of a magnitude he didn't want to think about. There was no going to the authorities. He had unlawfully entered the apartment after all. And what would his explanation be? And although he knew his way through the labyrinth of the American legal system, who knows what subtleties or snares lay hidden in the Polish one. No, clearly he had no choice but to put a bullet through the unconscious man's head and get the hell out of there. The one blessing in this whole episode was the fact that Zweig's Glock had the silencer already attached. Normally a smart move, a protection. This time it helped his opponent. Neither

Zweig's failed gunshots nor the ones Jack would empty into him would be heard.

Jack aimed the Glock two feet above Zweig's chest and squeezed the trigger. The man's body jumped, spasmed momentarily, then went lifeless as the holed heart held the bullet and the blood braked in his arteries and veins, forever. After unscrewing the silencer from the nine millimeter, Jack leaned down and stuffed it in the mouth of the dead killer then tossed the gun in the toilet. The gusset of the glove on his right hand had ripped open and a small cut in the web of skin between his thumb and forefinger bled. This did not please him, not because the injury caused him pain but because now he could not be sure his own blood wasn't somewhere on Bernard Zweig's body. Nothing he could do about it now. The cut was small; the likelihood that they'd find his blood then be able to link it to him was very slim. But the detective hated the idea that there was any possibility at all.

Jack Grady took a long, deep breath; he deserved it. He had survived what was surely a life and death struggle and the adrenaline rush had catapulted him back in time to the days when he lived off such a high. These infusions were better left to youth. Years ago he would have felt invincible; today he just felt lucky.

Bernard Zweig, a militant existentialist, once thought himself invincible as well. It would be five days

before the effluvium of his rotted corpse would be discovered. The final irony of his presumed insuperability would come from a Polish Coroner who'd remark after the autopsy, "Truly the most wretched, indomitable stink from a man I have ever smelled."

CHAPTER FIFTY-SEVEN

Cory laid in the second of the two beds in his hotel room, having sweated through the sheets of the first during the long night. Relieved of the agony of his symptoms now, he watched outside as the first smoky haze of dawn rolled back the darkness. Had the misery of his fever not been so unsparing, he would have thought his present condition distressful but at that moment he was grateful simply to be able to breath, focus his eyes, and conceptualize anything beyond his own pain.

Four hours earlier, at 2 a.m. he could fight the sickness no longer. Bedraggled with sweat, unable to get to the bathroom and a splash of cold water without first stopping at the divan half way between for a brief respite, and with barely enough strength to turn the spigot at the sink and hold himself upright, he realized that he could not beat this thing, as he so often did, by riding it out. Cory shambled to the phone and called the Hotel Hollywood.

Udo, the night security guard in charge of answering the phones because of his passable English, answered. “Dobry wieczor.”

“Udo?” Cory asked.

“Yes.”

“This is Cory. I’m dyin’ over here. Could you wake Carolyn for me, please. It’s an emergency.”

“Yes. Wait one minute, prosze.”

Sitting alongside the bed, Cory rocked like human metronome. He felt as if his head were splitting in two, cleaving to make room for another.

“Cory, what’s wrong?” Carolyn’s sweet voice came through the phone.

“I know you wanted me to try and make it through to the morning, until you could take me to the clinic, but I can’t. I can’t take the pain, I tell you. My head literally feels like it’s going to explode and I can barely focus with my eyes. I’m burning up, Carolyn. I need something for the pain.”

“All right. Just hold on. What’s you’re room number again?”

“662,” Cory responded.

"I'll have someone there as quick as I can. Try to hang in there."

"Okay. Thanks."

As he hung up the phone, he calculated how long it might take. Surely Carolyn was on the phone that moment getting in touch with a doctor. He knew they had a list of medical personnel at their immediate disposal. But this late? Who would it be? How long would it take to get a hold of them? And how long after that before they arrived? Minimum twenty minutes, maybe as long as an hour. No way he could last that long. At least that's the way he felt. He began rocking again. Maybe the movement would help. Sitting still was like waiting to die. He began pinching himself along the muscles of his forearm, naming every one as he worked his way up attempting to distract himself from the agony.

"Extensor indicis, extensor pollicis longus, extensor pollicis brevis, abductor pollicis and flexor pollicis longus…"

Yes, this was the distraction he needed. Cory continued naming every muscle of the arm, including points of origin and attachment, reminiscing now and again about his days in the physiology labs at the university, the camaraderie, the fascination with the human body, the narrow escape of expulsion when Dr. Winkler, who always demanded the utmost respect for the cadavers, caught him juggling three well preserved hearts trying to impress Cynthia Black.

"Iliopsoas, quadtratus lumborum, internal intercostal, external intercostal…shit, shit, shit." Cory's head hurt so bad he couldn't even think. He fell into the fetal position on the bed and gathered up the comforter in his fists. "Iliopsoas, iliopsoas, where the fuck does it originate?" He imagined himself in the lab, pulling back the diaphragm of a cadaver and counting backwards along the vertebral column of the spine, up from the sacrum - L5, L4, L3, L2, L1, T12. "T12. That's it, motherfucker. Iliopsoas originates along the T12 vertebrae and the twelfth rib."

A knock at the door.

"Thank god." He whispered to himself. Relief at last.

The Doctor looked as if he'd been awakened from a restless sleep, tufts of brown and gray hair like loose fitting thatches along the roof of his head. He didn't speak. Arrayed in a hound's-tooth sport coat with elbow patches, a tawny turtleneck, beige slacks, and workman's boots, he carried a russet leather bag from which he pulled his stethoscope and listened to Cory's breathing. He felt his forehead, took his temperature and his pulse then removed from a tiny box a blue and white pill the size of a bottle cap.

"Take this." The Doctor slipped into Cory's bathroom and returned with a glass of water. "Why do you wait so long?"

"I thought it would pass with some rest." Cory offered meekly.

"Your brain is boiling. Few more hours maybe you have scars in your brain."

For some reason the idea of scars on the brain made him laugh - the absurdity of it. He swallowed the pill then finished the glass. Scars in the brain. Nothing new to him. Cory Sonne could tell this Doctor about scars in the brain. He felt them every time he'd run his imaginary fingers across memories of his past. Perhaps the Doctor had stories to tell as well. Perhaps that's why he was so taciturn and unfriendly. Didn't everyone? The older Cory got, the more he realized that nearly everyone gets fucked up somewhere along the way. Human nature he supposed. Georgia, even Lani who had every possible advantage and privilege and yet still couldn't find a way to identify with her father. People do it to people. We do it to each other.

Scars on the brain.

They were there all right. He just didn't need any more.

The Doc was there less than eight minutes. Cory remembered because he'd looked at the clock when the knock at the door came just to remind himself of how long he had endured the wait - twenty seven minutes. That was twenty seven minutes longer than he could have thought possible. He had left a foil sheet encasing a half dozen pills, different from the first one, smaller, and a prescription to be filled immediately that would last him for the next five days. The only word Cory could read on the paper was: INFLUENZA. Same in Polish as it was in English - as a word and as a sickness. The damn flu had knocked him out, and but good. One mean, motherfucking flu Cory thought as he lay down on the bed.

The pain was gone within minutes. He could relax. He could sleep. Turning his head to the window, he watched what he thought was a full moon in a dark but clear sky. Or was it the reflection of the desk lamp with its oval crown distorted to a perfect circle? Not a second to spare on sorting it out before sleep came like a ton of feathers.

Just past dawn. The familiar gray light. Hadn't the sky been clear last night? Something had awakened him, a weight on the edge of his mattress, the sounds of coiled springs under compression. A callused but tender hand upon his forearm, the same forearm he had anatomically scrutinized just hours before. He turned his head and strained to open his eyes fully.

"Georgia?" Cory asked. "Am I still dreaming?"

"Dreaming about me, were you?" She spoke softly and continued stroking the ridge of his wrist.

"What are you doing here?"

"Carolyn told me about your call in the middle of the night. Said you sounded pretty bad."

"It was bad all right. I'm not lying when I say my head has never felt that kind of pain. Now I know what the Colonel's fuckin' chicken must feel like dumped into the fryer."

"I wanted to come by and make sure you weren't dead."

"Maybe that would solve some of your problems," Cory replied.

"You know as well as I do, solve one, anther one inevitably shows up to replace it."

"I just don't want to be one of your problems."

"You're not. In fact, I actually look forward to seeing you every day, for the most part."

Georgia's hand found its way up to the matted hair hanging in Cory's eyes. She tucked it back behind his ear.

"I must look like shit?"

"You look like you've been through the wringer."

"Literally."

Their laughter was followed by a long silence.

"Georgia, I'm sorry."

"Don't worry. You didn't do anything. Another place, another time. Be a different story."

"In that case, I wish I were H.G. Wells."

Georgia's eyes fixed on his lips as he spoke but her mind wandered. Where would that time and place be? Nowhere? Never? Could she live with that?

Cory's words reclaimed her. "It's just that I've never, well, I haven't had...that kind of experience. I guess I wasn't thinking. Being selfish, you know. I shouldn't have put you in the position of having to refuse."

"I didn't refuse." She interrupted boldly.

"No?"

"No, I escaped." She wanted to tell him how close she had come to throwing off the shackles of her resistance. Just a kiss, just the desire for a kiss, just the serene surface of desire like a placid pool of water. There was no wading in, no dipping of the naked foot, only diving. If she made the leap, there would be no going back. She would be fully submerged, and if she stood at the edge of this luscious eddy long enough there would be no way she could not immerse herself. The water of his being was the Song of the Sirens. Such a beautiful undoing.

"I'm sorry."

"Stop saying you're sorry. It's been this way long before you entered the picture." She stopped suddenly, realizing the intimate details she had just blurted out.

"I don't mind if you want to tell me. I'm a good

listener, really."

Georgia released Cory's hand and walked to the window. More snow. It just kept piling up on an old, charcoal gray city that seemed to have surrendered under the weight of so much persecution and pollution. "You're young, Cory. You haven't learned the terrible compromises you have to make to stay in a marriage, about the complexities of love and love turned maddening."

"You don't have to be old or married to know that kind of madness. You only have to have experienced it." Cory volleyed.

She turned to him. "What do you mean?"

"Madness undid my family. It undid me," Cory paused. Could he find the words? Everything about his past had been kept so tightly sealed in the padded room of his mind. If he spoke of it, uttered syllables that carried away atoms of his interior universe, would the galaxy of his soul begin a collapse onto itself like some dying star? Would madness ensue? How could he? How could he take the risk?

"You never speak of them?" Georgia sensed his turmoil. Her words urged him to unburden himself. Her own pulse quickened. She wanted to know.

"My mother, Becky, she was beautiful…and he tried…and tried, year after year…slap after slap, punch after punch…to beat that beauty out of her…and to punish us, Ray and me, for…I don't know what…for loving her more than him, for not being good enough. Hell, he'd beat us for nothin', for dropping a fork at the table or throwin' a shadow across his path, he was so superstitious. But he was a man who lived by the razor strap and the backhand and the anger that drove him to it. And so we had to. We had to endure. My mother had to endure…and…even until the end…even after all the blood and broken bones and all the violence…she still loved him. Is that fucking madness, or what? She believed she still loved him…but I couldn't…I couldn't help it…I…" Cory couldn't go on. Either the memory of it or the emotion of revealing it for the first time to anyone choked him. Maybe both. He focused his entire energy on simply breathing.

Georgia returned to his side. He was barely keeping it together. Tiny whimpers escaped his throat like steam released. She placed her cheek against his and held the other with her hand and whispered into his ear, "You brave and beautiful boy."

Cory Sonne could fight no longer. Not against the river of his inner tumult, the blood that flowed against the dam of his heart.

Georgia's embrace was an explosion of caring, a cleaving sympathy. That dam burst. And out came every last tear that Eli Sonne had forbid him to cry at the risk of being beaten to death. His eyes flooded. His

mouth stretched wide and leaked a low, steady wail. His torso convulsed - all into the arms of Georgia Hart. Ready or not, she would be the iron cast into which the paraffin of his tortured past would be poured. And, like it or not, he would re-emerge from it, re-solidified with her shape forever affecting his form. From then on he would burn like a devotional candle for her, with her, unavoidably a man shaped by love. Her love.

CHAPTER FIFTY-EIGHT

In the dark chambers of the Berlin Hospice Center, Lars Rostock brooded deeply. The ordeal at Schaferberg Castle played over and over in his mind with the image of Vera Gosler, the only woman he had ever, well, cared about, dropping her bathrobe to reveal her naked form to the boardroom filled with kingpins of the neo-Nazi vanguard.

They had spent the previous hour admonishing him for sending Bernard Zweig to Krakow to keep tabs on a movie production intent upon spreading vicious lies and ill-fated propaganda against his biological father, Hans Frank. Lars found it rather odd that they should be so opposed to this practice. It was Wilhelm Hauer's

father after all who had placed the infant Lars with a foster family after the Krakow Governor had entreated the elder Herr Hauer to care for the boy. As a young scribe being indoctrinated into the Organization, Lars had uncovered his true heritage. It was Herr Hauer himself who had encouraged him to emulate the legendary Nazi. He had built his life around this guiding principle and now they wanted him to call off his dogs.

Promises were made that evening with the Organization reserving a lofty position for Lars and he vowing not to unleash his terrorist tactics on the Hollywood propagandists. But never once did they consult him about this most personal sacrifice. Did they think he would naturally consent to Vera becoming part of their ongoing, kinky experimentation with the Fuhrer's progeny? These Teutonic tycoons had taken the desire for retribution for his father's defamation from Lars, and now they were taking his woman.

Yes, that was it. His woman. Vera was his. He knew it. She knew it. That was the reason for the wounded, apologetic yet imperative look in her eyes when they brought her in to that boardroom and proceeded with their ceremony. That night, they had taken her away from him and made her theirs. Lars' sense of aloneness, of abandonment, once again reclaimed its reign over his soul, and with it came the dissolution of his sense of purpose.

The non-stop pounding of his fist had fractured the small bones on the lateral portion of his right hand. He cradled it with his left, wincing with pain as he remembered how the overhead light of the chandelier in the boardroom had given the contours of Vera's body such shadowy definition.

The twelve men around the table had remained seated. Except for a bespectacled man with a silver-white tonsure circling his otherwise bald head. He flipped up the lid on a black attaché case in front of him, and removed a long hypodermic needle.

"Gentlemen, once again we are pleased to have found such a suitable and willing volunteer for our supreme purposes. Miss Gosler's participation marks the fiftieth year anniversary of the in vitro procedure that has produced twenty two sons of the Fuhrer, our esteemed colleague Thomas Macke included among them."

Again the hands pounded the table in applause. Thomas Macke dipped his head in recognition.

The guard moved to Lars' side and motioned for him to stand. When he did, the chair was removed from the end of the table, leaving an opening where Dr. Schikel positioned Vera's naked body. Lars watched as the doctor with the needle turned her body around and helped her up onto the edge of the table, "Now, just lay down on your back, my dear."

She spread out before the fathers of the New Reich like a female feast. Their eyes were riveted, their throats undulating with suppressed desire. Lars' skin crawled with rage. How could they do this to him? How could they expect him to go along with it? Although the security guard was not restraining him, he knew that any motion he made in Vera's direction would warrant an immediate intervention by the Stasi-trained sentinel. Besides, she was, as Herr Hauer mentioned, a willing participant. The agony of having to watch what was about to happen seared his temples. He ground his molars together and clamped his mouth shut. They would not get the satisfaction of watching him squirm.

Herr Hauer spoke, it seemed mostly to Lars for the others were well aware of the ritual. "Over fifty years ago, our beloved Fuhrer had the foresight to preserve his precious semen in copious supply with the good doctors of the Fertility Institute. Through the process of in vitro fertilization which, unknown to the outside world, we developed into a reliably predictable procedure at the hospitals of Mathausen and Belzen concentration camps, we have managed to produce twenty two scions of the Fuhrer himself, all of whom have gone on to serve the New Reich in valuable ways. We can only hope that tonight's ceremony will produce an equally fortuitous result." Herr Hauer motioned to Dr. Schikel. "Doctor."

Schikel addressed Vera as a conductor might

signal a soloist. "Miss Gosler, you may begin bringing yourself to climax."

Not a body stirred. All eyes were on Vera, laying on her back on the table, legs spread, knees up with the soles of her feet flat on the onyx surface. The saliva on the crest of her lip generously lubricated the index and middle finger of her right hand. She placed it on the hood of her clitoris, a petite berm of flesh no bigger than the seed head of an oyster plant, and rotated it in small circles of gentle pressure.

Dr. Schikel continued to speak as she massaged her genitals. "One of the risks of the in vitro process is in the fact that the zygote develops at a slower rate than the natural embryo and the synchronizing of its development with that of the endometrial tissue is aided by consistent and repeated orgasm in the host female. It is most crucial at the time of injection and in the subsequent twelve hours."

A perverse tingle of pleasure seized Lars as he watched what was once a scene from their own intimate theater, her masturbation to a hip-thrusting orgasm. He was not alone. Every cock in the room stiffened as Vera's lithe body responded to her own stimulus. And still, his stomach churned. As he looked from face to face, the nausea began to overtake him. She was giving herself away to a roomful of strangers and taking away the only true intimacy, sordid though it was, Lars had ever known

in his solitary life.

There was a time when he thought that he had loved Vera Gosler. If so, that time had come to an end when she climbed on the table in front of him. But the real blow to his heart came when he heard Dr. Schikel's last comments before injecting her with the fertilized egg, the embryonic Fuhrer-to-be. "It is incumbent upon each of you gentlemen in your hour with her following this implantation to bring her to orgasm at least twice within the hour. From what I have seen of this girl's performance, I do not think you will have any trouble."

They were all going to fuck her.

Vera's familiar moan echoed in the wordless minutes that followed. Lars knew she was about to come. That knowledge, the picture of the doctor poised to inject her with the needle, and the idea that every man in the room would partake of her unparalleled sexual pleasure sent Lars over the edge.

It was as if someone had slashed open his abdomen with a dull knife, pulled out each of his organs then crushed his bones one by one.

"Noooooo!" He woke up screaming in his dark office at the Berlin Hospice Center, the echo of Vera's orgasm bouncing from his memory to the walls of the room and back. Sweating, flushed with a fever-like heat, enraged by the recollection yet again, he rushed to a window and threw it open, breathing in the crisp air. He

would never forget what his own eyes had seen, what his ears had heard. And he would never forgive her.

The phone rang. He watched it. Who could he possibly want to speak to? What if it were Vera? He imagined himself picking up the receiver and crying into the phone, "Why, Vera? Why?" But he knew her answer already. From the moment he had met her he knew she hungered for a greater contribution. She knew he knew. She would expect him to have been understanding. The darkness in her that made her a good soldier, a willing accomplice, could not deny this blacker destiny. After all, they were in it together. Would it have made any difference at all if, all those nights he had longed to speak words to her of his caring, of his need for her, if he had told her of them? Could she have been his and his alone? He had never intended to share her with the lust of the "cause." And yet how could she know that for he had never spoken of his desire one way or the other. He had been only grateful to have her return advances. And now he had lost her.

The phone kept ringing. Maybe it was Vera. Maybe he could tell her now. Maybe there was a way past all this, a way to get back to the two of them?

Lars lunged for the receiver. A voice spoke at the other end. It was not the voice he had hoped for. In fact, it was a voice he had never expected to hear at all. They had spoken only once before, and it had been an uneasy conversation, two men dancing around very different expectations, two men who the outside world would presume had nothing to talk about. No, he had not expected to hear this voice again but even more shocking, the information contained in the words.

"Bernard Zweig was dead."

CHAPTER FIFTY-NINE

Mercifully, Cory's bout with influenza had passed and his strength returned. By Saturday morning he was up and around and even went down to the breakfast buffet where Eric and Yuri had welcomed him to their table. It was good to have the company. They had known he was sick and apologized for not stopping by to visit but they were well aware how nasty the influenza bug was and wanted desperately to avoid the risk.

"Back to your old self again, I see." Eric commented as he watched Cory strip a dozen hard-boiled egg halves of their yolks.

"Yes, my body craves protein." Cory answered.

"Mine craves young girls with tight asses." Yuri

added, plopping a spoonful of runny orange scrambled egg into a piece of folded toast.

"It's getting to that point; isn't it?" Eric said.

"What point is that?" Cory asked.

"When you've been on as many movie sets as we have, you realize how predictable things are. The first two weeks are all about the excitement of getting started, discovering exactly what kind of project you're undertaking. Then, when people fall into the routine of their work habits and adjust to the new environment, it happens."

Yuri stopped talking. Neither of them appeared ready to go on with the explanation.

"What? What happens?"

"Sex," Eric stated.

"Correction, the desire for sex. People begin trying to find that willing partner that they can romp with for the next two or three months. You'll see. Many pairs will start popping up. Some understandable, others completely unlikely. It's just human nature. People have a desire to be intimate, to mate. A movie set is a microcosm for society where couples find each other through all sorts of circumstances. The beauty of it is that we all get to figure it out, watch it, gossip about it. It's your own built-in soap opera." Yuri was obviously tickled by the idea.

"It will provide you with entertainment, whether

you find yourself involved or not." Eric added. "Just don't let it get in the way of doing your job."

"No, cardinal sin." Yuri added.

"The only thing worse is getting involved with the director's wife." Eric mentioned casually. Cory swallowed hard, choking on a dry egg white. He grabbed for his glass of water. A long drink calmed him.

"I don't think we have to worry about Georgia Hart." Yuri said. "She's the consummate pro. That woman is all talent, all business, and no bullshit."

"And as nice as they come. Andrew's a talented and lucky motherfucker," Eric added.

Cory was only beginning to realize the deepness of the shit he was in.

Had the invitation come from Georgia, no way in hell he would have attended. The way things had been going with her and considering the warning shot Andrew had fired over his bow, he would make himself as scarce as possible. But it was Jerzy who had called to invite him on Andrew's behalf to Sunday Brunch at the Hotel Hollywood and sent the car at 10 a.m. Cory found himself seated at the dining room table with Andrew, Georgia, Lani, Niki, Carolyn, Sean, Jack and two visitors, Raymond Teller, Andrew's business advisor, and Marcus Johnson, head of marketing for Peloton Studios.

The visitors had arrived the night before and kept

Andrew up late in teleconference meetings with the studio over how to sell the bleak and unsavory love story. Since copies of the dailies had been forwarded to the Melrose Lot, seemed some of the big wigs had been getting a little nervous. "Dark" was the word that kept popping up from Marcus and the crackling voices at the other end of the line.

"Of course it's 'dark.' It's a brutal relationship at a brutal time in our history. And the absence of light only underscores that."

"But audiences don't want to sit in the dark and watch the dark and be in the dark. Something has to 'enlighten' them." Marcus attempted to attach some aesthetic to the word but Andrew knew him better than that.

"Don't bullshit me. You don't want enlightenment; you want action. I've given you action, Marcus. I've given you action in nine different pictures to the tune of two billion dollars. And now, I want to delve into character. And I will. You know why? Because 'Crooked Lines' did over four hundred million world wide, and we have a very lucrative contract for the both of us to do 'Crooked Lines 2', or 'Crooked Lines: The Sequel', or 'Crooked Lines Gone Straight', or whatever the hell you're going to end up calling it. That's why we'll make this picture the way I want to make it, dark, detailed, methodical. And I *will* find a way to fill the seats in those theaters. I guarantee you that. So get off my back and realize that for once you're involved in making an important motion picture." When Andrew was through with him Marcus packed his papers in his briefcase and sat with his tail between his legs. The voices on the other end resumed their superficial tone, their dissent duly noted.

The next morning was a much different story. The load had been lightened. Nothing left for Marcus and Raymond but attend to the details of business and enjoy their visit together. This pleasant demeanor, this expression of victory on Andrew's face and subjugation on those of his associates, was what Cory noticed during the meal. Andrew seemed to be a little more at ease with everyone, including his wife's trainer.

On the way in that morning, Cory had just enough time to stop in and say hello to Dante and Leyt in the security room, neither of whom he had seen since Wednesday, and to check in with Jack, who seemed genuinely glad to see him.

"We missed you around here." He said, putting his big bear arm around Cory's shoulder.

"I'm trying to follow your advice and lay low," Cory responded.

"You didn't have to get sick to do it." Jack laughed.

"Rather dramatic, I know. But in keeping with

the mood."

Lani and Niki gamboled down the stairs, having just had their "Melrose Place" fix via videotape, a special service had been employed to tape all episodes of "Melrose", "Seinfeld", "The Simpsons", "Mad About You", and anything else Andrew or the girls had circled in the TV Times. The girls got the programs five days after their air date and forbade any of their friends calling from the states to discuss anything about the shows in the interim.

The two of them hugged Cory at the landing as if he were their brother.

"Don't tell me. Billy dumped Amanda." Cory remarked.

Lani slapped him. "No, Billy would never dump Amanda. You're a meanie. You know how I hate it when you make fun of Billy."

Niki stepped in between them. "Speaking of Billy. Did you hear that Lani has a new beau? A Polish boy named Pavel?"

Lani beamed.

"No, really. Does he speak English or do you just use body language?" Cory teased her.

"He's perfectly adorable, speaks broken English but wants desperately to learn. And I'm going to teach him."

"Where did you meet this hunk?" Cory asked.

Niki answered for her. "At the orphanage, of all places."

"Yes, he's a volunteer. Isn't that just *too* noble?" Lani answered, obviously infatuated.

"Isn't that just like you. Your mother sends you to the local orphanage to do some good public service since your stint on the set turned out to be nothing more than a social hour, and you meet the handsome prince. You live a very charmed life, my dear. Does he know you're Andrew's daughter?"

"What's that got to do with it?" Lani's tone of voice turned instantly accusatory.

"Nothing, I suppose. Just wondering if the gentile pole knew he was dating the Jewish daughter of a world famous filmmaker."

"This is almost the twenty-first century, Cory. Things have changed." With that, the two indignant high school girls stormed off to the dining room. The brief moment of camaraderie had dissipated like helium from a rogue balloon.

Cory caught Georgia out of the corner of his eye at the top of the stairs. Dressed in an exquisitely tailored Versace jacket, with wide lapels, a tailored waist and gold piping along the seams and sleeves. Her hips were hugged by a tight pair of black pants that flared at the cuff just enough to hint at the bell bottoms of the seventies. She was amazingly haute couture for brunch and for Krakow.

"What are you wearing?" Cory couldn't help himself. He had never seen her in anything like it before.

"Oh, don't be a fuddy duddy. I bought it in Paris on the way over here and felt like trying it out. Are you telling me you don't like Versace?"

"Versace. Ah, so that's Versace. Yes, I'm telling you I don't like it. Is that all right? I'm sorry if it offends you. But it's so, so…"

"So what? Hip? Glamorous?"

"I'm sure it's all those things. It just seems so…discoey."

"How come Sharon Stone can get away with it and I can't?"

"Who says she gets away with it? Not with me."

"Oh, you have no fashion sense."

"Maybe not. You're going to show up for brunch in that and Andrew's gonna wonder what's up."

"Andrew knows I have wild taste in clothes. In fact, he encourages it. He likes the attention I get and the press."

"There's no disputing that you'll get some attention in that outfit. If that's what the purpose of it is then it serves its purpose well. Forget I said anything." Cory opened the door to the dining room for her.

"I already have."

Inside, the rest of them had already taken their

seats. Andrew rose to greet Georgia and gave her a peck on the cheek after commenting, "Versace never had a better advertisement than you, dear."

'Dear.' He really called her that? The appellation signaled the clear difference between the generations. No married woman still in her thirties could possibly covet such a geriatric greeting. Besides, such a sexy woman? And in that outfit? How could 'dear' even come to Andrew's mind? At least 'honey' or 'sweetie.' But 'dear?'

The only other empty chair at the table was across the table from Georgia and next to Jack. Cory took it; Andrew came over and shook his hand. "Feeling better I hope?"

"Yes, thank you."

"I hear it's a bastard strain of the virus. Knock on wood none of us come down with it here at the HH." Andrew knocked on the corner of the table on the way back to his chair. "These are friends of mine from Los Angeles, Marcus Johnson and Raymond Teller." Cory nodded to the two stiff looking gentlemen.

Among mundane conversation about the progress of the shoot thus far, came snippets about school, trips they were planning for their spring break, what the latest news was from home and more. Cory listened intently, not uttering a word. Except when Raymond asked him about how to get rid of his overhanging mid-section.

Always the same questions. Women wanted smaller, tighter thighs; men wanted smaller, flatter bellies. Of course none of them wanted to pay the price of disciplined eating and sustained exercise over the many months it would take. They wanted quick fixes. And for the problem of excess fat that had taken them years to accumulate. Always the same questions. Always the same answer: good diet and exercise. Followed by the standard joke. I do it by cracking the whip, or a lipo surgeon can do it by hooking up the vacuum.

Cory new that Raymond Teller would carry that spare tire with him for the rest of his life, which would be significantly shorter than necessary given the statistically proven correlation between extra abdominal fat and coronary disease.

Machek and Renata served up a splendid pasta salad made with yogurt, honey mustard and fresh vegetables and a turkey meatloaf that he was proud to announce to Cory and the rest of the table was very lean but still quite tasty. Then of course there was the ever popular broccoli soufflé that combined some egg whites and nonfat sour cream with the pureed crucifer which made the vitamin and beta carotene rich concoction tremendously palatable. Whole wheat rolls, jam and an assortment of cereals for those still in the breakfast mode.

They all ate their fill, except Georgia who nibbled on small portions of turkey and soufflé but drank prodigious

amounts of water.

It was Dante who interrupted the meal and the Krakow homicide detectives who ruined it.

CHAPTER SIXTY

One of the darkest days of the Berlin winter was behind her now at the end of one of the most exhaustive weeks of Vera Gosler's life. Her head ached, her throat was dry and her breasts were swelling and becoming extremely tender so that even the soft abrasion of her silk brassiere across her nipples irritated her.

The medication Dr. Schikel had been pumping into her persisted in making her nauseous. She considered it a minor miracle that she'd endured the marathon fuck session from the fathers of the New Reich, all of whom might as well have been faceless Johns from the streets of the Reeper Bahn in Hamburg, the sex was so passionless. While they licked at her, massaged her clitoris, vibrated her, pounded her, grunting and gasping, she had kept her mind focused on one thing - history. With this child and this opportunity, she would notch a significant place for herself in the history of this great land, in this pantheon of political and cultural preeminence. Every climax she had came not from these men and their lethargic cocks, but from the idea of a resurgent Aryan demagoguery in which she would play her part. If they only knew how easy it was to endure their lust, their sloppy kisses and slippery semen. Dr. Schikel's was the only injection that mattered, and she would parlay that into a position of power far greater than being some Reichstag slam-piece or the mistress of a terrorist Lothario.

After long hours of testing, in which Dr. Schikel concluded with reasonable certainty that the potential for pregnancy favored success, she was finally back in the comfort of her own modest flat. Schaferberg castle was nice, and Herr Hauer a worthy host, but nothing quite like home. The smell of it, the warmth, the familiarity. These quaint thoughts evaporated quickly when she flicked on the living room light switch and found Lars sitting in the easy chair nearest the window.

Vera clutched at her breast. "Lars, you startled me."

"Did I?" Lars remained seated. He had been perched at the window since four in the afternoon watching the day fade away, waiting for the familiar Audi sedan to pull into the garage below. And now she was here in front of him. In the preceding hours at his office he had decided there were two things he must accomplish before he could go on with his work concerning the New German Alternative. The first piece of business had brought him to Vera's apartment. And yet all the things he'd imagined he might say to her, the questions, the confessions, they deserted him now.

Vera removed her coat and hung it in the closet then slipped out of her heels. "Can I get you something? Or have you helped yourself?"

"I believe it is you who have helped yourself." Lars' jaw tightened. The image he had not been able to shake for the last twenty four hours came screaming back into his brain. A door, behind which lay a room with a soft bed, on which lay Vera, legs spread, cunt wide open, swollen from the friction of cocks, many cocks, and dripping with the excess of cum her communal pussy could not hold. And outside that door, a line of men, smoking cigars and drinking port, waiting patiently for their turn. It was, to say the very least, a maddening image, and it plagued him.

"You should be happy for me. This is an honor quite unlike any I could have imagined. I told you once how, as a little girl, I was fascinated by military heroes, the medals, the valor, the respect they were given. I wanted that; I wanted it all. That is why I joined up out of primary school. But it was not what I expected, and the treatment of women was far from honorable. I knew I would have to find my own path to that place of importance, and I also knew I would not be denied. I am on that path now." She moved towards him with the soft steps of stockinged feet, her hands loosely reaching out to him.

Lars remained at the window but did not resist her hands. Vera slipped her arms around him and laid her head against his chest.

"You should have consulted me, my dear. You should have consulted me."

She turned into him, opened his jacket and pushed back the lapels. Her lips zigzagged across his torso, kissing his body through his khaki sweater. The familiar role of the scolded child came easy to her. They had played this game for years, and she crouched as she worked her way down his belly with her mouth and began undoing his belt with her fingers and teeth.

Lars remained indifferent, watching her gorgeous countenance enmeshed in his own loins. He violently whipped his head to the side, attempting to dislodge the profane image of the door, the line of men, the room behind them filled with Vera's groans. But he couldn't. It was a video loop that kept circling back on itself, and as Vera inserted his cock into her mouth, it was suddenly not Lars she was fellating but the whole of the New Reich, no the whole of Berlin, no the whole of the Fatherland. She was once exclusively his, once his indefatigable lover. He had cherished her in a wholly unique and satisfying way, and now she was a mouth and a cunt available to every hard prick the world had to offer.

Rage. Rage overtook him. He reached down for the back of her hair and yanked her up to his face. The look in her eye was not one of surprise or shock for she knew what was coming. She had spent too many hours tangled in the web of him not to know, and she threw her fate into his hands once again. This time, however, his hands moved to her throat. She pleaded with her eyes for him not to do it then uttered one phrase, words she knew would save her life or speed her death, “Let this be our son. You shall be his father.”

Lars paused, still gripping her throat firmly in his hand, her chin pointed up to a spot over his head and out the window, indicating a star somewhere past the blanket of the night; her nostrils flared in anticipation of his answer. He looked into her eyes, her lavender blue eyes reminiscent of the Tollensesee spring meadows of his youth. Vera Gosler was truly his and his alone, his in a way no other man, nor club of men, could ever possess her. His heart began to melt; he resisted it, his grip tightening around her throat but to no avail. The blood from his heart seemed to leak into the cavity of his body, his knees trembled, his lips quivered, his eyes began to water. Now it oozed out of his pores; he was sure of it. She was doing this to him - Vera Gosler. She was making him weak. That stare, that Nazi whore's glare behind whose eyes lay the sinister plan for co-opting him into surrogate fatherhood.

Then and only then did he fully realize what she was asking. She wanted him to be the foster child of a stranger's son. And it all came crashing down on him. It was his own past, his own childhood, his own foster father, or monster father as he so often referred to him. The beatings, the rat cellar, the tolerance of his foster mother, the uprising and eventual murder of the man. Pain. Blood. A flurry of fists. Tearing, scraping, shoving and stumbling. Die. Die. You Bastard.

This was the future Vera had suggested to him. A son that was not his own rising up against him. The picture of his father's fist, of him trapped in the barn cellar, rats crawling all over him, of Vera spread out on the boardroom table masturbating for the good of the cause, old men lining up to fuck her. No more. No more.

Lars spun her head quickly around, wrapped his left arm across her torso, and clasped his right hand around her lower mandible. In one swift and powerful tear, he yanked her chin as far and as fast to the right as he could and snapped her neck. She made not one sound as her body went limp in his arms.

Breathing, breathing as if stopping in the middle of a chase, Lars released her. She slid down his shaking body and toppled onto the perimeter of the rug, her body oddly incorporated into its overall design.

Lars stood over her. The familiar voice of his foster father trapped in the barn cellar himself, being slowly bitten to death by rabid rats, echoed in the back of his head, pleading for mercy. In that moment he thought it strange how eerily similar the voice recollected sounded to that of Hitler's own. He looked from Vera's dead body towards the sky and uttered words of penance.

"My apologies to your son, Mein Fuhrer."

This first piece of business had concluded. Now, to Krakow for the second.

CHAPTER SIXTY-ONE

"I know what you're doing, Andrew." Georgia yelled across their bedroom at Hotel Hollywood while she pulled her sweats on over her thermal underwear. "You're intentionally starting a fight. You do this every time you want something from me. What do you want, Andrew? Just come out and say it. What do you want?"

Andrew fiddled with his digital watch just to have something to do. He had already set its alarm for six in the morning, a habit he continued despite a twenty-four hour staff whose duties included a wake-up call. "Don't be silly. I don't want anything from you. God knows I'm aware of the thin ice that is your personality when you're shooting a film. Far be it from me to tread there. I'm simply stating the obvious, G. You don't have to be a soothsayer to discern your attraction to the kid."

"You're the one who hired him. You're the one who wanted him along, who thought it'd be good to have a professional keeping tabs," she shot back at him.

"And you're not maintaining a professional relationship with him. You're buddies now. Taking him with you skiing, inviting him to the set, to brunch. We've had this discussion before, G, the inner circle is sacred, remember. You're exposing him to delicate matters, making him one of the family."

"He's a good human being, Andrew. Not spoiled or carnivorous like the sycophants that constantly kiss your ass."

"And yours, my dear."

"And mine. Yes, I know. That's why I like him around. He's not like the rest of them. It's a refreshing change."

"I just don't want him to become a distraction. You can't afford to be building friendships when you're playing a character whose world is being decimated around her." Andrew set his watch on the night stand and slipped under the covers, sitting upright against the headboard and neatly folding them over his lap.

"That's what this is all about. I knew it. You tell me right now, dammit, if you've got a problem with my performance. Right now, you son of a bitch. Don't play games with me; do I have a problem? Do I?" Georgia fumed. Andrew was unmoved by her intensity.

"No, what you've been doing up to this point is magnificent."

"I hear a 'but'."

"Yes, but, but, but we have intimate love scenes coming up, we have tragic revelations about the fate of Anna's husband, family and friends. I'm just very nervous about getting it right. I don't want anything or anyone fucking up my movie."

"Your movie? Your movie? It's always about you. Your ego is immense. How can you get your head into a hat in the morning is what I want to know? I've been married to you seventeen years and yet I continue to be shocked at the degree of your self-centeredness. It's no wonder your daughter treats you like a stranger."

"Oh, I see. You're so good at this, G, so, so good. Let's turn the conversation on Andrew. So clever the way you take it, reshape it, then hang it on me like a fucking anchor. And don't bring up all that old baggage about Lani. We've been over this territory time and time again. Let's just drop this whole goddamn thing. Please, just don't let it affect your performance. That's all I'm saying. There isn't supposed to be a glint in your eye; there's supposed to be resignation and fear." The surrender in Andrew's voice trailed off.

"I'll get it right, goddammit. You do your job.

I'll do mine. And leave Cory out of this. The poor guy's ten thousand miles from home, a home where he has no family of his own, and he's busting his butt to do the most professional, the most thorough job he can, even to the point of taking on a lot of extra responsibility where the girls are concerned."

"Oh, so passionate about Cory. Poor Cory. Cory's trying so hard." Andrew's sarcasm sizzled off his tongue.

Georgia paused. She thought she knew this man, the body beside her night after night, year after year, and in the last few there had been more secrets revealed than she ever imagined. What she had been discovering all this time was not the man she had married but the man he had tried to conceal in a failed quest at family conventions, the hidden darkness of his predilections, the deviances, the emotional treason.

He hammered her for showing kindness to Cory, for paying attention to a smitten young man flattering her. But Andrew was wrong. She hadn't given him the slightest reason for distrust; she had kept her nose clean and her ducks in a row. At least in action. And now, as she searched for a way to understand his volatile reactions of the moment, it came to her.

"I think I know what this is all about," she said to him as she sat at the foot of the bed. "You're jealous. You want him for yourself; don't you?"

Andrew slid down into the covers and flopped to

his side feigning an effort to sleep. "Don't be silly."

"He's a beautiful boy." Georgia hovered over him; he ignored her. "Is he your 'type', Andrew? Golden boy? The kind you and your insatiable friends dressed in tight underwear and had prancing around your luxury hotel suites?"

Not a word, not a response from Andrew. Truth in stillness perhaps. At least that's what Georgia thought. She grabbed his watch off the night stand. "You disgust me, Andrew. We're in this thing together. I don't deserve to be judged like this. And least of all by a man whose deviance has known no bounds."

She stormed out. The guest bedroom would do just fine. Anything to be away from him. She would have trouble sleeping tonight anyway. Her world, her life, were suddenly unfamiliar to her now. Lying in the crisp sheets of a small bed and staring at the stucco ceiling, Georgia Hart would ask herself the same question over and over, "What's happening to me?" Anna Kamenski seemed so far from her now and Cory so near. Could Andrew be right after all? Maybe she couldn't be objective about it. Especially not after Zermat, after being in his arms in that intimate way, nearly tasting him in that cold night air. A part of her urged the immediate fleeing to the Hotel Orbis. It would be so easy, so…comforting. That was it. Comfort. She needed that now, more than anything. Cory would be elated most likely. But what about afterwards? There would be an afterwards. There always was. No, she couldn't do that no matter how tempting the idea. She would just lie there and try to sleep, to think of Anna Kamenski and what would be expected of her tomorrow morning when the crew moved to the concentration camp of Auschwitz-Birkenau for five dreaded days of bone-chilling shooting.

Georgia hated Andrew for the way he treated her, accused her, about her performance, about Cory. Their marriage was getting to the point where she was hanging on by the promissory thread of a worn and rusted vow. There was no doubt in her mind that if he weren't dying, she would definitely leave him at the end of this picture. But he was dying. And death always makes a difference.

CHAPTER SIXTY-TWO

The cut on his hand had scabbed over, and now Jack Grady couldn't seem to leave it alone. It itched him as he sat across from Gunter Strauss in the bar of the Krakow airport.

"You sure you can't let me buy you dinner in town?" Jack asked the slender Austrian Interpol Chief and espionage expert with a face like a whippet and jet black hair slicked back behind the ears.

"No, I've got to be back in Vienna tonight. We're in the middle of cracking a high level arms smuggling outfit. Technically, I shouldn't even be here, and, as I'm sure I don't have to tell you, I'm not."

"I'm very grateful for your not being here," Jack

cracked back.

Gunter opened his titanium briefcase with a thumbprint identification on the lock.

"Nifty," Jack said, impressed.

"Our budget ballooned after those vicious commuter subway gas attacks last year. Anti-terrorism is big business now, for everyone. At any rate, we've got all the latest gadgets."

He dropped a file on the table. Jack opened it and leafed through the photos on top.

"Lars Rostock. He was Zweig's boss. Naturally, when I heard of Zweig's expunging, I honed in on Lars with everything I had available to me." Gunter looked his friend squarely in the eye. "Shot through the heart with his own gun. Must have been some experienced soldier to pull that off on a Stasi trained assassin, wouldn't you say?"

Gunter wasn't really looking for an answer to his question, only a look. The look of confirmation from his friend whom he suspected had been at the other end of that gun

"Must have been," Jack returned.

"That's what I thought. That man was lucky, I think. Probably didn't know what he was up against." Gunter blew into his hands. Despite being indoors, the lounge was still chilly. "You know, the first thing I tell my rookie recruits is that killing a man in the field is a good way to limit your effectiveness and most likely shorten your career."

"Yes, I know. Are these recruits Darwinists by any chance? Possessing a keen sense of self-preservation?"

"Most. They practice it from afar."

Silence. No more words needed on that subject.

Gunter explained the photos. "The top one is the most recent of Lars. The one below it is a picture of him and his girlfriend, a former demolitions expert named Vera Gosler, taken a few months back. This is Vera this morning."

Jack stared at the picture of Vera's body curled up on the floor of her apartment, dead.

"Broken neck. We suspect by Lars himself. Seems the woman was pregnant. Who knows what happened. Could have been someone else's; he could have freaked out about the idea of being a father, anybody's guess." Gunter indicated a much older photo. "That's a picture of Lars and Zweig taken in Cairo in the late sixties. Have you ever heard of something called the Xavier Project?"

"No."

"I thought not. It's a testament to the security of the New Reich that so very few people know about. We could use that kind of loyalty in our own secret service branches." Gunter snapped his briefcase shut and set it on the floor beside him, blowing into his hands once more then folding them on the table in front of him. “Hold on to your hat. This one’s going to spin your head.”

Gunter began a detailed account of the Xavier Project, a sinister plan that had been the crown jewel of the East German Bacteriological Warfare Department (BWD) and the Lars Rostock’s deviantly fertile mind.

“Lars had made a name for himself as somewhat of a biochemical boy-wonder at the University of Berlin when he was secretly recruited to the BWD. Let me backtrack a little. During World War Two, doctors at Mathausen and Sobibar concentration camps had been experimenting with infectious diseases, subjecting Jewish prisoners to all kinds of viruses, bacteria, sores, etc., and measuring the symptoms. One virus in particular had caught their fancy. They called it the Xavier virus, named after Jolanta Xavier, the mastermind behind these hideous experiments who was later indicted for war crimes and executed. They eliminated the man but not the research. Quite a few East German virologists picked up where he left off but it was the twenty-two year old genius, Lars Rostock, who went to central Africa and really documented the most thorough work on the subjects of malaria parasites and simian immunodeficiency virus or SIV. Sound familiar? It should. It’s the primate counterpart to HIV.

“Africa is where Lars met Zweig, who was an

aggressively ambitious agent in the North African operation. His parents had been anthropologists and he spoke many of the local dialects. He had been commissioned to be the courier from Lars' labs in Africa to those in Berlin.

"Lars Rostock's brilliant contribution to science and to the twentieth century came on that fateful day when, cocooned in his laboratory in Kigali, he successfully mutated the SIV virus into the virulent HIV-2 virus, different from all previous HIV-1 strains which had existed perhaps for centuries and been passed from monkeys, mostly mangabeys, green monkeys, mandrills and chimpanzees, to humans, but not proven particularly lethal.

"Initial tests apparently went better than expected. Of the two dozen patients that he injected and kept careful track of, all died within four years. At a secret conference in Berlin in 1970, he presented his astoundingly successful research to a rapt military panel of the BWD and Xavier took on the utmost clandestine status. From then on it was to be treated as a secret weapon.

"The first horrendous large scale test came when, working under the guise of an international relief organization clinic, they vaccinated several hundred thousand Black Africans. Black mind you; the antithesis of Aryan supremacy – in Zaire, Rwanda and Burundi.

They ostensibly were vaccinating for polio but using HIV-2 tainted simian blood. Is it any wonder that today that continent is decimated by the inevitable end product of AIDS that results from these infections?"

Jack slowly shook his head. The idea that one man could feverishly pursue the task of destroying millions of lives boggled the mind. But why should it? Lars' own countryman had annihilated six million Jews in pursuit of the same goal of ethnic cleansing.

"Horrifying as that may be, there's more. The East Germans, in conjunction with the Soviet Union, expanded the output of the Xavier Project and mass-manufactured the virus, dispensing it at clinics all over the African continent where they had connections. But Lars wanted more draconian measures. He and his superiors devised a method to introduce the disease into the population of their arch Cold War enemy – the United States.

"Knowing that the spread of the virus needed to be from blood to blood, they implemented two plans. The first, unveiled when Lars took a position as a clinical physician in Key West off the coast of Florida. Are you familiar with Key West?" Gunter asked the rapt Jack.

"Yes, yes, my wife and I went there once for vacation. It's gorgeous but a little too foofy, if you know what I mean." Jack wiggled his limp hand as if he were waving a jellyfish.

"Obviously, you know the place is a haven for homosexuals. Lars knew from his studies in Africa that the disease was easily transmitted by anal sex. He injected everyone that came through his clinic in the early seventies. And you know the sexual habits of young men? An inordinate amount of them take on multiple partners, day in and day out. In the twenty five years since that time in Key West, you can imagine the geometric progression of infection.

"The second thing he did - and the CIA documented this when they uncovered KGB dossiers on the subject after Glasnost - was to gain access to all the Cuban prisons through Castro and the KGB's influence. He indiscriminately injected a huge portion of the criminals with the virus shortly before the asylum of the eighties where the U.S. opened its borders to all Cuban refugees. Castro then emptied his jail cells into the panhandle of southern Florida. And what do you suppose the last thing was they were told before their short journey across the sea to the land of the free? He told them that they would be paid good money to donate blood in America. That's right. Infected Cuban refugees inundated the blood supply of the gulf coast with HIV-2 tainted blood. Are you getting the picture my friend?" Gunter asked, pausing to take a swallow from his beer.

"Unfortunately, yes. It's staggering to think that one man could think all this up and then do it."

"He's the worst kind of genius. It'll take a thousand lesser scientists, trillions of dollars, countless grief, and many years to undo this one man's work."

"How come someone hasn't put a bullet in this guy, and how did he get into the terrorism racket?"

"The mind that generated the terror may well be, in the end, the mind that finds the cure. Those select few officials in the BWD that know about this whole project recognize that the possibility exists of the disease getting out of control and creating a compromising position for even the good citizens of their own nation. They protect him. As much as we'd like to eliminate him, we agree with their assessment of his abilities and reluctantly have to keep him around. They don't see an outbreak in Germany as very likely, however, and are content to let it run its course, ridding the world of homosexuals, drug users, prostitutes and the sexually promiscuous denizen that tear away at their idea of the 'essential fabric of society.' Between the ills of the African continent and the rapid spread through North America and Asia – you know of course that by the year two thousand and ten, a hundred million people will be infected – you can see where they relish bringing these regions to their knees."

"Do you suppose they have a cure and are just keeping it to themselves?"

"It's possible."

"If Interpol knew all of this, every step of the way,

why didn't someone intervene?"

"We didn't know. No one did. What I have told you is a history that has been pieced together over many years. The clear picture has only recently come to the forefront. Many of those KGB documents expedited our handle on the information."

"And now? Why Lars' radical change in direction? How did he get into the explosives business?" Jack asked.

"Oldest answer in the world. Power. Seems everything he did for them with the development of the virus, its dissemination, he still wasn't commanding the kind of respect he felt he deserved. He'd been a temperamental entity to deal with all along but they always managed to find a way to placate him. Mostly empty promises. And when he came calling in his markers, they only wanted him to stay the course of Xavier. He broke off four years ago and formed the New German Alternative, recruiting young zealous neo-Nazi's disillusioned with the reunification with the west."

"Man, this guy has a major beef with the world. With such big fish to fry why is he bothering with Andrew?"

"Andrew's making a film about Hans Frank, correct?"

"Yeah, so what?"

"Hans Frank is Lars Rostock's real father. To put

it plainly, he's obsessed about the connection."

"Jesus H. Christ. Gunter, don't get me wrong. It's been great to see you but I kinda think I might have been better off not knowing about all this. Truth be told, I'm a little intimidated by this guy." Jack took a sip of his coffee and loosened his collar. The lounge seemed to be getting warmer in equal proportion to his java's cooling.

"My intention was not to intimidate you, Jack, but to warn you."

"How so?"

"Lars Rostock flew to Warsaw this morning."

"You think he's coming here?"

Silence from Gunter was as good as a yes. Jack had barely been able to process the scope of Lars' evil work and now he had to deal with the notion that he would most likely be stepping into the man's cross hairs. Suddenly, a drive through East L.A. policing gangbangers didn't seem like such a bad duty.

CHAPTER SIXTY-THREE

The sets had been ready for days and the weather reports showed a warm front moving in from the North West at the end of the week. Andrew needed cold and snow for at least three more days as they filmed the crucial Auschwitz-Birkenau portions. He got exactly that.

The first scene on that numbing Monday morning, where teeth-chattering was a common greeting, was the execution of Anna's husband Janusz outside of cell block eleven. Externally, block eleven hardly differed from the others – same lifeless, naked looking brick buildings whose very appearance quashed all hope to any newcomers urged in at the point of SS machine guns.

Despite the sign overhead at the main gate, "Arbeit Macht Frei" – work shall make you free – few prisoners at Auschwitz-Birkenau harbored the delusion of a return to freedom.

Three stone steps led to the front door. To the right of it hung an insignificant, small black sign with the number 11. Through the glass panes of the door one could see the dimly lit hall and the iron latticework of a door which separated the front and back of the building – where those in their final days and hours were stored until disposed.

Unlike the other blocks, however, the cell windows were almost entirely blocked up, with the exception of a narrow strip about the width of a palm to let in the daylight.

The yard between block ten and eleven was surrounded by high stone walls which connected the front and back parts of both buildings and protected them from curious eyes. A massive wooden gate with a peephole, closed from the inside, barred entrance to the yard. The windows of the next block were secured by wooden cross boards, and even the most unassuming observer would know this yard served some special purpose.

The inside of the stone wall of block eleven was black and constructed of thick black isolation plates stacked high like tarred railroad ties. The procedure was primarily always the same. Prisoners, one or two at a time, were escorted from the dark, stinking cells where some had been cramped for weeks, maybe months, clad in dirty white and blue rags, their faces apathetic, the will to survive completely beaten and drained out of them. Charged with fabricated crimes of treason or insurrection that most times amounted to nothing more than the pilfering of a potato, obtaining one undergarment too many or smoking during work, or at worst, having escaped and been recaptured, a sure path to execution, they'd be pushed into the wall, face first and beleaguered with the command, 'Proste', or straight. A small caliber gun was then fired at a distance of two or three feet, the bullet piercing the back of the skull, and blood running down the back as the bodies slumped over. The shooter would then step on the forehead of the man with his boot, pulling back the eyelids to make certain. Often a groan would ensue and an extra bullet through the forehead or eye socket would be necessary. Two prisoners on each end of a stretcher would cart the bodies off to the crematorium and a third with a small hand spade would cover the foaming puddles of blood with fresh snow in the winter, sand in summer.

Such was the death of over seven thousand men at Auschwitz-Birkenau during the years 1940 through 1944.

Andrew wanted this protocol authentically reproduced. For the master shot they started with a one camera set-up outside the front wall's open gate. The dolly would track in right as the prisoner was being lead out of block eleven and an SS Officer would come into the left side of the frame as the camera passed him as if he were shutting the gate behind us. The brick walls of blocks ten and eleven would border left and right sides of the shot, the snow and dark gray sky would frame top and bottom. The camera would move past three SS Officers, waiting with their hands crossed behind their backs, one of them with the loaded pistol, readying himself for the kill, up to the execution wall where the camps enforcing regulators - who were often as brutal as the Nazi's themselves – would turn the prisoner around to reveal to the camera his identity – Janusz Kamenski.

Anna's husband, whom Frank had given the order to execute, would die in the movie at dusk on the very same evening that his love would be laying down in the bed of the Nazi governor and giving herself voluntarily in hopes to save him from that very fate. Andrew planned on intercutting between the two scenes – the preparation for death and preparation for sex, the climactic moments before his life is taken and before the orgasm, the gun firing into the back of his head, the ejaculation into the wife of the murdered man.

That's the way Andrew saw it; that's the shot they were preparing.

Cory had fallen back into his routine at Hotel

Hollywood. Only on this Monday morning the girls and Georgia had swapped workout times. She didn't have to be out to the set until one o'clock, and particularly didn't want to be around to watch the scene of her screen husband's execution. After all, she's supposed to believe he is still alive.

Lani and Niki seemed in good spirits that morning, going through their buddy stretches with intermittent spurts of giggling. They didn't even object to the circuit of calisthenics and plyo-ball exercises which were normally met with mammoth groans. Owing to their newfound work ethic, Cory decided to push them to their limits by trading off ninety second hill climbing intervals on the treadmill with sets of twenty slow, body weight front squats and reverse glut raises on the bench. Their legs and butts would be very sore tomorrow but he'd be able to point out that such was the path to firm legs, something for which they'd confessed they were in the hunt. They would curse him later on that day when the lactic acid started jamming up the works in their muscles as they squatted to play with small children at the orphanage that afternoon. But then with Pavel there, it hardly seemed like Lani would be complaining at all.

Cory went into the office and chatted with Carolyn as she and Jerzy made the final arrangements for Sunday's dinner with the Prime Minister. Andrew was to be the guest of honor at Ludwisia, Krakow's premiere palace of elegant dining. There would be tremendous interest in the affair and all the publicity this nascent democracy could muster. Cory noticed a shoulder holster with a small caliber, ivory handled revolver slung over the back of Jerzy's chair. He wanted to ask about it but thought better of it.

Shortly after ten, Georgia arrived in the gym looking like she hadn't slept a wink.

"I know, I know. I look like shit. Fucking Andrew did this to me intentionally. He knows I'm supposed to look like shit in the movie but instead of letting me act tired he wants to make sure that I am tired. So he picks a fight and tells me something he knows will eat away at me so I won't be able to sleep."

"I'm sure he didn't mean it," Cory said, though he didn't know why.

"Oh? You can't begin to know the devious depths to which he can sink. I'm sure he meant it." She moved over to him, standing above the stretch mat, and leaned into his torso, setting her right cheek against his chest and letting her arms, lost in the sleeves of her oversized sweatshirt, dangle at her sides. She closed her eyes; Cory could see that in the mirror across from them. "I could just go to sleep right here."

"Did you eat something?" Cory asked softly, not wanting to move. He could stand there forever he thought.

"Renata brought me breakfast but I just didn't feel like egg whites this morning."

"But you had coffee. I can smell that."

"Of course. But it didn't help. I'm still half-dead."

"As far as I'm concerned coffee doesn't' 'help' anything."

"I know. I've heard your lecture," Georgia moaned.

"And skipping breakfast isn't a good idea either; breakfast…"

Georgia mocked Cory's tone. "…is the most important meal of the day. Starts the furnace burning and gets the metabolism working for the rest of the day, it's like the accelerator of a car…blah, blah, blah."

"Hey, the facts are the facts. And your svelte body is living proof," Cory reiterated.

"Svelte? Svelte means lithe and sensual. I thought I was just skinny?"

"Oh no, you're thin all right. But there's no denying you're sensual. Skinny would be totally inappropriate."

"Well, svelte, huh? I'll take it, then."

"I'm working on finding the right words these days. I can see from the reading material you've been giving me that you have to pay careful attention to the thing observed and the words you use to communicate your experience of the thing." Cory smiled proudly.

"Hey, not bad. Very Rilkian."

"Thank you." Cory bowed theatrically then clapped his hands together. "Now, to work."

"Can we just do some cardio? I don't think I have it in me for one of your kickass workouts." Georgia moved away towards the treadmill before he even answered. She had made up his mind for him.

"Sure."

They spent the half hour making small talk. Lani's newly discovered crush on Pavel, Niki's parents coming for a visit in the spring, the difficulty they were having with school, and more. But nothing about last night, about Andrew or the fight, and a lot of long quiet pauses that Cory let linger, taking her pulse now and then to monitor her work level. From what Cory had read on the call sheet in the Orbis lobby that morning, the days ahead were to be some of the most emotionally taxing of the movie. He'd taken Jack Grady's words to heart and more than anything, did not want to get in the way of Andrew or Georgia or the movie itself. So he stood quietly watching Georgia jog, breathe, sweat and delve into the psyche of Anna Kamenski, a woman being sent out to the death camp to verify that her husband was still alive.

Like the pain of Eli's fiendish beatings, this agony of reaching out but not touching, of feeling but refusing action, this unbelievable locus of love-thwarted would also pass. And when it had fallen away, this euphoric rush denied, would it, too, define him so clearly as the blood his father had drawn?

Could he live with love or would he repeat the cycle of the fathers before him and kill it as well?

CHAPTER SIXTY-FOUR

All morning long the bulk of the crew had been dressing the set of the famed Auschwitz front entrance with its double walls of electrified barbed wire on both sides of the long brick building whose high, arched opening below the tall guard tower facilitated the coming and going of passenger trains dumping Jews into the frozen, barracks-laden acres of the camp, into the cauldron of the Nazi's nefarious Final Solution.

The vintage locomotive possessed a smoke-spewing, rake-fronted engine, six freight cars and the soldiers' caboose. The establishing shot would be from inside the camp as the SS guards watched the approaching train make its way under the arch and into the compound. Yuri and Andrew had placed the camera on a crane and planned on taking it from ground level as the train drew nearer up over the engine, letting the pillar of billowing smoke pass right through the camera as it cleared. Rory's zooming lens was supposed to find the visage of Anna looking down from the window of the main guard tower over the railway arch. A tricky, detailed shot that would require a good forty-five minutes of preparation each time they had to shoot it. Andrew was insistent upon doing it no more than twice.

Anna Kamenski had been driven the thirty miles from Krakow to Auschwitz in one of Hans Frank's private Daimler-Benz sedans with blacked out windows and then secretly ushered up to this temporarily vacated guard tower. Schlesinger and one other SS officer were the only ones aware of her visit and allowed her this hawk's-eye view of the camp at Herr Frank's insistence. He had followed behind them in his own car and met with Commandant Hoess before joining them in the tower, bestowing a lavish crate of Kentucky whiskey, Belgian chocolates, and Vienna's finest sausages on the Camp Director in return for the small favor he had arranged.

Four hundred acres of low-ceilinged wooden barracks arranged in rows, sectioned off to divide men, women, and children and surrounded by tall fences of barbed wire in groups of six to ten buildings. A large open space, the width of a luxury liner, split the camp in half. But luxury was nowhere to be found in the flatlands outside of the industrial town of Oswiecim, except within the confines of Commandant Hoess's private yard.

At the far end of the camp, a half mile down the main, snow covered road, were two square black smoke stacks. Anna could not have possibly imagined, staring out the window, that the ash fluttering in the crisp breeze comprised the remnants of the brothers and sisters, fathers and mothers, the very children of her own race, whose Zyklon B poisoned bodies were incinerated daily by the thousands.

Crippled by long journeys and freezing weather, passengers in their threadbare coats and emblematic yellow stars, crammed wall to wall inside the freight cars like cattle, no, worse than cattle, forced to stand and survive in their own excrement, hanging on to life without having eaten, bathed, even breathed fresh air for those unlucky enough to have been stuffed in the middle, stumbled out of their boxcar prisons and into loose formations in the space molded by the direction of SS gun barrels.

Having been stripped of their possessions at the journey's inception, they clung to the small bundles they managed to stow away for the trip as tightly as they held their children. A tall, somewhat debonair man in a long bluish-gray coat, flanked by two SS Officers scanning clipboards, stood at the front of the lines that had formed en route to his position. Armed with only a stethoscope and a long, bony finger, he sorted through the swooning, coughing, grumbling crowd, examining them, sometimes with his hands, sometimes with the scope, mostly by sight and intuition. He sent them either left or right. Most often in this initial segregation, mothers were separated from children, the elderly and the weak from the young and the strong. Amid soldiers false guarantees in Polish, Czech, Rumanian, Hungarian, whatever the origin of the train, women with barely the strength to stand wailed in horrifying pleas for reunification with their children that deep inside they knew would not be coming. It was the agonizing good-byes that severed Anna's heart as she watched forced separation and long marches away from the train.

"Doctor Mengele is weeding out the healthy from the sick. By the time they get here, the line between life and inevitable death is very fine." Frank spoke to Anna as he entered the room.

"A line you drew when you tore them away from their homes." Anna retorted caustically.

"Now, now, Anna. We have an agreement." Hans tried calming her down.

"The magnitude of your barbarism is so impossible to process in my mind I can't remember my own name."

"And the name of your husband? After all, isn't that what we are here for? You have held up your end of the bargain. This is mine." Hans turned to Schlesinger who had retreated to the door. He addressed him. "Bring in Professor Kamenski."

Schlesinger opened the door at the top of the stairs and motioned for then to come up. Anna covered her mouth with trembling hands as she heard the ascending footsteps. After all this time, everything she'd been through, the unimaginable hell he himself must have been through, she was finally going to see him, lay her swollen eyes on the face that rested beside hers on their nuptial pillows for so many what seemed now, by contrast, blessed years. Dry, her mouth. Hysterically subdued, her shuddering torso. Resurgent, her hope.

In the white and blue prison uniform, a man's body fit, slumped and haggard, his crook nose angled off at an unfamiliar slant, his sunken eyes traveling along the floorboards. The facial hair was speckled with gray; she'd never seen it that way before. Schlesinger stopped him in the middle of the room where the broken man continued staring at the floor, straining to lift his head and address the woman standing at the window. Slowly his chin rose.

Anna stared at him in disbelief then looked to Frank, confused and inquisitive. She pleaded with the stranger, "Who are you?"

In a measured response, as if he had just read the name off a gravestone, the man replied, "I am Professor Janusz Kamenski."

She looked back and forth between them, baffled. "This is not my husband."

Without so much as a wink of hesitation, Frank responded. "Yes, yes it is." He addressed the man. "Tell her."

The stranger spoke methodically and without inflection. "My name is Janusz Kamenski. I am a doctor of philosophy at Jagellonian University. My wife's name is Anna. I resided up until recently at twenty-nine ul Komandosow in the city of Krakow and now am a prisoner of the Reich." He recited into the floor, never once looking at Anna.

"There you see. This man is your husband," Frank remarked.

Anna remained perplexed. "What are you saying? I have never seen this man before in my life."

Frank turned to the man, his patience growing thinner. He pointed a fisted hand, gloves clenched in its grip. "Is she or is she not your wife?"

The moment of betrayal was upon him. To deny what he had been ordered to do would mean death, and though he had no knowledge about the fate of the real Janusz Kamenski, that man was most certainly dead. Either answer was about to crush this woman's soul;

should he die too for the sake of speaking the truth? There seemed to be no value in it.

"Yes, this is my wife."

"Liar!" Anna shouted. She lunged at him and slapped his face. He did not move, nor did he seem pained by it. Schlesinger pulled Anna away from him back towards the window. Outside, on the frozen train platforms, Doctor Mengele continued the selection process, marking innocent people for annihilation.

"Are you saying this man is not your husband?" Frank asked.

Anna's hysteria had turned to tears. She could not answer. The game, the fate of her beloved, were beginning to dawn on her and the tragedy of it all had begun to compress her, spinning toward the center of a black hole, where time stretches into something unrecognizable and mass collapses into a density that permits no room for light, breath, blood.

Frank struck the stranger with the back of his hand. Still he did not shrink away or cry out. "I want the truth. What is your name?"

"I am Professor Janusz Kamenski. I am a prisoner of the Reich."

"Well, one of you is lying. Anna? I will ask you again. I realize it has been some time since you have seen him and the condition of his forced labor has no doubt changed his appearance but are you sure this man is not your husband?"

Through her fits and sobs, Anna whispered in a grievous voice, "You know he is not my husband, you evil bastard."

"Very well, I believe you. And since you have indicated this man is a liar, and since lying to an officer of the SS is considered treason, I am left with no alternative but to have this man executed immediately." Anna pulled her head from her hands and turned back towards the stranger. There was still no visible reaction from him, even upon hearing of his own death sentence.

"For the sake of this man, Anna, who clearly believes he is your husband, I will give you one last chance. Look carefully at him. Do you see before you, your husband?" Frank looked between them.

She stared. Was this the way Janusz looked before he died Anna wondered. His eyes so sullen and his skin sallow, his spirit broken, his will to live deserting him? She looked at him, scrutinized him for the first time, the man before her, not the man she had envisioned, dreamt about seeing these past few days. In the few seconds she had to make her decision she realized that he, too, probably had a family somewhere, perhaps a wife whose heart would shatter at the news of his death. Despite her own new nightmare, she knew at this moment that her husband was gone and that she had the power to save the life of the man in front of her. There was no room for truth now, only the choice to live. "Yes," she said. "This man is my husband."

"Cut!" Andrew yelled from behind the camera at the top of the stairs in the guard tower.

"Reset, please. Back to one." Peter spoke to the handful of crew that fit into this tiny room. "Make-up on Anna and Vladi," he called down the stairs, then admonished the P.A.'s outside through his radio. "Jonathon, we see everything outside at the train, remember. Remind these extras that they're supposed to be fearing for their lives not waiting for Michael Jackson to show up."

Yuri checked the back light at the window. Keeping the action out on the train platform in focus was a difficult proposition. He'd had to pull a few tricks and didn't want to end up in the dailies watching this immensely expensive and complicated scene become unusable.

Andrew pulled Georgia aside. They had been walking on eggshells around each other all day after their confrontation last night. The tension between them was palpable, even to the crew who were most often too busy to notice such things.

"I don't know what's going on, Anna. But it's not there. It's not there." Andrew turned and pretended to watch the extras piling into the train cars equipped with portable heaters for warmth between takes.

Georgia reminded herself to listen first to the man as her director, not as her husband. If he felt, as the *auteur*, that she was not delivering, then he had a right to point it out. But how much of this was him getting back at her for her words the night before? How much derived from his jealousy over her defense of Cory? It was hard to tell. Part of her thought he was merely trying to aggravate her, add to her frustration in an effort to get it out on screen. But it wasn't working out that way; it was distracting her.

Andrew knew this; he could sense her displacement. "I don't know what else to tell you, G. Anna just found out her husband is dead. That should pull her stomach right out of her through the bottoms of her feet." She did not respond. Inside, she was reminding herself to keep her cool. "But then I guess that's bad direction on my part, because in real life, that's your secret wish. I'm sure you'd love to be rid of me, you'd be able to fuck your little trainer boyfriend."

Smack! Before she even knew why, Georgia' hand flew from her side and slapped him ferociously across the face. And before he knew what hit him or why, he retaliated with his own slap that spun her head back over her left shoulder so powerfully it knocked her silver hair clip onto the floor.

The room froze. All eyes on the two of them. Georgia paused, stunned. She had never hit him before, and he most certainly had never hit her. Things had indeed changed between them. How much more could she possibly take?

She spoke to him calmly, resolutely. “I know you’re frustrated and afraid, Andrew, but don’t you ever hit me again or it will not only be the last time you touch me but the last time you see my face.”

And then she stormed out.

After five minutes of abject silence at the window, looking out at the remnants of a once horrific landscape seemingly come alive again, he turned to Yuri and spoke plainly. “We’ll shoot around her for now.”

CHAPTER SIXTY-FIVE

Although three inches of snow had settled onto the runways by Monday noon, a snow so aerial it seemed not like snow at all but rather an icy fog that whirled about the air-field like the breath of a million ghosts caressing the ailerons of the jets, Lars landed in Warsaw that afternoon without incident. From there it was a bumpy taxi ride to ul Gordinka just past Praski Park and the zoo to Slasko's Military Surplus Store. Waiting for him there was Ivan Golebami, his brother Max, and their comrade Victor Bok, local black market gun runners and members of The New German Alternative's brother organization in Poland – "Pazur Ryzy", The Red Claw.

"Did you find what I need?" Lars asked Ivan as

they settled in the bunker-like back room of the shop.

"There is a sanitarium outside Kielce which is on the way. It will require a number of payoffs, and very large ones."

"Money is no worry," Lars replied.

"And they want it in Deutsche Marks," Ivan added.

"Of course they do." Lars pulled a letter-sized envelope out of his coat pocket and tossed it onto Ivan's lap. "You all do." Ivan smiled; they all smiled.

Ivan tucked the envelope in his jacket without counting the money then handed Lars a folder filled with information about the movements of the film production – photos identifying the chief players, photos of their locations, copies of all the call sheets that went out to the crew daily and all related addresses.

"I have been in contact with Sanzia at Wawel. He was the last man to see Zweig alive." Ivan explained.

"Correction, the last man to see him alive was the man who murdered him. And that man is mine to kill. Are we clear about this?"

"Yes, Herr Rostock." They all nodded.

"Sanzia seems to think this is the man who killed him. Jack Grady." He indicated Grady from a set photo. "Goldman's Bodyguard. Seems Zweig mentioned to him that Grady had the look of a soldier."

"I'm well aware of Jack Grady, and, if I were a

betting man, I'd put my money on him as the assassin."

"So there will be bloodshed after all?"

"Very discriminating blood shed, and only on my orders. There will be no punishment until I say so. Understand?" Again they nodded silently. Their tacit compliance reassured Lars. He realized he had picked the right men for the job. What steadfast Nazi's they would make. Their preparation was excellent, their fealty unquestioning. Only their courage remained untested.

"Max will show you the weapons," Ivan proceeded.

On an old printing press with a sheet of plywood thrown on top that doubled as a table, Max laid out a series of automatic weapons, slick handguns, and enough ammunition to wage a small scale war. "Choose what you will, comrade. These are especially nice." He pointed to a pair of 5.56mm Enfield Weapon System rifles. "Single shot or automatic first strike capability, burst selector, interchangeable sub-assemblies, laser sighting, muzzle launch grenade ability. They even conform to NATO specs. An excellent assault weapon, an infantryman's wet dream."

"Yes, these will do nicely." Lars inspected the weapon then gave a reassuring nod to Ivan. "How long is the drive?"

"Three hours to Kielce, an hour to Krakow from there."

"Are they expecting you at the sanitarium tonight?" Lars asked.

"Yes. They said to come after ten."

"Then we will go at eight o'clock."

"We'll be ready," Ivan remarked, turning to his compatriots and getting a confirming nod from both.

Lars took in a deep breath and gathered his thoughts. Running through the mental checklist, everything seemed in order. The priorities were set. Now he listened to the prodding of his hungry stomach and attended to secondary considerations. "Now, where can a man get a good kielbasa around here?"

The laughter of four hardened killers filled the back room. Outside, it had finally stopped snowing. Their drive to Krakow would be that much easier.

CHAPTER SIXTY-SIX

The Hotel Hollywood felt deserted. Most everyone had made the trip out to Auschwitz to partake of the historic filming inside the camp. It had taken Andrew many months of negotiations to achieve this unprecedented feat. Committees had to be appeased, organizations had their coffers lined with golden American dollars, and a rickety government trying to make sense of its newfound social democracy had to approve. After so much trouble, Andrew was going to milk it for all he could. Americans and Poles alike wanted to be there when he recreated some of the national nightmare.

Cory dared not attend. He knew thin ice and

chose to stay behind. After a morning of touring Wawel Castle for the second time, this time at his own pace, and making some wonderful discoveries he was eager to share with Georgia, he had taken a taxi over to Hotel Hollywood to use the gym for an intense two hour workout of his own.

Only Jerzy remained behind in the office with Dante in the security room as the lone guard. Machek labored in the kitchen whipping up some salmon, new potatoes, stuffed Cornish game hens for those who eschewed fish, and a whopping chopped salad with so much diced produce it resembled vegetable confetti. Renata's whistling was the only human sound that coursed its way through the upstairs as she changed the linens and straightened the rooms.

Owing to the fact that the gym had nothing heavier than fifty pound adjustable dumbbells and a one hundred and fifty pound weight stack on the multi-station machine, Cory had to resort to a high rep workout for himself. He didn't mind the fact that he would lose overall strength over these four months but he would do his best to stay lean and muscle dense. Besides, sets of twenty to thirty gave him a great pump.

He was finishing up his fourth mile on the treadmill when he heard a commotion in the hall followed by a door slamming. He shut down, toweled off, and stepped out of the gym. Lani's door was closed and he heard muffled voices from inside the room. The girls weren't expected back from the orphanage until after four. Maybe one of them is sick, he thought. He knocked on the door.

"Lani, Niki? It's Cory. You guys all right?"

The voices stopped. After a long pause and a little whispering, Niki came to the door, stepped out of the room and shut it behind her.

"What's up?" Cory asked.

"Well, it's kind of a long story…" Niki was reluctant to speak.

"Is Lani okay?"

"Sort of. Just had a major heart trampling by Pavel."

"Oh. I see." The picture came into focus for Cory. No serious emergency. A sense of relief washed over him. After everything Jack had been telling him, he found himself worrying about the girls more than usual.

"He told her he couldn't see her anymore," Niki continued. "His parents made him quit his volunteer work." Cory realized she probably wasn't supposed to tell him anything but she couldn't resist putting it out there.

"Why? Seemed just like the kind of guy Lani needed around her."

"I guess when he told his parents that he was working with her and had a crush on her and everything they just flipped out. In a wholly unpositive way, you know."

"Let me guess. Because she's Andrew Goldman's daughter and she's Jewish."

"Niki?" Lani called from inside.

Niki looked at Cory and nodded, an exaggerated, wide-eyed nod, before slipping back inside.

Cory whispered to her just before the door shut, "Well, tell her I'm sorry. Really." He was alone in the hallway, sweat still trickling down his torso. "Poor girl," he said to himself then realized how absurd that sounded. He went to shower.

When Cory entered the office to ask Jerzy to call a taxi Andrjez turned to him. "Yes, Cory. I am supposed to take you to the Hotel Orbis. Mrs. Goldman is waiting for you there."

"Georgia?" Cory was sure he'd made a mistake.

"Yes." Andrjez remarked. Cory looked to Jerzy. He confirmed it with a nod.

"I thought she was filming all day at the camp?"

"Yes, well there was problem. She say to me to bring you as soon as possible to talk to her."

"What the hell does she want to talk to me about?" Cory knew they had no answer.

CHAPTER SIXTY-SEVEN

Cory lead Georgia down the last five stone steps in the dim light of intermittently placed, electric sconces. They were the only two people in the great crypt, whose short columns and cushioned-style capitals dispersed into cross-ribbed vaulted ceilings barely eight feet high that gave the daunting chamber the look of a great arcade roof with its legs cut out from under it.

With a glass of Sophia twirling in her hand, Cory had found Georgia at the bar in the Hotel Orbis watching American Heavy Metal Groups on European MTV, mystified.

"Why are these kids so angry?" She had asked him when he sat down next to her. "They aren't old

enough to be so disillusioned."

"Georgia? What are you doing here?" Cory asked. She gently placed her hand on top of his. The electricity shot through him. He noticed the slight swelling on her left cheek.

"I needed…to talk to you. To get away from Andrew." She paused, not hearing any of the ear splitting sounds coming from Big Head Todd and the Monsters. "Can we go for a walk?" She asked.

"I've been trying to get you to walk this city with me for three weeks."

They marched over the Vistula and up the rampart to Wawel Castle where Cory had a big surprise for her. Georgia spoke very little and mostly listened while Cory reveled in the joy of her unexpected company and talked on about Rilke's poem "Archaic Torso of Apollo" and how the last line – "You must change your life" – brought such fascinating closure to the piece.

"He fills you with the tormented sense of our human incompleteness from which practically leap the demands for transformation, for change."

Georgia laughed, bundling herself tighter against the cold as he went on, every inch of his six-four frame the excited schoolboy. Her heart smiled for she had always intended him to enjoy the wonders of great literature but never imagined it would so decisively "transform" him into the hungry student.

The snow kicked up from their boots as they struggled, heads cocked against the chilling breeze. An afternoon snow had descended. Perfect for Andrew's exterior shots she thought as they looked out at the whiteness of an Eastern European world driving ice crystals against their stinging cheeks and narrowed eyes with a foreshortened view of everything.

They were sufficiently dried by the time they had ducked into the sepulchral room below the main chancel in St. Stanislaus Cathedral inside Wawel Castle grounds.

"This is your big surprise? A tomb?" Georgia chided him.

"But look whose tomb." Cory motioned for her to read the name engraved on the gold medallion embedded on the face of the black marble sarcophagus.

"Adam Mickiewicz. No kidding?"

"This is the guy, Poland's greatest poet." Cory added, even more excited than when talking about Rilke.

"How did you know about this?"

"The first day I came to train you at your house in Beverly Hills I was waiting in the gym, checking out all the equipment to see what kind of condition things were in and his anthology was there on the seat of the recumbent bike. I opened it and saw where you had marked the passage. Something about a woman becoming a huntress, wearing a bear-skin and returning from the field where she was often mistaken for the

Prince himself."

"Yes. From Grazyna. You read that passage?"

"It was just sitting there. And you were ten minutes late coming down to the gym."

"Cory Sonne. You are full of surprises." She grabbed his hand and squeezed it from over the top of the coffin. It was the second time in less than an hour she had reached out for him. The sheer joy of these stolen moments with her made him light-headed. He smiled and drank her in.

"This is the guy," he repeated just for something to say.

"This is the guy. I wonder why Judy didn't show us this on the tour?" Georgia remarked.

"Probably thought the girls wouldn't appreciate seeing the tombs of a bunch of dead guys. I mean this whole Church is like one pile of memorials to the dead - Kings, Bishops, Saints, Heroes in the ongoing struggle for Independence, Poets." He indicated the sarcophagus.

"Look at you You really are fascinated by it all."

"Yeah. Aren't you?"

"Yes. But I'm older. I always thought I was a bit odd for being so intrigued by everything. Always thought that a thirst for knowledge was a by product of being an actress and wanting to be armed with information."

"Huh. I don't know why it interests me so much.

I've always been eager to learn, pretty much so I didn't end up like my parents - ignorant."

Suddenly, the lights went out. They stood there listening in the total darkness of the tomb. "Do you think they'll come back on?" Georgia asked.

Cory pressed the light button on his digital watch; it glowed green. "It's four o'clock. I think that's closing time."

"Maybe we're the only ones in here. They probably didn't see us come it."

"We're not alone. We got Mickiewicz. And across the way is Prince Josef, Cardinal Vasa, Casimir. Even Kosciuszko is down here somewhere. We've got a legion of famous dead guys."

"Cory, I'm scared," Georgia said, sounding like a little girl.

"You? Nonsense."

"Where are you? It's so black I can't even see the nose on my face."

"Take my hand."

Cory and Georgia both reached out into the darkness and slowly waved their hands in the air until they found each other somewhere over the marble coffin of Adam Mickiewicz. They held on tightly until they got to the opening of the crypt. He led the way, feeling carefully for the first step then waiting as she found it herself before going on and up into the emerging light at the top of the stairs.

When they came out from the royal tombs into the main body of the Cathedral, they were alone. The fading afternoon light cast opaque planes of illumination from on high across the pews of the church. They walked towards the closest row and sat down, breathing a little easier and still holding hands – two small bodies in the vastness of the monumental basilica.

"I guess you're better with the darkness than I am," Georgia admitted.

"Spent a lot of time in the dark when I was a kid, you know, closets, the basement and crawl spaces under the house, the barn cellar."

"To escape your father?" She asked looking up into his down-turned eyes.

"Yes."

A long silence.

"Something happened, Cory, with your father. Didn't it?" No response. "You can tell me."

"No, I can't." Cory stared at the broken corner of a massive, marble column. "I promised I'd never tell anyone."

"Who did you promise?"

"My mother."

"But she's passed away, Cory."

"And I promised myself." The instinct to run overtook him; he tried to pull his hand away. His past was here to destroy the most valuable moments of his life, right here next to Georgia. She grasped it more firmly.

"I tell you what. Let's make a pact. I'll be your priest, here in the church and you can confess your sins to me. Then I'll do likewise."

"No, you don't have to..." Cory stammered.

"I want to, Cory. I want to. Is that a fair deal?"

Cory drew a deep breath. Could he find it in himself to dislodge his crucial history? Could he put it into words? Could he bear the pain of remembering? And of telling it to Georgia? She would surely be frightened of him then and things would never be the same. This was so intoxicating, the way things were right now. It would change. If he told her the real truth, he would never be able to look her in the eyes again.

But something spurred him on. He began anyway because he knew that if he were ever to realize his greatest fantasy – the complete and utter possession of her – he would have to come clean. Pure. Truthful. To her and to himself. That's how we would want her. And so he prepared to give of himself as he would expect her to give.

The words came.

There were things she already knew about Eli, about how he had beat him and Ray and Becky, about how his mother still loved his father at the end, about how he couldn't help it. He couldn't help "it". But he had never told Georgia what that "it" was.

"I told you about my recurring nightmare. About packing my father's valise with his things, wrapping his belt around my fist and feeling the pain of every lick I ever took with it, and walking through the plum orchard toward the stump on a tide of rotten plums but never being able to escape."

"Yes, I remember." Georgia encouraged him with a sweet whisper.

"Well, that really happened. But I wasn't trying to escape. I was going to bury those things in the grave I had dug for my father's body." Cory continued talking through his tears. My parents had thrown everything into the pot, trying to keep the farm alive. One day the broker, Mr. Stevens from the bank, came out to serve us papers. I was fifteen then and home alone with my mother. She begged and begged for them not to take our home and our land. She told him that her uncle had died, which he had, and she was going to come into some money soon, which was a lie. But she just couldn't bare the thought of losing everything. He took pity on my poor mother and told us we had thirty days to come up with all back payments which we both knew wasn't likely to happen.

"Well, Eli came home drunk that night. He had heard in town that Mr. Stevens had been out to the house and was liquored up to prepare for the worst. He pulled up in front of the house. I came out onto the porch to meet him and explained that mother had persuaded Mr. Stevens to give us thirty more days. He went ballistic with rage and started screaming about what a whore she was and he knew that she had fucked him so he wouldn't take the house. I mean he kept saying that over and over as if he couldn't get the image of her fucking Mr. Stevens out of his brain. He made a dash for the porch stairs, yelling for me to get out of the way. I knew he was going in to beat her within an inch of her life. And I just decided right then and there that no matter what the price was, the beatings were going to end. I didn't move.

"He thrust out his forearm at me to shove me aside but I rebuffed him and pushed him backwards. He stumbled down the porch steps and ended up face down in the dirt with a bloody lip. 'I'm gonna kill you, you son-of-a-bitch' he shouted out at me. My mother was at the window upstairs. She cried, 'Eli, no.' He picked himself up, grabbed a half of a rotten plum out of the bed of his truck, threatened to kill her, too, then heaved the plum directly through the window at my mother, shattering the glass.

"I don't know what happened to me but this pent up rage just surged through me, my muscles tensed, my fists clenched, my eyes literally saw red, I mean literally all the light from the porch and from the moon, even from the cab of his truck, it all turned red, and I leaped off the porch and attacked him. We traded punches and fought and rolled on the ground. He clawed at my eyes, that's this scar here." Cory indicated a small scar over his right eyebrow.

"My mother had run downstairs and pulled me off of him for a moment. As he rose off the ground he took a roundhouse swing, not at me, but at her, snapping her head around and knocking her to the ground. She hit the side of her head on the porch railing and got a concussion. And then I just lunged at Eli, and with every ounce of strength I had I took him down to the ground and choked him and beat his head in until I had completely exhausted myself. I don't even know how long he was unconscious before I finally stopped but I rolled off of him and lay there next to his body, panting and sweating in the dirt. He didn't move. I had…I had killed him."

Cory looked up from the pew to the altar in front of them. The Sigismund Chapel stood before them. The "Pearl of the Renaissance north of the Alps" it had been called. The mellow red marble, the gold inscriptions, the arcaded niches flanking the golden dome with ornately carved statues of the saints. Sitting among such intricate and antique beauty with the most radiant looking woman he had ever seen next to him, Cory could hardly imagine himself a murderer. But that he was. And, although he had been trying to for his entire adult life, he could not run from it.

"I spent the rest of that night digging the grave by the old stump. I dragged his body over and rolled it in face down, to make sure he had a good view of where he'd be going. Then I went upstairs and packed his things, thinking that if the police came investigating we could at least point to his missing personal items. My mother just stood there by the shattered window, looking out over the orchard at night, sobbing. That's when the cover-up began. I've been living that lie ever since. You see, I'm a rotten person, that's why I dream of rotten plums."

Georgia placed her hand under his chin and spoke directly to his face. "No, you're not, Cory. You did the only thing you could do. If you hadn't, he'd have killed you or your mother or both of you. If I had picked up the morning paper and read this story, knowing nothing about the people involved, I'd say the same thing to you that I'm saying now – he deserved to die. I know it sounds callous but it's the truth. Somebody's got to stand up for the innocent people in this world who have been victimized. You did. You did the right thing." Georgia placed her thumb on his forehead and with a loving smile made a tiny sign of the cross, "I absolve you, Cory Sonne, of all your sins."

Through the trail of his tears, he returned the smile. "If it were only that easy."

CHAPTER SIXTY-EIGHT

Just then the creak of a heavy and ancient door opening echoed through the back of St. Stanislaus Cathedral. Georgia stared at Cory for a split second then clutched at his hand, stood, and dragged him from the pew, across the aisle and into the confessional, pulling the burgundy curtain closed behind them.

The two of them sat there on the narrow wooden bench, Georgia on Cory's lap, Cory's head wedged into the nape of her neck. He smelled her, the greasepaint mixing with the almond praline scent of her Parisian soap, with just a hint of jacaranda, which he had come to cherish. Outside the confessional in the main body of the church the footsteps methodically plodded along.

Someone was pacing down the northern aisle across from them, pausing at the openings to the many alcoves, chapels and tombs lining the far side of the Cathedral.

In their rush to be seated and silent, Cory's hand had slipped up underneath Georgia's jacket and sweater. He felt the cotton fabric of her undershirt then found himself doing something he could not prevent, pulling it out from its tuck in the back of her jeans. She didn't say a word or move to avoid it. His fingers found the warm skin of her lower back, and he caressed it, running the tips across the tiny ridges of her spinal processes then along the slight convex of her erector muscles, then up until he could spread his full palm across her back then around in a full circle. So smooth.

They listened to the footsteps coming closer as the curator or security guard or whoever swung around to the southern wall of the church, the wall with their confessional flush upon it. Cory's hand up the back of her shirt never wavered in its touch.

If this was penance, he would surely sin again.

The footsteps came closer and closer until they were just outside the curtain, pausing for a moment, presumably to look into the Chapel of Bishop Zalucki which abutted the confessional. An eerie quietude was marred only by the sound of congested breathing from the Cathedral custodian inches away. Cory thought about the massive heart attack they could give this poor

schlep if they burst out of the sacred closet right now, screaming. But they waited, still, silent, him reveling in the warm smoothness of her back, her in the gentle caresses, their bodies converging radially, like a crystal towards a center.

After ten more minutes of shuffling footsteps and the concomitant shriek of the closing door in the back of the church, they were again alone.

So little light in their cubicle and yet Georgia could see his eyes so clearly in the luminous beam coming from the crease between the top of the brocade and the door frame; there was no mistaking his want. It started with his heart and made its way to his hand and now his eyes, and every other tangent of his body she could sense. It was her want, too.

And so she kissed him.

Their lips found each other in a passion so piercing, a rassling of mouths so ardent, it was as if her face so severely wanted to occupy the same space as his own that it pressed every last tear from his eyes. He was crying again, and not because he had re-discovered the killer in his soul but for the discovery of something new – love.

Love fulfilled in the act.

Georgia's hands roamed through the soft sward of his hair; his arms wrapped around her back with his hands firmly grasping the opposite sides of her torso.

They swarmed at each other minute after minute with hot, hungry busses. She pulled at him, squeezing his face into her chest, resting her chin on the top of his head. Unable to resist the impulse any longer, he spoke. "I want you."

All movement stopped as she cradled his head in her arms. Finally, she broke away from him and exited the confessional only to re-emerge alongside him in the layman's cubicle next door with a semi-translucent screen between them. She whispered with her lips so close to it, he could feel her breath on his cheek.

"It's my turn to confess, Cory. Please, hear me out."

"As you wish," Cory complied, his pulse still pounding.

"I married Andrew when I was very young, and I saw in him all the things I wanted for stability in my life which I never had growing up. And I wanted the things Andrew could provide. For me and for my children. He was a kind and loving man, brilliant and fascinating, I learned so much from him and he has this unquenchable thirst for knowledge, which you've probably seen plenty of evidence of, that's very sexy in its own way. He was very supportive of my career which I was adamant about pursuing. But after Lani, and as my success continued, though it never really rivaled his by any means, we found ourselves settling into an antagonistic relationship that neither of us could understand. He was not a good father as it turned out, virtually ignoring Lani in many ways. And his physical affections became less and less frequent. I learned to live with that. I was getting a vicarious fix of affection and feeling through the roles I was playing but as you can imagine it wasn't the same thing. It's very easy to fool yourself into thinking that you are needed, you know. After years of this, I resigned myself to the notion of doing without that part of my life. Instead, I longed to have another child. I told you this already. But he agreed to that, probably out of guilt, but his virility had waned considerably and we made love so seldom that it took years, and when it finally happened, I was so excited. I made it my reason for living. This was over four years ago."

Cory leaned his head into the screen where their cheeks touched in the millimeters of openness between the mesh.

"The story I told you before about having a rare tissue disorder that contributed to my miscarriage. Well, that wasn't entirely true. The real story is much uglier. As fate would have it, two weeks after I found out I was pregnant, nearly six weeks along, I came home one night to find him stinking drunk, sitting on that huge couch in our living room, listening to Vivaldi at an ear-shattering decibel level. There in front of him on the coffee table was a physician's paper with the results of his insurance physical on them. His blood test had come back HIV positive."

Cory could barely contain his shock, ""No! My God. How?" He bit nervously at the inside of his lip as she went on.

"It all came pouring out of him that night. During our entire marriage he had been having homosexual relations with many different men. He had always been bisexual but thought that falling in love with me and settling down would tame that wild streak in him. He said he managed for almost two years to quell it but that for the last ten he had been discreetly seeing his male lovers behind my back. I gotta admit; he was damn good at his deception. I had no idea. It took a long time for me to quit blaming myself for being so blind and stupid. And, of course, he could not process the horror of what had happened to him or what he had done to me and the unborn baby. You can bet I was at the doctor's office the next day for my testing. Two weeks later it was confirmed. I, too, was HIV positive."

Cory buried his head in his hands. The overwhelming silence of St. Stanislaus Cathedral was the language of the dead. All around them lay the crypts, tombs, altars and sarcophagi of legends long since expired – a necropolis high on the castle hill. He felt suddenly cold. A chilling breeze moved through him as if the ghosts of these great beings were all reaching out, waving their spirit arms and clutching at the flesh and blood of this warm and vivacious woman next to him.

Georgia was more akin to the deceased than he could have imagined, and thus her great fear of the dark. It struck him now. He had always seen her as a pillar of strength, and the truth was that she was the most fragile of creatures, vulnerable and facing an impending death in a palpable way even he had never known in all his spilt blood and beatings.

"The doctors immediately put me on medications that would protect the fetus. They assured me that if I followed their plan and consulted with them regularly for careful monitoring there would only be a one in three chance of the baby being born with HIV. I heard what they were saying but something inside me had no faith in those odds. Something inside me closed down to the possibility of bringing an AIDS baby into the world. That was my mentality at the time. And so, God, Cory, I can hardly bring myself to say it, but you see I am just like you, we are the same. I sabotaged myself and refused to eat. I stopped taking the medication and walked through the hills every day at such a brisk pace that I forced myself to miscarry. I'm sure you're well aware of the risks of hard exercise during pregnancy. But so was I, and I ignored them. I deliberately denied my baby a chance at life. Oh, God. It was horrible." Georgia's voice sputtered into convulsions of pain and sorrow. Her crying then was as essential as breathing.

Cory came around into her cubicle, picked her up off the bench and held her so close to him he felt as if he were a wall surrounding her on all sides, attempting to protect her from an agony he could not reach, a demon that stirred from within.

The echoes of her sobs played like primal music in the regal caverns of the Cathedral. Cory Sonne and Georgia Hart, locked in that embrace, dwelled in a moment that existed separate from the temporal. It could not be measured by ticks on a clock or the sweeping hands of a watch, only by its primordial reflection back into the dawn of the universe when desire formed the cosmos. A couple bound in sharing grief with loving intent, they were a mirror shining back the light of God. And if Godliness were measured in the need of aching hearts, then this grand church never succored two more Christ-like parishioners.

In her delicate ear he whispered words never before formed in his breath. "I love you, G."

She pulled back from their embrace and resumed kissing him as if his face were a blackboard and her lips the eraser. As they danced there in place, the material world faded around them - concentric rings of still water displaced from a stone tossed.

With both his hands on her waist, he lifted her onto the bench in the confessional so that her torso was nearly at eye level then lifted the front of her sweater and undershirt with his right hand, undoing the snaps of her 501's with his left. He peeled back the flaps of her worn jeans, revealing the top panel of white silk on her French cut panties with an embroidered "G" on the front triangle. Cory hooked his thumb around them and pulled them down far enough to fully expose her taut belly. There was no resisting him as he pressed his head into it and kissed it with his whole face, this gorgeous womb that had miscarried a son, poisoned now in the blood. She felt, as he rubbed her and kissed her, as if he were some tribal medicine man attempting to heal her, and she was right. He wanted to be the healer of her womb.

But he wanted more than to touch it, and his hands untied her boots and began sliding her jeans down her thighs as he continued devouring her through her panties with his mouth. She found herself lifting her feet one by one and letting him remove everything. It was only his words that stopped her. "I want to be inside you."

"Cory. No. We don't have any protection." Her voice went guttural as his tongue slipped under her lacy hem and lapped at her vulva.

"I don't care." He undid his own pants.

"You can't, if there's blood it's like committing suicide."

Cory responded with a strong and resolute tone as if he'd prepared for this moment. The way she had put up virtually no resistance, had accepted it as almost inevitable, she wondered if she hadn't as well. She remembered the first time she laid eyes on him when he had walked into their home that day, remembered his posture, his riveted look, the sheer strength in the way he stood.

Her recollection was usurped by his poetic words spoken with more passion than anything that had ever pierced her from the page. "Having you is pure living. I'd gladly die tomorrow for making love to you right now."

And with that, he ripped her panties instantly in two, wrapped his large hands around her back and pulled her from the bench into his arms. Her legs enfolded his hips; her lips cavorted across his face. While one hand cupped her ass, palming her tailbone and supporting all the weight of her, his other hand grasped the shaft of his granite cock and guided it up inside her.

There was a force that swept up from the furrows of her soul as she felt him parting her from within, a question of emptiness in the shape of folded hands held open to the rain that filled with the storm of himself. His heavens were clashing and pouring down a torrent of pure passion that she brought to her mouth and drank, quenching a long thirst.

Cory's hardness, inside her and around her, seemed so utterly reassuring. She felt his strength, as if he could hold her like this forever. The muscles of his upper back contracted and her fingers kneaded them as he gently rocked her hips in his hands and over his swelling urge.

An image flashed through her floating mind, a picture of horses from the Ilapalakua Ranch on Hawaii's Big Island where she had visited as a little girl. While her father proposed business with the resort managers she had meandered over to the stalls and watched as a shimmering brown stallion mounted a golden mare. Even then the power and the need of the animals had drastically impressed her. Cory's need and his power were so dominant in these moments she had no choice but to give in. And so she flowed with him as he moved, pitching, quaking, undulating. He was her stallion, and as she arched her head back in ecstasy and felt her hair feathering her shoulder blades, she thought of it as her mane and the act of their bodies united as a force of nature undeniable.

The churning of her hips into his own grew frantic and the sheer notion of his impending release yanked her from the patient absorption of her pleasure to the brink of an orgasm the likes of which she had never experienced before. A thousand rifles could have been pointed at her now and the command to desist barked into her ear and she could not have stopped. She burned with pleasure from the very center of her being as every breath expelled the demon of her long buried lust.

Tensed with the contraction of every muscle and leaking out a steady moan, Georgia came. Her protracted climax reached high into the rosette rows of the basilica, into the crevices of the arcaded walls, the ears of statued saints in their separate niches, spilled into the seventeen distinct chapels, washed over the tombs of Sigismund, Casimir, Jadweiga the child queen. Even Adam Mickiewicz in his black marble coffin must have snickered at the echo of a prayer quite unfamiliar. Without a doubt, this Cathedral had never heard such a chorus of desire fulfilled.

So, too, Cory exploded. Screaming, unearthing every buried instinct to love that his sordid past had taught him to suppress. Spurting the flood of himself into her womb and dying *le petite mort* in her arms.

The two of them struggled to catch their breath, to catch each other's breath. They had sealed a fate they had been spinning toward for some time now. They looked at each other, unsmiling, still possessed by an electricity that circled them like the wild streak of a loose charge traveling the web of conduits ensnaring them, looking for a place to negate itself. But it couldn't and so it persisted.

Still wrapped around him in an ineluctable

embrace, still enveloping his hardness in her wet opening, Georgia finally whispered, "How can stupidity seem like Heaven?"

And it was.

CHAPTER SIXTY-NINE

They walked into the Orbis lobby shortly after 6 p.m. and ran smack dab into Jack Grady in a near panic over her whereabouts.

Cory and Georgia left Wawel at around five thirty in order to get back to the hotel before it got too cold. Much to their dismay, when they stepped out of St. Stanislaus the reliably gray western sky had cleaved and displayed a celestial pathway of fading blue. A radiant crescent sun was sinking into the corner of the Tatra Mountains – the first sunset of their stay in southern Poland. The two of them, inebriated on love rendered, watched the light succumb. "All things rise and fall." Georgia had said mysteriously.

“You gave me a bit of a scare, you two.” Jack said in a chastening tone.

“Really, Mr. Grady,” Georgia had said, “What would they want with me anyway?”

The question went unanswered but he knew well enough what kind of a target she presented, and he was just grateful to have her back in his sight. He had a car waiting to drive her back to Hotel Hollywood.

Georgia turned to Cory and, trying to be nonchalant, asked, “Will you come out to the set tomorrow, Cory?”

“Do you really think that’s a good idea?” He replied. How could he possibly shield what happened from Andrew? Ray had always teased him about lacking a good poker face; he knew he was not adept at deceit.

“Just come. Please.” She invoked.

“Then I’ll see you tomorrow.”

On his way through the lobby to the elevators, still high from his confessional experience, Cory was summoned by Sean into the bar where court was in session with Yuri, Mikola, Hiam and others.

“Join me, my friend,” Sean requested as he stood and corralled Cory in private.

“What’s up?” Cory asked.

“Maybe you should tell me?”

“What do I know?”

“Didn’t I just see you walk in with Georgia?”

Sean commented, putting up two fingers to the bartender who was familiar enough with his famous patron by this time to know exactly what he meant.

"We just went for a walk. She just wanted to blow off some steam."

"Oh, I see. You weren't on the set today; were you?"

"No."

"She needed to blow off steam because Andrew hit her, slapped her one good on the cheek. Not a smart thing to do to your leading lady if you're a director. But there's obviously something deeper going on there than either of us know about. Seeing the way she's cozied on up to you, I just feel compelled to warn you. You see, movie sets are strange things. It's not the real world. It's a fantasy world that you create for a very short period of time. It's as if people are exiled together, compacted in this little microcosm and because of the nature of the work and the long hours, their emotional levels are heightened. Love affairs spring up, people start coupling and copulating willy-nilly, and feuding sometimes as well. But whatever it is, you have to remember, it's not real."

"I think I can tell the difference between what's real and what's not. I may be a novice on the set but I've worked with my share of famous clients."

"Maybe you're right. But Georgia and Andrew have been together for a long time. Relationships like that, that lengthy, evolve in strange ways; they aren't all peaches and cream. Sometimes, and I'll admit this sounds perverse, but sometimes a man and a woman thrive on torturing each other."

"What are you saying, that Georgia wants to torture Andrew?"

"Maybe. I see her interest in you, and I think to myself what's going on there? Younger man, good-looking. Just the kind of guy that might make Andrew jealous. Maybe it's payback for something he did to her. All I'm saying is - you never know. Just be careful because believe me, when you're playing with movie people, you're playing with fire."

Cory took one sip of the Pilsner Urquel, and slammed it back down on the bar. "Thanks for the advice." He didn't believe Sean for one second and was determined not to let it interfere with his euphoric mood. And so he left. Sean zipped on his merry face and rejoined the drunken cartel.

That night, Cory lay in bed, reading Rilke's poems and Georgia's notes to herself in the margins before falling into a deep sleep and dreaming of a white-winged angel of mercy named Georgia Hart floating through the Cathedral on a cloud chorus from euphonious choirboys.

CHAPTER SEVENTY

Jack and Georgia had returned to Hotel Hollywood just as Andrew and the girls were sitting down to dinner. She took her usual place and proceeded as if nothing unusual had happened during the day. Not with Andrew, not with Cory. And he didn't ask where she had gone. He nervously wolfed down a second dessert. Surprisingly famished, she ate two helpings of Machek's turkey stew.

Afterwards, Andrew took her aside and apologized for his hostile – a word he phrased in air quotes - behavior. She accepted gracefully but still retired to the guest room that evening, away from him. Georgia felt neither contempt nor pity towards him. It seemed to her now that he was simply a man she could live without. Whereas living without Cory, who had planted his passion deep inside her, would be a travesty of a woman's dream unrealized.

Like Cory, Georgia too fell immediately asleep just past eight thirty and slept for three hours until awakened by Lani. Niki had broken out into the familiar frenzied sweat indicating the heinous flu had claimed another victim. The doctor was called to administer the requisite horse pill. After that he administered a flu shot to the rest of the household and advised them to get plenty of rest that evening and drink as much water as they could possibly stand, repeated trips to the bathroom be damned.

Following that small crisis and after comforting Niki with cold compresses, Georgia found it difficult to fall back asleep. She lay there in her single bed staring at a murky black ceiling washed in a half moon's light.

Cory. Cory. And more Cory. It was the only thing worth thinking about. The excitement of the film, the role of a lifetime which could bring her the kind of critical acclaim she had sought since her fledgling days at the American Conservatory Theater, even the meaning of her privileged, guarded and gated life with Andrew, all these things seem to pale in comparison with the discovery of the day – that she could give herself to another human being, find solace in that escape and have that feeling returned in kind. The impulse to leave Andrew had been there many times during their marriage long before Cory Sonne and for legitimate reasons. Now, it was more than an impulse. It was a necessity. Slowly, gradually, thought by thought and want by want, as the evening shadow overtakes the light, Georgia came to the decision that she would make the leap with this brave young man who kindled a fire within. A fire whose promise of continued warmth was worth risking her entire life as she had known it.

Yes, that was it. Consequences be damned. When this film wrapped, when she was back in the states, she would follow her doctor's lead on new protease inhibitors to fight her HIV, she would leave Andrew and would begin again. She didn't give a damn what he had to say about it or how he felt. And Lani? She'd be all right. She was used to Georgia and Andrew living separate lives. She'd be off to college next year, anyway.

It dawned on her that the idea of it no longer began with the question, "What if?" but rather "I will." Tears came to her eyes and she longed to touch Cory, to hold his face in her hands, to breath on him and hear the brass-plated resonance of his voice.

Shortly past 2 a.m., unable to sleep, she walked downstairs and into the office, excused Udo for some privacy then rang Cory at the Orbis.

"Hello," came the voice on the other end, still half-asleep.

"Hi. It's me." She whispered like a schoolgirl.

"Hey. Are you all right?"

"Yes. Sorry to wake you."

"Are you kidding? It's better than dreaming about you waking me up."

"There's something I didn't tell you at the Cathedral that I should have." She paused.

"Something else. Seemed like you covered a lot of territory." Cory answered mercurially, a little apprehensive, trying to counter the seriousness in her voice.

"Yes, something else. I love you. I should have said it then; I certainly felt it but I was too chicken."

"You said it; just not with words."

"I knew you'd understand."

"I'll always understand, Georgia. Even if I'm exiled tomorrow, I'll always understand."

"I don't want to exile you. In fact, I want to be with you. Can we do that, Cory? Can we be together?"

"I know I can. Can you?" Cory asked, his voice quivering.

"There's so much to talk about." Her voice trailed off into the unfrequented hours of the night.

They spoke to each other quietly, longingly. The wistful conversations of lovers with an aching need to connect. They talked about soft lips, rapturous smells, natural chemistry, about things they could do together, places they could go and what they would do when they got there. Possibilities. Delightful possibilities. Even amid the admitted turmoil that they knew would follow, their hearts were light and ascending the niche of Heaven they had carved out for themselves.

They agreed to be patient and discreet. To meet their obligations on the film and sort things out when they returned home. Cory said he could do it. Georgia confirmed she would. They would steal time whenever possible but sustain themselves with the sweet notion of what was to come.

Shortly after 3 a.m. they fell into the same sleep, into the same dream with the same besotted hearts in separate beds.

CHAPTER SEVENTY-ONE

Szania Lipski opened the Vasa gate at the entrance to Wawel just after midnight when Lars and his gang had finally arrived in Krakow. Ivan and Max unloaded the gear while Victor escorted their prisoner into building number five, the former Royal Kitchens, now mostly used as a storage facility, administration building and staging area for renovators. The broad-shouldered man under the hood with his thick hands tied behind him was Tog Welonski, a mentally disturbed sex offender and serial molester who stumbled along with a symptomatic lack of coordination. In the advanced stages of syphilitic dementia, he was little more than a weak-kneed, drooling, compliant marionette pulled along by Lars' promises of the chance to feed his habit. They had "purchased" him from the sanitarium in Kielce for a mere two million zloty and a case of vodka.

"Are we set for tomorrow?" Lars asked Szania, shaking his hand.

"Yes. The package containing all the updated information was in the post office box just as you said, and I have prepared the holding cells."

"Good." Lars could see apprehension in Szania's face. "What is it, my friend?"

"About Herr Zweig? The killers?"

"Killer. We know who the man is. No need for concern; he will be dead before this whole episode is finished."

Szania breathed a sigh of relief. Lars Rostock instilled confidence. When he spoke about something that would be done; Szania felt it would be done. Though he was only a boy at the time, it was precisely the way he had remembered the man's father. The confident lawyer turned SS henchman. Amazing how all these years later the two of them would conspire together at this castle the way their fathers had in the early 1940's. Like his father before him, it gave him great pride to know he was in the service of a brilliant man battling Jewish pestilence.

"I was curious, Herr Rostock, what my duties would be tomorrow. I am no good with a gun and am far from agile."

"Don't you worry, Szania. I only need you to keep watch at the gate, be expedient in letting us in and delivering the ransom package. I remember your father as a capable man; so you must be. Am I right?" Lars asked him, putting an arm around his shoulder.

"Yes. These things I can do."

"Good." Lars patted him on the back.

"Yes, well come inside, please, and warm yourself. I have hot tea ready."

Lars stopped at the door to the gift shop, turned and took a long reverent look at the castle grounds. "How remarkable it must have been back then, hey, Szania?"

"Yes. A remarkable time, Herr Rostock."

"Wawel Castle, to be our servant once again."

They slipped inside, followed shortly by Ivan, Max and Victor. Tea and strategy warmed their bellies while the dark of night teamed with the collusion of lovers and criminals.

CHAPTER SEVENTY-TWO

By noon the next day, the dependable gray haze of morning turned whimsical, splitting overhead into a vaulted river of indigo blue and vivid sun, reflecting off the flat expanse of white snow and providing so much unexpected light that Yuri was unable to match the exterior shots involving all the camp extras.

"I can't close the apertures any narrower or we'll lose all the depth of the field. I might be able to use filo-filters and a different film speed but I can't guarantee it will be as crisp chromatically."

"Shit. Shit. Shit." Andrew stammered in disgust. "We'll lose a whole day by resetting and we'll need all these extras tomorrow as well."

"You're talking a fifty thousand dollar swing, Andrew." Erasmus chipped into the conversation.

"I know what it's going to cost." Andrew snapped back. "Yuri, it's your call. You know me. I don't want glaring inconsistencies. I'd rather take the setback and make these scenes perfect."

"I can't do it, Andrew. Not now, not with all this sun and snow. Much too disparate. It won't match; I'm telling you."

"Fine. Then that's the final word. We'll shoot the barracks scenes now and finish the rest tomorrow morning at first light. Can we count on the overcast in the morning for at least four hours do you think?" Andrew directed his question towards Peter and Yuri, as if they could predict the weather.

"Generally, yes. But with the mountains it's not as predictable as other parts of Poland." Yuri added.

"Well, let's keep our fingers crossed. Hold the extras in case of a drastic shift later on this afternoon but get Anna and her mother ready. We'll break for lunch now and start with the mother's deathbed scenes after."

Peter barked through the megaphone, "Let's set-up the barracks for scenes eighty-seven a and b. Then we break for lunch." The extras swarmed into the heated train cars for warmth as the dozens of crew members hustled the equipment across the frozen yard to the four women's barracks buildings that had been restored to

authenticity but given the added amenity of five industrial-sized coil heaters connected by cable to the main generators. They were all grateful to be indoors with at least the chance to stay warm through the afternoon.

With the absence of her cohort from school, Lani caught a break from Judy Breslau and cut out early at noon. Waldek and Cory picked her up in the Audi and headed straight out to the Auschwitz set where she would have the opportunity to watch her mother's dramatic scenes and rekindle her flirtation with Sean and Chuck or any other uncovered cutie who would help put the memory of Pavel's rejection behind her.

The half hour ride was filled with Waldek's latest imported cassette – Toad the Wet Sprocket's "Dulcinea." The soothing sounds from home coupled with the first real day of sunshine made for a pleasant drive to an otherwise portentous destination, the death camp.

Waldek pulled up across from Georgia's trailer just as she was returning from the make-up cabin. Cory stepped out of the car and looked over its roof at Anna Kamenski, smiling and coming towards him.

Lani hugged her mother.

"How are you feeling, honey?" Georgia asked.

"Fine."

"I know how you two girls share everything; you

sure you're not coming down with this thing as well?"

"I'm sure. Other than a World History headache from listening to fractured English all period."

"Well, Sean isn't in the next scene so you can bother him for the rest of the afternoon; take your mind off your troubles." She kissed her daughter on the cheek then winked at Cory as mother and daughter disappeared into her trailer.

Cory found Jack near the lunch tent scanning the grounds with his mini-binoculars while keeping watch over Andrew's trailer door.

"Cory. Decided to come join the fray, huh?" Jack teased him. "You got a lot of balls, kid. I always liked that in a partner."

"Jack, you wouldn't want me as your partner. I'd just slow you down and screw you up."

Cory stood next to him and they made small talk, Jack regaling him with some of the toughest cases he'd worked on in homicide all the while making full survey of the surroundings.

Erasmus walked toward them making demonstrative gestures to a rapt, bearded gentleman with a notepad. "Who's that?" Cory asked.

"Name's James Howard. Special correspondent from the New York Times. I'm informed this morning that he's shadowing Andrew for the next week or so, all the way through dinner with the Premiere, to do some big story on the flick. One more thing for me to worry about. As if you aren't giving me a major pain in the ass already." Jack gave him the knowing look. No use fighting it, Cory thought.

"I can't help it, Jack. I'm sorry." Cory dropped his head and kicked at the snow.

"Hey, I know it's not your fault. Seems like those two were out of sorts long before you arrived on the scene. I don't blame you really. She's awful gorgeous. Wish I was your age again." He paused. "No, I take that back. I never got women like that even when I was your age. Just don't do anything stupid; if you can help it."

"I'll try." Jack slugged Cory on the shoulder. They listened as Erasmus and James Howard approached.

"What we are about to shoot is one of the most crucial points of the story." Erasmus spread his fingers and pulled his hands apart as if tearing an imaginary loaf of bread. "In a tender moment, Frank takes Anna, his prisoner up until this point, to see her dying mother. They make an emotional goodbye and as she passes away we see for the first time, the human face of Frank, his compassion, his sincere reflection on mortality, that small corner of his heart that has not been blackened by hatred and lust for power. Anna sees it, too. And at this moment she realizes that she has no one else in her life to turn to for her grief and so she embraces Frank for comfort, and he comforts her. It will be magnificent."

James scribbled furiously on his notepad as Erasmus knocked on Andrew's trailer door. It opened and he welcomed them in, holding a small bottle of Perrier in his free hand and offering them something to eat or drink. As he moved to close the door his eye caught Cory's, standing aside Jack. The muscles on the sides of his jaws tensed, and his eyes narrowed. There would never be kind words between them again Cory thought as the door closed.

Jack must have seen it, too, because he muttered under his breath, "Gonna be a long shoot."

Less than half a minute later, Peter opened the trailer door. "Jack, can I see you a moment." Jack nodded at Cory then stepped inside.

A feeling of nausea overcame him. Cory could not help but project what was happening. The uneasiness that clamped down on him rivaled the elation he had felt this morning upon rising and realizing that his time with Georgia in the Cathedral was not merely a dream.

What once was a carefree, fascinating opportunity, training Hollywood clients on the European location of their movie, had now turned into an intricate drama of passion and deceit. In the beginning, he'd taken these people at face value. Now, however, he was aware of how quickly they could turn on him. Lani had. Andrew had. Why not Jack? And Georgia? Though she professed to disdain it, she was as much a part of this lifestyle as any of them. In fact, she had been her whole adult life. She was in it, around it, because of it. Mostly, she was "of it."

Cory's uneasiness amplified. Any of them, all of them, even Georgia, could put the proverbial knife in his back. What good reason would they have not to? They could undermine him, embarrass him, emotionally bankrupt him. After all, hadn't he undermined Andrew? Stolen the affections of his wife from behind his back? No, not stolen. She had given it to him. It wasn't his fault or his conniving. It was simply what had happened, and it was glorious. But he doubted Andrew would see it that way. Perhaps nothing was as it seemed. All of them in that trailer now, discussing something.

The remnants of his breakfast threatened re-emergence, forcing Cory to seek out the port-a-potties behind the trailers. He passed Andrjez and Waldek on their way to the lunch tent.

"Cory, they are serving roast beef sandwiches today. We save you a place at table, no?" The always friendly Andrjez asked.

"No, go ahead. I'm not eating." He may have not been eating but he was being eaten. By the ill-will he felt directed at him that very moment. How could he be so stupid to think that Andrew Goldman wouldn't want something done about him? He had seen the look in

Andrew's face on more than one occasion and knew that he was being interpreted as a threat, and was, truth be told, the most serious threat of all. Like it or not, he was now "the other man." Oh, this was all too much. He would drop out of sight for the rest of the afternoon, sit in the Audi and wait for the first car going back to town if necessary.

These thoughts raced through his head. How to stay out of the way. Then he saw, out of the corner of his eye, the event that would instantly change his life.

CHAPTER SEVENY-TWO

Around 11:30 a.m. Ivan parked the unobtrusive white van to the side of the service road near the Auschwitz-Birkenau camp. Forty minutes later Lars flipped off his cellular phone and listened over the short wave radio to the sound of Peter's voice. "Break the extras for lunch now. Grips and electricians are back on at the barracks in five." The team had been listening in on the production bandwidth since their arrival, waiting. Waiting for a clear signal that their objective would be unimpeded.

"We go," was all Lars said. The plan had been laid out the previous night and everyone was familiar with their roles and orders. Ivan started up the van and

slowly drove it into the maze of trailers shielding the talent and crew from the frigid elements.

The information which Szania picked up from the post office box had proven quite accurate. Georgia's trailer was precisely where the map had shown and Ivan turned the van between the rows of E-Z Comfort Coaches so that the side cargo door slid open right in front of Georgia's trailer door where they could read her name in bold block letters.

The whole thing took less than twelve seconds. Click. Rolled open van door. Yanked open trailer door. Armed Max and Victor hop into the trailer. A startled Georgia and Lani are bagged over the head and shoved out the entrance, down the two coach steps and pulled in by Lars as Ivan watches ahead of him and in the mirror, seeing no one. Van door rolls closed. Gears shift. Tires spin on frozen dirt. Van takes off. Kidnapping is successful.

"What you are feeling on the back of your head is the butt of a machine gun. Do not make a sound or I will crack you like a baseball." Max smiled at his comrades; he liked his Americanized analogy. Lani and Georgia lay on their stomachs on the floor of the van while Victor tied their hands.

"Lani, are you all right?" Georgia asked in defiance of the command.

Max nudged the side of her face with his gun butt.

"Did you not hear me?"

"I'm all right, mom." Lani responded.

Victor lightly smacked the back of her head; she quietly began to cry. They did not speak the rest of the trip.

Feeling queasy enough to vomit, Cory had wracked himself with guilt and paranoia. Throwing up seemed the best solution. But his upheaving was suspended by the sight of a suspicious looking van driver turning into the alley between Sean and Georgia's trailers. The wicked face drew Cory's attention as much as the slow pace of the driving, as if unfamiliar with the terrain. His jog toward the port-a-potties slowed as he watched the van come to a stop at Georgia's door. They were a good fifty yards away from him and as the trailer door came into his view, he caught sight for a split second of what he thought to be Georgia and Lani being rudely ushered into the van.

"My God," he uttered. His mind tried to process the picture. Is this really happening? Are they really being kidnapped? Jack had warned him to keep a close eye out for anything suspicious and this had alarmed him. But the preposterousness of kidnapping Georgia and her daughter. It was almost too much to believe. Could it all have been some kind of gag they were playing on Andrew? Or he on them? These notions blipped across the radar of his reason but the one that registered most and remained was the danger signal.

Think, man. Think. Trying not to panic, Cory wondered whether or not he had time to run back to Jack. But to get there, make them aware of the situation and get back in pursuit would take almost two minutes. As the van turned and circled around the trailer's end and back towards the main road, Cory knew it was time he didn't have.

Right next to him was Waldek's Audi. He pulled open the door and checked for the keys. In the ignition. Pure instinct took over. It was the only thing he could do. To lose contact with them could prove fatal. That was all he could think of. "I can't lose them. I can't lose them."

Cory pulled onto the road a quarter mile behind them and headed out the Auschwitz gates to the north in pursuit. They weren't driving particularly fast, he thought, and his Audi narrowed the gap rather easily. Maybe they're checking to see if they're being followed. Yes, that's what they're doing.

As they slowed to a red light in the town's intersection, Cory pulled off into a gas station and waited. The mechanic came out of the garage and spoke to him in Polish indicating for him to roll down his window. The light turned green. Cory didn't budge. His eyes were fixed on the van. Would they take the overpass or turn onto the ramp heading west?

The attendant spoke again, this time a little louder. The van made its way up the overpass and over the highway. They were going east. Heading back to Krakow probably. There was no other road. Cory peeled out of the gas station.

Having no idea what the protocols were for tailing a suspect, he pulled onto the highway behind them and made a decision. If they believed he was following them they could very well harm Georgia or Lani. Cory didn't want to take that risk so he punched the accelerator and pulled out into the fast lane. In a minute or so he was pulling up alongside the van; he continued on and passed it without so much as a glance over. This would be his strategy; he would follow them from the front, never getting too far ahead.

Flying by snow-covered farm houses, barren groves of trees and threadbare hedgerows, Cory kept between a hundred and a hundred and fifty yards ahead the entire drive into the city limits. What in the name of God was he doing? He was unarmed; they were surely armed to the teeth. He had no idea where he was going; they knew exactly. They were no doubt experienced criminals; he was a personal trainer. Twenty-five pull-ups and a three hundred pound bench press weren't exactly weapons from the anti-terror handbook.

As they approached the banks of the Vistula river

bending in towards town, he watched in his mirror as the van pulled off the highway at ul Konopinickiej. Cory slowed as he approached the next exit. He saw them merge into traffic on the bridge heading back over the river and towards the center of town. Determined not to lose them, he sped up the off ramp, flew through a red light and cranked the car around the corner onto the overpass going parallel to them now. Lucky for him he had been through this part of the city a number of times during his morning runs. He knew he could make a left up ahead at ul Stradom, cut over, weave through the Bohentarin Park and come out close to the main intersection of Konopinickiej and Kanonicza.

He prayed as he snaked through the icy streets, nearly spinning out of control twice. "Be there. Be there." He repeated to himself. As he rounded the corner of the park he could see the van, third in line at the light, making a right turn towards the roundelay at the plaza below Wawel Castle. He pointed the Audi directly through that intersection and watched them as he sped through the long light, favoring the traffic coming from his direction.

"They're going to the castle," he exclaimed to himself, not quite able to believe it. Less than twenty four hours ago he and Georgia had made love inside those walls and now she was someone's prisoner. It defied rationality.

As he skirted the plaza and came to a rolling stop, he watched as the van drove up the cobblestones of the southern rampart. The armorial gate opened for them as if they were expected then shut just as hurriedly. Cory parked the car and continued on foot.

CHAPTER SEVENTY-THREE

Szania had prepared everything. The idea of actually using the holding cells of the old castle dungeon had excited him. He had to rummage for the proper turnkeys in the armory but that had been on his list of things to do anyway as Andrew Goldman's people were interested in possibly shooting some scenes there in the spring. This kidnapping ploy would be well over by then, and he would have his own fun bringing the film crew into the very place where Georgia and her daughter had been captive. He was following the example of the venerable villain Lars Rostock and learning to enjoy the potential misfortune of others.

Victor and Max sat the two women in chairs

facing the door, untied their hands, and re-fastened the ropes so the two of them could sit comfortably but secure. When they were finished, Lars spoke to Victor.

"Bring the drooler." Victor nodded and exited the dungeon. Fortified in the castle renovation of 1906, the stone room at the bottom of the Senatorska Tower still maintained the ominous aura of the damned. Dirty bricks and oxidized red mortar comprised the western wall with a small arched window thirty feet up and providing a concentrated shaft of light in an otherwise dark and frigid prison. The floor was made of large uneven flagstones. There was no furniture other than the two chairs and only one way in and out - a heavy oak door with a barred window at eye level about a foot square.

Max retreated to the hallway to stand guard, leaving Ivan and Lars to unmask the women.

"Now, that went rather smoothly. Wouldn't you say?" Lars asked them in a calm voice.

Georgia thought about maintaining total silence and letting this parched looking maniac in front of her do all the talking. But she couldn't help herself. After ascertaining that Lani was all right, the bile came pouring forth.

"Who the hell are you, and what the hell is going on?"

"Now, Georgia, you and Lani are going to be with

us for a little while. Don't you think it would be best to conserve your energy and make things as painless as possible?" He smiled.

She hesitated. If she had to withstand torture, so be it. But the thought of watching them torture Lani in front of her would be unbearable. For her sake, Georgia calmly went along with him.

"That's better. My name is Lars Rostock. I don't mind telling you because, you see, I want the publicity. I represent the people of the German Republic. No, I'm no politician; politicians don't represent the people. They represent the money and they make sure it stays in the hands of the few. No, I am the real mouthpiece of the people, and unfortunately, your husband..." he looked to Lani, "...and your father…is in the process of undoing our work over the past decades and reawakening our national nightmare. We have done quite an excellent job I'll have you know of calling into question the validity of the so-called Holocaust. The generations coming up behind us today even wonder if the whole thing wasn't just some big lie perpetuated by the Jews in order to keep the world from permitting the rise of a unified and supreme German state. And now, this little Hollywood escapade threatens to push us backwards. Any other filmmaker, perhaps not such a worry. But, Andrew Goldman? We simply don't like the smell of it. And so, quite simply, to avoid this perhaps far-reaching Jewish

propaganda we are willing to trade your return for the termination of production of this movie. A fair trade; don't you think?" Lars moved behind Lani and ran his fingers through her hair.

"I don't believe you. This isn't the first Holocaust movie and it won't be the last. And from what I understand; you don't even need a denial of this horror to motivate a good portion of your arrogant masses."

"You are not German, Georgia. And yet you know the German psyche so well. Perhaps this is true. But I am quite familiar with this story; I have even seen some of the footage."

"So you stole the dailies?" The pieces were beginning to fall into place.

"Yes. The magnitude of the lies you are telling about Hans Frank is inexcusable to me, personally. This man was one of our greatest Nazis, and your story is defamation of the worst kind. It's a preposterous fantasy to think he would have behaved in such a way, falling in love with a vermin Jewish whore like Anna Kamenski."

Something about the passion in his voice struck Georgia as odd. She egged him on. "Oh, yes. It's all true. Thoroughly documented. Why do you think the book won the Pulitzer Prize?"

"Conspiracy. Exactly the kind of thing my organization is poised to fight."

"Your beautiful Nazi, a butcher of thousands,

perhaps millions, was inches away from repenting his sins for the love of a woman, a Jewish woman who taught him that love was stronger than violence. You just don't want to face that fact."

Lars raised his voice for the first time and got right up into Georgia's face. "He may have been a womanizer; that I do not deny. But he never loved a Jewess. His sole mission in life was to eradicate that stinking filth from the face of this earth. The story is a lie. A lie your husband is packaging as the truth."

"It is the truth." Georgia insisted.

"It is not the truth." Lars returned.

"How do you know it's not the truth? How do you know?"

"Because I was born here in this castle in 1944. My mother was his mistress, a patrician woman who was the daughter of the Polish Minister of Finance. I know because although I never knew the man personally, I know everything about him. I know who he was, how he lived and why he did what he did. I know because he was my father."

Georgia's eyes went wide. Not only had the madness of the man begun to seep out in his vehemence but something else about him struck her, an instinct, a guess. She had no way to be sure but it dawned on her that this man in front of her, this raving Nazi was,

perhaps, not only Hans Frank's son but the offspring of the true Anna Kamenski as well.

"You are the son." She uttered.

"What?"

"You are not the son of some Polish mistress. You are the son of Frank and Anna Kamenski."

"Don't be absurd."

"They had a son. He was taken away by the SS shortly before the fall of Krakow, only weeks before Frank's capture. You are he."

"Foolish woman."

"You are her son."

"I said I am not and that is that."

"You have done the research. You know a great deal about the man's life about his years of butchery here in this city. So you know that what I am saying is true. You yourself are a Jew."

Lars turned and smacked the back of his hand across her face, marking the same cheek Andrew had tattooed only yesterday and Cory's lips had sweetly kissed. She thought about Cory for a split second surprised at the pity she felt not for herself but for him.

"Lies. Lies. Lies." Lars shouted. "Where is Victor with the drooler?" He screamed to the ceiling. Ivan moved for the first time, stepping outside to find his comrade before Lars went ballistic.

"Let me tell you how it went, how it ended for

your mother." Georgia began.

"No." He insisted.

But she would not desist. "Despite all the horror, he had fallen in love with her..."

"I said, no!" Lars shouted. But he did not move towards her. He stood frozen in the middle of the room. He quelled the urge to beat her. He had made an agreement not to hurt her and had already overstepped his boundaries. But the real reason he did not move was that some small part of him wanted to listen. "Where is the drooler?" He yelled again but Georgia continued.

"You know the story, Lars." Addressing him personally would drive the point home she thought. "But what wasn't detailed in the book, or the early drafts of the script, but is in there now, taken from the author's own notes of the interview with the doctor who delivered the child is how it all ended, or in your case, began..."

CHAPTER SEVENTY-FOUR

Anna screamed. The medication she had been taking over the last few months had made her almost numb but now, grunting and sweating, she was delivering her child. And there was pain. In a strange way she welcomed the pain; it made her feel alive again.

So much had been surrendered in these last few years, her husband, her mother, her own being, it felt good to fight, to wrench out a cry for life. New life. This was her son. His son. There was nothing she could do now to prevent his birth. Hans Frank would have his progeny.

He had seen to it that this second pregnancy would not end like the first, in a miscarriage. She would

bare him a child no matter what the cost. Although there was no proof, he was almost certain she had intentionally aborted the first fetus in protest. She blamed him for the death of her husband but had laid with him despite that tragedy for the sake of her mother. But Sarah had died of disease, a natural death, nothing he could prevent. Yet she blamed him for this as well and withdrew from him. He had forced himself on her many times since then but abhorred the way something wonderful and fulfilling had turned cold and utterly foreign, forcing him to return to his past behavior. He beat her but it seemed to pain him more than her and so he stopped. For months he had agonized over how to win back her love. When he had begged for her to forgive him she gave him one alternative. The only way she would return his affections would be for him to repent his sins and stop the killing. To Hans that meant undoing everything that had forged him into the man he had become. He could not do it. It was at this time that she discovered her pregnancy. And since he would not honor her one request and since, in her mind, he had taken her husband and mother from her, she would take his child. And she did.

But not this time. On this day, in this bed, her spread legs would deliver into the hands of the doctor a son, his son. He had had to resort to extreme measures to assure success. It ripped a part of his heart away to hear her cries in the room down the hall six months ago when,

after she had tried to abort the second fetus, he had Doctor Mengele amputate her hands and feet and cauterize the ends of her limbs into blunt stumps. But he felt there was no other way to bring about the birth of her son than to prevent herself from ending it.

Anna would no longer harm herself nor would she run. She was his captive. And if she would not love him nor permit him to love her, he would take from her the thing he wanted most outside of her affection - a child.

Deep, deep screams percolated in her throat then catapulted into the castle walls. Her body was soaked in sweat, her hair, cropped short for convenience, matted in spiked bangs across her forehead. The baby's head had made its way out of her vagina into the hands of the doctor, tearing her labia open in the process. Then followed the pink body and the tiny feet. Anna sucked at the air, her chest heaving, her eyes watering from the tears of pain and pain subsided.

The doctor grabbed the infant boy by the bottom of the feet and spanked the first breath of life into him with the palm of his hand. The cry of a child filled the spaces vacated of Anna's screaming.

The nurse wrapped the child in a blanket wiping away the remnants of the placenta and birth sack and headed to the door almost immediately with the doctor.

"Where are you going? I want to see my child. I want to see my baby." Anna cried.

"Do not worry about our son, Anna. I will make him a god, an Aryan god." Hans sat at her bedside as the door opened and the nurse exited. The doctor hesitated and looked as if he were about to speak. "That will be all, doctor. You are dismissed." Hans barked.

"Where are they taking him? Oh, please. Please, Hans. Let me see him?" Anna begged him, placing the stump of her right forearm on his thigh, thinking in her mind, still, that she was reaching out with her hand, a hand that was no longer there. In an instant, seeing no hand, just the abrupt and obscene end of what used to be her delicate arm, she knew she would never see her baby. This man who was his father, this madman who had ordered the death of her people, her husband, demanded love from her in exchange for the life of her loved ones, who would not, despite the awakening of an understanding and compassion that could have saved his soul, learn to love anyone, this same man would persist in his cruelty and never let her see her child.

But things were beyond that. Beyond even Anna's comprehension of her relationship with Hans.

"Because you understand Schopenhauer, I will tell you this. You have tried valiantly to convince me that all life is governed by love, that love is the energy source of the universe. But you are wrong. Violence governs, and destruction is the energy source of the universe. In fact, the universe is but one big explosion that is still happening, and particles of atoms colliding make up all things. And as far as who I am, who you are, who anyone is as a human being and what we are capable of, again I call on Schopenhauer who explains that there is only a single point, other than imagination, at which any one person has access to the world - within the self. When I see my body or its activity, then what I perceive or imagine is still only recognized, still only representation, imagination. But in my body, I feel the urges, desire, pain, pleasure, anger which simultaneously, as I feel them, present themselves to my imagination and the imagination of others. But only within myself am I myself, and that which I observe about myself and which others observe about me. Only in myself do I experience that which the world is, in addition to the thing that is presented to me or imagined to be the world. The world outside has only an imagined 'inside'; only in myself am I that 'inside' myself. That is what he meant by 'Will.' This is my will. I am the inside of the world, and the world is the most incomprehensible complex of energy based on destruction. That is the imagined world and it is inside me. I am what the world is. And this is why I will do what I must do."

From the minuscule black leather case of his holster, Hans removed a silver bullet. He held it between his thumb and forefinger and showed it to her.

"This bullet, Anna, do you see it?"

She nodded. It was clear to her now why she would never see her son. It was clear to her now what his intentions were. It was all becoming clear to her now.

"This bullet I love. Do you know why? I love this bullet because I had it especially made for you, my darling. That wonderful hair clip, the one you cherished from your childhood, the one I used to love to watch you remove as it allowed your beautiful hair to cascade down around your shoulders, that very same hair clip has been forged into this bullet right here."

Hans rubbed the bullet through her hair, along her face, as if her flesh might recognize it. He felt the softness of her warm cheek with the back of his hand.

She whispered, "Schopenhauer also said, 'The will to live is the source and essence of things.'"

Hans smiled.

"It is better this way." He whispered back as he inserted the single bullet into the clip then slid the clip into the heel of the Walther PPK.

Anna did little to try and sway him. She did not cry or curse or beg him. A serene acceptance emanated from within her. At last she was achieving the fate she felt would be hers all along. The strength that flowed through her to bear the deaths of her loved ones, the willingness to give love to the man who had brought about their undignified end, her resolve, her hope, and, most crushing of all, the desire to see her child, these

things had all deserted her. For nothing was there left to live. Schopenhauer be damned.

Hans leaned in slowly and planted a lingering kiss on her forehead before standing and pointing the barrel of the gun at the same spot.

Anna's last words to him came calmly and with genuine affection. "It is love that has driven you to this."

The words hit him hard; his hand began to shake. The steady aim of the pistol wavered. He turned his face from her, rubbed his eyes and refocused on her forehead, repeating to himself in his mind, "Do not look at her eyes; do not look at her eyes."

A surge of courage rushed from his heart. He squeezed the trigger. The bullet pierced her skull, searing the flesh of her forehead as it burned through on its way to the middle of her brain so that only a thin trickle of blood slithered down her forehead, slowly making its way into her eye as he stood there, finally able to look into it.

Anna Kamenski lay dead in her bed. Her eyes wide open but seeing nothing. Lifeless. As stiff as Lot's wife caught looking back. A pillar of salt.

As Hans Frank opened the door to leave this execution room, the wail of a baby echoed through the hallways. He stepped outside, a father now, chasing the cry of his son.

End of story.

CHAPTER SEVENTY-FIVE

Cory had climbed up the western slope of the castle and over the Bernardynska gate. In the pitch black shadows of the former hospital wall, he stealthily slid along the bricks until he could get a glimpse around the corner. Across the eastern courtyard he could see the van parked next to the building that used to house the royal kitchens. A quick sprint through the moonlight, ducking into the alcoves of the defense wall twice to verify there was no sentry, and he made it to the opposite corner. He inspected the windows of the south face. None would open. A narrow trellis at the furthest corner climbed close enough to the second story balcony for Cory to spring up and swing over.

The first set of double doors he checked was open. A cramped living quarters with piped in heat. He listened for sounds of inhabitancy. None. As he opened the apartment door, a man's voice came from the hallway and down the stairs.

Two seconds after he stepped out to get a better look and listen, he realized he'd made a mistake. The footsteps were coming up the staircase. He ducked into the nearest doorway. Locked. And the next. Locked. A third. Open. He slipped in just as the voices came to the top of the second story landing.

They spoke in clamorous Polish. He heard the sound of keys then of a door unlocking. They seemed to be summoning someone from within. A few moments later they retreated down the hallway.

Cory cracked the door a sliver as the voices began to fade and caught a glimpse of two men leading a third man, a tall, sickly man, down the stairs. He followed, clinging to the walls on his way to the granite railing.

When they were gone, he knocked cautiously on the doors of all the locked rooms upstairs, calling in a loud whisper, "Georgia? Lani? Are you in there?" But there were no answers.

At the window at the end of the hallway, he paused, watching the two men escort the third across the courtyard to the side entrance that lead into the Senatorska Tower portion of the castle, the part he had read about but was off limits to the public. It contained the document rooms, the lapidary, the main storehouse of Oriental treasures, and in its lower depths, the dungeons.

"Shit, the damn dungeons," Cory said to himself then crept down the stairs and towards the door. There seemed to be no one around. It was the last thing he thought as he stepped out the front door in the direction of the Senatorska Tower and something crashed down on him from behind. Things went instantly black.

"Intriguing. Very fascinating fiction, Georgia. I would expect nothing less than heinous lies from a writer who upholds the Jewish experience during the war with such honor and dignity," Lars commented, following the finish of Georgia's story of the birth of Anna's son and her subsequent, shocking death.

"You can deny with your words but you know the truth in your heart," she added.

"I have no heart." Lars said, laughing. "Mark my words. That is how history will remember me when my work is done."

The heavy door swung open. Victor and Szania shoved Tog Welonski inside.

"Ah. The drooler has arrived." Lars moved over to him and took the corner of his untucked shirt tail delicately in his fingers. Without so much as a flinch from Tog, he wiped the saliva from the crease of the drooler's mouth where it threatened a slow slide down his chin. He grabbed him by the loose belt of rope that fastened at the waist of his over-sized fatigues and urged him forwards towards the women.

"This man is in the advanced stages of syphilitic dementia, a disease which he contracted years ago from his priapic and insurmountable impulse to stick his penis into everything passing on the affliction both anally and vaginally to over a dozen boys and girls much younger than even you, my dear." Lars looked at Lani; her eyes bulged in silent terror.

Untying the rope and removing it so that Tog's pants fell immediately down around his ankles, Lars pointed to the man's enormous genitals. Tog's penis was swollen and festering with open sores, and a slight smile crossed his lips as the cold air enveloped his exposed member.

"If our demands are not met, namely that Andrew Goldman pack up and go home and put an end to this vitriolic proselytizing, Tog here will have an opportunity to feed his habit and invade every orifice of your bodies with his instrument. Starting with you." Lars pointed to Lani. She looked to Georgia and shuddered so severely, she nearly fell over in her chair.

The morbid episode was summarily interrupted by the heaving sound of Ivan who entered the open chamber with a body slung over his shoulder. "I found

this one stalking around the tactical operations center."

He threw the body to the ground at their feet.

"Cory!" Georgia shrieked. Either the sound of her voice or the pressure of Lars' foot on his chest rolling him onto his back woke him.

"Well, well. What have we here?" Lars asked as Cory shook his head and squinted trying to get his eyes to focus.

As the view of Georgia and Lani tied to the chairs appeared before him, he spoke. "Are you all right?"

Lars intervened before they could reply. "Of course they're all right. The question is who are you and what are you doing here?" Lars yelled. "Szania, find us another chair; Max, bring some rope."

"I followed you from the camp." Cory offered.

Lars shot Ivan a glaring look. An embarrassed and frustrated Ivan kicked Cory directly in the ribs. He rolled onto his side in pain.

"Ivan." Lars reprimanded him for his show of force.

Cory attempted to get up but the barrel of Ivan's weapon in his forehead discouraged further movement.

"Your courage is exceeded only by your stupidity, my friend."

"I may not know what's going on here but I do know for certain that I am not your friend." Cory replied.

"We shall see."

Szania and Max returned with the chair and rope and the three of them secured the intruder quickly in the seated position aside Georgia.

"An unexpected turn of events but nothing to be alarmed about." Lars turned to Szania who had been waiting with a clipboard and pen in hand. "I guess we'll have to rewrite that letter, Szania. Inform them that we have a third prisoner, a late arrival whose name is..."

Georgia looked to Cory; his eyes darted around the room and landed on Lars, then Szania. She could see his mind racing as he interrupted Lars. "Coory Sonne!" He pronounced it with a "u" sound. "That's Coory with two O's, motherfucker. At least you can spell it right you backwards cocksuckers."

Lars looked at him and raised a hand as if he would strike. Cory's stern face seemed to welcome the hand and it gave Lars pause. He withdrew it. Georgia kept quiet. She had no idea what he was doing but he guessed he must have had his reasons. Her attention returned to Lars as he came towards her.

"Now, to go along with our ransom note, I need an artifact as a little sign that you are indeed in our possession." He kneeled in front of her and removed a switchblade knife, clicking it open. "Let's see. How about a lock of hair? No, too romantic. A finger? No, too messy." He grasped the hem of her long skirt, pulled it up from the ankles and ran his hand up the gap between her thighs until her panties were partially exposed.

Georgia gasped.

"Ah, there we go. I would imagine Andrew would recognize these, wouldn't he? I hope so, for your sake. Otherwise, I would speculate that maybe you'd be wanting for a little lechery, and then a little go round with Tog might not terrify you at all but rather please you. And that would be no fun for me." He slid the blade under the hem of her panties at her hip bone and sliced them off quickly, taking a leering look at the triangle of her pubic hair before dropping her skirt back down over her knees.

Behind him, Tog had begun to pant like a retriever poised for a fetch.

"Get him out of here before he loses control." Lars instructed Victor. "This ought to do the trick," Lars stated, smelling the panties then smiling before handing them to Szania who stuffed them in a padded manila envelope along with the rewritten letter. "You know what to do," he said. And Szania was off.

Lars turned to his bound audience of three. "And now we wait."

CHAPTER SEVENTY-SIX

The package arrived via common taxi at Hotel Hollywood at 8:03 p.m. that same evening. Jack and Jerzy, Andrew and Erasmus, the Krakow police, and a Special Forces unit had set up a staging area there where they interrogated the unsuspecting taxi driver. He told them simply that a short, nondescript man had approached him just outside of the square where he was waiting for a fare and paid him 500,000 zloty to deliver the package to this address. That was all he knew. After a heated interview lasting nearly a half hour, Thomas Vlaski, the head of the anti-terror task force was finally satisfied that he was telling the truth.

When Peg had come to retrieve Georgia from her

trailer for the start of filming after lunch, the chain of suspicion and panic was set into motion. The production shut down quickly and the local police were called. They had immediately phoned the President's office and an anti-terror team, lead by Vlaski, had been dispatched to Krakow at 3:30 p.m.

After the bomb squad had checked the manila envelope and verified the absence of explosives, it was opened in the Hotel Hollywood office. The collective gasp at the sight of the panties being pulled out by Vlaski's gloved hand sucked all the oxygen out of the room.

"Can you verify that these are hers, Mr. Goldman?" Vlaski asked him.

"Oh, my God." Andrew's eyes fell onto the embroidered "G" on the front panel. "Yes. Those are hers. You don't think..."

Vlaski knew what he was about to ask. His experience told him in situations like these to always assume the best. Until the dead body was right in front of you, always imagine the person alive and unharmed. It really was the only way to make it through the mind-numbing anxiety. "Don't panic. This doesn't necessarily mean anything. Most of the time it's just a scare tactic." Vlaski calmed him then read the note out loud. "'We have in our possession Georgia Hart, Lani Goldman, and Coory Sonne.' Who's Coory Sonne?" he asked.

Jack answered. "They've got Cory, too? His

name is Cory, with one O, and he's the personal trainer Mr. Goldman hired for Georgia."

"Yes, he's with us." Andrew reiterated, still somewhat bewildered by the whole affair.

Jack read over Vlaski's shoulder. "They must have misspelled his name."

Vlaski continued. "Perhaps, but everything else seems grammatically correct. Let's not overlook it." He went on reading the note out loud. "'They are unassailed, and we are prepared to trade them in return for the immediate cessation of the propaganda ploy you call the 'Pillar of Salt' movie production. We also require that Andrew Goldman be prepared to state in front of the international media that the so-called Holocaust never existed and was itself an intricate work of the Jewish world conspiracy as indicated in the text 'The Protocols of the Elders of Zion'. When this has been done and the last camera has been packed away and shipped off and the last crew member has flown the country, they will be safely returned. There are other demands that can be discussed in person. We await your call at the untraceable cell phone number 675612162 in order to arrange a meeting. Do not underestimate the severity of the threat. It would be our pleasure to torture and kill all of them in case of non-compliance. The New German Alternative.'"

James Howard, the New York Times journalist

scribbled furiously in the background as Andrew looked to Vlaski for some sign of what would be done.

"Hand me the phone." Vlaski dialed the number. A voice on the other end of the line answered calmly. "This is Thomas Vlaski of the Federal Anti-Terror Task Force. Who am I speaking to?" A voice responded; Vlaski repeated the name. "Lars Rostock." Jack lowered his head. It was just as he expected. They looked among themselves knowing that everything Jack Grady had shared with them out of Gunter Strauss' Interpol file was true. They had a Nazi tiger by the tail.

As the conversation ended and Vlaski had his instructions about the alleged meeting that would take place tomorrow, Dante, who had been manning the laptop computer Jerzy had converted to police use, leaned over the desk and took a glance at the actual ransom note. Something about the misspelling of Cory's name had made him curious. "Coory," he whispered to himself. "Double O's". And then it struck him. Cory was trying to tell them something.

"Excuse me." Dante spoke so softly among the din of agents desperately rattling off ideas, no one heard. He raised his voice. "Excuse me."

"Dante, what is it?" Jerzy asked.

"I think I know why Cory's name is misspelled," he stated plainly.

Vlaski's attention turned from the phone and his

men. "What's that comrade?"

"Well, you see, Inspector Vlaski, sir, I've been teaching Cory to play chess..."

"Dante, please. There is little time; these men have work to do." Jerzy apologized for him to the entire room.

"Let him continue," Jack demanded.

"It's just that I've been showing him how to write the moves down on paper so that one can follow the game without seeing the board." He looked up. All eyes in the room were on him; he blushed.

"Yes, go on, son." Jack implored him.

"It's called denotation. And, well, if you write down two zeros, that is the symbol to castle your king to the short side of the board. Double O's means castle."

Total silence.

"Wawel." Jerzy was the first to say it but the others were thinking it.

"Wawel." Jack repeated. "Wait a minute. Wait just a go'l darn minute. Gunter told me that Lars believed himself to be the son of Hans Frank, your Hans Frank, from the movie, and that he may have actually been born here in Krakow."

"Wawel isn't the only castle in these parts." Erasmus added.

"No, but it's a good place to start." Vlaski stammered. He had a hunch. Having read Grady's

information from Interpol and knowing the twisted minds of men just like Rostock, he knew that, if indeed he was the son of Hans Frank or even believed himself to be, returning to the place of his father's greatest triumph, at least in Lars' mind, made perfect sense. He turned to the Police Commissioner. "I want everyone you can spare."

"Please, be careful," Andrew pleaded with Vlaski.

"Don't worry," Vlaski returned.

Don't worry. The lives of his wife and daughter were hanging in the balance. How was he supposed to remain composed? For Andrew Goldman, possessor of a poisoned body, a poisoned marriage and a poisoned dream of a movie, there was nothing but worry.

CHAPTER SEVENTY-SEVEN

"What's going to happen to us?" Lani stuttered out her first calm sentence since their abduction. Lars and Ivan had taken Tog away from their cell and Szania had left to deliver the ransom envelope. The three of them were alone except for Max's scrutinizing eye that looked in the window of the door every now and then as he stood guard over the chamber.

"Don't worry, Lani. If they were in it to harm us, they'd have done so by now." Georgia tried to reassure her daughter though she herself had misgivings about the immediate future.

"Andrew will do what they say, right?" she asked.

"Of course he will." Georgia spoke to Cory. "Are

you all right?"

Cory's face was pomegranate red. He had been virulently contracting his lats and biceps against the wood frame of the chair in which he was tied. "I'm fine. If I could just..." he strained again.

Snap!

The left dowel cracked in two. With a ferocious lateral yank, the right one gave way easily. He had slipped the rope out from around the chair's back and freed himself. The women watched as he rolled to the ground on his back, elevated his legs, hips and lower back, spread his arms, still tied at the wrists, as wide as they would go, and wiggled his butt through them. With his knees flush against the sides of his face, he was able, with a tremendous tug and with the flesh around his wrist tearing as he pulled, to bring his hands up and over his bottom then over his feet. He stood, hands bound but in front of him now.

"Cory, if they catch you, they're going to hurt you." Georgia whispered.

"The two of you just act like nothing's wrong. I'm going to try and lure him into the room."

"But..." Georgia began.

"Cory, you're insane. They'll kill you." Lani snapped at him.

"Shhh! Cory put a finger to his lips. The ropes around his wrists had loosened enough that he was able

to slip his hands out. He quickly placed the broken chair over by the far wall under the window, taking one dowel from the backing and gripping it between his teeth. The portal may have been thirty feet high but the gaps between the bricks were wide. Somebody athletic and brave enough could conceivably climb up the wall and out. At least that's what Cory hoped the guard would think the next time he looked in and found Cory gone.

He himself dashed to the left side of the door and used the outcropping of brick around the jamb and the small crevices between stones where the mortar had eroded away to climb over the entrance to the cell where he held on with the skill and tenacity of a rock-climber. All those wrist curls were finally paying off he thought to himself. He held on tightly with one hand, his body pressed face and chest first into the wall, the tips of his toes resting precariously on the small brick ledge above the door. With his free hand he took the dowel from his teeth and slammed it into the hard floor in front of the door. A loud slap echoed through the bowels of the castle.

As expected, Max came to the window. His eyes bulged when he did not find Cory where he expected and caught a glimpse of the chair by the far wall. He fumbled for the key and threw the door open but did not enter right away. He reached around the hinges and made sure the door opened flush against the wall, well prepared

for the possibility of Cory lurking behind it. He clicked off the safety on his machine gun. When he did decide to enter, he came in low and with his weapon scything back and forth across the room at gut level.

What he did not expect was to be ambushed from above. Cory released himself from atop the door frame, turning deftly in mid air and crashed down on the back of the sentry.

The HK 23E 5.56 caliber machine gun bounced on the flagstones. Cory grabbed the back of Max's head by the hair, pulled it three feet off the ground then slammed it down into the floor with such force it shattered the man's nose and knocked him out cold.

After two minutes of quivering uneasiness followed by three seconds of sheer exhilaration watching their friend pounce on the enemy, Georgia and Lani winced at the picture of a man's face caved in by someone they had previously seen as an employee, a chaperone, a member of the entourage, and, in Georgia's case, a lover. It had never struck them that he was capable of such violence.

Cory grabbed the weapon. He checked the magazine. Fully loaded. He needed to know. As quickly as he untied the two women, he had Max bound and gagged with his own shirt and dragged into the corner away from view of the door.

"Come on." Cory entreated them, leading the

way out, the barrel of the machine gun preceding them. Jack had promised to teach him to fire a weapon. A little late for that now he thought to himself, checking to make sure the safety was off. That much he knew from the three thousand hours of gunplay he had seen in his movie and television watching. He was relying on action-movie instincts now and hoping the flicks provided some semblance of authenticity.

"Don't make a sound and stay close," he told them as they climbed the stairs out of the dungeon.

Cory's immediate thought was to get them to the Vasa gate by the armory. It was the easiest one to scale and only a ten foot drop to the rampart abutting the northern face. But that meant they'd have to make their way through the east then the north wings of the castle; through the promenade between the castle proper and the Cathedral, then through the church itself, out the front door, and exposed for maybe fifty yards in the courtyard. All before they could begin their ascent over the wall.

He was lucky for two reasons. One, he had been through the castle now on two separate tours and was somewhat familiar with the layout. And, two, he had trained these women for almost seven weeks, had made them stronger and was well aware of their physical capabilities. He was confident they could climb the wall.

In the warmth of Szania's front room Lars and

Ivan had been going over the details of their meeting with Vlaski tomorrow when Victor interrupted them. Lars had ordered him to call Max on the radio every half hour to check up on the prisoners. Only this time there was no reply. The three of them grabbed their automatic weapons and scrambled for the Senatorska Tower, leaving Szania an M1 Rifle to man the administration building.

Cory rushed the women through the ground floor of the castle, reminding them to keep low when they went by windows or portals which, lucky for them, were recessed under the shadowy, arcaded front of the courtyard facades. They passed through the tapestry room, lined with 16th and 17th century Brussels and Florentine masterpieces from floor to ceiling, then through the Turkish tent room, through the Renaissance gallery with its baroque decor and portrait series of Polish nobles.

Just past the cloak room, the east wing elbowed into the north. Georgia and Lani waited for Cory's signal from across the grand hallway then darted through the doors of the military display room. Behind velvet ropes and glass cases was the collection of swords and various coats of mail used over the centuries. A gun exhibit on the south wall surrounded a huge mounted shield emblazoned with the Vasa Family Crest - the eagle and the sheaf of wheat. They had all examined these things before on their tour with Judy, one that went at a much more leisurely pace than this flight from danger.

At the western entrance to the castle proper, Cory opened the huge door and stuck his head out into the promenade. It was approximately thirty feet from the edge of this northern wing over to the back doors of the St. Stanislaus Cathedral. Not far at all. But it opened up into full view of the courtyard directly across from the administration building where he had been apprehended. If they could bridge it undetected, getting to the gate through the church would be easy.

Cory scanned the open area in front of him. Nothing. "The two of you go ahead, one at a time. I'm going to cover you with the gun. The doors should be open, remember? Judy said they have no locks."

Lani looked to Georgia. "I'll go first."

"I know you hate it when I tell you to work harder in the gym but I'd sprint as fast as I could if I were you," Cory advised her. Lani simply nodded. No backtalk from her for once. Cory nosed out from behind the alcove's column and pointed the gun in the direction of the open courtyard. "Go."

Lani scooted across the gravel path, temporarily lit by the moonlight, her blonde hair flying behind her, then disappeared into the shadows of the Cathedral's back entrance.

"Now you." Cory touched Georgia on the

shoulder.

“Okay.” A smile tickled the corner of her mouth but was gone in a sober second. She hadn’t taken but two steps out of the alcove when a spray of bullets danced in the gravel between the buildings, sending her scurrying back to Cory’s side.

“Mom!” Lani yelled from the doorway.

“I’m all right, honey.”

“Lani,” Cory called out. “Go. You know where you’re going. You’ll recognize it when you go out the doors. It’s the same place we came in with Judy. Now go. You’ll make it.”

“No, I don’t want to leave you.” Lani cried.

“Just go.” Cory ordered her.

“But...” she yelped, on the verge of tears.

“Go!” Georgia yelled back. “You’ll be fine.”

“I love you, mom, Cory.” She spoke then turned into the dark of the church and was gone.

Cory looked out into the courtyard. He could see no one but there was no chance he was going to risk running out in the open. He craned his head behind him then looked up.

Scaffolding. Between the castle’s Sobieski Tower on the northwest corner and the Cathedral roof. He grabbed Georgia’s hand, pulled her back inside and through the front gallery to the Senator’s stairs that led up to the tower.

There were large portal openings on the second and third floors of the tower but the planks lay across the scaffolding bars only near the top where they were working on repairing the gutters of the church roof. They stopped on the second story and looked out. It was too far away from the ledge. They bounded up the next flight of stairs to the highest window. From there, they could step out onto the ledge, grab the scaffolding pole then work their way over to the long planks that lay across the interstices.

"Can you do it?" Cory asked her as she got an eyeful of what was required. She nodded. "Looks like those pull-ups are going to pay off after all."

"When this is over, if I'm still alive, I'm going to get fat and lazy. You can bet your ass on that."

"Not you; not in a million years." Cory responded. She knew he was right.

"You do know me." She kissed him. "No regrets." She said to him.

"What?"

"The name of my perfume. It's called 'No Regrets.' I promised I'd never tell but since I've already broken so many other promises I figured what the hell." He kissed her again and smelled in the nape of her neck the familiar, subtle spice of her perfume mixed with the alluring oils of her skin. "See you on the other side."

Sliding hand to hand and foot to foot, she made

her way along the two crossbeams until she had come to the center of the scaffolding. She pulled herself up to the level of the planks then swung her leg up and onto it like as if it were a tall and broad horse. It wasn't but a moment that she was safely on the walkway between the buildings when a second volley of bullets bounced with a dull thud off the bricks of the window ledge and a high-pitched ping off the metal scaffolding.

"Hurry!" Cory yelled to Georgia. She scrambled across to the Cathedral roof as the second round of fire chewed up the boards in front of her. The planks clattered on the metal crossbeams of the scaffolding, splintered and broke away. Georgia's footing was gone. She made a desperate lunge for the corner pole of the assembly and wrapped her arms and legs around it just as the last plank fell away from under her feet, crashing to the gravel below.

Cory looked down and saw Ivan on one knee at the corner of the Sigismund Chapel aiming at them again. He pointed his machine gun in Ivan's direction and squeezed the trigger. Nothing happened. "Shit!" He yelled. He examined the gun with no idea what he was looking for. He tried again, squeezing the trigger. Still nothing. What was he doing wrong he thought. He removed the magazine quickly and banged it on the side of his head as he'd seen so many soldiers do in Nam movies. Something about it settling the rounds into proper position. After reinserting it, he fingered the trigger again. Still nothing. If he had known anything about machine guns he would have known that very few of them fired with a closed bolt. All he had to do was pull the bolt back and he'd have fifty rounds of rapid fire power per second. But Cory had a sophisticated weapon with a closed bolt, no knowledge of the fact that he needed an open one, all of which amounted to having nothing.

Lars' voice echoed in the courtyard. "Ivan! Hold your fire." He appeared at Ivan's side shortly thereafter. They looked up at Georgia, hanging onto the scaffolding pole for dear life.

She was only a foot away from the church wall, thirty feet off the ground. In her mind, her only option was to slide down the pole slowly until she was opposite the stained glass window below her. Hand over hand she maneuvered herself into position then karate kicked the first pane. It shattered but only in an opening the size of a toilet seat. Four more kicks at various angles and most of the glass had fallen away. She reached for the window ledge with her foot then shoved off the pole with a strong push. Avoiding the shards still protruding out of the iron casings, she ducked into the Cathedral.

Inside she found herself right above the chapel of the Holy Cross. Mounting the back of a marble angel, she shimmied her way down onto the top of Casimir

Jagiello's ornate tomb. From there it was a six foot drop to solid ground. She had made it.

CHAPTER SEVENTY-EIGHT

Cory stood at the portal ledge, knowing that Georgia had made it safely inside and keeping a sharp eye on the two terrorists below. They seemed to be speaking to each other. He yelled down at them. “I know you can hear me.” His voice echoed through the courtyard. “I’m tossing down my weapon. I am unarmed.” He took one last look at the machine gun. “Nothing but trouble,” he said, then watched it sail out through the air and bounce in the gravel below.

Ivan and Lars separated. Lars entered the north wing of the castle at the gallery doors and Ivan appeared to be circling around to the front of St. Stanislaus to go after Georgia. Cory had to act fast. He leaped out onto the scaffolding and began traversing the crossbeams as quickly as he could, hand to hand and foot to foot, just like Georgia had, only he had to make it completely across this way and before Lars got to the third floor window.

Inside the Cathedral, Lani had made her way cautiously to the front western doors. The coast seemed to be clear. She knew that having no one on her tail was a good sign for her but probably bad for her mom and Cory. But she would do what they had told her and get over the wall to go for help. Once outside the western entrance to the Cathedral she had recognized immediately where she was. It had taken her less than thirty seconds to get to the Vasa gate and begin climbing the square stones with just enough ridge for her finger and toeholds. She felt strong and motivated, never once looking back but keeping her mind focused on the task at hand - getting over the top.

When she had scaled the ten foot barricade and lay with her torso across the top bricks where she could see for miles into the sporadically lit city, she was shocked to the point of tears when she saw coming at her, two dozen police and unmarked cars with a pack of armed officers and gray suited men running towards the gate. Jack Grady, Jerzy, and Dante were the only ones she recognized but she knew the rest were there to help. For a girl who had just summoned enough willpower to elude killers and clamber up a castle wall, she suddenly went weak and bawled like a baby.

As Lars ascended the landing of the second floor of the Senator's stairs, he caught site of Cory from the corner of his eye shuffling across the scaffolding towards the Cathedral roof. He changed direction immediately, went back down, exited the gallery doors and snuck into the church across the promenade while Cory's eyes were fixed on the corner of the roof and safe passage.

Inside, he bolted for the bell tower and hastened up the narrow, steep stairs that were expressly built in the 14th century for tiny, patient monks who rang the eleven ton, six foot high, nine foot wide bell on important church Feast Days and occasions of national importance.

Ivan turned the corner into the western portion of the castle commons, towards the armory gate, just in time to see a legion of Special Forces officers spreading out over the grounds. Uncharacteristically exposed and vulnerable, the leader of The Red Claw was caught completely by surprise. He pointed his weapon into the crowd and opened fired. All bodies ducked out of the way, behind cars or buildings or hit the dirt in front of them. A hail of gunfire came right back at him so fast and furiously, that he staggered backward ten feet before dropping his weapon, careening and falling onto his back, riddled with fifty bullets.

Inside the church, Georgia leaned against the

doors. She had just made up her mind to open them and make a run for the gate when she heard the thunder of gunfire. There was so much of it, and so many voices talking when it had stopped, she knew somehow instinctively that help had arrived. She opened the door a crack and peeked out. The first face she saw was that of Jack Grady, flanked by an array of officers in black garb and flak jackets. Her heart leaped into her mouth as she burst out the door and in their direction.

"Jack. Jack. Thank God you're here. Quickly. Cory is in danger." She led them around the outside of the Cathedral towards the promenade, warning them that there were others and that they were armed with automatic weapons.

Cory had just gotten onto the roof when he, too, heard the gunfire at the western entrance. He scaled across the steep pitch on hands and feet as quickly as he could without losing his balance. To start a slide on these tiles and on this side would not only send him over the edge of the Cathedral but over the castle wall as well. There was little doubt in his mind that he would not survive if he lost his footing now.

Traversing as far as he could on the roof still did not bring him to a vantage point where he could see over the facade of the Cathedral's west entrance. His best bet was to climb the outside of the bell tower and start down from there but to do that he would have to let himself slide down the roof and aim for his momentum to be stopped by the bricks of the southeast corner of the tower. Cory took a deep breath and did just that, his butt bouncing over the tiles until the soles of his spread feet planted onto the tower wall and stopped him cleanly on his line.

The portal was less than a story above him and there were plenty of places to grab onto as he made his way up the face. With one last heaving effort from his tired back and aching forearms, he pulled himself up and into the tower itself. He lay there on his back for a few seconds, breathing hard, thinking of all the training he had done - conditioning, power-lifting, fartlek, intervals. But it was fear that gave him the strength now. For himself, he had never been so scared in his life, but now he was scared for Georgia as well.

The huge bell hung there, monopolizing the tiny room at the top of the belfry. Cory could see in the moonlight the Polish Coat of Arms and the Latin inscription underneath. Something about God, Sigismund, Poland, valor and ending with the date: 1520. It flashed across his mind that this bell had been ringing shortly after Christopher Columbus had discovered America. Incredible.

He circumnavigated the instrument and was turning the corner to the stairwell when - BAM! - out of nowhere a fist hit him square in the jaw. He stumbled backwards and grasped at the only thing that could save him from a six story fall down the center of the tower - the rope. Swinging around under the rim of the bell, he lashed out with his feet, trying to plant them back on the flooring. One time around, he pushed off the huge clapper suspended from the middle of the slightly swaying, eleven ton monster. It slammed along the bell's inside and sent a tiny metallic ring out into the clear Krakow night. Everyone on the ground below stopped to look up. They could barely make out the two figures in the belfry.

Cory had finally achieved enough momentum on the rope to swing up to the other side but by the time he rolled onto the deck, Lars was right on top of him. The battle began, mano y mano, fist to fist.

One hard, pulverizing punch after another Lars threw at the off balance Cory, ripping his lip open with a left hook that sent him into the wall. Cory retaliated with a precise elbow to Lars' throat that forced him to gasp for air and allowed Cory the advantage. He grabbed him by the back of the neck and shoved him up against the ledge of the northern facing portal.

The group had gathered below. Two of the officers had apprehended Victor who had surrendered his weapon immediately. Vlaski had Szania banished to the back seat of his car and Tog locked into one of the vans. Lani had told them about Max in the dungeon and

two officers had been dispatched with Jerzy to bring him out. But Georgia, Jack, Lani, Vlaski and the others watched from the ground below the bell tower as Lars' head appeared now over the portal railing.

Cory didn't know what he was doing. His instinct was driving him to throw Lars out the window to certain death. But his reason began to take over. The thought of Eli's bloody face popped into his brain. He'd already beaten one man to death, murdered him. And he had promised himself he would never take another life. One, was too many. He would die first. That's what he had constantly told himself. Never again.

He pulled Lars back in and let up on him for just one moment, and that one moment of hesitation turned the tables on him. In a fit of blind rage, Lars grabbed Cory up under the armpit, hooked him with all the force of his legs, hips and right arm and launched him towards the portal opening. Cory's body impacted on the wooden railing and seemed on a trajectory of defenestration impossible to avoid. But in sheer determination, in an act of pure self-preservation and an athletic display of power, he made a desperate grasp with his right hand that caught the railing and held him in place as his body slammed into the external wall of the bell tower.

Two Special Forces officers were on their way up the stairs but by the time they got there they were forced to wait as Cory's life lay in the hands of Lars, poised over

him and whispering. They planted themselves at the top of the stairs, weapons at the ready.

"You are a fool, boy." He moved in close to Cory's face, placing his hands over Cory's, which hung onto the railing for life. "This whole thing was nothing more than a publicity stunt - for both sides. Goldman knew about it; he agreed to it. You'd have been free in a matter of days. But no, you had to be a hero. No one was going to get hurt. But it's too late for that now. You wanted a fight; you wanted to challenge me, Lars Rostock. Now, you are going to die."

Cory looked into the eyes of the only man who could save his life and saw the familiar evil of Eli Sonne. He held out no hope of being pulled back in as his body dangled from the bell tower and his hands burned in their effort to hold on.

Click. Lars had removed his switchblade, reversed it in his fist and steadied it over Cory's left hand. "Let's just get this over with, shall we?" He jabbed the blade directly into the back of Cory's hand between the tendons of his middle and index fingers.

"Ahhhhhh!" Cory screamed. The agony shot through him like a lightning bolt. Every instinct of his body was telling him to let go to eliminate the pain, and every instinct of his rational mind was telling him to hang on despite it.

"Cory!" Georgia shouted from below.

“Cory. Cory. Such a pity.” Lars mocked him. He twisted the knife. The intensity of the torture swarmed over him. Cory could feel himself starting to lose consciousness. Lars’ malevolent face above him faded indistinctly in and out of focus. Surely this must be Satan’s face he thought. This insidious man devoted to the rise of a murderous legion of neo-Nazis, an assassin who exterminated with supreme glee, surely he must be the curator of hell.

There was no other choice left but to do it. In the final moments of his life, he would break his own promise. He convinced himself that what he was about to do was not taking the life of the monster above him but giving his own so that others would not perish. That’s the way he chose to see it.

“Georgia!” He knew what was about to happen, that these were his final breaths, and with those breaths he wanted to say her name one last time and say it so she could hear him, so that she would remember it was the last word he had spoken, howled actually into the clear night like some kind of coyote straining to make contact.

Cory summoned every last ounce of his strength and holding on with his left hand, still pinned by the switchblade, he let go with his right and lunged at the snickering face of Lars Rostock. He managed to secure a handful of Lars’ leather jacket and closed his fist around it as he both pulled and let his falling bodyweight yank

his nemesis right over the railing and out the portal.

Lars flailed with his arms, attempting to grasp at something, anything. But he gathered in only air at his clutches. He had come right over the top, right over Cory's body. The combined weight of the two men ripped Cory away from the wall of the bell tower, leaving only a shred of his hand's flesh affixed to the switchblade still stuck in the railing.

Lars' shriek started at the top and continued all the way down. He had yowled "No!" from the second he realized he was going over in the most adamant denial of the greatest certainty of his life. The certainty of gravity. Yes, he was falling to his death. Yes, he was going to die. Yes, it was a long time coming, but he had finally received his comeuppance.

From Cory, on the other hand, there was no sound. He had mourned his tainted life for so long and learned only recently to celebrate it, without reproach and with passion. He fell silently, almost serenely with his back to the earth and his face looking toward the blanket of unfamiliar stars. The montage of his life flashed before the eye of his mind. He had felt this way once before when he was very young. Falling. Falling from the railroad bridge. Looking up and seeing Ray's horrified face. Ray came to him now. In a nanosecond wish, he prayed for Ray's happiness, for his release from the demons that the two of them had wrestled with as

young men searching for their identities. The need to tell him had never dawned on Cory before but as he plummeted he released this sentiment: *I love you, Ray.*

Becky's face was there, too. And Eli's. Her sad smiles and healing hands upon his wounds. His weathered skin and belt wrapped around his fist. And there were plums. Plums and more plums. There were always plums it seemed.

But the last images that flickered through the projector of his recollection were those of Georgia Hart. In Armani suits, in baggy sweats with morning hair, Georgia as adoring mother, Georgia as taciturn wife, Georgia as Anna, Georgia as G., as the sculpted back on the pull-up bar, as the flexible, leggy client on the stretch mat, the chimera and the chameleon, athlete and actress, student and mentor. She was laughing, discussing, listening, teaching, learning, weeping, breathing and sweating and confessing and making love to him.

The split second before Cory's bones cracked, before his spine shattered and splintered, before blood was pulverized then leaked onto the legendary execution stones of the courtyard - in the moment when Cory had always thought he'd see God - the instant before certain death, he saw instead, the face of Georgia Hart. And he smiled with a peaceful acceptance of his Fate.

EPILOGUE

Darkness had fallen.

Georgia rose from her seat on the verandah and moved to the railing. I followed. The sun had set on us somehow without my noticing. The lights of the patio were on. On timers, Georgia explained. Some kind of sensor that brought them up gradually as it detected the fading light.

Raoul came out with a tray on which were a plate of four perfectly quartered quesadillas made from flour tortillas with a combination of cheddar and jack cheeses with salsa, a tall glass with some sort of blended drink, for Georgia, and a Weisbier. I inspected the label.

"Andrew drinks only German beers, Bavarian

actually. Says everything else is just piss water."

"And you? What are you drinking?" I asked as she picked up the glass with a mean thirst.

"A whey protein shake. Cory got me hooked on them. A perfectly engineered food, he used to say, a good supplement. I drink one or two a day."

Georgia called Raoul over and whispered something to him while I enjoyed the evening breeze and gazed at the stars emerging on the cusp of night.

"Souls? Blinking back their light from the heavens?" Georgia asked me.

"That's what my mother used to say," I confessed, a rush of nostalgia running through me.

"Maybe she's up there." She added. "Maybe they both are."

"He had this aura about him," I said, "despite everything that happened to him as a kid. Nothing could deter him or kill his spirit. Nothing." I bit on the quesadilla. The salsa was above my limit for spicy.

"The irony of this whole thing is that everything had happened as if Andrew had planned it all. The movie has done over two hundred million dollars world-wide, received nine Academy Award nominations, myself included, secured Andrew's legendary status, allowed him center stage for an audience of a billion people when he takes the podium for his acceptance speech. And you know what? He did actually plan it that way."

"What do you mean?" I asked.

"Jack Grady verified everything. He came to me with a horrifying tape of a recorded phone conversation that this terrorist Lars Rostock had in Berlin. Interpol apparently had his phone bugged for some time. There was a voice on the other end imploring him to come to Krakow for reasons they had already discussed. An amount of money was mentioned, dates, even my name. The voice on the other end of that phone was Andrew's."

"Then it's true?"

"Killed two birds with one stone. Took away what he felt was the distraction to the film and generated the biggest publicity this side of the O.J. Trial. And, when we got back to L.A., Jack did some more investigating. He found that Andrew's agent, Bill Michaels, had received a script some years back that was all about the neo-Nazi revolution taking over the world. Apparently, it was so shocking and plausible that they contacted the writer, some German scientist, and were actually thinking of making the movie. The whole thing fell apart but you know who the writer was?"

"Lars Rostock?" I guessed. It seemed only perversely logical.

"Yes. Andrew had dealt with him before."

"I can't believe this. I can't believe people would go to such lengths."

"Believe it. This is the way Andrew's mind works.

It's what I've been trying to tell you. He was marketing the film before the shooting was even finished. After this whole big charade about neo-Nazi interference, which the world, to this day, accepts at face value, every paper in America and around the globe seized on the story and has stayed on the path of the movie ever since, driving it to this immense popularity. It's a juggernaut and will be all the way up until the acceptance speech where the world is waiting to hear what Andrew, who has adroitly avoided comment throughout, has to say. It will be his first public commentary on the events of the film. He has played every card more shrewdly than even I could have imagined."

I shook my head. "Wow." It was all I could say.

"Wow, indeed. But let me tell you something only two other people know."

I sat up, leaned forward as she lowered her voice.

"Andrew doesn't even know who or where he is. He will be dead within a month. This game of his? He lost. And I'm still standing."

She finished her drink and set the glass down. Raoul again came with his tray. Only this time it held a book with a white envelope protruding from within the pages and a cellophane wrapped video-cassette entitled Pillar Of Salt.

"I'm sorry if that sounds cruel. But it's appropriate, don't you think? Given what I've just told you?

"I don't even know how to process this, Georgia." I laughed awkwardly. *Georgia.* I found it strange to be calling her Georgia. She was a global celebrity who, up until today, didn't know me from Adam. "What happened to Cory's body?"

"Ahhh…" she said, handing me the book from the tray. "At the time I was so distraught I couldn't see straight, couldn't eat, get out of bed. For days. Andrew had gone to great lengths to conceal everything and downplay the incident. Including the location of Cory's body. He told me Cory had been cremated. I don't know why I believed him. I was simply devastated. Not myself. Then, when I returned to the states, and the depths of his deception became apparent, I started to question everything. Everything, Ray."

"Including…" she knew what I meant before I even said it.

"Yes. Open the book. Read what's underlined in the preface on page seven."

I did. "*Rose, oh pure contradiction, joy of being No-one's sleep under so many lids.*' What does it mean?" I really had no idea.

"What does it feel like?" Georgia asked me.

I had to speculate. I reread it and made a stab in the dark. "If the rose is no one's sleep, then does that mean it lives on forever?"

"Yes. Even though we think of a rose as blooming for a very short time, not only are there other roses and always will be, but the experience of the rose lives on in us. Rilke often used the image of the rose as the presence of Orpheus, meaning beauty and love, but Orpheus was caught between the two worlds of life and death. Rilke lived in both those worlds as a poet and wrote to express the life he was living. The contradiction is of being and non-being. 'When there is poetry, there is Orpheus singing, and singing is being.' Rilke was really all about this. Rilke, Orpheus, Cory. They lived beautifully, each in their own way. They will always be there when there is singing, or poetry, or the radiant imagery of a painting. Art. The rose symbolizes art. Rilke was an artist wrestling with an angel; he is the rose. And when you read what's in that envelope, you'll see that Cory is the rose, too." Her lip quivered, and her eyes glassed over with a film of nascent tears.

"Cory was right to put his faith in you." I sucked in a deep, balmy Beverly Hills breath. "Do you want me to read the letter."

"Yes. But first come with me. Bring the book."

As we walked upstairs, I summoned the courage to ask her, "After all you've learned, everything you've shared with me how is it you stayed with Andrew?"

"Someone once told me that in the end the devil always gets your soul; you either sell it to him or he takes it from you. I guess that's how I feel. I feel as if I've already surrendered my soul." She took a deep breath. I felt as if she was thinking about Cory right then. "I know my staying with Andrew must seem incomprehensible. Cory was the greatest, most pure thing that ever happened to me. Cherish is the word that comes to mind in the way that I remember him. But that really doesn't come close. It's almost like worship, but not in any religious sense. As I said, Cory was like a god, my god." Georgia bit the inside of her lip and shook her head, an innate response against her inability even now to believe that he was gone.

"Remarkable," I said.

"Besides, and maybe this is still part of my answer to your question, there are other reasons. Like Anna, I have my dark side and I am deriving some deep, inscrutable satisfaction in watching Andrew deteriorate in front of my eyes even as he reaps his greatest fame. Attending his death is retribution of sorts. But there's an even more important reason."

We had arrived upstairs. In the bedroom across the hall from Georgia's, a small Mickey Mouse night light cast a multi-colored glow onto an elegant, sparkling enamel crib with the most heavenly baby sleeping inside.

Georgia whispered to me. "His name is Cory. But he's not your brother; he's your nephew."

I looked down on him in awe. "He's beautiful."

Little Cory stirred as our breath settled on him like a mist of words. "But I thought, you know, that you were HIV and you mentioned there was so much risk. What made you change your mind this time?"

"How could I not? With everything that has happened? Cory's child? When I realized I was pregnant, it was near the end of the filming. We went on, obviously. It was the strangest finish to a film I have ever known. Andrew manipulated my grief perfectly. The sense of loss that was with me every day, every hour - I still think of him a hundred times a day; I see him in the face of his son. But it seemed during those months that followed his tragic fall that I just turned into Anna Kamenski. In fact, sometimes I feel that her character has taken over my life, as if I am still her today, transplanted into another time, another city.

"I went on with the film, discovering that I had this life inside me, and I flew my doctor into Poland and started taking the latest drugs and kept on them all through the pregnancy - Saquinavir and Indinavir, both of which you combine with AZT and 3TC. It's all very technical. They've made some significant advances in AIDS and HIV prevention, you know. All that money and effort, finally paying off. Except for cases in the advanced stages, like Andrew. But for me, the doctor says I could live to be a hundred if I'm careful, and the end result you see before you. And it's Andrew's money and my love that will nurture this beautiful child." She turned to me suddenly. "And now I need you to do something of me."

"Certainly. Anything."

"Please open it." She pointed to the envelope sticking out of the back of the book.

I removed it. There was a photograph inside that I recognized instantly. A memory of long ago, one of the few happy moments of our childhood.

"I put that in there. Cory had it with his possessions at the hotel."

"We were eleven and seven years old here. For one of her painted landscapes my mother had won first prize at the county fair - a Polaroid camera. She had taken pictures of me teaching Cory how to juggle plums. Already you can see how good looking he is. His face is chiseled like a sculpture. My mother tried not to but she doted on him; she was always running her hands over his face. She was never mean to me, Becky, but it was clear he was her favorite."

I pointed to Cory's tongue. "It was always hanging out when we were goofing around. Look at him concentrating on the plums. It was one of the few photos we ever had of us. Eli had come along some minutes later, taken the camera from my mom, screaming something about how we were always slacking off from our work and smashed it on the ground."

The second thing in the envelope was a scribbled poem. It had the wear of repeated viewing. I recognized the handwriting immediately.

"It came to me only last week. No return address. Please read it out loud."

I did.

"In the 'What if' box in the corner of her heart...
...was a life she may have lived and loved in
...from which no backwards look had spared her
...I would have gladly licked the salt that is my
wound.
What If...
...my pacing in cramped circles had not paralyzed
Me
...she had plunged into her will to do and undo
What If...
...the poverty of longing were the currency of
possibility
...the infinite space we all dissolve into tasted of us
Both
What If...
...in flinging our arms towards each other we found
we could fly
...we were truly given over to the moment of our
making
What If...

...our own two solitudes greeted each other

...they penetrated through the lyre's strings

...they gave off sparks, songs, selves

...they were allowed

What If...indeed...What If..."

Georgia Hart, the most beautiful and famous actress in the entire world pleaded with her eyes. "What do you think?" she asked, her voice as hopeful as the first light of sun on the fringe of dawn.

There was truth in the words.

My words shocked the both of us, "I think he's alive."

22062927R00346

Made in the USA
San Bernardino, CA
18 June 2015